PRESUMED GUILTY

Junius Podrug

A TOM DOHERTY ASSOCIATES BOOK
NEW YORK

This is a work of fiction. All of the characters and events portrayed in this novel are either products of the author's imagination or are used fictitiously.

PRESUMED GUILTY

Copyright © 1997 by Junius Podrug

A Forge Book
Published by Tom Doherty Associates, Inc.
175 Fifth Avenue
New York, NY 10010

Forge® is a registered trademark of Tom Doherty Associates, Inc.

ISBN: 0-812-55507-4
Library of Congress Card Catalog Number: 97-16925

First edition: September 1997
First mass market edition: November 1998

Printed in the United States of America

0 9 8 7 6 5 4 3 2 1

This is for Robert Gleason,
who has done it all.

ACKNOWLEDGMENTS

I would like to thank Natalia Aponte and Steven de las Heras at Forge for their hard work and support, Carol McCleary of the Wilshire Literary Agency for creating miracles, my personal editor Hildegard Podrug for being there, and G. Steven Jones for technical support.

I

When will the devil come for you?

—Aleksandr Pushkin

ONE

St. Basil's Cathedral, Moscow

Lara Patrick stood near a group of tourists in Red
Square. Night had fallen and the brazen lights of St.
Basil's Cathedral glowed before them. The tour guide
was speaking.

"This cathedral was built with blood," the woman said,
"and Moscow was founded on murder, its whole history
rife with death and intrigue."

But Lara didn't hear her words. A woman standing
closer to the cathedral had turned around and stared
straight at Lara, freezing her to the soul. The woman was
the spitting image of her mother.

My God, is she alive? At the same time Lara's mind
screamed the question, doubt gripped her. She strained to
see the woman's face, but the woman was nearly a hundred
feet away, standing near a group of tourists about to enter
the cathedral. She realized it was the clothing—the woman
was dressed in the distinctive style of her mother and had
turned to face her as if Lara were a little girl coming home
late from school. But her mother was supposed to have
been dead for over twenty years, blown away in a strange
accident after Lara was found brutalized.

The clothing, Lara thought, she's wearing my mother's coat. The old-fashioned, long, dark brown military-style coat, double-breasted with large metal buttons . . . and the hat, not a *shapki*, the stovepipe fur hats worn by most Russians, but a soft leather cap with a stiff bill, reminiscent of the caps worn by the Bolsheviks who stole Russia in 1917. It was her mother's outfit, the funky clothes she wore to show her contempt for the Soviet bureaucracy that had forgotten the ideals of the Revolution, a fashion statement by a 1960s Berkeley political science professor exiled to Moscow.

She remembered the scarf, too, bought from an old woman, a babushka on a street corner. During the city's zero weather her mother had worn the hand-woven red scarf around her neck, covering the lower half of her face—the same way the woman in the square was wearing it.

It's the outfit her mother wore the last time Lara saw her, the day that . . . that . . .

Her mind rebelled at evoking the memory of what had happened to her that last day in Moscow, keeping it in her subconscious where it had lain rotting for two decades and only now was seeping out little by little, like poison draining from a sore. She didn't believe the official explanation of that day's horror, remembering her mother as a warm and wonderful woman who loved and cared for her, who was more likely to give her a kiss on the cheek and slip an extra cookie in her lunch box than to have harmed her.

As she stared, confused, her heart racing, an uproar exploded as demonstrators marching along the Moscow River embankment suddenly poured into Red Square from the access near the cathedral.

"Communism *Yes*! Communism *Yes*!" Shouts fractured the thick night.

All eyes in Red Square went to the disturbance—except those of the woman facing her. Even Lara glanced at the mob marching into the square but when she turned back the woman had not moved. *She's staring at me.* Don't panic, she told herself, I'm not a little girl, other people are in the square . . . but she felt the fear swelling in her chest, choking her throat as the solitary figure in the frozen night threatened her with an eerie presence.

Lara was not a tourist. She had been drawn to the cathedral by a picture, a grainy old police photo of a naked woman slashed and mutilated on the floor next to a bed, murder in black and white. Lara was certain the dead woman was her mother, certain that the photograph exposed as a lie the police version that her mother had gotten high on psychedelic drugs and did unspeakable things to Lara before dying in a fiery crash that left nothing to bury.

The picture had arrived at her San Francisco office in an envelope without a return address, but the postmark was Moscow. As she stared at the photo, Lara knew she would have to return to Moscow to unravel the mystery behind the crime that had left her American mother dead and herself a battered and violated seven-year-old orphan.

She left her job as a prosecutor with the San Francisco District Attorney's Office, packed up her condo and boarded her cat, to return to the Moscow she had last seen as a schoolgirl.

Now she stood in Red Square on a black night and faced a silent menace from the past. How could this be her mother? Her mother was dead, the victim of an insane mind. No, the woman facing her wasn't her mother, it was the person who had lured her back to Moscow, to Red Square, to the cathedral itself where she had been brutalized in its inner sanctums.

The woman in the long brown coat turned and joined the tour group entering the cathedral.

Lara suddenly woke up to the crisis going on around her. A group of American tourists had clustered around the Russian guide near her and were being told by the guide that because of the demonstrators entering the square, it would be wiser for them to return another day to see the inside of St. Basil's.

I have to get into that church. She rushed to the guide and spoke to the woman in Russian. "I need to get into St. Basil's."

The woman shook her head. She was in her fifties with a stout Russian figure and hair the color of wood ash. She wore a fur *shapki* and her heavy coat and pants were brushed leather with sheepskin liner. Completing her outfit were *valenki* boots, thick felt knee-high boots—hers had black soles as thick as tire treads. "That was the last tour. We have to get out of the square before there's trouble."

With pounding boots, blazing torches, and Communist banners, the demonstrators marched toward the little tour group standing innocently in the middle of the square. At the other end of the square, riot police formed into a shadowy defense line of bulletproof vests, helmets, face shields, and clubs.

The tourists, eight retired phone company operators from Chicago, gathered around the guide and her "follow me" umbrella like anxious sheep.

Lara impulsively pulled a wad of money from her coat pocket and slipped it into the guide's hand. The woman's hand squeezed the wad as she looked at Lara with surprise. Neither knew how much money had just been passed but the wad was thick.

"Get me into the cathedral."

For a moment, the woman's eyes went wide and her ruby cheeks puffed full of air, red balloons ready to pop. Raising her umbrella high, she yelled to her flock, "Follow me!" as she swung around and headed for the church.

The group of confused women blundered after her, anxiously asking each other why the guide was leading them into a head-on collision with the mob.

"Don't worry, ladies," the guide shouted back, her umbrella up, her great breasts proudly erect, Mother Russia leading her brave little band in battle, "just ignore them and follow me."

Ice needles, frozen rain, pricked at Lara's exposed cheeks as she marched behind the guide, the woman's words drizzling back on clouds of breath fog. "Red Square was not named for the Communists. The word 'red' meant beautiful in Old Russian and the translation is Beautiful Square. You have already seen the mighty Kremlin palaces behind those walls to your right and now you are about to experience one of the great churches of all Christendom.

"It is said that Ivan the Terrible used the blood of his enemies in the mortar. When the cathedral was completed, Ivan had the eyes of the architects gouged so they could never create anything as beautiful again."

Lara heard gasps among the women but she was sure it was because the front runners of the mob were only a few dozen feet away and it was going to be a photo finish as to whether the little group would make it without being trampled by the mob or getting caught in a cross fire with the police. For a moment Lara forgot about the fact she had been shaking in her boots from cold and fear earlier, ignored the icy rain pricking at her cheeks, paid little attention to the tour guide's drizzling words—she could see the faces of the men at the head of the mob, big angry men, overlarge in their winter clothes and mean spirits.

"Even Stalin," the guide shouted, "the beast himself who killed thirty million people, dared not desecrate this cathedral that symbolized all of the cultures of the Russian Empire. Stalin was superstitious about St. Basil's. He refused to enter after he had a vision that the ghosts of those he had murdered had come back to kill him."

The men at the head of the stampeding pack were almost upon them. The guide suddenly shifted gears and shot forward with a burst of speed, Lara and the tourists breaking into a run behind her. A heavyset older woman carrying shopping bags stumbled and Lara quickly grabbed her arm with both hands and pulled her out of harm's way as the mob surged by.

"Thank you," the older woman gasped.

"That's all right." Lara laughed nervously, a little breathless, watching the mob trampling by. "Something to talk about when you go back home."

"You're an American," the woman said, surprised. "We heard you speaking Russian."

"American," Lara murmured, turning to the cathedral, mesmerized by its tall, spiked central tower and the surrounding exotic cupolas. The cathedral was a startling clash of cultures, barbaric and eerie in the black night. The blazing torches of the mob ignited the brilliant colors on the eight cupolas, casting the reverently barbaric cathedral into an even more bizarre light.

"They say you can feel the haunting," the older woman said.

Yes, the haunting. *I can feel it.* Twenty years ago terrible things had happened to me in there. If terror has an essence, then part of me is still in there, she thought, left behind by my screams.

The tour guide, a little breathless, her great chest rising up and down, stood with her back to the church and grinned triumphantly. "In the new Russia we must find new ways to solve old problems."

"I almost had a heart attack," a silver-haired woman said.

"Good, good," the guide said. "Now we enter the great St. Basil's. Remember that it is still a church and we must show respect."

The woman whom Lara helped was beside her as they lined up to enter. Matronishly full and rounded with unlikely red hair, she carried shopping bags and swung the bags like paddles as she waddled along.

"Ivan the Terrible killed millions, you know," she said to Lara. "The guide told us yesterday that Moscow itself was built because of a murder, some prince or another avenging the death of his brother at the hands of an unfaithful wife. Were you with us when we went past the Place of Skulls? That's where the tsars used to have people's heads cut off.''

She was layered with clothes, a bulky overcoat, two scarves, heavy wool pants, boots, leaving only her chubby cheeks and flaming hair exposed. Her frumpy looks reminded Lara of an old Russian word, ''*kutatsya*,'' used to describe women who put so much clothing on to keep warm that they looked like a bundle of rags.

The woman's fat cheeks were on fire from the cold and her words rode on clouds of frozen breath.

''I love cities with dark histories, don't you? Like London and the Ripper, Paris and the Hunchback. I went to Milwaukee to look at the house where Jeffrey Dahmer ate those people . . .''

TWO

I nside the vestibule the group paused as the guide explained the tour. Lara looked beyond her at the tour group that had gone in before them and was now getting ready to exit. The woman in the brown coat was not with them. Lara asked the man guiding them, ''A woman in a brown coat and red scarf was with your group . . .''

The man shook his head. ''Everyone in my group is here.''

''Something wrong, dear?'' the older woman beside her asked.

''No, I was . . . was just asking about a friend.''

''It's wonderful that you speak the language. I only wish that I—'' The woman stopped as the guide started explaining the church.

"Earlier you saw the frescoes of the chapels. As you will recall, the cathedral is like no other in the world because it is actually not one church, but nine separate chapels, each built as a monument to the battles Ivan the Terrible won. Now we journey into the inner sanctum, the area that the public is not allowed into except in the company of an official guide. There are many stairways and you must stay close together."

"Who's that singing?" a woman asked.

"The Don Cossack Choir is making a Christmas broadcast from the cathedral. Can you imagine, ladies? Three quarters of a century has passed since the last national Christmas celebration took place. Then the tsar, his wife, his four daughters, and his young son were murdered."

Lara shuddered at the thought of the massacre, the helpless victims waiting to be murdered, especially the children. Wasn't one of them very young, a frail little boy. What went through his mind—

Stop it! She shook off the dark thoughts. I have to keep my mind clear, she thought. Maybe it's all in my mind, maybe the woman in the brown coat was just another tourist. Moscow is cold and hungry . . . paranoia is blowing through the damn city like bad breath and I'm sucking it all in. I have to get control of my nerves. My imagination is playing games with me.

"Was your friend the woman in the brown coat?"

Lara swung around, almost gaping. The question had come from the older woman. "You . . . you saw her?"

"I guessed you were asking the guide about her because I saw you looking at her when we were outside. Maybe your friend left by another door."

And maybe she was inside, waiting for me. She started to tremble and calmed herself . . . I'm not a little girl anymore and I'm not alone.

She fell into line as the group started up a stairway. The older woman who had befriended her was awkwardly lugging the two bags and Lara asked if she could help with the bags.

"I'm old and fat, but I'll make it. There's nothing in them anyway. You could have fired cannonballs down GUM's aisles and not hit any merchandise. You look pale as a ghost, my dear," the woman huffed. "Are all of these horrible stories about murder in Moscow getting to you? If I hadn't paid for the trip six months ago I wouldn't have come. Shops are empty, people all scared, nobody knows who'll be in charge tomorrow. People think the president will be assassinated before New Year's. Got a chill, dear? You're so pale."

"Just a little cold." Lara touched her neck and self-consciously pulled her scarf higher. She knew the scars didn't show but it was an unconscious gesture on her part.

It was as cold as a headstone in the stairwell and the brooding voices of the Don Cossack Choir came to Lara as music at a wake.

"Isn't that music somber?" the older woman said, puffing as she climbed the stairs.

The song was of Christmas among the Volga boatmen but the tone was of hardship and toil, voices rising from the black soil of Mother Russia, evoking images in Lara's mind of peasants stooped over golden wheat fields and frozen tundra, of retreating Russian armies scorching the earth and torching cities, of famine, grief, cannibalism, and the mad dreams of tsars.

A memory suddenly rushed at her, fueled by the dark tones of the Cossacks and the grave chill of the stairwell.

She was in the second grade at the little school just off of Red Square.

"Your mother's come for you," her teacher said, standing at the window and pointing down at the woman waiting outside.

The woman was bundled in the long brown coat,

black hat, and red scarf her mother always wore,
the scarf pulled up over her mouth and nose to protect
against the treacherous windchill.

They left the school together and walked down
Red Square to St. Basil's. She skipped alongside the
woman, holding her gloved hand, her own cheeks
nipped by the biting winter wind.

They entered the cathedral and went up the dark
and deserted stairway, higher and higher toward the
110-foot summit of the main tower.

She asked her mother why she had been taken out
of school, why they had come to the cathedral, what
was at the top of the high tower.

The woman didn't answer and they were near
the top before Lara saw the woman's eyes . . .

"St. Basil's was built to commemorate the victory of
Ivan the Terrible over the Tartars at Kazan and Astra-
khan," the guide told them as the group paused on a landing to remove coats and scarfs.

Lara kept her coat on. She was trembling despite the
perspiration wetting the sides of her face. Her skin was
clammy, her throat raw and dry.

"Russia had been under the brutal heel of the barbaric
Tartars and paid tribute in the form of gold and golden-
haired maidens. Tsar Ivan drove the hordes from our cities
and in turned raped their cities and women."

"Isn't that interesting?" the older woman said to Lara.
"Ivan was mad, you know. Killed more Russians than foreigners. He and Stalin. Stalin's wife killed herself. Or was
it his son? Maybe he killed both of them. Crazy, too, you
know. Aren't you going to take off your coat, dear? You're
sweating."

"I'm cold," she lied.

"You've got to come, my dear."

"What?"

"We're moving on, up, up, up," the woman said.

Lara shook away the memories and kept her wobbly legs moving on the stairs. "You're right, that music, the Russians are so damn soulful, aren't they?" she said, using the sound of her own voice to beat back the nightmare awaking in her head. "It reminds me of the hardship and suffering of slaves in the Old South."

"Were your parents Russian?"

Lara shook her head. "American and British. I . . . I was born in Moscow, went to school here before I returned to the States."

"Oh, parents in diplomatic service. I so envy people in the diplomatic corps." The woman went on about how hard, though, it must be for the children.

Let her think my parents were diplomats. It would shock the woman if she knew who her parents really were.

"Coming back for a visit now that communism has fallen?"

"Yes, for a visit," Lara repeated mechanically.

"I got so scared when I saw that mob coming I forgot to take out my camera. But I'll find out if anyone else . . ."

Lara tuned the woman out and looked up the stairway. The main tower, the 110-foot central spire of the cathedral. That was where the woman in the brown coat had taken her.

THREE

At 5:30, closing time, the door guards left their positions at the cathedral entrance and went down the corridor to watch the famed Russian choir. They left the door unlocked because the tour group in the stairwell, the last for the day, would be leaving shortly.

One of the guards had a clipboard that he used to keep track of the number of tourists coming and going and he stared puzzled at the figures.

"What's the matter?" the other guard asked.

The man with the clipboard shrugged. "Counted nine coming in, eight going out on that tour that left a few minutes ago. I must have made a mistake. Nobody would stick around to wander around the towers at night."

FOUR

Memories chased Lara's tail as she went up the dark winding stairwell. This was the way, she thought, the stairway I was taken up.

A spike of pain shot between her temples. She stopped and leaned against the wall. Her throat was constricting, tension around her neck creating the sensation her windpipe was closing.

The older woman edged away a little. "Got a touch of the flu, honey?"

Lara half smiled and nodded her head, shoving away from the wall. *I've got to keep going; keep putting one foot in front of the other, that's all it takes.* And keep remembering.

She had left school that day, was taken to St. Basil's, up the stairwell, but what had happened in the tower was a blur. The next memory was of being in a car, a dark car. Two men were in the car with her. They put her on a plane, she remembered that, and remembered a stewardess giving her a hug. And a stuffed animal, a teddy bear or something another child had left behind. The stewardess covered her with a blanket and put the toy next to her.

I remember going to school that day, I remember the airplane, but what happened in the church . . .

Somewhere in the upper recesses of the great Russian cathedral was the answer to that lost time; to the dark images that made her wake up screaming every night during her first days in America until a doctor "cured" the nightmares with a drug that put her into a deep, dreamless sleep at night.

The tour guide's voice floated down to her as she paused at another landing.

"Ivan had a passion for blood at a very early age," the guide said. "He was only thirteen years old when he ordered a prince ripped apart and fed to his dogs. At the age of fifteen he had a nobleman's tongue cut out because he didn't like something the man said. In his last days, as he grew madder and madder, his brain eaten by fever, he chased priests up this very stairwell, chopping at them with an executionor's ax."

A tempest pounded in Lara's head, fed by the somber music that blew up the stairwell as a powerful wind, a crazy mumbo jumbo of thoughts and fragments of images—a mad Russian tsar chopping up priests with an ax, blood flowing down the steps . . .

A small room, hardly more than a cubbyhole, somewhere in the upper reaches of the great tower.
She was so small, so scared. The red scarf and hat covered most of the woman's face but she saw the eyes staring at her . . .

Burning eyes. The eyes of her mother . . . No! They weren't my mother's eyes.

In the dark room a hand had reached out for her, a muffled whisper from a shadowy figure beckoning,
Come closer . . .

The guide's voice jarred Lara back from the memories. "This is the end of the tour. We will return to ground level by a stairway on the other side."

As the group moved down the corridor toward the descending stairs, Lara hung back. The older woman with the bags was conversing with another woman as the tour disappeared around a turn in the corridor.

Lara stared at the steps leading to the top of the tower. I have to go up there, that's where the room is, that's where she took me. If I don't go up there it's all useless, my coming back to Moscow . . . to clear my head, to clear my mother's name. A memory came, of a cold night when she snuggled beside her mother in bed with a cup of hot chocolate and listened to her mother tell stories about the father Lara never knew and a life in a place called America Lara had not yet seen. Somebody took my mother's life, took her from me, and violated her memory. Not even a grave or a headstone marked her time on earth.

Thinking with heart and soul, sure, but she had spent too much of her life relying on logic. She had to go up the dark stairs, find the room where it all began, and unlock the past.

One step at a time, she thought, I'll take one step at a time and make it all the way. As she took her first step she heard a noise to the rear and stopped. It had sounded like footsteps on the stairway where the tour group had just been. She stood still and listened but no more sound came.

There are good reasons for people to be on the steps, she thought. It's a church and Russian Orthodox priests, with their flowing black robes and large headdress, had passed by the tour group.

The powerful music was a hand at her back as she went up the steps. These were the same steps she had been forced to go up as a child. Her body heat rose and she loosened the scarf from around her neck.

At a landing two flights up she paused at a point where the stairwell split, one set going to the right, the other to the left. She hesitated, unsure of the path she had followed as a little girl and finally chose the one to the left.

The direction she chose led to a dead end and she went

back, stopping in her tracks as she heard a creaking noise, the sound of a heavy foot on a wooden step. Not able to discern whether the noise came from above or below, she paused where the stairwell split into two paths.

It occurred to her that if someone had been following her the person could now be above her. Determined not to fall victim to her own imagination, she forced herself to move forward and slowly went up the stairway on the right.

As she went up the narrow stairway a dark figure came down, a priest wrapped in the heavy black robes and cloak. She kept her head down, pretending to be preoccupied with her footing on the rough steps, just a tourist wandering around, hoping that the priest saw enough tourists to not question her being there.

At the top of the stairway she stopped in an open doorway to a small room. The room was cast in shadows and deep holes of darkness. Wooden crosses against one wall were visible in the dim light pushing in from the corridor. Dark objects hung on every wall . . . priestly robes, it was a storage area for robes and crosses.

Nothing about the room stirred a memory except the cold knot of fear she experienced just being at the threshold. Staring at the darkness, a piece of the past flashed in her mind.

I was in this room . . . I worked my hand loose from hers as she tried to pull me farther into the room . . . she took something out of her pocket . . . something . . . a rope, oh, God, she took a piece of rope out of her pocket and tied it to an overhead beam.

Her throat constricted—she gasped for air, the spasms in her throat choking her.

The woman turned to me and held out her hand. I remember looking at her, trying to see her eyes again . . . it was so dark in the room.

> *Come closer, the woman had said, holding out*
> *her gloved hand for Lara. The woman pulled her closer*
> *and started to . . .*

Her mind rebelled at the memory. She undressed me. She took off my hat and scarf, unbuttoned my coat and took it off and took off my dress—the memory repulsed her. I was naked. I stood in this room in this cold damn room and I shivered and tried to cover my nakedness as the woman touched me.

Tears that wouldn't flow burned her eyes. She wanted to run, race back down the stairs and back to her hotel room and hide her head, but she knew if she did she would never be able to face the past—or the future.

Footsteps sounded from the stairway and she spun around to face the door, her nerves on fire.

Someone is out there.

She sank back, deeper into the darkness as the steps grew closer. *There's no way out of the room.* The thought nearly paralyzed her. Window shutters rattled on her right, pushed by the wind outside. The window was a glassless opening, the shutters were unhooked and appeared ready to part with a push, but it was a hundred feet down to Red Square.

I'm trapped. Her throat muscles constricted and her breathing came in shallow gasps. The footsteps grew nearer and emotions overwhelmed her as she relived the birth of her nightmares.

The woman had pulled her closer, not toward the window but to the wall behind her. Something was dangling from one of the low beams . . . a rope.

The woman had hung a rope from the beam. The end of the rope was knotted into a noose.

Lara swayed dizzily, the memory billowing in her mind as a dark cloud. A black form moved by the doorway and continued down the hall. *A priest, another damn priest.*

As her vision cleared she continued to stare across the small room. Something was hanging from the ceiling and her eyes slowly brought it into focus.

A brown coat and cap. A red scarf around the collar of the coat. She backed away, a scream welling in her throat, and turned to run when a black form filled the doorway. The priest.

He lunged at her and she stumbled back in shock, falling as her heel caught on the rough flooring. She fell backward and hit her back against the wall, banging her head against the frame of the window. The legs of the priest tangled in hers and he tripped, falling forward, his sudden charge slamming him against the shuttered windows—the shutters burst open on impact and Lara heard a gasp and saw the black form sweeping over her.

She lay on the floor and stared at the window next to her head. *Mother of God, he's gone out the window.*

In a daze she grabbed the windowsill with her hands to pull herself up. As she came up a hand slapped onto her hand and a dark figure rose from outside the window.

She jerked back—crying out—and turned and ran in blind panic out of the room, bouncing off the wall in the narrow corridor. Turning to go down the steps her ankle twisted under her and she fell, clutching frantically at the wall beside her but there was nothing to grab on to.

II

My mother was a pious woman,
but who knows?
The soul of another is a dark forest.

—Anton Chekhov

ONE

═══

C ross your legs," the doctor told Lara. "Uncross."

The metal examining table was cold on her tush. She was limp and tired and sore after being found unconscious at the foot of a stairwell in one of the world's most famous cathedrals.

"Lift your arms above your head," the doctor said. "Relax now while I touch up some of these cuts. Be thankful that you only fell down steps instead of being pulled out that window. You might have fallen over thirty meters."

"The steps felt like a thousand feet."

A young woman whimpering in pain in the examining room next to Lara was driving her crazy.

"What's wrong with that girl?"

"Her boyfriend broke her arms because she wouldn't fuck someone in exchange for drugs."

"Can't you give her some painkillers? She sounds like she's in terrible pain."

"Painkillers? We have a small ration to ease the last hours of the terminally ill. Antibiotics are even more scarce. Painkillers for women giving birth have to be bought on the black market by husbands. X rays, those we ate for lunch yesterday."

She studied him as he cleaned a scrape on the side of her head. He was young and harried and worried . . . no, she thought, not worried, grim. He was losing hope, had stopped worrying, and had simply turned grim and determined. He couldn't be more than her age, though he seemed older; tension marks had already formed at the corners of his mouth and worry lines creased his forehead as a perpetual frown.

Compared to high-tech American emergency rooms where the profit margin was more outrageous than in jewelry stores and cosmetics counters, the Moscow emergency room struck her as dated, a 1930s ambiance, the equipment big, heavy, and basic.

"You keep touching your neck," he said. "I don't see anything significant. Just a little redness."

"I don't bruise easily."

The strangling sensation was still with her and she knew she had to work with herself to get rid of it. She wasn't surprised that the doctor hadn't noticed the scar on her neck—childhood surgery had erased it from the public eye. But she knew it was there and sometimes she unconsciously touched it.

"Everything is being rationed in Moscow. Even life and death," she murmured, not really talking to him, but thinking aloud.

"Life and death are becoming black-market commodities," the doctor said. "A child died last week in this hospital because staff members were watering down medication to sell some on the side. Mothers and newborns become infected because there are three or four women at a time in delivery rooms and bedding doesn't get changed after delivery."

"It's better than living under tyranny. The problems will iron themselves out."

"Tell yourself that the next time you go into a store to buy tampons. If you didn't bring a supply from America, you'll have to carry a big wad of cotton in your purse as Russian women do.''

The young woman in the next room screamed again and Lara felt her pain in the pit of her own stomach. "If you're finished I'll get out of your hair.''

"You're paying with hard currency. That makes you a priority patient.'' He looked up and gave her a tight smile to take the edge off his words. "Just joking.''

He wasn't kidding and she knew it. Her U.S. dollars had an exchange rate of nearly a thousand rubles to a dollar with the ruble deteriorating every day. She felt instantly guilty that she was getting special attention because she could pay with hard currency when the poor girl next door was suffering.

"It's not good to practice medicine when you don't have the right tools,'' he said. "We have more thermonuclear warheads than incubators for sick babies. Anyway, that's our problem. Your problem is that some crazy attacked you. I suspect that you passed out more from fright than the fall. You don't seem to have a significant head injury.''

"I hurt in fifty places.''

"Small hurts. Nothing broken. Having on heavy winter clothes helped cushion the fall.''

Her hand went to her throat again.

"Do you want me to check your throat again?''

"No, it's an old injury. It still sometimes constricts on me, feels like my air is being cut off.''

"That may have been the sensation that caused you to black out.''

The doctor's name was Shukhov. He was a harried thirty-year-old, new to medicine at a time when Russia was in the middle of its second revolution. He glanced up at Lara as he sat on a revolving stool and filled out the patient sheet on her. Height about 1.68 meters tall, 5'6" in her own country. Hair long and chestnut with natural red highlights, falling onto pale cheeks, hair he'd like to run his fingers through . . . MINOR ABRASIONS TO HEAD, he wrote.

Eyes were hazel . . . round and wide, eyes that have seen hurt, he thought, noticing a subtle caution in her searching gaze. Was it that she didn't trust people and was probing to see if there was someone else behind the mask? EYES CLEAR.

Her cheeks were too pale, he thought, even though they were lovely cheeks. He liked the softness of them when he checked a slight bruise on her left cheek.

"You need some vodka to put color in your cheeks."

"I don't drink. A warning from my mother. She said a little liquor turned my father into a wild man."

He shifted on the stool so she couldn't see his grin as he thought of what it would be like to be around her when she turned wild and crazy from a kiss of vodka. He wiped the grin off his face and swung back around.

There was a little redness to her nose, probably from bouncing off of a step. He touched it. "Hurt?"

"A little. Not much."

Her nose turned up a little at the end, adding more emphasis to her full lips. No lipstick because she didn't need it—her lips were a natural cinnamon rose. Her smile was neither an invitation nor a greeting to the world, but a device she hid her real feelings behind. Her chin was strong, a little pushed forward as if she sometimes led with it. A natural dimple, visible only on second look, was carved on her chin.

It was a face that was interesting rather than pretty. She brought to mind a line from a translation of Shakespeare's *Henry VIII* his mother had given him as an early Christmas present: *There's language in her eye, her cheek, her lip*.

Like King Henry's woman, there was a story etched in Lara Patrick's features and the doctor wondered how so much had been written during such a young life.

"Will I live?"

"What?"

"You were staring at me. Have you found something terminal?"

"You'll live," he said shortly, blushing a little at his secret thoughts. He was not good at expressing himself to women and he sometimes hid it behind professional curtness.

The next entry required his opinion of her chest. He thought about the luscious curve of her breast line—

"Excuse me, Doctor, there's a policeman here to see you," a nurse said, poking her head through the curtain.

He wrote CHEST CLEAR on the report. "He'll probably want to talk to you," he told Lara as he left the examining room.

A plainclothes police officer in a cheap overcoat was waiting down the corridor as Dr. Shukhov came out of the examining room. As he approached the policeman, the doctor wondered if the inexpensive overcoat was the sign of an honest cop—or just bad taste.

"Detective Yuri Kirov," the cop said, showing his official identification as a member of the Moscow Militia, the city police.

The doctor's first impression of Yuri Kirov was that he was probably in his mid-thirties but he looked a little older because something in life had taken the shine off of him. Part of it was Moscow pallor from too many cigarettes and too little sunshine. Maybe the rest of it, the tough stare, the angry mouth, went with the job, the doctor thought.

"You're treating an American, Lara Patrick."

"She's lucky to have just cuts and bruises. Someone tried to kill her."

"Perhaps." Yuri Kirov took a pack of cigarettes from his pocket and shook out a cigarette.

"There's no smoking in the examining area."

Yuri shrugged and pushed the cigarette back into the pack. "Cigarette smoke would probably kill some of the germs in this place."

"I'm busy, Detective. This is an emergency ward. Do you want to talk to the woman?"

"I don't need to talk to her. We know her story. She made a visit to our office as soon as she got off the plane a couple of weeks ago. You don't have to make an official report."

A tone in the policeman's voice caused the doctor to tense. "What do you mean, you know her story? She was attacked by a maniac at St. Basil's."

"By a maniac no one else saw. A maniac who fell out a window with a thirty-meter drop and then reappeared."

"You know how St. Basil's is built, it has more tiers than a wedding cake. Was there a ledge outside the window?"

As he spoke, he studied the police detective. Russian doctors didn't have the independence—or the respect and wealth—of doctors in the West and he was used to obeying the dictates of authority. But he also had a lot of anger caged up and he wanted to grab the police officer and shake him and tell him that Russia wasn't a police state anymore, that he couldn't flash a badge and have a doctor snap to attention.

"Was there a ledge?"

The policeman said nothing.

A lifetime of intimidation doesn't fade in a relatively short period of chaotic freedom and the doctor kept the anger out of his voice as he said stiffly, "It's my duty to report treatment for injuries caused by acts of violence."

Detective Kirov shook the cigarette back out of the pack and lit it. Somewhere down the corridor a woman in labor screamed and begged to be killed. A door slammed and the woman's pleas became muffled as the two men stared at each other, the doctor full of frustration and anger, the policeman with his secrets.

Detective Kirov blew cigarette smoke from his mouth and nose. "You're right. You must report all acts of violence. When the violence actually occurs. You see, we know all about this woman . . .''

Lara was slipping on her last boot when the doctor came back in. His grim but friendly demeanor had changed. He avoided her eye.

"I didn't finish cleaning your wounds."

"Is the police officer still out there? I'd like to know if he found out anything."

"He's gone. He said you can drop by the police station tomorrow and file a report."

"I was almost murdered and I'm supposed to stop by and file a report? Did he say if anyone saw the woman who pushed me out of the window?"

"You said it was a priest who attacked you."

"I told you I thought it was a woman dressed up as a priest. I never saw the face but it had to be the woman I followed in. There isn't any other explanation."

"A woman with a brown coat and red scarf." His voice was deliberately neutral and it sent a shot of anger through her.

"Yes, brown coat, red scarf, black hat. What is it? What did the policeman say?"

"Just like the last time."

"Yes, just like the last time." Her voice lost its control. "He told you I was crazy, didn't he? That's how they treated me when I went to the police and tried to reopen my mother's—"

"This is what he told me." His words were carefully chosen. "That you came back to Moscow after leaving here as a child. That you have visited the police and questioned the cause of your mother's death that occurred over twenty years ago. That you were brutalized as a child, a priest found you hanging in the church tower, sexually—"

"And reliving the past, I threw myself down a stairway. Great theory, saves police work. He told you my mother hurt me when I was little but that's a lie. She was a caring, loving—''

''Your mother was a foreigner, an American political radical. There was a question of psychedelic drugs.''

''That's a lie, too.'' She dug money from her purse. ''Thanks for the help. The rest is to buy painkillers for the girl next door.''

His angry voice followed her out of the room.

''We have enough problems in Russia. Why don't you go home and be crazy.''

Detective Yuri Kirov sat in his unmarked militia car a block from the hospital and watched Lara come out the front entrance and get into a taxi.

It was the dead of night, the time of utter darkness when not even the moon or stars shined, a frozen night made bearable only by the heat of cheap cigarettes as he waited for her to come out of the hospital.

He couldn't see her face from the distance, but her body language was stiff with anger.

He started the car and followed the taxi down the deserted street.

TWO

Lara skipped the elevator at her hotel, using the stairs up to the third floor. She avoided the elevator because it sounded asthmatic and ready to collapse with the next coughing spell. Like the equipment back at the hospital, the elevator was big, solid, and didn't always work.

Reaching the top of the stairs and taking in a lungful of air, she decided that the hallway had the cold, fleshy smell of a meat locker.

She shook her head coming down the hallway. *I'm let-*

ting my visit to the hospital get to me. Besides, the hotel corridor was probably too cold for anything but frozen food. Even the rooms were kept just chilly enough so she was never quite comfortable.

What a dump, she thought, walking past wallpaper that had peeled from the wall. She hated the place, hated the sturdy, graceless fixtures and furnishings that seem to boast that a society that was classless was also faceless.

It was going to take weeks, maybe even months to get the information she needed and the Gorky was the best she could afford without running up an enormous tab on credit cards that she wasn't sure she would be able to repay.

Her hand shook as she inserted the key in the lock to her room door. There was no dead bolt on the door and once inside she placed a chair under the handle.

Sitting on the edge of the bed, she held her head in her hands. Her head was pounding and her stomach had gone sour. She needed to cry, her mind and soul needed the cleansing, the release, but tears failed her now as they always did. Much of her anger was pent-up fury at the way her mother's memory had been defamed.

Angela Patrick had been a household name in the turbulent 1960s. A young Berkeley professor, she had been a leader of anti-war activists, firebrands that took the cry against war out of the classroom and into the streets. Sure, her mother had been a campus radical, but she had fought for life, to get the U.S. out of Vietnam and save lives on both sides of the war. When a demonstration went to hell on a Berkeley street and someone got killed, her mother had found herself on the police list even though she had not caused the tragedy. She fled to Canada and later accepted an invitation to teach in the Soviet Union.

If the Soviets had been looking for a propaganda piece in her mother, they had been mistaken. She was not a Communist and refused to get involved in anti-American dialogue.

In Moscow her mother had fallen in love with Keir Thomas, a wild and impulsive Welshman. Born in a poor coal-mining town, Keir was a poet and social revolutionary—a lover, a drinker, and a fighter, he was, like Angela, a child of the sixties. Some drunken talk in a pub about blowing up Parliament on Guy Fawkes Day had turned him into a political fugitive.

True to their nature and those heady idealistic days of the sixties, Lara's parents had not bothered formalizing Angela's pregnancy with a wedding ceremony. Conventions like marriage and planning for your children's education meant nothing to a generation that tried to conquer the world with the power of love, pot, and T-shirts that said FUCK THE DRAFT.

Lara never met her father. As fiery and idealistic as his poetry, Keir joined a group of other young foreigners living in Russia who went off to Africa as unpaid mercenaries to remove some last outpost of European colonialism only to be caught on the wrong side of a tribal war and killed by the people he had come to liberate.

He had been in Africa when she was born, but she knew him through the stories her mother told her. She had felt his love through her mother. They were wonderfully passionate people, Lara thought, filled with a zest for life and love for all living things.

Her mother had given Lara that same passion, instilling in her a love for life and people, but the passion had been smothered in her when she was still a child. She had to find that passion again, just as she had to find a murderer.

In her heart she knew it was all a lie, everything they claimed about her mother—the acid trip, the battering and molestation of her own daughter, the wild driving that took her into a fiery head-on collision with a gasoline tanker truck.

Lying on the bed, her thoughts went back to that last day in Moscow, her and her mother in their snug little apartment with winter's frost outside, hearing again her mother tell her she'd grow up skinny as a bean stalk if she didn't finish her hot mush, her mother packing Lara's school bag while Lara dressed. On the landing in front of their apartment she remembered being impatient as her mother made a last-minute adjustment of Lara's coat and scarf. At seven years old you were more concerned about running and joining your friends en route to school than things like catching cold. As they stood on the landing her mother slipped an extra cookie into Lara's coat pocket . . .

The landing. Something about the landing, about that last normal moment with her mother gave rise to an unnamed fear in her, fear swelling in her chest and throat. What was it about the landing at their apartment that morning . . . ?

She told herself that the landing wasn't important, that it was St. Basil's where the terror began, but the shadow of a memory hung over her like an ax ready to fall.

> *When her mother had finished fussing with Lara's coat and scarf, she gave Lara a kiss on the cheek and slipped an extra cookie in her side pocket.*
>
> *Lara turned to race down the stairs when something caught her eye on the landing above them.*
>
> *A nurse in a white uniform was stepping out of the apartment above . . .*

A nurse in a white uniform. Eyes staring down at her. The same eyes she stared at when she looked up at the woman in her mother's brown coat taking her into St. Basil's.

A headache exploded between her temples and the fear welling in her chest turned into nausea that surged up her throat. She ran for the bathroom. It was rushing out by the time she made it to the sink, the spoiled contents of her stomach boiling up her throat and out of her mouth.

She flushed her mouth out with water and brushed her teeth three times. Afterward she stared at the grim image staring back at her in the bathroom mirror. She had noticed that the doctor had been attracted to her. She never thought of herself as pretty, never thought anyone else would consider her attractive, but in the last few years as her life seemed to be going the way of a dried prune she had wondered if her brain didn't need an overhaul.

She knew she wasn't exactly the most approachable person on earth when it came to meeting men. The "ice queen" is what one frustrated attorney called her after she rejected several lunch dates.

"What's wrong with you," she asked her reflection. "You have nobody because you're scared. Admit it, you're afraid to get involved. You're afraid to show any emotion."

She was almost thirty and had not had anything more than casual relations with men—and no close women friends. No close friends, period. And no relatives that she knew of now that her grandmother was in the grave.

"Why haven't I ever experienced a love like my parents?" Lara asked herself.

Her mother's death made Lara a seven-year-old orphan whose only known relative was a grandmother halfway round the world in San Francisco. The subject of the death and of what had happened to Lara on her last day in Moscow had been taboo in her grandmother's house. The only comment she had heard her grandmother make was that the Soviets had killed Angela, but Lara had never accepted it.

Her grandmother had considered herself a failure. Her husband had died years before she was ready for widowhood, and her only child had gone overnight from a bright-eyed flower-loving peacenik to a front-page fugitive. She had found refuge accepting Jesus and hiding behind biblical quotes until an ill wind carried her daughter's child to her. Raising Lara had been a burden, not a penny from heaven.

Lara had left Moscow with secrets metastasizing inside her like a cancer. The pain had lain dormant for over twenty years while she grew from frightened child to cautious woman, never probing that corner of her mind where mad dogs played.

For most of her life she had simply accepted her role, a determined workaholic respected by police officers and her fellow prosecutors for her bright mind and assertive actions. But the bubble burst when the cryptic summons to Moscow arrived and she started reliving the past. And thinking about all the lost years in between. "My parents were wonderful, passionate people who loved and lived," she told the wall. "And I didn't have a date for the high school prom."

She closed her eyes and had started to doze off when pounding erupted at her door. Grabbing at the telephone by her bed, she fumbled and dropped the receiver. Getting it back in hand, she called the front desk, her heart beating.

No operator was on duty at this time of night. Would the front desk clerk answer? The pounding came again and her blood pressure surged.

Leaving the telephone off the hook so it would keep ringing, she went to the door, hoping it was just the floor warden complaining about not checking in with her.

"Who is it?"

"Gropski."

Gropski was hotel security, a short stump with fat lips, wide nose, huge head, and ugly brown blotches on his flesh that gave him the appearance of a frog left out in the sun too long, a not too likely scenario in Moscow since sunshine was not a threatening commodity.

"What do you want?"

"You asked me questions."

A slur to his voice suggested he had had too much vodka, a common diagnosis in a country where the leading cause of almost everything was too much vodka.

"I asked you questions in broad daylight," she said, "it's the middle of the night."

"You've been gone."

"What do you want?"

"I have information for you," came through the door in a drunken slur soaked in lust.

Thinking of his round face, watery jaundiced eyes, and fat nose, she imagined a frog in heat.

"Put it under the door."

"The door? Lady, don't be stupid. The information is from my mouth."

Definitely wouldn't fit, she thought. "Look, I'm not opening this door. And I have the front desk on the line and I'm going to ask them to send someone up if you don't go away."

From where she stood she could hear the constant ring of the phone. Still no answer from the front desk.

"Send someone up? This is Gropski, I'm the security officer. You call, I get sent up."

"Gropski, listen to me. Tell me what you want or I'm going to make a complaint with the ministry in the morning."

She left it open as to what ministry she'd be complaining to because she didn't have the faintest idea as to which one administered hotel security officers now that the KGB had crashed and burned.

"Information has a price," he purred, with all the sexual innuendo the little frog could muster.

"Tell me what you're offering. If I think it's worth anything I'll slip some money under the door."

"No money, we can make other arrangements."

"I'm calling the ministry!"

"All right, all right, on Lenin's grave, I'm just trying to help. You asked me to find out how you can arrange access to, uh, certain matters."

"Yes."

"I have made contact with the man who can make the arrangements. He is a master of blat."

Blat. The fine art of peddling influence to get things out of the government. A master of blat could supply anything from a refrigerator to a thermonuclear missile. With the fall of communism, the billions of documents detailing over seventy years of Soviet atrocities were being bid for. She wanted access to records about her mother's death, records that would show the hypocrisy of the official version.

"There's a price," the frog whispered through the door.

There was always a price.

"Who is this person?"

"I have the information written down for you. Open the door and I'll give it to you."

"Slip it under the door and I'll put a hundred dollars under."

"Money first."

"We'll do it at the same time."

No honor among thieves or anyone else in Moscow, she thought. These were hard times. Before the Fall people like Gropski had a small amount of prestige, even as a security officer at a fleabag like the Gorky.

Lara grabbed a hundred-dollar bill from her purse and bent down by the door.

"I'm ready," she said.

Gropski slipped just enough of the paper under for it to poke out on her side. She slid the bill slowly under, pulling in the paper as he reeled in the money.

She got to her feet to read the message, her aching bones reminding her of her injuries.

MR. BELKIN
8:00 P.M. TOMORROW
PATRIOTIC PARK

She leaned closer to the door. "Why do we have to meet in a park at night when there's a lounge downstairs. Gropski? Gropski?"

The frog had left.

She leaned against the door and sighed wearily. All

alone, no one to hold her, comfort her, share with her. Even her damn cat was halfway round the world.

She staggered to the bed, pausing to put the phone back on the hook, and crawled under the blankets, aching and miserable.

III

Fear has the largest eyes of all.

—Boris Pasternak

ONE

≡

Detective Yuri Kirov's life was layered with secrets.

Most people followed a straight course through life, a spinal path of ups and downs through birth, marriage, career, and death. Yuri's life was a dark and stormy road filled with dangerous curves. And he knew there was no guardrail as he sat in the dark and watched a good-looking woman take off her clothes for a man with a big hairy belly.

Blue-gray smoke from his cigarette curled in the flickering light of the movie projector, adding a little cabaret ambiance to the dingy room.

He watched the film from his bed, an old army cot with a thin mattress atop a rusty steel mesh. It was the only place to sit in the room. The stool that the projector was on had been borrowed from the boiler room next door. He sat on the cot with his back to the wall, feeling the warmth from the boiler radiating through the thin wall, feeling himself getting aroused by the woman taking off her clothes.

A small refrigerator, hot plate, and sink were against the wall opposite the army cot. The bathroom, hidden behind a curtain in the corner near the sink, was so small he could sit on the toilet and stick his feet in the shower stall at the same time.

The dark little room was an afterthought in the ass of a dreary building. The room would have been depressing to most people. To Yuri it was a womb, someplace he could crawl into and hide, curling up with secrets that would destroy him if exposed to light.

Now he sat in his room and watched a moving picture that was somehow connected to the web entangling his life.

The woman undressing was young, probably no more than twenty. The black and white film only told him that the girl's complexion was light and her hair pale, but to the right of the screen, propped against his wall, was a more recent picture, a publicity photo of a woman fifteen years older than she had been when she undressed for a man with a hairy belly.

The woman was being coy with the man, taking off her clothes slowly, acting embarrassed and innocent, pulling her sweater off over her head, revealing full breasts straining at a bra that had been designed more to expose than contain.

Earlier in the film the man had eagerly stripped down to boxer shorts. Now his belly quivered as he watched her undress. He had tried to approach her a couple of times and she had slipped away to build up his sexual tension.

As he watched the film Yuri tried to figure out where the hidden camera had been placed. The bedroom had a country look to it and he decided it was a dacha outside the city. The camera must have been placed in the ceiling of the bedroom, probably at the base of a light fixture or air vent.

The clandestine filming had been done by the KGB. Handwritten serial numbers identifying the film had been put on a chalkboard and filmed. Crude, but who needed professionally prepared credits for the thousands of surveillance films taken by the KGB?

It wasn't hard for Yuri to guess the motivation for the film. The man was probably married and the woman was setting him up. Even though Soviet politics had been brutal, Soviet social life had been strictly puritanical—one could gain a promotion for shooting a boyhood friend in the head if the friend was suspected of anti-Soviet thoughts, but a career would be ruined by an extramarital indiscretion—or by a blow job caught on film.

Yuri had learned who the man was from the same place he had obtained the film: KGB archives, easily assessed by an "official" request from a Moscow police officer now that the KGB had been disbanded.

The man in the film had been a deputy minister in the Communications Ministry. The young woman had been an entry-level broadcast employee. From the file that came with the film Yuri learned that the woman had cooperated with the KGB.

The man had no redeeming social value. The woman was a slab of flesh to gratify the pulsating bulge between his legs. He would fuck her and probably go home and crawl into bed with his wife. And maybe the next morning shoot his boyhood friend in the back of the head for harboring anti-Soviet thoughts.

The man was history—someone somebody sometime wanted something on.

The woman was also history—current events. She was good, Yuri thought, a real prick-teaser. She had stepped out of her skirt, revealing bikini panties and no nylons or panty hose.

The man was wriggling and looked ready to explode in all directions.

Yuri wondered about the woman who used her body to gain advantage in place of the hard work other women used. Yuri had no respect for her and as he watched the action he became angry that she was giving a treasure of her womanhood to a swine to get a promotion at work. Not liking the woman made his job easier to do.

The woman now knelt in front of the man. As her head disappeared under the quivering belly, Yuri reached over and shut off the projector and turned on the lamp by the bed.

She had let herself be used by the swine and by the KGB to break into broadcasting. Now she was known to millions. He wondered how people who religiously turned on the Moscow Evening News would react if someone slipped in a film showing the country's leading anchor-woman earning her first stripes in broadcasting on her back.

He rewound the film and put it in its canister. He hid the canister under the sink, lifting up a board he had loosened for the purpose, then replaced the board.

To cover his ass if someone broke in and searched his apartment, he set a porno movie next to the projector. The film came from the same street vendor who had sold him the old projector.

The fact someone might break in was well within the bounds of possibility. The Soviet system was still reaching out of the grave to pull people under.

Yuri's mind went to the American woman, Lara Patrick. He had not spoken to her, although he had been close enough to reach out and touch her when he followed her through the airport the day she arrived. Since then he had only watched her from afar but she had made contact with him in a different way, invading his nights, coming into his bedroom at three o'clock in the morning and tapping on his mind, causing him to wake up and stare up at the darkness and think about her.

He liked the way she walked, the way she carried herself with assurance but modesty. Her gentle but assertive voice when she dealt with taxi drivers and waiters told him she was a caring, thoughtful woman, but one who fought back when pushed. He had almost interceded at the airport when a taxi driver locked her luggage in the trunk and tried to extort an enormous fee from her. She handled the situation and didn't lose her cool but threatened to have his license revoked.

He thought about a lot of things, dangerous roads that had kept a woman like Lara Patrick out of his life.

He kept a tight grip on himself, on his emotions and facial expressions, even his innermost thoughts. Something about Lara Patrick opened the flood gates and as he lay awake at night a motion picture would go on in his mind and he relived moments of laughter and joy.

And moments of horror he couldn't switch off.

I V

<hr>

It always comes out the same, a journey,
a wicked man, somebody's treachery,
a deathbed, a letter, unexpected news,
I think it's all nonsense, Shatushka,
what do you think?

If people can tell lies why shouldn't a card?

—Fyodor Dostoyevsky,
The Possessed

ONE

By eight o'clock Moscow had been dark for hours and the street outside the Gorky was a shade past midnight.

"They're rationing the streetlights," the porter told Lara. "Turning off the lights at every other sector to conserve energy. Tomorrow night we'll have lights. Very democratic."

Was he trying to be funny with the last comment? No, she thought, there was no humor in him. He was small and wrinkled, with white hair, rotted yellow teeth, and unhealthy gray skin. In his heavy uniform of tattered purple wool and tarnished gold epaulets, he looked like a dwarf king from Alice's Wonderland.

"No taxis again?"

"No, they're all at the better hotels. They're rationing the petrol for buses, too," he said. "Buses run out of gas on their route." He shook his head. "Just like the war, the Great Patriotic War. Everything was rationed. People are hungry again. Just like the war."

He went through the same routine every time she spoke to him. Fighting senility and fear at a time when the whole country was going through convulsions, he found comfort in having survived worse times.

His mind lurched back to her transportation problem. "Do you want a taxi called?"

"They never come."

"That's true. They stay around the better hotels. They're low on gas, too. It was like that during the war, but then there were no lights anywhere. The bombers . . ."

Leaving him in the embrace of his remembrances of the Second World War, she stepped out onto the street, gasping a little as the below zero air burnt her throat and lungs. She quickly covered her mouth and nose with her scarf and pulled her hat down until only her eyes were visible. The cold even attacked her eyes, making her blink as they smarted.

How big was the sector that had been blacked out? Streets were dark in every direction. Was the intersection where she was meeting the man named Belkin also suffering a blackout?

Damn damn damn. That idiot Gropski should have set up the meeting at the hotel lounge, at *any* hotel lounge. Hell, she would risk his friend in her room rather than walk dark and frigid Moscow streets.

She had slept most of the day and had crawled out of bed only a couple of hours earlier. To change the meeting place she had tried to find Gropski, but he was out, no doubt living it up with a bottle and a prostitute on her hundred dollars.

No taxis, no buses, dark deserted streets, it was insane for her to go out by herself . . . but it's only eight o'clock, she told herself, and it's just a few blocks. Like hell. She turned around and went back to the hotel. She gave the porter a five-hundred-ruble note. "Stand outside and watch me as I go up the street," she told him.

"Watch you?"

"Muggers and rapists."

He nodded as he followed her outside. "The streets aren't safe. Nothing works, not even the police. They say now we're free, but when the Communists ran the country our jobs were safe, the streets were clean, and the buses ran on time. What's the use of being free if you have to be scared? Back during the war, if a mugger was caught . . .''

Lara hurried in the direction of the rendezvous, the street deserted except when an occasional car drove by, headlights setting the darkened street aglow, tires hissing on the wet road. The Gorky was located in an area of government offices that became deserted when buses stopped running at seven in the evening after hauling away the last of the workers. The buildings were all Soviet generic: big, solid structures of dull concrete, with no character, grace, or even architectural interest.

Her feet crunched on packed snow. The municipal street cleaners still managed to keep most of the traffic lanes clear of snow, but they piled the snow along the gutter as a long dirty mound that spilled over onto the sidewalks.

She looked back over her shoulder, making sure the porter was still keeping watch in front of the hotel.

Cold cold cold.

She hated being cold. With a California ski jacket, woolen pants, long underwear, boots, heavy socks, sweater, hat, and scarf, she was bundled up for a Himalayan trek and was still cold, still shivering.

One of the few pleasant memories of the Moscow she left as a child was the clean white snow at Christmastime. Moscow was no longer a lily white city and she wondered if the damn place had gotten colder, too.

She stopped at the corner a block from the hotel and silently cursed. The street was dark for blocks. Behind her the porter was no longer in sight and she hesitated, unsure of whether her feet were going to race her back to the hotel or continue on toward the meeting.

She gritted her teeth and hurried down the street, her eyes darting toward the dark entrances in front of each building, at the street behind her, at the spaces between buildings.

Can fear make you colder?

Her fear of someone jumping out of a dark alley or doorway got the best of her and she stumbled over dirty snow and started running down the street.

Half a block from the rendezvous, she spotted him, a big, solid, well-fed slab of Russian beef.

He was standing in the shadows just outside the glow of the streetlamp on the corner, reassuringly conspicuous. She was grateful that the park was not part of the blackout.

As she stepped up on the sidewalk on his side of the street, he suddenly turned and started walking down the park path, signaling her with a look to follow him.

She fell in wordlessly behind him, telling herself that Russian parks weren't like American ones, that they belonged to the people, not gangs and perverts, and that there was nothing wrong with a stroll with a strange man in a dark park at night.

Right.

Other people were around, young and old, even a couple with a baby carriage. But she wasn't going to follow him off the main path if he decided to communicate with nature.

He suddenly paused to let her catch up, his eyes searching the path behind them. She pulled her scarf off of her face as she approached.

"Expecting someone to join us?" she asked.

"No," he snapped. "Are you?"

"Only you." He's more paranoid than me, she thought. "Could we go someplace warm?"

"This is better."

He was an obvious fat cat—his hat sable, his overcoat cashmere lined with fur. Everything about him spoke of an *apparatchik*—one of the middle management bureaucrats who ran the country. But there was another quality about him, one that made her uneasy. His pockmarked face, fat cruel lips, black, slicked-back hair—the brute-brained look of an old-line Communist, down to a wide-lapel suit coat and pants tailored for tree trunks. He conveyed a sort of menace, that of a cold Soviet bureaucrat who would walk down a line of peasants kneeling before a mass grave and put a bullet in the head of each . . .

"You have murder on your mind."

"What?"

"You're not fooling me," Belkin said. "I worked for the government. You believe your mother was murdered years ago and now you have come to hunt down the killer. Am I right? Yes, I am right."

She took a deep breath before answering. The man really rattled her cage. She almost told him it was her own murder that she was most concerned about at the moment.

"At the time of your mother's death I was in a position to know a little about it."

His words electrified her.

He saw her reaction and beat a retreat. "What I am saying is that I was in a position to have read reports that were not released to the public. Your mother took a psychedelic drug, LSD or some other hallucinogenic drug. She went crazy, attempted to harm you, her own daughter, and ended up driving a car at high speed into a petrol tanker truck. Boom!" He threw his hands in the air. "That was the end of it."

"Not exactly. My mother was a 1960s Berkeley radical and it's easy for people to immediately identify her with acid trips, but I know that wasn't true. My mother didn't take drugs. She was an anti-war activist, not a hippie. She was a college professor and intellectual—"

"Like Professor Leary, the American drug guru?"

"An idealist and pacifist and health nut. She was not the acid-taking radical that the newspapers tried to portray her as after her death."

Winter night bit at her exposed cheeks and stung her nose. She wanted so much to tell this arrogant bastard to screw off, that her mother's memory was too precious to be debated with someone like him.

Lara turned her head so he couldn't read her thoughts.

An apparatchik had the soul of a metal desk, but it wasn't his lack of sensitivity that suddenly struck her. There was something else, an almost subliminal signal underlining his words. Her instincts honed from years of prosecuting liars and thieves were going off like a heart monitor during cardiac arrest. He was dangerous—and couldn't be trusted.

The dark night was falling closer to the ground in an icy mist. Streetlights cast a gloomy pallor on the lamps and exposed shadowy trees stripped to skeletons by winter's cold hand.

Light glowed in the distance and she heard music. She glanced back over her shoulder and he caught her eye. "Just paranoid about being in a park at night."

"Parks belong to the people of Moscow, day and night," he said. "We have not yet given them up to criminals as you Westerners have. But now"—he lifted his hands as if there were a Communist heaven that would hear his plea somewhere in the darkness above—"with the new regime . . ."

"We should have met in a restaurant," she said. "I don't know how you people can stand this cold. My feet are frostbitten."

"Tell me about the photograph," he said.

She continued walking without responding. The meeting had been set up so she could gain information, not hand it out. She decided to tell him as much as Gropski knew since Gropski had probably already filled him in. "It's a black and white police crime scene photo of a woman who had been slashed with a knife."

"And what do you want from me?"

She had given that question a lot of thought and was ready to reach for the golden ring.

"I want access to secret KGB files. The ones stored at the Lubyanka."

TWO

Lubyanka. The word hung between them, suspended in the frozen night as they walked.

"This woman in the photograph," Belkin said, "it was your mother?"

"I'm sure it's my mother. The woman's face is partly under bedcovers, but she's the same age and size as my mother was. Besides, there would be no reason for anyone to send me the picture if it wasn't my mother."

"The message that came with the picture. What did it say?"

"There was no written message."

Belkin stopped and stared at her. "No message?"

"Just the picture. Postmarked Moscow."

"And you came halfway around the world . . . because of a picture with no message?"

"I came to Moscow because the picture itself was a message. I know my mother didn't get high on drugs and run her car into a tanker. The person who sent me the picture knows it, too."

"You were a child, yes."

"I'm not a child now. I came back to Moscow a couple of weeks ago and one of the first things I did was go to the accident site, a deserted stretch of road about fifty miles east of the city. There's a small village nearby and I checked the police records there for the day my mother was supposed to have died. The village police still have their handwritten records going back to tsarist times. They were proud to show them to me." After she had greased the palm of the constable in charge, she almost added.

"The day of my mother's death there was a report of a farm tractor stuck in a ditch, a wife complaining about her drunken husband, a tire stolen from someone's car. A tractor stuck in the mud rated eighteen lines but a horrendous accident involving a head-on collision between a passenger car and a petroleum tanker, an accident that killed a famous American peace activist, wasn't even mentioned. It had to be the biggest event that happened in that village for decades and yet there's no record of it.''

''An accident involving a foreigner would not have been handled by village police,'' he said.

''I know, it would have been handled by the KGB which had jurisdiction over everything concerning foreigners. But that doesn't mean a significant event wouldn't have been noted in the police ledger.''

''This picture of a woman, this message without words, show it to me.''

''I don't have it on me.'' She was ready with the lie. Gropski had already demanded to see the photo. ''I keep it in a safe place.''

''There was no safe place to keep something from an official of the government before. Now . . .'' He looked back up to the Communist heaven.

''I, uh, showed it to the crime lab people in my San Francisco office,'' she said, to fill in the void left by her refusal to show him the picture. ''They provided me with a psychological profile of the person who committed the crime.''

''Psychological profile?''

''A profile of the mental state of the person who did the killing. It's obtained by analysis of the wounds.''

Another grunt. No doubt he was used to analyzing criminal behavior with a rubber hose, Lara thought, not with a computer.

''It was a crime of passion?'' he asked.

''A crime of insanity. The . . . the woman,'' she couldn't say her mother, ''was mutilated by a savage attack that included slashing her sex organs. She wasn't simply stabbed—the killer was in an insane frenzy.''

"I remember a similar case," he said, "it occurred around the same time, over twenty years ago. A seventeen-year-old boy killed a woman in the building where he lived. The woman was a foreigner, Scandinavian. No doubt the woman brought the attack on herself by provoking the boy."

Jesus, what an ass.

"Swedish girls, that's what she was now that I recall, are notorious sexual deviates. This type of crime would not have been committed in the Soviet Union without foreign influence."

Oh, bullshit. Beria, the old KGB chief, used to have his men grab women off the streets of Moscow at night so he could rape and abuse them. Fathers and husbands who objected ended up dead or were sent off to forced labor camps. The crimes never officially happened.

"You have wasted your time coming to Moscow. The woman in the picture is not your mother. Give me the picture and I will have the jokester who sent it to you tracked down and punished."

Eagerness. It slipped through the tough hue of Belkin's voice. She had noticed the same tone from Gropski at the hotel. It sent a little shiver through her. Other than to her, what was so important about the picture?

"As I said, I believe that the person who sent me the picture was sending a message that the official version of my mother's death was not true."

"Nonsense! Your mother's death was investigated by the proper officials. The findings are not open to question."

"I went to the university where my mother used to teach. There's no record of her. I checked the militia files here in Moscow, there's no report on my mother's so-called accident. I went to the apartment building where we used to live. The manager from the old days has passed away but I persuaded her daughter-in-law to show me the tenant book from that time. A page was missing, the page that would have registered our stay in the building. Do you understand?'' It was almost a plea. ''It's as if someone spat on the slate and wiped my mother off of it. An entire life is missing.''

''So it is your belief that the KGB was involved in your mother's death.''

She shrugged. ''Who else could make a person invisible in the Soviet Union? But no, I don't think that the KGB was responsible for my mother's death. A different form of insanity than politics caused my mother's death.''

Her feet were frozen and she wasn't sure if her toes had broken off and were bouncing around her boots. Her whole body had become cold.

''What's the matter with you? You're shaking. Are you ill?'' Belkin asked.

''No. I'm not used to this cold weather. It's much warmer in San Francisco.''

''It's the weather that makes us Russians strong. We fight the winter with vodka and hot beds.'' He tried to slip his arm around her waist and she moved away, pretending to smother a cough.

The sound of music had gotten louder. ''I hear music,'' she said.

''Yes, there's a carnival. We will see it.''

Lights from the carnival created a glowing dome in the freezing mist ahead and the music gained volume with each step. Only the Russians would have a carnival tucked away in a dark park on a freezing night, she thought.

''That's Christmas music,'' she said. She quickened her pace and followed the sound around a bend. The path straightened and led down to an old-fashioned carnival with Ferris wheel, carousel, and booths selling chances to win prizes.

''Amazing,'' she said. ''They've put Christmas trim on the booths, but those elves hustling people look like—''

''Gypsies.'' The look on his face told her Gypsies were bugs to squash.

Off to the right, on a massive monument to the "Heroic Workers of the Ural Mines" who had provided the steel for Soviet tanks, chubby, rosy-faced children sang Christmas carols to a larger group of beaming parents.

"Gypsies dressed as elves and children singing Christmas carols on a Communist monument."

"Blacks and Mafia," Belkin said about the Gypsies.

Three giggling teenage girls ran by, eager to get to the carnival games. Belkin stared at their backsides as if they were pieces of meat to hump; his big paws opened and closed as if he were squeezing a succulent piece of their anatomy.

She realized who Belkin reminded her of. A man she prosecuted a couple of years ago, a Market Street stripjoint owner who had beaten one of the girls, then had taken his big hands and squeezed her inflated breasts until the silicone implants burst. In court, as she had turned from the jury, she had met his dead eyes and saw his big hands squeezing the end of the counsel table . . .

She cleared her throat. "I need to make arrangements," meaning payment, "to, uh, inspect my mother's KGB file. Mr. Gropski said you could get me access to the KGB archives."

It was a moment before he spoke. "Freaks. They have a freak show. And a dwarf."

The freak show was ahead of them on the left side of the midway, the wall of the show tent lining the midway with pictures of deformed people. A small person in a tall Cossack hat and heavy fur coat, Belkin's "dwarf," stood on a platform and shook his cane at the crowd passing by, urging the people to come in and see the Fat Lady, Snake Man, Tattoo Man, and the Crocodile Woman.

"Freak shows are outlawed in America," she said.

"Freaks fascinate me."

His response surprised her. She would have guessed that nothing fascinated the man. Apparatchiks were not given to imagination.

"And disgust me. Human deformities. Have you ever met a freak?"

She didn't know how to answer because she never considered disabilities as unnatural.

"I know one," he said. "I have made a study of a freak. They are interesting because they are . . . abnormal. Am I right? Yes, I am right."

Her uneasiness increased. Something in his voice . . . a message? A warning?

Keeping her fear and dislike of him under control was getting more difficult. She wanted to pay him and run, but he seemed to enjoy having her beside him as he strutted along, glaring contemptuously at everything he saw. With a clipboard he would have looked very much like a petty apparatchik recording names of people who dared to enjoy themselves.

"Look at these fools," he said, "they worry about food for their children, they use the same bone for three soups, and they come here and throw their money to thieves."

People who should have been worried about bread were lined up several deep at every booth, trying to win a stuffed animal by getting coins to stick on slippery plates, tossing plastic loops at vodka bottles, throwing knives at balloons. Knives were so much more Russian and Gypsy than darts, she thought.

At a shooting gallery, a group of drunk Russian paratroopers wearing Afghanistan and Chekian campaign ribbons were having a wild contest shooting pellets at metal ducks.

Tall, hoary old Grandfather Frost and Snow Maiden walked among the sideshow crowds selling colorful wrapped "gifts."

"Those bastard thieves should be sent off to Siberia for reeducation," Belkin said of the Gypsies. "Along with the fools who give them money. Not so long ago we would have swept the park clean of this trash."

"Let them have fun," she said. "The economy is getting worse, everyone is expecting another political coup, something like this is a good diversion. Besides, look at the faces in the crowd, the adults are as excited as the children.''

She glanced back over her shoulder again.

''Are you certain you were not followed?'' he demanded.

''Why would I have been followed? I don't know anyone in Moscow. I just got a little frightened walking from my hotel in the dark. I'm going to take a taxi back.''

''You need a man to protect you. Am I right?''

What she really needed was a gun.

A little boy carrying a balloon on a stick got too close to Belkin and he popped the balloon. He held up his hand in mock innocence to show Lara a huge diamond ring. ''An accident.''

Lara glanced back sympathetically at the little boy.

The child gave her the finger.

Russian kids weren't much different from the home grown.

''They are selling human meat in the butcher shops,'' he said.

''I read something about government inspectors finding a human knuckle bone in a batch of pigs' feet. But there are always crazy rumors during bad times.''

''Cannibalism,'' he said smugly. ''We had it after both wars and it is coming back again. Strangers attacked on the roadside and the bodies dragged into the forest to be butchered. Mark my words—it is no coincidence that we have this invasion of Gypsies just as we find human meat on our shelves. If those of us capable of running the country do not return to power you will see Gypsies stealing Russian children and selling their flesh. Am I right? Yes, yes, I am right.''

An old Gypsy woman, a small person, similar in size to the man hustling for the freak show, came up beside Belkin and touched his arm.

"Let me reveal the future to—"

"Get away from me, you diseased old hag." He jerked his arm away with such force the woman stumbled back and fell.

Lara rushed to her and helped her to her feet. She looked back at Belkin. His expression told her he had just stepped on a bug. "I'll be with you in a moment," she told the bastard. "I've never had my fortune told."

She tried to force a smile but couldn't manage it. She never really had a desire to be a man—but every once in a while she wished she had the strength of a 220-pound San Francisco linebacker so she could kick the crap out of some ass who sorely deserved it.

Following the Gypsy to a small booth near the freak show, she sat on a rickety wooden chair across the table from the woman and glanced over her shoulder to make sure Belkin was sticking around. He was looking at billboards displaying the oddities and deformities of the freak show stars.

Dark Gypsy eyes studied her. "You are tall and fair. Much too thin for a Russian winter. My Gypsy brothers would be attracted to you. The man you are with is not worth the price of your beauty."

Lara blushed. "The man is not a friend. He is providing information about . . . a personal problem. I'm sorry he was rude to you."

Keen eyes in a wrinkled old face drilled into hers. "I know he is not your friend."

"Can you really tell the future?"

"You are not Russian," the Gypsy said, "though you speak almost as one."

"You're not Russian either. And your accent is much worse than mine. Are you Romanian?"

It was as good a guess as any, she thought. Romania was famous for Gypsies and vampires.

"I am from many places," the woman said, "and from

none.'' She didn't smile but kept her intense eyes burning into Lara. ''That man,'' she said, nodding in Belkin's direction. He had wandered over to a booth selling magic novelties and love potions. ''He is not a good man. He does not mean well for you.''

''That's true,'' Lara said. ''I've already figured that one out.'' Afraid she'd lose Belkin, she took a wad of rubles out of her purse and slipped a thousand-ruble bill from it—about a dollar at the current rate of exchange and not far from the official minimum daily wage.

''I'm sorry for the way he pushed you.'' She put the money on the table and got up.

The woman slipped the money up her sleeve.

''You are troubled,'' she said.

Lara shook her head. ''I came to Moscow for personal reasons. I think winter is getting to me. Everything is so cold and gray. I'll feel better when I get home and see some sunshine.''

''A shadow walks in your footsteps.''

''Sounds like an old Gypsy tale,'' Lara said, leaving the tent.

The Gypsy woman's words caught up with her as she was walking away. ''This shadow brings death.'' The woman jerked shut the curtains that closed off the front of the tent.

Lara stepped back to the tent but hesitated at pulling the curtain open. It was just an act, part of the game, she told herself, but the words hacked at her and she jerked back the curtain.

The woman was gone. She had slipped out the back.

Lara stepped around the small table in the middle of the booth and fumbled with the curtains. Finding the opening, she stepped through, coming out behind the tent.

The fortune-teller was nowhere in sight, but a tall man with thick black hair, no hat, and wearing a cheap, loose-fitting overcoat was leaning against the streetlamp. His hands were in his coat pockets and he had a cigarette dangling from his mouth.

"Hello," she said with a smile, "did you see the fortune-teller?"

Taking the cigarette out of his mouth, he nodded toward the back door to the freak show.

"She went in there. Probably to put on her crocodile skin for the next show."

"Thanks."

She slipped back into the booth feeling like a fool for chasing after a dwarf fortune-teller who doubled as a crocodile woman. Too bad the guy smoked, she thought, as she headed for Belkin. There was a rough sensuality to him, a little Al Pacino, a tough guy with a big heart. But she didn't like men who smoked.

The Gypsy woman had turned her paranoia on fire and she glanced back at the path leading into the carnival.

Just part of the act, she told herself.

Just part of the act.

Behind the Gypsy tent Yuri cursed his bad luck.

She had seen him.

That changed the way the game had to be played.

Belkin was still at the booth that sold magic and love potions. His back was to her as she left the fortune-teller's tent. Crystal flakes, sprinkles just big enough to be called snow, had started falling from the night sky.

The Gypsy woman's words had shaken her. She needed to get out of the park and back to her hotel, away from the weird Christmas celebration with freaks and Gypsies and a throwback to the old regime.

This is crazy. She had to get control. She couldn't let an old Gypsy woman get to her.

Why hadn't Belkin mentioned money? It bugged her. Everyone from the hotel security man and clerks at government offices to the taxi drivers in between had been on the take.

Why did he want the picture?

As she came up behind him, he turned to face her, a bloody dagger sticking in his chest.

THREE

Lara stared at the dagger, her eyes glued on the blood. She worked her jaw muscles and finally it burst out of her, a scream that stopped all the action around them.

The hustlers stopped hustling, the marks stopped pulling money out of their socks, the dwarf on the platform in front of the freak show cut his spiel in midsentence, his cane raised overhead. Every eye on the midway went to her and Belkin.

Belkin's expression slowly relaxed. One of his big paws went up to his chest. The dagger came away with a wad of plastic blood. A chuckle began deep in his chest and exploded as an almost girlish giggle as he pointed up at the "magic" sign above the booth.

Tension snapped and people all around them began to laugh; a shrill cackle from the little man hustling the freak show pierced the night.

She wanted to crawl into a hole and die.

An elderly couple walked by and the old woman shook a finger at her. "Silly girl."

Belkin was still chuckling as they walked away from the carnival.

Lara began to wish the bastard really had been stabbed.

The freezing night, the crazy carnival, the old Gypsy,

and the bastard had worn her nerves and patience to the breaking point.

"Mr. Belkin, this meeting was set up to help me access KGB files in the Lubyanka. Can you help?"

"Have you ever been in the Lubyanka?"

The question sent shivers down her back. The Lubyanka was not just KGB headquarters, it was the brutal prison where dissenters or anyone else the old regime squeezed with its steel fist were taken. Some people never came out alive. The lucky ones ended up in the forced labor camps of Siberia.

"No, but if you can make the arrangements, I'll be happy to, uh, pay an appropriate fee."

His grunt told her that the money was meaningless to him. So what was he after?

"You will be disappointed even if you find the file you seek. You will discover that the KGB was the most important organ of the state in ensuring that justice was administered evenly and democratically, that the stories you have heard about excesses are just that—stories. Certainly if a woman was brutalized, the KGB would have been the first to seek punishment for the perpetrator without political considerations."

Lara could imagine the man beside her using his authority to paw and molest young women. He even looked like her mental image of the notorious Beria. When Beria was dethroned and executed by Khrushchev, it was not for his crimes against women, many of them teenage girls, but for his political ambitions.

"Look at the litter in the park and along the streets," he said. "Soon the city will be as dirty as American cities. Drugs are pouring into the country. Next there will be drive-by shootings."

She cleared her throat and reached deep into her almost-dry well of patience for just a little more to tolerate this insufferable man. "I suppose the streets were cleaner and, uh, much better maintained under the Soviet regime."

He pointed up at the night sky, at the light snowfall drifting down. "Even the snow was cleaner under us Soviets."

"About gaining access to my mother's file in the KGB archives . . ."

"I have made the arrangements. But my fee is the picture. A copy of it," he assured her smoothly.

"Okay. A copy of it. But not until I get what I want. Can you get me into the archives?"

"I can get you into them. As I told you, it has already been arranged. Now let me see the picture."

"I don't have it. It's back in my room."

His eyes shot to her purse and she needed every ounce of control to keep from tightening her grip on it. If he had suspected it was in her purse he might have simply grabbed it. She thanked her courtroom experience, the never show surprise when the other side drops a bomb at your feet.

"I have it well hidden in my room," she said, thinking at the same time that Gropski had probably already searched her room and might have told Belkin it wasn't there. "And I dropped off a copy to the American Embassy," she lied. "In a sealed envelope. If I get admission to the archives I'll give you a copy of the picture."

Tension in his huge shoulders relaxed a fraction.

Jesus, I made it.

"I want to see the picture—"

"First the archives. Look, Mr. Belkin, I don't mean to be rude, but I've had a couple of unpleasant days. If you want to make a deal, fine. If not, there are people on almost every street corner offering the Soviet's old secrets for a price."

"You will see your archives. And when you are finished, you will give me a copy of the picture. If you do not . . ."

There's nothing like an unspoken threat to really get across a point.

"How do I get in?" she asked.

"Tonight at one o'clock in the morning you will meet a man named Minsky at the Lubyanka Square metro station. He will be in the tea shop."

"Tonight? In the middle of the night? Can't we—"

"Don't be a fool. This archive contains top-secret KGB files. Would you prefer to present yourself tomorrow morning at the Ministry of Security and tell them you wish to sneak into the archives?"

"What do I pay—"

Belkin slapped away the question with the back of his hand. "Minsky will take care of those details. He will charge you five hundred American dollars." He stopped walking and faced her. "You are not to show that picture to anyone, not even that fool Gropski. Do you understand?"

"Yes."

"When you return from the archives I will be waiting in the tea shop. We will return together to your room and get the picture."

"You can see the picture in my room, but I'm not giving you that one. We can have a copy made in the morning."

She didn't know if the explanation annoyed him or if the look on his face meant he was disgusted with her, the situation, and life in general because he had to negotiate with fools like her rather than crush them.

"Tonight," he said.

He turned away and walked toward the corner where a group of people were waiting to cross the street.

She deliberately started in the other direction, heading away from him to find a taxi. When she was fifty feet away she turned to see if he was following her. The broad back of his camel-colored coat was visible in the crowd waiting for the light to change at the corner.

Turning back, sighing, wondering why God put creeps like Belkin on this earth, she heard a crash and swung back around. A truck had stopped at the curb a little farther down the street and a crowd was starting to gather around someone lying facedown in the gutter.

The person was wearing a camel-colored coat.

She ran back, nearly taking a fall as she slipped on new snow. People surrounded the prone figure in the gutter but she pushed through them to get a look at the man in the gutter.

Belkin.

Voices babbled about what had happened.

"The man fell in front of the truck."

"He was pushed."

"He's dead."

"The man's injured. Has anyone called an ambulance?"

As Lara moved toward the gutter to get a closer view an elderly woman shoved her back, not about to give up her gawking space. It was the same woman who had called her "silly girl" earlier when she screamed about the bloody dagger.

Ignoring the woman, Lara stood on her toes to get a look. She felt someone uncomfortably close to her backside as a raspy voice whispered in her ear.

"*Come closer.*"

Before she could react, a hand went between her legs and clawed at her crotch as another hand gave her a shove. She fell forward against the old woman, taking the woman to the ground with her.

"Bitch!" the old woman snarled.

The old woman got on her knees and clawed at Lara as her husband tried to help her up. Lara pulled herself away and looked around wildly for the person who had assaulted her.

"Did you see that nurse?" somebody asked.

"Nurse?" Lara's voice quavered.

An image flashed in her mind.

The landing outside their apartment. Her mother bundling her up for school. Someone in white . . . a nurse coming out of a room at the next landing.

"I saw a nurse standing by you," the woman said. "I called for her because she could have helped the injured man, but she walked away. That's the trouble with . . ."

Lara hurried away. Her throat began to tighten and her head started to pound, the words slashing at her.

Come closer . . .

V

So many lips have fell silent,
so many eyes have closed forever.

—Tusya Gabbe, Russian
book editor, talking about
the victims of Stalin's Terror, as quoted by
Lydia Chukovskaya,
The Akhmatova Journals

ONE

Her knees shook as she walked across the lobby of the Gorky.

The clerk was bent over a newspaper spread on the front desk, supporting his chin on his hands and elbows. He looked up as she approached.

"May I help you?"

"Gropski, the security man, where is he?"

"Mr. Gropski is not on the premises. Do you have a problem regarding security?"

"Yes—no, I'm checking out."

"Yes, of course. You wish your bags transferred—"

"No, wait, I'm not checking out." A wave of nausea hit her and she leaned against the counter for support.

"Not checking out. Does Madam need a doctor?"

"I need a—" She almost said gun, but held her tongue. She took a deep breath and tried focusing on the clerk with glassy eyes. "I—I'm sorry, I'm not checking out, not tonight, I'll check out tomorrow. I have to do something tonight."

Turning away from the clerk, she headed for the elevator. She had never taken the elevator before, it looked as run-down and anemic as the city was becoming, but tonight her weak knees wouldn't carry her up the stairs.

Leaning back against the elevator wall, she unintentionally snubbed the friendly, smiling woman operating the lift.

Safely in her room, she slammed the door behind her, too drained mentally and emotionally to barricade the door. She sat on the bed and stared down at the floor. Her mind had been scrambled since the incident on the street and now she forced herself to set things out in order.

Belkin had been hit by a truck. He was hurt, how serious she didn't know. From the conversations she had heard around her she had the impression that he wasn't dead but she couldn't be positive about that.

Right now she wasn't positive about anything. Except that she was being stalked.

That was a certainty.

The incident with Belkin might have been an accident . . . but that would be too much of a coincidence. The person stalking her had pushed Belkin into the path of the truck.

Why? Because Belkin was helping her, because he wanted the picture, because . . . she didn't know all the becauses, she just knew it couldn't be a coincidence.

Last night a woman disguised as a priest attacked her in the cathedral.

Tonight it was a nurse.

The two people had to be the same.

The childhood memory came to her again, the nurse emerging onto the landing from the apartment above as Lara was leaving for school, Lara and her mother looking up . . .

The memory gave her an immediate throbbing at the temples. She shook her head and put aside the image, unable to deal with the past any longer. It was after nine. The appointment with Minsky and the KGB archives was set for one in the morning in a subway station.

How could she go through with it? How could she go

out on the dark street and make her way to a rendezvous halfway across the city? She didn't have the strength or the guts. It was too much. She wanted to go home, recuperate. But she couldn't. Someone had lured her back to Moscow, someone who knew words from her nightmares.

Why after over twenty years? What had happened? Who was hiding a dark secret from the past that she threatened to expose?

One thing was clear about Belkin—he was not simply a go-between brought in by the hotel security man. Belkin knew something about the picture. If not the picture, then about her mother's death. Perhaps it arose from his job in the KGB.

She was sure he was ex-KGB. What had he said? That he had been in a position to know things about her mother's death that were never revealed to the public?

He wanted the picture. For what reason? To protect someone? Blackmail? Advancement? Revenge?

She shook her head. Too much speculation, too many roads for her mind to travel. Right now she had to concentrate on the most critical problem: someone had lured her back to Moscow and was trying to terrorize her . . . and kill her. And she had to go back out onto Moscow's dark streets to the KGB archives.

What does a person do when someone wants to kill them? she asked herself. Not just ''someone'' but probably a maniac.

Get the police to investigate. But the police were a problem. Nothing worked quite right in the city, not even the police. Before the Fall the KGB had handled most of the internal security and everything involving foreigners, leaving the local police, the militia, to handle traffic tickets and petty offenses.

The KGB was gone and the militia lacked the training, equipment, and leadership to fill the gap.

She heard a story at the American Embassy of a young French girl who had been murdered, probably by her Russian boyfriend. The police horribly botched the investigation, never even taking fingerprints from the crime scene or preserving blood samples. The killer was still free.

But her problems with the police went deeper than their competence and the fact they thought she was a nutcase from California. It had to do with leaving the dead buried.

When she first arrived in Moscow she went to the Criminal Investigation Unit of the Moscow police. She had expected courtesy, cooperation, and information. What she received was cold water in her face.

With the city under attack by a crime wave that included the birth of the Russian Mafia and a massive drug trade, a crime that had been solved two decades ago didn't provoke any interest. When she started talking cover-up, the deputy commander escorted her firmly by the arm to his door and told her to go back to America. "We are not resurrecting the past to punish the living and defame the dead," he had told her.

After the incident at the cathedral, they really believed that she was a nutcase.

She fumbled with the predicament, certain she had neither the courage, fortitude, nor stupidity to go traipsing around dark and dangerous Moscow in the middle of the night. Lying back on the bed, she pulled the covers over her, too cold and stressed even to take off her boots. She needed a plan. She had to make that appointment, but she wasn't walking out into the dark streets by herself.

She'd hire Gropski to go with her. He was probably the worst choice. But who the hell else could she get to help her break into KGB archives?

At thirty minutes past midnight, she went down to the lobby. The night clerk was sleeping with his head on his folded arms on the countertop.

"Excuse me, sir, excuse me."

The man rose from his slumber and leaned back, taking a deep yawn, nearly falling off his chair.

"May I help you?"

"Has Mr. Gropski returned?"

"No, he hasn't reported in."

"Who's in charge of security when he's gone?"

"Mr. Nosenko."

"I'd like to speak to Mr. Nosenko."

"He's on vacation at the Black Sea."

Her temper rose a notch.

"Then who is—" No, she knew the routine by now. "Gropski's not here, Nosenko's not here, so no one is in charge of security at the hotel while they're gone. Is that it?"

The clerk tried to shake some of the sleep out of his head. "Nosenko's in charge of security when Gropski's—"

"But Nosenko's at the Black Sea!"

"Yes, but when Gropski is gone, that means—"

"Forget it." So much for the bodyguard.

She spun on her heel and started for the front doors, steaming. These people have had the government telling them what to do for so long, they've forgotten how to think.

She followed the sound of snoring to locate the porter. He was spread out asleep on a luggage bench in a tiny alcove just behind the porter's desk.

Awoken, he came out of his cave buttoning his uniform coat and apologizing.

"I want you to walk with me over to the Metrope Hotel so I can get a taxi."

"You want me to carry your luggage?"

"No luggage. I don't want to walk alone in the dark."

"I can call you a taxi."

"Will it come?"

He shrugged. "Probably not."

"Then let's not call one. I'll give you five American dollars if you come with me."

Sleep popped out of his eyes and he literally snapped to

attention. "I'll accompany you. It's dangerous for a woman alone at night."

She pushed open the front door. Moscow freeze attacked her the moment she stepped outside. Pulling her hat down over her ears, she adjusted her scarf until it covered her nose.

The porter followed her into the night, stuffing his shirt down his pants, buttoning his heavy wool jacket.

"I'm leaving this hotel," she told him. "There's no security, the restaurant is poisonous—on those rare occasions when it decides to open—and there are no taxis. And the damn place is freezing."

"Yes, yes," he huffed beside her. "Ah, but the old days—"

"When the snow was cleaner," she snapped.

"Yes! Yes, it was cleaner. Why, back during the Great Patriotic War—"

"There's a taxi!"

A taxi was approaching the hotel and Lara turned to hurry back to the entry to meet it.

"Perhaps you'd like a different taxi?" the old porter told her as he hurried beside her.

"I'll still give you the money."

"This taxi is a good one. Only a few dents . . ."

Two men in business suits, ties askew, a breeze of vodka following them, exited the taxi. From their accents they appeared to be Ukrainians. One of them reached for her arm as she moved by them to take the taxi. "Pretty lady, join us for a drink," came out in poor Russian as she pushed aside the arm and got into the taxi, slamming the door and locking it.

She wasn't flattered by being called pretty—her scarf covered most of her face. "Pretty" to a drunk was anything wearing women's clothes.

She rolled down the window just enough to give the porter a five-dollar bill as the taxi pulled away.

"Men in this country are a century behind in women's

rights," she told the driver, who was a woman.

"Russian men are bastards," the woman said. "I like the foreign ones, especially the French and Italian. They know how to treat a woman right. American men think sex is something they get for dessert if they buy you dinner. Where am I taking you?"

"The metro station at Lubyanka Square."

The woman shot Lara a look in the rearview mirror as she moved through the light street traffic.

"A taxi to a metro station?"

"I'm, uh, meeting a friend," Lara said.

The woman shrugged. "Not that you shouldn't take a taxi, the metro's not safe at night. They're talking about putting Afghanistan War veterans with assault rifles on the trains to protect honest citizens. Pretty soon the city will be like New York. Criminals will have more guns than the police."

Lara wondered if the woman was a defense plant layoff. She had the look of a professional. She had heard of engineers and scientists driving taxis because of layoffs at all types of plants. A group of prostitutes dominating the bar at the best hotel in town were formerly engineers at a defense plant.

She had to admit that prostitution was a slightly better way to feed your kids than cannibalism.

TWO

Lara stared at the Lubyanka as the taxi entered the square. True to Russian logic, the "square" was circular. She had seen the building in the daytime when she was making her rounds trying to dig up information about her mother, but the most notorious building in Russia took on a sinister cast in the gloom of night.

"A friend of mine has Dzerzhinsky's left toe."

Lara glanced at the empty pedestal where the huge statue of the founder of the CHEKA, an earlier predecessor to the KGB, had been pulled down after the August coup attempt. She wondered if Dzerzhinsky's left toe was as valuable as a piece of the Berlin Wall.

Lara gave the driver a generous tip and hurried away.

The stairway to the underground was littered with newspapers and two men sharing a bottle of vodka. She stepped quickly by the men, wishing the mysterious Minsky had chosen somewhere on street level for their meeting.

The tea shop was a makeshift kiosk with a few tables scattered out front. There was only one customer seated and he stared apprehensively at her as she approached.

"Mr. Minsky?"

He winced and looked round to see if anyone had heard the name. The only other person in the kiosk was a beefy woman behind the counter washing cups.

Lara sat down across from him, thankful he didn't have Belkin's brutal mentality written on his face. In fact, he looked more like a rabbit than KGB middle management.

The woman washing cups looked over to her and Lara shook her head no, she didn't want anything.

"Mr. Belkin sent me. He said—"

"Yes, yes, I understand, we don't have to discuss it."

The rabbit was a nervous wreck. She wondered if he had heard about Belkin's accident. If he hadn't, it didn't seem the right thing to mention when he was shaking in his boots at just the sight of her.

He spiked his tea with a splash of vodka from a flask and downed the drink, allowing a little to dribble on his coat front where it joined the residual of previous meals and drinks.

He was older than she had expected, probably in his sixties. Definitely not a Belkin fat cat, Minsky's clothes were winter heavy but threadbare, the shoulders of his coat littered with dandruff.

He had the look of a shop-worn bookworm rather than a night watchman. His straggly hair was dirty white, his eyebrows driven snow and bushy, protecting eyes that had a hint of pink. His face had mostly sunk into jowls that weren't clean-shaven but had faint white hairs pointing straight out like tiny needles of an albino cactus. He reminded her of a big-footed rabbit, old and scuffed and . . . odd. One that had just crawled out of a hole and was looking around, amazed the world was still here.

He slammed his cup down on the table and coughed onto the back of his coat sleeve. Picking up a piece of the newspaper he had been reading, he rattled it at her. "Look, look at him, imitating the old aristocracy."

He was referring to a newspaper article about a Moscow entrepreneur, the enfant terrible of the new Russian rich, who had bought a museum-palace on the outskirts of the city from the workers committee that had managed it before the Fall. The whole country was talking about it because the man had taken possession of national treasures and was fighting the government's attempt to get them back.

"He's trying to make serfs out of us poor people," Minsky muttered. "He's stolen a palace and calls it his dacha. KGB one day, next day a millionaire." Minsky's hands shook as he held up the newspaper.

He was so damn nervous it was making her nervous.

"The money. American," he whispered.

She took five hundred dollars out of her purse and put it on the table. "Mr. Minsky, I—"

He slapped the paper on top of the money and stared at her wide-eyed.

"Sorry," she said, kicking herself for exposing the money transfer. She wasn't used to being covert. Being a prosecutor, passing bribe money was the sort of thing she saw in police snapshots and hidden videos.

Minsky glanced over to make sure the counter woman had her back to them before he slid his hand under the paper to take the money. After another furtive look around, he counted the money, keeping it and his hands beneath the table.

"There's only five hundred. I must have a thousand."

The Moscow hustle.

"The deal was five hundred. I'm not paying any more."

"New deal," he said, with an attempt at looking tough that came out more whining than hard. "Most people pay a thousand to get into the archives. I can lose my job, my pension."

A train was coming into the station and she watched it, resisting an impulse to blow at him. The metro closed at one o'clock and the train that pulled in let off a couple of people and didn't take anyone on.

She couldn't afford to pay a thousand dollars. "Mr. Minsky, the price I was quoted and accepted was five hundred dollars. If that is not good enough, give me the money back. And"—she leaned in closer talking a little louder—"before you entertain any notions about keeping my money, let me tell you I will be at the Ministry of Security when it opens in the morning if I don't get every cent back."

His pink eyes bulged and his face turned crimson. "Come with me," he croaked.

She followed him into the station and down the high-ceilinged corridor.

Overweight, arthritic, and asthmatic, he wheezed as he inhaled and wheezed as he exhaled. "The government with its capitalistic ideas is making thieves out of honest men."

She glanced at the derelicts in the underground and didn't see an honest man. It occurred to her that he might be talking about himself.

"They're trying to kill off the old people. The new Russia is for the young. They don't want to pay pensions to the old. They're killing us off with cold and starvation. Why don't they just shoot us. Better to die fast."

If whining was infectious, the old man had a near fatal dose of it. She changed the subject.

"Are you a night guard at the archives?"

"I was once a KGB historian." A moment's pride fell before self-pity. "Now there is nothing to record. The KGB is gone and a wet-nosed ministry has taken over. Once I made a record of history. Now I sit in a chair and smoke cigarettes and watch history grow dust."

She suddenly felt sorry for him. He had spent a lifetime under one system, worked, planned, saved, and was ready for retirement when the system fell and inflation soared not into double digits but into the thousands of percent.

"Because I no longer earn enough for meat in my soup I am turned into a criminal by foreigners who want to peek into our secrets."

Bypassing escalators leading up to the street level, he led her behind the mechanical steps to a door with a sign that warned against entry. A dim lightbulb in a wire cage caked with dead bugs hung above the door.

He pressed a button concealed on the side of the door molding and a moment later a judas window opened and an eye examined them.

Just like a Roaring Twenties speakeasy, she thought, keeping a straight face.

The door swung open and a dour man with a bushy mustache and huge belly let them in. The door was thick and solid enough to secure a walk-in bank safe.

The guard station consisted of an iron chair with a pillow on it. Newspapers, lunch, and a thermos bottle were on the floor next to the chair. The guard gave her a hard stare and she met his eye. Another pensioner, but this one looked mean and cranky.

"You have to pay him two hundred dollars," Minsky said.

"What?"

Minsky looked away.

"I already paid him," she told the guard.

"Now you pay me."

"I'm not paying you anything. I paid him five hundred."

The man glared at Minsky. "So little? You give away the KGB's secrets for small change?"

Minsky shrugged. "I'm a hungry man."

"You're both—" She cut it off, knowing she couldn't win. She dug five twenties out of her purse. "I'll give you a hundred dollars. If that's not enough I'm leaving."

The man took the money without a word and she saw a look pass between them. They would be splitting the total take later.

"There had better be no more surprises," she told Minsky as they walked side by side down a dank corridor.

He wheezed.

The concrete corridor was poorly lit. Rusty pipes, sweaty walls, dead rats, and small streams of water made up the decor.

"Where exactly are you taking me?"

"To the archives." He wheezed again.

"Are we under the Lubyanka?"

"You'll see, you'll see," he muttered.

What the hell did that mean? The old man was worse than Belkin. Belkin would have been manageable with a little sex and flattery. Minsky was a hole she threw money in and got wheezes in return.

What kind of life was her path taking? Here she was in a dank tunnel with a strange old man who wheezed and limped as he led her under the most infamous building in Russia. If places had soul, the Lubyanka's would burn in eternal hell for the crimes against humanity committed there. People were beaten and tortured and even killed in the place. She shuddered at the thought that her mother might have been one of those harmed.

Another door that would stop a tank was waiting at the end of the corridor.

Another guard, another chair, newspapers, a jug of coffee.

Another hundred dollars.

"That's it," she told her wheezing guide. "Not a dollar more. I have enough money left on me for a taxi back to my hotel. That's it."

"What's a hundred dollars to a rich American?"

He started coughing and leaned against the wall for a moment to catch his breath. She realized that somewhere in the convulsions was laughter.

"You won the war and now you pay," he said, laughing. "Isn't that how you Americans always do it? You win the war and then you pay."

They arrived at another door and this time she blew.

"No, no," he wheezed, "this is my station."

On the other side of the massive door was a well-lit corridor. After going a dozen feet, he led her through tall metal doors and into a different world.

Storage walls soaring twenty feet high created narrow, poorly lit aisles that seemed to go on forever in every direction. The walls were swollen with containers—cardboard boxes, wooden boxes, plastic bins, metal containers, and filing cabinets out in the open, behind mesh screens, behind steel bars.

She walked around a little, taking it all in, feeling as if she had stepped into the belly of a dinosaur. Cobwebs and dust, the smell of old paper, yellowing and decaying—wrongs and atrocities disappearing as the paper disintegrated. A rat scrambled across an aisle and down another.

"The KGB archives," she said more to herself than to him.

"Yes, but some say that the most secret documents are in Mr. Yeltsin's sugar bowl."

"Ones that can be used politically?"

Minsky shrugged and wheezed.

She understood why the world's scholars were frantic to get inside. It all had to be here, seventy-five years of skullduggery, plots and spies, murder and mass murder, blackmail, treachery and atrocities. Thirty million people were killed under Stalin.

Perhaps the record of each was in this vast concrete cavern, she thought, a last testament written by their executioners: "Ivan confessed to anti-Soviet thoughts just before he was shot attempting to escape."

She felt the pathos, the human drama. These were not documents about the grain harvest, but about lives—people of flesh and blood, people like her mother with pride and prejudices, fears and ambitions; all that was human or inhuman about them now stored in boxes like paper souls.

"Where is my mother's file?" she asked.

Minsky turned away from her and watched a bug crawling up the wall. "Your mother's file?"

"My mother's file. The file I've spent nearly a thousand dollars between you, your friends, and Gropski to see tonight."

Wheeze. He folded up a piece of newspaper to use as a swatter, watching the bug with what appeared to be great interest.

"You wanted to get into the archives to find your mother's file. My task was to get you in so you may do your search."

"So I can—" She shot a glance around her. It would take a team of scholars months to find a barking dog in the vast paper jungle. The saving grace would be a good index system.

"Fine. I'll find it myself. Where's your index?"

"Index?"

THREE

"You bastard!"

Minsky backed up, his fat jowls trembling, the bug swatter held up in self-defense as she stalked him.

"I'm going to have you thrown in prison. You won't have to worry about the price of vodka for the rest of your life. You're a thief, a liar—"

"You bribed me, an official of the—"

"I'm an innocent American tourist who was lured here under false pretenses and robbed. By the time I get through telling my story to the American public, Russia can kiss foreign aid away. And you're going to prison. I'm leaving now, but I'll be back tomorrow to hold a news conference on the front steps of the Lubyanka."

He slowly sank to the floor on his knees, sweat rolling down his jowls.

"Please, my pension . . ."

A pang of pity hit her but that prosecutor's go-for-the-kill training kicked in.

"Where's my mother's file?"

"As God is my witness, I don't know."

A Communist swearing to God?

"How do I find it?"

He waved his hands in front of him. "You can't, not tonight. If there's a file here it would take many days to find. And you would need more information than just her name."

"There's no indexing system?"

"No indexing system, I swear it."

It rang true. Another element of control, like no phone books.

"Then how do you find anything in this . . . this . . ." She waved at the cavern.

"Most of the filing is done by KGB department, further divided geographically."

"By year?"

"Sometimes, but there would be a hundred different places to look for any particular year."

"How do you find anything?"

"Find anything? We don't find anything. We don't look. No one wants the past to come alive." He wheezed.

"Get off your knees," she told him.

Minsky climbed laboriously to his feet.

"Sit down."

He sat down. So far, so good.

"Now listen to me, you sold me information and you're going to come up with information. I don't care if you have a coronary. Understand?"

He nodded and wiped sweat off his jowls with the newspaper he was going to kill the bug with, leaving black streaks.

"You and Belkin must have discussed this and come up with a plan. Or you both lied to me from the beginning and—"

"Please, please, we discussed it. I told him I would not be able to find your mother's file. But there might be something."

"What?"

"Belkin said your mother was killed in an accident involving a truck. Do you have the name of the truck driver?"

"Yes, but that's all I have about him. A name from over twenty years ago. I haven't been able to locate him."

"We might be able to locate his file. If he was KGB and if the accident took place near Moscow, he probably worked for the KGB's local motorized division. There are only a small number of those files here. Knowing his name and the year he drove for the KGB will help you find his file and obtain information about the accident from it.''

"I never said he worked for the KGB."

"You said it was an accident that didn't happen. Only the KGB could make things not happen."

An hour later she found the file of KGB motor pool driver Joseph Guk. He had worked for the mobile support division, Moscow Area, for over thirty years, and retired five years ago. He had had the same rural address for most of the thirty years and, if he was like most people in the country, probably still had the same address today. If he was alive.

The file confirmed all her suspicions about the accident: there was no mention of it.

To the contrary, Joseph Guk had received annual commendations for being accident free, including the year of her mother's death. He had only two fender benders during his entire career. Neither was judged his fault and both incidents were duly related in characteristic Soviet detail.

But not a word about a fiery collision between his petrol tanker and her mother's car that supposedly destroyed both vehicles.

She was tired and dirty by the time she found and read Guk's file. At nearly three in the morning Minsky got out of his chair and lumbered along to escort her out.

He asked nothing about her findings and she volunteered nothing.

She wanted desperately to wash the filth of KGB archives off her hands but the only water she'd seen was the rusty stuff on the floor and walls of the concrete corridor.

Minsky, like Belkin, didn't compute. She feared a setup and wondered if he had more of a relationship to Belkin than he pretended. She decided to test the waters.

"By the way," she said, "I forgot to tell you, tonight as Mr. Belkin was leaving me he was hit by a truck. I think he might have been seriously injured."

A hoarse expulsion of breath, not a wheeze but something more akin to a death rattle, gurgled from Minsky's throat.

He backed away from her, then turned and ran.

FOUR

Back in her hotel she braced the door with a chair under the handle.

After washing her hands and face, she climbed into bed with two sets of long underwear still on and pulled the covers over her head.

Minsky's coronary reaction to Belkin's accident had sent her own paranoia soaring. She knew she should be on the next plane out of Moscow, back to a nice safe job of dealing with killers and perverts.

Something was seriously out of kilter in Moscow.

She couldn't be the first person to buy his or her way into the archives. Minsky and his cohorts had a well-rehearsed act going. So why was he ready to croak every time she opened her mouth? And nearly did when she mentioned Belkin's accident.

The questions spun around in her head like a dog chasing its tail. It all seemed to come back to the same question.

Who had sent for her?

Just before she fell asleep, another question slipped through a crack in her mind to add to her confusion: that wasn't an ordinary storage room she had been digging into, but an archive still classified top secret because it recorded the brutal atrocities of generations of Soviet secret police.

What was the file of an unimportant truck driver who had retired years ago doing in the country's most important KGB archives?

* * *

It was early morning when a noise at her door jerked her awake. The door was being forced against the chair wedged under the handle.

A man cursed. "She's jammed it with a chair!"

VI

We kill everybody, my dear.
Some with bullets, some with words,
and everybody with our deeds.
We drive people into their graves,
and neither see it nor feel it.

—Maxim Gorky

ONE

She jumped out of bed and ran at the door, yelling, "I've called the police! I have a gun!"

"We are the police! Throw your gun out or we'll shoot!"

"Wait. I don't have a gun! Don't shoot!"

"Sonofabitch." Then silence. A man's calm voice came through from the corridor. "Remove the chair."

She pulled the chair away from the door and it opened with a push from the other side.

Two men were standing at the door, one oversized, one normal. They wore the standard uniform of Russian plain-clothes cops: cheap suits, wrinkled white shirts with yellowing collars and top button undone, ties sloppy and askew, and shoes that had seen too much mileage.

She backed away from the door as they came into the room, the smaller man leading the way. A look from the men reminded her she was still in long underwear and she grabbed a blanket off the bed.

"What do you want?" she asked.

The bigger man had a Cossack handlebar mustache, bald head, and powerful torso. He automatically looked to the other man for an answer to her question.

"What's your name?" the smaller man asked.

"What's your name? And let me see some identification before I start screaming."

He raised his eyebrows at his husky partner. "First she has a gun, now she's a screamer." He flashed her an identification card. "Detective Kirov. My partner is Detective Stenka."

She examined the card closely. Detective Yuri Kirov was with the Special Division, Moscow Militia. The local police.

"Now let me see your identification, please," Kirov said.

The "please" was not polite. Her hands were shaking as she fumbled for her passport. She knew she was going to be arrested for bribing her way into the archives. She was so stupid. Hidden cameras probably recorded the whole thing.

Kirov was quick, intense, professionally curt. He wandered around her room as she fumbled with her bag, taking in everything while Stenka folded his arms and leaned quietly against the wall by the door.

She gave Kirov the passport. He ran his hand through his thick black hair while he studied the passport.

She noticed his eyes. They were unusually dark, what some Russians would call Gypsy eyes. And then it hit her.

"Wait a minute, I've seen you before," she said to Kirov. "Last night. You were at the carnival, behind the fortune-teller's tent."

"Correct. You were chasing a dwarf at the time."

She blushed. "I . . . what were you doing there?"

"Police business. Why have you come to Moscow?"

"Visiting."

"Visiting who?"

"Moscow. I'm a tourist."

"You speak perfect Russian. Your family was Russian?"

"American. I was born in Moscow." Her insides were

shaking. How could she have been stupid enough to break the law in a foreign country. It was probably a setup, a sting operation. She was surprised she hadn't been arrested coming out of the archives.

"What is your relationship with Nikolai Belkin."

"Belkin? Someone I met here in Moscow."

"Met him for what reason?" Detective Kirov wandered around the room a little more and opened her closet.

"Excuse me, but do you have a warrant?"

"A warrant?" He turned to Stenka and threw up his hands. "How rude of you, Stenka. Show her our warrant."

Without a change in expression the Cossack opened his coat to expose a 9mm automatic in a shoulder holster.

Kirov pointed at Stenka's gun. "In Russia, this is what gives you permission to search."

"This is crazy. I'm calling the American Embassy." She went for the telephone next to her bed.

Kirov spoke as he went through her clothes hanging in the closet. "Your phone doesn't work. Stenka had the hotel operator turn it off." He looked back at his partner and shook his head. "Tough cop. He's from the old school." He moved to her dresser and started riffling through the drawers as he talked. She felt totally helpless.

"Why are you staying at this hotel?"

"Why not?"

"It's a dump."

"I'm not rich."

"You're an American."

"Don't believe everything you read about Americans."

"Are you a prostitute?"

"What? You have no right to ask me a question like that. Get the hell out of my room. Better yet, I'll get out. I'm going to your supervisors. No, I'm going to report you to their supervisors." She started for the door.

Stenka raised his eyebrows at Kirov who shook his head. "Let her go. She'll freeze to death in her underwear before she catches a taxi."

Shit. She had forgotten how she was dressed. She came back into the room with the blanket trailing after her and stood toe to toe with Kirov, her face burning.

"I'm a prosecutor in my country and I work with the police. I know the difference between someone being harassed and a real police investigation. I saw you last night. You have—"

"All right, all right, calm down and I'll tell you why we're here." He backed away from her and flopped into the stuffed chair by the dresser and lit a cigarette.

"I don't like smoking in my room."

"So don't smoke."

She sat on the edge of her bed and stared coldly at him. She ran her fingers through her own hair and they caught in tangles. I must look like hell. She pulled the blanket tighter.

Kirov blew smoke in the air. "I apologize for the prostitution remark, but"—he counted with his fingers—"one, you are in a cheap hotel that does not cater to foreigners. Two, you have been registered here for two weeks and appear to be neither a tourist nor on business in Moscow, and three, last night you were in the company of Nikolai Belkin about the time the subject took a nosedive in front of a truck. Belkin is well known to the Moscow police as a sausage waver. You know what I mean."

She knew what he meant. In her office they were called flashers—a guy who liked to pull his penis out and startle women. Relief flowed through her. They were investigating Belkin's accident, not her invasion of the archives.

"And four, an elderly woman at the scene of Belkin's accident stated that a young foreign woman who had been with Belkin had been acting strange. The good citizen is willing to testify that the young woman was under the influence of drugs. There is also the fact you were behind the Gypsy tents when I saw you. As you are no doubt aware, Gypsies are importing drugs into Russia in great quantities."

"Now I'm a drug runner?"

If it sounds like drugs, it probably is drugs, a San Francisco cop would say. But Belkin didn't strike her as someone who would be involved in drug trafficking. Blat, a little perversion, yes, but not drugs. He was Old Guard, not Yuppie. But she couldn't defend herself by telling the police she had met Belkin to steal state secrets, not sell drugs.

"I was looking for the fortune-teller because of something she said. I don't sell drugs, I don't use drugs, and I seriously doubt Mr. Belkin is a drug trafficker. That's what you're investigating isn't it, drugs?"

"I wasn't investigating him last night. We know him from the past. I was on another case last night when I spotted you with him. What's your relationship with Belkin?"

"Nothing that is any business of the police. We're just friends." Great, what a thing to say about a sausage waver.

Kirov looked at Stenka and gave him a "it takes all kinds" shrug.

She went a shade redder but kept her mouth shut.

Kirov blew more smoke and asked, "Have you violated any laws while in Russia?"

She leaned against the bedpost, crossed her legs, pulled the blanket snugger, and gave Detective Kirov her best smile.

"Why don't you give me a list of laws, Detective, so I can tell you which ones to arrest me for?"

Stenka chuckled, and Kirov gave him a dark look but then suddenly smiled, a genuine smile, as he ran his hand through his dark wavy hair. The smile broke up the rigid intensity of his features and made him look younger. She estimated his age as the late thirties, but his features had the cast of a man who had seen more life than that. She knew the smile was to disarm her. If being friendly didn't work, he'd go back to tough cop.

"We're here because Belkin was injured last night. In

his pocket was a slip of paper with your name and hotel on it. A woman fitting your description was observed leaving the scene of the accident. As I already said, witnesses say the woman was acting peculiar and left in a hurry."

"Why don't you ask Belkin about the situation?"

"An excellent idea!" He jumped to his feet. "Get dressed. We can question you together."

"Together? What about?"

A radio blasted on in the room next door, someone's wake-up call. The music was rap.

Kirov jerked his thumb at the wall.

"This is what our young people are learning from their exposure to Western culture—drugs, sex, and bad music. Get dressed."

He politely left the room and Stenka followed him, leaving the door open a crack.

In the corridor Yuri Kirov lit another cigarette and positioned himself so he could watch Lara through the crack as she dressed.

"Checking for weapons," he whispered to Stenka.

The big man leaned against the corridor wall and folded his arms. "We didn't have an investigation in the park last night."

TWO

It was Lara's first ride in a police car as a suspect. Stenka drove, his big frame overwhelming the driver's area of the small militia car. She sat in the back with Yuri. Neither of them spoke. He had rolled down a window and hung his cigarette out and tried to blow his smoke out, but the smoke came back in, along with a lot of frigid air.

She was determined to keep her mouth shut about everything. It was not the time for a lecture about the evils of secondhand smoke.

As the car approached the hospital, Yuri told Stenka, "Park in the rear, near the basement steps. It's the quickest way to his room."

As she followed Yuri down a flight of cement steps into a rear entrance to the hospital's basement, Stenka's big frame behind her, she wondered how seriously Belkin had been hurt. He obviously wasn't critical if cops and suspects could waltz in and out of his room.

Yuri flashed his ID at an attendant's station near the entry door as he walked quickly by, moving down the drab corridor at a pace fast enough to make Lara stretch her legs to keep up. The hospital corridor was colder than the corridor at her hotel. And with a real meaty smell.

Yuri pushed through a pair of swinging doors into a room with white walls and glaring lights and she flew behind him. He stepped to the side and with the pressure of Stenka coming on her tail she was almost on top of a gurney before she stopped.

A naked body, a man's hairy body with its penis poking up in full erection, lay on the gurney. Belkin, black and blue marks down the left side of his body, his arm broken and separated, an open wound at his hip, was very dead.

She recoiled in shock, knocking away Yuri's hand as he reached for her. "*You sonofabitch.*"

Shoving by Stenka, she knocked the swinging doors open, bursting back into the corridor, nearly bellying over a gurney being pushed down the corridor by an attendant. A sheet slipped off and she pulled away as an old woman with dead eyes and gaping mouth in death's rigor stared up at her.

She ran down the corridor and out the steps leading back to the parking lot. It was while going through the door at the bottom of the stairs that she saw the sign by the attendant's desk: HOSPITAL MORGUE.

Halfway across the parking lot, Yuri Kirov caught up

with her. He walked beside her without speaking.

When she reached the sidewalk, she stepped off the curb to flag a taxi.

"I'm sorry," he said. "I needed to know your reaction."

"My reaction? How the hell did you think I would react to something like that?" She was shaking.

A taxi spotted her waving and swerved across traffic lanes to get to her.

"You set me up by lying about his accident injuries. Then shove a dead body in my face. I hope it gives you and your pals a big laugh when you get back to your office."

She had opened the back door and started into the taxi when he said, "I told you he didn't die from a truck hitting him. That wasn't a lie. He was murdered. Later."

THREE

Yuri Kirov's dark eyes fascinated her.

The tune to the old Russian love song, "Oh, Shishonya," "Oh, Dark Eyes," played in her head as they sat across the table from each other in a coffee bar. The coffee bar sold espresso, cappuccino, café mocha, and desserts. A sign on the wall said it was a joint venture of an Italian company and Russian entrepreneurs.

Most of the patrons looked like foreigners, which wasn't surprising—cappuccino and espresso were a thousand rubles each and the average Russian could buy food for a couple of days on that kind of money.

He insisted upon a cup of regular coffee. "I'm not into designer drinks. That's what the world's gone to, designer clothes, designer cars, designer sex. Designer drugs are becoming the next big problem in Russia. Right now most of the drugs are expensive. But to get money to feed their families, half the unemployed chemists in the country are making synthetic drugs in their kitchens. Either that or vodka. And some of the homemade vodka is deadlier than bad drugs.''

"You told me you were going to explain how Belkin died.'' She noticed Yuri wore the same cheap overcoat he had on when she saw him at the carnival. A sign he was honest? Moscow police officers probably made less than a hundred dollars a month, she thought.

He took a sip of coffee. "In a moment of great personal fear when I thought you were going to knock me down and let the taxi run over my head, I told you I would explain how Belkin died. But—''

"No buts.''

"But if I explain immediately, like the magician I will have revealed how the trick works and lose my audience. Can't we just sit and relax for a moment and enjoy this wonderful treat the Italians have invented for us?''

She leaned across the table toward him. "Detective Kirov—''

"Yuri, please.''

"Detective Kirov, you strike me as a hardworking and dedicated officer. The only time you strike me wrong is when you pull dirty tricks on me . . . or try to be nice. Don't try to be nice. It doesn't suit your character. Just tell me what happened to Belkin.''

"He was killed.''

"Murdered?''

"The matter is still under investigation. His death may have been an accident.''

She groaned. "You told me a few minutes ago that the man was murdered.'' Getting information out of Yuri Kirov was not going to be easy. "Is this going to be one of those cases of suicide where the dead man shot himself in the head, stabbed himself in the back, then hung himself without a chair?''

"Suicide? What are you talking about?"

"A stupid attempt at humor. My reaction to you being evasive. How was Belkin killed?"

"An injection of potassium. It may have been an accidental injection. We are still trying to find the nurse who administered it."

Her gut wrenched. She fumbled with her cappuccino and took a sip to hide her reaction. "A nurse? One employed at the hospital?"

"We're not sure. One of the night attendants saw a nurse enter Belkin's room last night. She didn't recognize the person but assumed it was a private nurse. Russian hospitals aren't always administered efficiently. Lethal injections are sometimes just part of the standard of care."

"Man or woman?"

"The nurse? A woman. I noticed when I mentioned the nurse you . . . reacted."

"Last night, after Mr. Belkin was hit by a truck, a woman, one of the people in the crowd, pointed out that a nurse left the scene when her help was needed."

"Did you see the nurse?"

"No."

"So you think the nurse who gave him the injection may have pushed him in front of the truck."

"He was pushed?"

Yuri shrugged. "We have conflicting versions. We don't know if he was pushed deliberately by someone or if he lost his balance from a surge of the crowd."

"You didn't see the accident?" she said.

"No, I was back at the carnival. I found out about it later."

She had an urge to tell him everything, about the photograph that had lured her to Moscow, her mother's "accident," what she had found in the archives, but she held back. It would be pretty stupid to admit to a cop she barely knew that she had spent the previous night bribing her way into government secrets. In America, she could count on being arrested. In Russia, who the hell knew what could happen?

And she wasn't sure if she could trust him. She liked him, felt very comfortable with him, sensing a caring and reasonable human being behind the tough veneer police have to maintain as a hazard of their profession, yet . . .

She desperately needed an ally but what did she really know about him? If he was the type of cop who took bribes, he certainly hid it well; besides the cheap overcoat, his suit was well worn, his shoes dog-eared, his shirt washed and ironed at home.

Hoping he wasn't married was a sudden thought that she quickly put out of her mind.

He lit another cigarette.

Next to being cold, she hated men who smoked.

"I know, you hate smoking."

"Can you read my mind? I know a carnival where you could get a job."

"I was reading your face. You said you were born in Moscow. Your parents were diplomats?"

"No, quite the opposite. Both my parents were fugitives from justice."

That got his attention.

"My mother was an anti-war activist. She was a teacher at Berkeley—that's a university in California."

"I know about Berkeley. Burning bras, sex in the street, fights with the police."

"She wasn't into burning bras or public sex, but a battle with the police is what made her a fugitive. She taught at the university, political science, and was a leader in the early movement for free speech and against the war in Vietnam. She was one of the organizers of a demonstration that got out of control. Someone was killed when a car that was turned over in the street caught on fire and blew up. Arrest warrants were issued for the organizers of the demonstration and my mother fled to Canada to avoid a murder charge for a crime she didn't commit."

"A person was killed regardless of your mother's motives."

"My mother was a pacifist, a caring person, she didn't even eat meat because she loved all forms of life. The last thing she would have wanted was for someone to get hurt. She felt, with some good cause, that she would be prosecuted as an example to scare others. So she ran.

"She went to Canada. After an attempt to extradite her, she accepted an invitation to teach at the Foreign Institute in Moscow. The motive for the invitation was probably to use her for propaganda, but she restricted herself solely to anti-war issues."

"And your father?"

She smiled. "I wish I had met my father. I read letters my mother sent home to her own mother. He was a very special person. He was a poet, a Welsh poet."

"Welsh?"

"Wales. It's part of Great Britain."

"I know Wales. Exploitation of coal miners by capitalist warmongers." He grinned to let her know he was joking.

"I've never been there but it sounds picturesque," she said. "Wild moorlands, crashing waves, sudden storms. Anyway, my father was a poet and, well, something of an anarchist. He got involved in some sort of foolish plot. A bunch of young college students with too much political passion and not enough brains talked publicly about blowing up Parliament on Guy Fawkes Day."

Yuri choked on a sip of coffee.

"You have to remember this was the sixties," she explained.

"Of course, I forgot, in the sixties it was permissible to blow up governments and kill people in political riots."

"Anyway, my father fled to the Netherlands. He was apparently quite well known for the socialist theme of his poetry. While in Amsterdam, he was invited to read poetry in Moscow by a young poets' association."

"Is he still alive?"

"No. He was . . . idealistic, impulsive—wild and crazy, I guess they'd call him today. A bunch of volunteer mercenaries were organized and sent to Africa to help some fledgling Communist ruler. In my father's mind, he was off to save Africa from the last vestiges of colonialism. He died there, in some battle, I think against the army of the very man they were sent to help.

"I really wish I had known him. I have some wonderful memories of my mother, more feelings than actual events. She died when I was seven. With my father I only have my mother's stories and the letters she wrote about him."

"Your mother, she passed away?"

"She was killed in an accident." Her voice faltered. She looked away for a moment before she turned back and locked eyes with him. "That's why I'm in Moscow. I don't believe my mother was really killed in an accident." She told him about going out to the police substation and finding no record of the crash. "It's not just the lack of a police report. Her existence was wiped out at the university, even at our old apartment. I'm planning to see my grade-school teacher. I expect to be told I never went to school there."

He listened and sipped coffee. His expression revealed nothing and it prompted her to tell him a little more.

"I was sent something in the mail. That's why I came to Moscow." She told him about the photograph.

There was a long silence between them. Finally he lit another cigarette and stretched. "In my opinion, you are making more out of the situation than it deserves. You assume that the woman in the photograph is your mother but admit the face is not visible. You also assume that there has been a cover-up of the brutal murder of your mother. But the truth is that under the Soviets we were so intent, so driven by the system to get things right, we never got everything done. I think you are confusing governmental inefficiency with a plot against your mother."

"You sound like Belkin."

"You discussed this with Belkin?"

"Well, yes, a little."

"And he was going to assist you in obtaining information about your mother before his accident intervened."

"Accident? You said he was murdered."

"That has not been established."

"Forget Belkin. What about the photograph and an attempt on my life."

He waved his cigarette hand at her. "You suspect a murder took place over twenty years ago. You have no evidence and no access to evidence. You tried to enlist the aid of Belkin who was probably only interested in your money—or whatever else he could get from you. You are wasting your time in Moscow."

"Wasting my time?" She fanned smoke away from her face. "You haven't listened to a thing I've said. And you sound like an apologist for seventy-five years of Soviet mediocrity. No wonder you people lost the Cold War."

"We ended the Cold War, we didn't lose it."

"Oh, excuse me, is that the current rationale for a system that couldn't grow enough grain to feed its own people?"

"A system that put the first man in space."

"Look, Officer Kirov—"

"Detective."

"Whatever. I don't want to argue with you. In fact, I don't want anything at all to do with you."

She stood up and fumbled in her purse.

"And I suggest you get on the next plane back to the United States," he said. "It appears that you have inherited the irrationality that runs on both sides of your family."

"I'm crazy, that's the official line, isn't it? Poor little Lara got hurt when she was small and is now imagining it all over again. The only thing I've imagined is that you're a good police officer. You have the brain of a metal desk like the rest of the bureaucrats in this country.'' She slapped five dollars on the table.

He leaped up, knocking over his chair. ''What's that?''

''I'm picking up the bill,'' she snapped. ''You couldn't afford—'' She closed her mouth and started to leave.

He grabbed her arm, forcing the five-dollar bill into her hand. ''You are in Russia,'' he said hotly. ''Men do not have their balls cut off in this country like your American men. I will pay.''

She jerked her arm away and walked out of the restaurant.

VII

The road to hell is paved
with good intentions.

—Karl Marx, *Capital*

ONE

The squad room at the Chekhov Militia station was a wide-open bay with a haze of cigarette smoke hanging overhead. Gray islands, four big steel desks bumped corner to corner, floated in the big bay on concrete flooring. The desks overflowed with paperwork, files, coffee and tea mugs, ashtrays, bread crumbs, and red tape.

When Yuri transferred into the detective unit his supervisor told him he lacked the three prerequisites for a good detective: big paws, thick neck, low brow.

All of the detectives were men. There was no issue of equality at the station: women either worked vice or pounded a beat.

Yuri met Stenka's eye as he came across the room. The big Cossack had his shirtsleeves rolled up, his tie undone and dangling, and his top button open, exposing a bushy growth. He had a cup of tea in one hand, a cigarette in the other—and he rolled his eyes when he saw Yuri.

It was their signal that Frolik, the chief detective, was on the prowl. Yuri was about to spin on his heel and head back out the way he had come in when Frolik spotted him from his cubicle and called his name.

Groaning under his breath, Yuri continued to his desk

next to Stenka's, flopped into his chair, lit a cigarette, and swiveled to face the attack.

Frolik, short and round with close-cropped yellow hair, came out of his cubicle like cannon shot. The layers surrounding Frolik's belly were pure, thick hard fat. The office joke was that Frolik carried his own bulletproof vest . . . but no one cracked the joke in front of him. His temperament was that of a volcano in perpetual eruption.

"What are you doing?" he growled at Yuri.

"Smoking a cigarette. Want one?"

"Fuck you. I have word that you're investigating an accident case and an American woman."

Yuri shot a glance at Stenka and got a blank stare in return. He knew Stenka wouldn't have told the supervisor.

"It's a case I came across."

"You don't pick up cases off the street like coins people drop. I assign cases, you work them. This unit works homicides related to drug trafficking, not people getting hit by buses. You understand?"

Yuri nodded.

"One more thing." Frolik raised his voice so it could be heard across the squad room. "Someone from this unit has been ordering up old KGB files from the archives. One of the files had a surveillance film in it. The file and the film never got returned and the records people are raising shit because sometimes this old surveillance stuff can be used for blackmail."

Frolik glared at the assembly.

"You know what I mean. Anyone order up the file?"

No one spoke.

The cannonball held out his hand and balled it in a fist and squeezed.

"I find someone dirty in my unit, I'll squeeze his balls until his eyes pop."

After the chief detective returned to his den, Yuri swiveled and said to Stenka, "Trust me."

Nothing changed on the big Cossack's expression.

TWO

It was colder than when it snowed, colder than when it rained ice, so cold the air felt stiff as Yuri walked toward the Bolshoi Theatre. He wondered how Lara Patrick was taking the cold. She had been born in Moscow but California living would have warmed her blood. California. The word was exotic to him. He had never met anyone from California, or even knew anyone who had ever been in California except Lara Patrick, but he had seen pictures of the place on television—white sandy beaches, candy-apple red BMW convertibles, movie stars and Disneyland, golden tanned people, women with small rears and big breasts, men with small rears and big pecs. And grins. From what he saw on television, people grinned in California rather than smiled. He'd heard that Russian crooks and businessmen—the words were synonymous in his mind—found California an easy place to make money, easier than big cities like New York and Chicago because Californians were soft from all the sunshine and glamour.

Lara Patrick didn't fit his TV-created image of tanned-blond-candy-apple-red BMW women. She didn't fit the mold of any woman he had met. No woman had ever entered the inner sanctum of his personal life, but the first time he saw Lara Patrick he felt as if all of his secrets had been stripped from him and he was naked and exposed before her. In self-defense he blew smoke in her face.

The Bolshoi Theatre was one of the strangest buildings in Moscow and also his favorite. But it was not his choice for a meeting with a man who planned to kill him.

The building that housed the world's most famous ballet troupe was physically just around the corner from the

Lenin Museum but was architecturally a couple thousand years younger, a Greco-Roman structure equipped with stately columns and a magnificent rooftop chariot with four charging horses and an imperial Roman whom Yuri assumed was none other than Julius Caesar himself. When he first came to Moscow, hating the cold impersonal brutality of the city, he sometimes sat and ate his lunch across from the grand old theatre, imagining that he was someplace else, a place where chariots and Romans were not so strange. Like California.

Ballet was as popular in Russia as baseball in America, but it was an art form and the strange path his life had taken had not left him with the luxury of loving art any more than loving a woman had been part of the scheme of things. He came to the square to look at the theatre, not ballet, but as he watched others come and go from the theatre he always wondered what it would be like to enter the Bolshoi with a woman on his arm, excited with anticipation about the performance, exiting a couple of hours later arm in arm earnestly evaluating the performances, perhaps pausing out front with friends to talk about the story or the music or a particularly fine performer, arguing the finer points of the ballet over a coffee or vodka later on.

He realized it wasn't the ballet itself that evoked the image as much as its normality. Most people were bored with their life, leading existences of repetition, up at the same time, staring at the same walls at work, interacting with the same people, back home at the same time and doing more or less the same thing that evening that they had done the week before and the year before. There was little normalcy about his life, little repetition. A moving target is the hardest to hit.

That was how he thought of himself, not as Yuri Kirov, Muscovite, Yuri Kirov, homicide cop, but as a target that had to keep moving.

He had the uneasy feeling of being followed from the

moment he had set out for a secret meeting at one of the most public places in the city and had attributed the feeling to the general uneasiness about the meeting. He knew little about the man named Gropski except what he had learned before Belkin died. Gropski was ex-KGB, a nothing when the KGB was something, less than zero now that the KGB was history. Security officer at the second-rate hotel where Lara Patrick was staying; relegated now to keeping panhandlers out of the lobby instead of spying on the minor regional officials and factory managers who frequented the hotel.

The message from Gropski had come in the form of a terse phone call a couple of hours before. Yuri picked up the telephone at his militia desk and identified himself and then heard, "This is Gropski. The Bolshoi, ten minutes to seven," followed by specific instructions on where to meet. And how much money to bring.

Seven o'clock was the time a couple thousand people crowded into the theatre for the evening performance. A strange rendezvous for a meeting with a man who was going to try to kill him.

There was no middle ground for the meeting to reach. When the man's blackmail attempt failed Gropski would realize that he had painted himself into a corner and would have to kill Yuri because he would be sure that Yuri would kill him. That meant that Gropski would have a backup plan, maybe an accomplice waiting to step in when Yuri refused to be blackmailed and didn't hand over the money, another ex-KGB type trying to squeeze gold out of flesh in a city where anyone without a gun or a gimmick was worried about the price of bread.

It was a quarter to seven as Yuri neared the theatre, walking a little slower than the people hurrying to enter before the performance started. It was a black, starless night on a winter day that had been so gloomy and overcast daylight had hardly swept over the city. For the last half of the block he kept his eye on a man across the street, standing near a Mercedes parked at the curb, punching a gloved fist into his other hand as he stared contemptuously at the people rushing by. The man was mostly hidden behind a heavy overcoat and fur hat, but his body language and mean lips had been a KGB trademark.

Yuri knew the man wasn't Gropski. He had gotten a quick look at Gropski when he had canvassed the hotel after Lara Patrick checked in, but he could be Gropski's backup.

As Yuri moved slowly up the sidewalk a man and woman came out of the building the Mercedes was parked in front of and got into the back of the car. The bully got into the front seat of the car and Yuri knew what the bully was. Ex-KGB, now bodyguard riding shotgun in a fancy car for a crook or businessman . . . who was probably also ex-KGB, Yuri thought.

He turned onto a side street before reaching the theatre. Gropski's meeting place had not been the lush red velvet and rich gilt interior of the two-hundred-year-old theatre, but a more unusual place.

Many important Moscow buildings had an anonymous gray steel door toward the rear without address numbers or other identification. The anonymous door at the Bolshoi was unlocked as Gropski said it would be and Yuri opened it and slipped in after taking what he hoped was a casual look around. He quickly stepped aside to avoid being silhouetted by the streetlight outside the closing door. He was in the back of the Bolshoi, not the stage entrance or the delivery area, but the special entrance everyone knew was there but no one talked about.

He stood still, letting his eyes adjust to the darkness. He wasn't in a room, but a space between the rear of the building and the rest of the interior. To his right a stairway went up a flight and made a left turn, connecting to a steeper, much narrower stairway that went up a wall and disappeared into the darkness above. As he stared at the upper stairway, Yuri realized it was little more than a ladder, less than three feet wide with wooden steps and a steel cable for a handrail.

As safe and fun to climb up as a trapeze ladder at a circus. He took the steps slowly, knowing where they were heading and in no hurry to get there.

A dozen feet up, the narrow stairs gave him a view of part of the backstage area. The performance had started and music vaguely familiar came from the orchestra pit at the base of the stage. He was late for the meeting—intentionally. A street full of hundreds of people converging on the theatre from all directions would have been a great place for Gropski to hide his backup buddy and Yuri had patiently walked the area, waiting for the sidewalks and alleys to become deserted, making his move for the back door after he was unable to spot anyone suspicious outside.

As he went up the shaky stairs he kept his face averted even though he was certain no one could see him. He recognized the music to the ballet. It was about the triumphs and madness of Ivan the Terrible.

An opening into the walk-space in the ceiling was where the stairs led. He knew that from what Gropski had told him. He had guessed the stairs and the opening had played a more sinister role in the Bolshoi's life than simply access for the maintenance crew.

Emerging into the walk-space, Yuri quickly got away from the opening, stumbling as he did. The area above the ceiling was even darker than the stairway.

He stood still, letting his eyes adjust.

The ceiling area was an enormous cavern with beams of light shooting up from openings in the floor. One of the openings was by him and he could see part of the backstage area through it. The light beaming up came from the lights in the theatre below. With the ballet in progress the lights were mostly at the rear end of the cavern. During intermission the lights in the great chandelier and hundreds of smaller lights in the audience area would be shooting into the ceiling area.

The ceiling cavern was hot and stuffy; the powerful tones and dark visions of the musical soul of the mad Russian ruler flowed up through the floor at his feet, rising as if part of the heat from below.

Shapes took form as his eyes adjusted.

A great swan stared at him, a creature of wood with painted face and feathers. Beyond the swan were wooden soldiers, the paint flaking from their rosy red cheeks and fancy uniforms. Beyond the soldiers he could see other props, a witch's cottage, a troika with plywood horses, a Greek temple. The attic was a city of dead scenes coated with decades of dust and neglect, a dirty snow that entombed the ghosts of plays past. The place was spooky and raised the hair on the back of his neck.

He smelled the cigar before he saw it.

The glow came from the mock troika. Yuri took his hands out of his coat pockets and slowly walked toward the glow. When they were a dozen feet apart Yuri recognized the man as Gropski. Underfoot Yuri felt the vibrations of the music as the dancers "rang" the great bells that were used to usher in each phase of the mad Ivan's life.

Yuri's eyes went to Gropski getting out of the troika, searching beyond him and each side, looking for Gropski's backup.

When they were three feet apart Gropski grinned at him and dumped the cigar on the floor, sparks bursting. As he stamped out sparks with his shoe, the hotel security man sneered contemptuously at the great cavern. "Now that the KGB's out of business, they've forgotten about this area."

Yuri's right hand swung out from his side with a gun in it and hit Gropski on the side of the head. The man went down and Yuri went down on top of him, pinning him with his knees, looking around quickly for Gropski's backup.

He shoved the gun in Gropski's face, trying to force it into the man's mouth, and Gropski twisted his head back and forth to avoid it.

"Where's your backup?"

"Tru-trusted you," he stammered.

"You don't trust your own dick. Where is he?"

"No one, no one."

Yuri carefully frisked him. No gun.

"Stay put." He got off Gropski and moved around, looking for the backup. Every step left an imprint in the snow dust on the floor. In the dim light he saw his footprints and Gropski's. No backup. No gun. Something was wrong.

"Get up," he told Gropski.

The man got slowly up, rubbing the side of his head. "You shouldn't have hit me."

"You shouldn't be fucking with me."

Sweat slid down the side of Yuri's face. The crescendo of heat from two thousand people below was suffocating.

"What'd you want from me. Tell me before I arrest you for attempting to blackmail a police officer."

Gropski moved around, ignoring the coat of dust on his clothes. He used a handkerchief to wipe blood from his ear.

"I heard you're tough but no one told me you were crazy. It's too bad times have changed. You would have made a good KGB operative. I could have had you placed."

"You could have had shit placed."

Gropski ignored the insult and walked around the roof, pausing to look down through peepholes. Yuri followed him, glancing down at the holes but keeping his concentration on the man and the surroundings. No gun, no backup, had him worried.

"I was assigned here early in my career, a plush assignment for a new agent. The dancers, directors, and musicians, always dissent brewing among them. They had the rare privilege of traveling abroad and we had to learn which ones were the most likely to suddenly make a dash for freedom in New York or Paris."

Gropski went from spy hole to spy hole, reliving the good old days when real men turned in their mothers for anti-Soviet remarks about the quality of bread.

"A real hotbed. People came to the ballet to pass seditious notes, to whisper plots. The bathrooms were a favorite of some plotters and we watched them carefully."

"I can see you were an important piece of the Soviet spy apparatus, peeking down into toilet stalls to see if toilet paper got passed under the stalls."

"I caught many dissenters," Gropski bristled. "I was in on the case when Olga Shishkin jumped ship in Boston to defect. But the people who were trying to sneak her four-year-old daughter out of Moscow as their own were caught at Sheremetyevo Airport. We sent Olga pictures of her daughter on the lap of our ugliest agent. That got her back into the flock immediately."

"You should be proud of yourself," Yuri murmured, keeping his hand on his gun that he had slipped back into his side coat pocket. He realized why Gropski had chosen the strange place for them to meet. Using the security office at the cheap hotel would not have impressed Yuri; even a restaurant would not have done much to enhance the tough ex-KGB agent image Gropski wanted to portray. But the Bolshoi, the assignment of his glory days before he was flushed down the piss hole of the organization, was meant to impress Yuri.

As he watched Gropski moving around the ceiling, checking out the audience below, he realized there was something . . . or someone Gropski wanted him to see.

Gropski knelt by a peephole and motioned Yuri to take a look. Keeping an eye on the other man, Yuri looked through the hole. He could see musicians in the orchestra pit and some of the dancers on stage—black-robed Ivan pranced around the stage dispatching the Mongol horde.

And then he picked up on what Gropski wanted him to see. A man and a woman in an orchestra box, a box reserved for royalty and high commissars in the days of Imperialists and Communists. The man occupying it now was Alexei Bova, said to be the richest man in Russia, not to mention the biggest thief in Russia, Yuri thought, the man at the head of the pack of nouveau entrepreneurs who were trying to see who could steal the most from the financial chaos created by the fall of communism.

The woman beside Bova was also familiar to him— Nadia Kolchak, Russia's top television news anchorwoman. Only the last time he saw her was in an old black and white film in which she took off her clothes for a man with a hairy belly. She had all of her clothes on tonight, though from his vantage point the clothes still managed to fall a little short of covering all of her body.

He was careful to allow no emotion on his face to reveal that seeing the two people had had any effect on him. Looking up, he saw Gropski studying him with an intensity that made the gears going around in his head almost visible.

He doesn't know anything, Yuri thought. Gropski had had him take the peek in the hopes that something in Yuri's body language would give him a clue. All he has are some names but he hasn't connected any of it up.

Yuri stood up and brushed dust from his pants.

"I could have bought a ticket if I had wanted to see the ballet. You told me you had information, information I would be personally interested in at a price. Tell me what you want."

"What do I want? It's a market economy, comrade. We are free to negotiate, to trade, to make profits. I want to trade with you."

"You have nothing to trade with."

"That is what I am selling, exactly nothing." As he spoke Gropski moved back toward the ghost village near the stair-ladder. "Silence is an absence of anything and that is the nothing I am willing to trade . . . for the hard currency I told you to bring."

He's fishing. "Tell me what you would be silent about?"

Gropski grinned and paused, resting his arm against the plywood troika. "About you . . . and"—he gestured back at the peephole—"them. And the situation."

Yuri almost laughed in his face. The man knew nothing. He knew of a vague link between Yuri and the two Russian socialites, probably learned through Belkin, but not even Belkin had known more about Yuri's interest.

But Gropski could be dangerous. He could raise questions about Yuri through his old contacts at the militia. Yuri's entire life could end up under the intensity of a magnifying glass when it would hardly bear the scrutiny of window glass.

The man was small-time and that was the most dangerous kind. Gropski didn't realize that he had put himself into a collision course with Yuri that could only end up in disaster. To deal with him with money was out of the question. Yuri didn't have the money to pay the man and even if he had enough to temporarily buy him off it would only open a flood gate of demands that the man would be too stupid to realize Yuri could not meet.

There was another approach, one in which he stalled the man, led him on until he was ready to make his move. But no matter how he dealt with Gropski the man would present an immediate danger because the man was so damn stupid. A smart blackmailer would never have come to a meeting unarmed and without a backup.

The cigar Gropski had discarded on the floor and stomped on was still glowing red, no doubt getting ready to ignite the dust in the attic and blow the roof off the Bolshoi.

"I'm going to have another cigar," Gropski told him, leaning over the side of the troika to the seat, "and maybe burn down the place. Napoleon did it once. Anyway, the theatre will probably end up as an American fast fo—''

As he spoke, he turned toward Yuri who saw the glint of light off a barrel. Gropski's backup was a 9mm with a silencer.

Yuri pivoted to the left, caught off balance, clumsily lurching for the man as the gun came around. He hit the gun hand above the wrist and the gun went off, a *zap!* sound, as he grabbed the gun hand by the wrist.

Gropski kicked at him and they grappled with each other. The man was barrel-built and strong, stronger than Yuri anticipated. He couldn't handle Gropski's weight and he let him slide past, tripping him, sending him crashing down to the floor with Yuri on top, still struggling for control of the gun as it went *zap!* again.

Gropski slammed his knee into Yuri's groin. For a second, Yuri went limp from the shock. Gropski used his strength to roll over, pinning Yuri to the floor. The vibrations from the music of the frenzied scene when Ivan chokes to death a rival who had dared sit on his throne pulsated at his back.

Gropski put his weight behind his grip on the gun, pushing it down, trying to maneuver it to get off a shot in Yuri's face or chest. Yuri struck at him with his left hand but Gropski blocked most of the punch with his shoulder. The muzzle of the gun was coming down toward Yuri's face. He reached out with his left hand, trying to get enough leverage to roll Gropski off of him. His hand touched the burning cigar on the floor—he grabbed the cigar and pushed it into Gropski's face, trying for the eyes. Gropski howled and jerked allowing Yuri to squash the rest of the smothering butt in his face. Gropski leaned back and then slammed forward again to pin Yuri as Yuri made another attempt at the gun, getting both hands around Gropski's gun hand. The gun went off and with each *zap!* Gropski's body kicked.

* * *

Yuri left the way he had come, down the ladder-stairs, his face averted, the pounding music from the ballet smothering the noise he made on the ladder.

He had put Gropski back where he found him, in the troika, perhaps to be covered with the dust-snow until he became just another part of the scenery that would be used in a future ballet.

VIII

═══

We had a belief that the first generation
of Russian capitalists would be nice guys,
but they are ruthless motherfuckers...
much worse than the American robber barons.
These guys take the fillings out of teeth
after murder...here we have a 1930s
situation in Chicago, except that Al Capone
has access to nuclear weapons.

—Seymour Hersh "The Wild East,"
Atlantic Monthly,
June 1994

O N E

Lara spent a day cooped up in her depressing room at the Gorky licking her wounds from the previous day. The physical aches and pains were healing better than the mental ones and she had twice reached for the phone to call the airport for reservations out of the country. The fact she was now in a taxi on her way back to Red Square had as much to do with the Gorky's inefficient telephone system as it did with her determination not to desert the quest to clear her mother's name.

She kicked herself over and over for getting into an argument with Detective Kirov at the café yesterday. It was insulting enough to embarrass him about the bill . . . did she really have to argue with him about the Cold War? Her big chance to make a connection with the Moscow police and she blew it over the price of cappuccino.

Story of my life, she thought. What would it be like to have a husband, kids, a house, and stay home in a cocoon? Her mother's generation had won the battle against the enslavement of women in a social prison. But every once in a while, when things that went bump in the night got closer, she thought about cocoons . . .

The gray gloom hovering over the city pressed down on

her, increasing her depression. She understood now why people living in northern climates with long dismal winters had high suicide rates.

St. Basil's had been the first challenge she had faced in coming back to Moscow. It had taken her two weeks and had nearly cost her life to enter the building.

The second piece to her nightmares was the Little School.

Lara felt a headache come as the taxi neared Red Square and the school. She wished she had brought her aspirin with her. Taking them right away usually got rid of the headache.

"I'm not turning back."

The driver glanced over his shoulder at her. "No English."

"It's all right," she told him in Russian, "I was talking to myself."

The Little School, as it was called by everyone even though it had an official name a foot long, was tucked away in a building a block off Red Square. The monster GUM department store was nearby. As a child, her way to and from the school had not been through Red Square, but from a street behind the square, even though the school could be reached from either direction.

It was indeed a "little" school, twenty classrooms carved out of the guts of an office structure. The closest thing to a playground had been a gymnasium above the classrooms. What the school lacked in size was made up for in prestige because only the brightest children of high-ranking Kremlin officials were admitted.

Her mother had not been part of the Inner Circle, but after Lara tested exceptionally high, a friend of her mother's at the Ministry of Education managed to slip Lara in on the grounds that she would provide a "cultural challenge" to the other children.

She knew the school still existed and that I. Malinovsky,

her grammar-school teacher, was still on the staff. That much she had learned with a telephone call. Separation by miles of telephone wire and trips to Red Square to stare at the cathedral had been as close as she had gotten to the school since her return.

She fought the headache as she made her way along an interior corridor to the steps that led up to the classroom level. She stopped at the administration office and asked the receptionist for directions to I. Malinovsky's classroom. "I. Malinovsky" was the only name Lara knew the teacher by. She didn't know what the "I" stood for.

"Last classroom on the right at the end of the hall." The woman checked her watch. "If you hurry, you'll catch her still in morning break before the children come back."

Lara remembered that I. Malinovsky would stay in the classroom during morning break to correct papers or read over a cup of tea but she couldn't remember what the woman looked like and wondered if her memory of morning tea was an actual recollection of what the woman did or part of a blur of memories about teachers at the school.

Walking down the corridor she heard the pounding of hundreds of young feet in the gym above. She remembered the gym. Gymnastics was the sport of the day for young girls when she went to the school.

Bits and pieces of other memories came to her; the smell of the white glue used to stick autumn leaves to classroom windows, a patriotic song the class sang each morning about heroic factory workers and farmers, being scolded for racing her friend Anna to the drinking fountain . . .

> Standing at a window with her teacher, the
> teacher pointing down at the street where a woman
>   stood,
> a woman in a brown coat and red scarf.
> "Your mother's come for you."

The door to the classroom was open and she paused before stepping in, taking a moment to study the woman seated at the desk in the front of the classroom.

I. Malinovsky seemed vaguely familiar but once again she didn't know how much of her impression was memory or how much was invoked just because the woman was sitting in the teacher's chair.

The woman was probably approaching retirement age. A few dark streaks still toned the hair she had pulled back into a severe bun. Wrinkles, certainly not from too much sunshine in Moscow, created the map of a hard life on her face.

No, Lara thought, not a hard life. The stern press to her lips that caused lines to scar her cheeks, the spinster frown that left creases in her forehead, and the harsh gray suit, more uniform than fashion statement, were probably the marks of a life *unfulfilled*.

"May I help you?"

"Yes, I'm looking for I. Malinovsky."

"I am Malinovsky."

Lara stepped into the classroom as the woman stood up.

"If this is about one of your children, school regulations require that you make an appointment."

"No, it's not that. I used to be one of your students."

"One of my students?" The woman studied her face. "It must have been quite some time ago."

"Over twenty years. My name is Lara Patrick."

"Patrick, yes, a little foreign girl. Your mother was an American Communist." The woman fumbled for words.

"My mother wasn't a Communist. She was an anti-war activist."

"Why are you here?"

"To say hello. It's been a long time."

"Well, we . . . we are happy when our students return to say hello." The woman's lips trembled as she smiled.

"Do you remember that day?" Lara asked.

"Which day?"

"My last day. It was near the end of the school term. You told me my mother had come for me."

"I don't remember."

"A woman dressed in my mother's clothes came to pick me up. I never returned to school. You must remember that. I was the only foreigner in the school."

"There are so many years, so many students . . ."

"Who took me out of the classroom that day and pretended to be my mother?"

"I don't know what you're talking about."

"I need to know who came that day and took me from the classroom."

"That was a long time ago. I don't remember such nonsense." The woman brushed away the years with a sweep of her hand.

"I never returned to the school. I was . . . hurt at St. Basil's. You must know that, there must have been rumors flying around the school, questions about why I never returned."

"I'm not responsible for what your mother did. You were a foreigner, you didn't belong here anyway."

"Why did you say it was my mother? Did you speak to her? Did she—"

"I remember nothing." Malinovsky stood up, her face dark with anger, her lips trembling. "Get out of here, go away. I don't want to hear this nonsense."

Lara shook her head. "Why are you acting this way? You knew who I was the moment I said my name. You didn't have to think back twenty years. You were expecting me."

"I don't know what you're talking about."

"Why are you so frightened? Someone has been to see you, haven't they? You were told I was coming and warned not to say anything."

"You have no right to come to my classroom and speak to me this way." She was almost yelling. "Get out, get out or I will call the authorities."

"Please talk to me. It's important."

"Important? Who are you to come here and make accusations after all these years. I am a schoolteacher—"

"I'm not accusing—"

"A professional teacher for over thirty years. My students have grown up and are running the country. They run the country and on weekends go to their fancy dachas while I sit and decay into an old woman with nothing."

"I need your help."

"My help!" The woman screamed the word. Spittle hit the breast of Lara's coat. "I can help no one, I can't even help myself. Get out, get out, go back to America. You're not wanted here. Poor Russians are trying to survive. Go back to your fat country."

Lara paused at the door.

"It was the woman who pretended to be my mother, wasn't it? She's been back to see you."

"Get out!"

Malinovsky collapsed back on her chair as if the shout had taken the last of her strength.

Lara heard her sobbing as she walked back down the corridor.

After Lara left, Malinovsky held her head in her hands and tried to stop the pounding. Fear had been with her for so long, lying dormant and ready to wake up and scream.

She knew something about the person who took Lara away that day and she lived with the fear that someday the information would be cut out of her heart.

She heard someone at the door and she looked up, expecting it to be a student that she would order back to the gym.

A woman wearing a red scarf across the lower part of her face and a long brown coat stood in the doorway.

"You were told not to talk to the American."

*   *   *

Lara's headache had become the terrible pain of having a vise clamped to both temples and tightened until her skull was being crushed.

At the bottom of a stairway she forced herself to turn left toward Red Square, the route she had avoided coming to the school. Her knees were weak and her head ready to explode but she forced herself forward, memories flying at her with every step.

Before her was the Place of Skulls, the stone platform upon which grisly executions took place in tsarist times. Farther to the right was the Lenin Mausoleum and the great Kremlin Wall. Through the gated entrances to the Kremlin were the buildings that housed the might and power of all the Russias.

She turned from the Kremlin Wall and slowly walked to her left, her throat muscles constricting until it felt as if dread would suffocate her. But she kept walking, determined to go forward, following where her feet were taking her even if her mind balked.

She stopped and stared up at the cathedral. It was the most incredible building in all Russia, a church not even Stalin had dared defile.

Blood pounded in her temples and a wave of nausea swept over her, turning her stomach, blocking her throat. Dizzy, unsteady on her feet, she forced herself to look ahead to the cathedral, her mind swirling with the memory . . . a rope hanging from the rafters, hands on her naked body . . .

She saw a woman in a brown coat with a little girl in hand entering the cathedral and her head exploded.

She swayed and felt herself falling as black dust swamped her mind.

TWO

Street traffic parted at the sound of the speeding ambulance's piercing siren. Lara sat on the metal floor in the back of the ambulance with a blanket wrapped around her.

"The factory for repairing stretchers is in Latvia," the ambulance attendant told her. "Latvia's declared its independence and won't repair Russian stretchers unless payment is made in advance with hard currency."

He seemed young to be a paramedic, no more than in his late teens, she thought, still fighting pimples and awkwardness with girls.

"New stretchers are made in a factory in the Ukraine," he said. "And they won't sell us stretchers without hard currency, either. Can you blame them? Every day the ruble buys less. Soon you'll need a wheelbarrow full to buy a bottle of vodka."

"So this board"—she nudged it with her foot—"is your stretcher."

"Temporarily," he said with a smile.

She liked him.

They had been near Red Square when they got the call that a woman had fainted in front of St. Basil's Cathedral. When they picked her up, he first inquired whether she was pregnant. After she told him that would have required an immaculate conception, he asked if she was starved. After a negative on that, finding out she was an American, he asked if she had AIDS.

The ambulance went around a sharp curve in the road, siren blaring, the driver's foot heavy on the gas pedal. A wide stretch of road opened up and the driver shot them down the middle divider, sending a militia traffic officer scrambling out of the way and cars swerving to avoid head-on collisions.

"Is all this necessary?" Lara asked. "You're just dropping me off at my hotel."

He grinned, exposing a metal filling in a front tooth. "Olga's a relief driver from the suburbs. She doesn't get many chances to race through the downtown sector at high speed."

Lara leaned back against the interior wall and closed her eyes. She was horribly embarrassed, fainting in Red Square in the middle of the day, cringing at the thought she might have been filmed and would make the Moscow Evening News. But the concern and good humor of the ambulance attendants had helped ease the embarrassment.

Misha, the attendant, was still curious as to why she had fainted, but other than telling him truthfully that she was under great stress, she avoided the subject.

She fell sideways as Olga took another hairpin turn at full gallop. Straightening up, Lara gave Misha a wan smile. "I'm going to throw up."

He grabbed a metal pot off a hook on the wall and shoved it at her. "Maybe we'd better take you to a hospital."

Bad timing. A fit of laughter hit her. Choking, she almost dumped the contents of the pot in his lap.

"People die," she gasped, "in Moscow hospitals."

The wail of its siren wound down as the ambulance pulled in front of her hotel. Misha opened the back doors and stepped out. He helped Lara down as a curious crowd gathered.

"Give my thanks to Olga."

Lara left a wad of five-hundred-ruble notes in the back of the ambulance because Misha had refused to take any money from her.

"Taxi shortage," she told the gawking porter as she walked by him and went into the hotel. It suddenly occurred to her that she had left the hotel yesterday morning in a police car and returned today in an ambulance.

Well, what did they expect when everything was going crazy in the city?

THREE

Two clerks stared at Lara from behind the front desk as she walked by and headed for the hotel security office. The only other person in the lobby was a sleeping man sitting on a couch with his head hanging back, snoring with his mouth open.

She opened the door of the security office, expecting to find Gropski in the room. A man cut from the same cloth as the frog, cheap pin-striped suit, belly buttons straining, shirt collar two inches short of being able to close at the neck, looked up at her from behind a steel desk. The desk and the steel chair he was sitting on were the only furnishings in the office.

"Yes?"

"I'm looking for the security officer."

"I'm Nosenko, the security officer."

"I'm looking for Mr. Gropski."

"Gropski no longer works for the hotel."

Lara stared at him. "Is he dead?"

The man's eyebrows shot up. "Dead? I hope so. He failed to report for duty and I had to cancel my vacation to cover for him. If he isn't dead now, he will be when I find him."

"Does anyone know where he went?"

"To hell for all I know." His eyes skimmed her up and down. "You have a security problem?" He started to rise. "We can have a drink—"

"Thanks, but I'm in a hurry."

She went back into the lobby. She didn't want to go up to her room. It was still morning. Finding another hotel was on her list of wants, as well as going to see Guk, the truck driver who had miraculously survived the crash with her mother.

Not able to muster the courage yet to turn up cold on the truck driver's doorstep, she left the Gorky and walked, ignoring the rare phenomenon of an available taxi in front of the hotel.

The taxi driver and porter stared at her as she walked down the street. She didn't blame them. Besides early morning visits from the police and being chauffeured in police cars and an ambulance, they could rack up the hotel security man disappearing after talking to her.

Had Gropski heard about Belkin's untimely demise and taken fright? Had someone paid him a visit? The same someone who frightened the schoolteacher?

She had the sensation of standing in a forest clearing as maniacs stampeded around her . . .

She wanted to call Yuri Kirov, to tell him she needed help, but she couldn't do it. I wouldn't ask for help if I was hanging from the ledge of a cliff, she thought. She knew how to give but had never learned how to take.

A ruthless prosecutor had been her reputation. Defense attorneys called her "Maximum Bob" after a retired judge who commonly handed out long sentences. Yes, she had been tough—but fair, she hoped. She knew in the back of her mind there had always been the suppressed anger and fears about her own childhood debasement and now she wondered how much of that had directed her in prosecuting people who hurt children.

No, the people I prosecuted were guilty and deserved what they got. The only thing they got from me was the maximum they earned for their crimes—that and nothing more. I simply didn't plea bargain with bastards.

She crossed the street to get off the busy, store-lined sidewalk and walk along a park on the other side.

It had snowed during the night, but a sky that was only partially cloudy allowed a little sunshine over the city. The sunshine helped uplift her spirits, but she still felt alone and vulnerable. No one to turn to.

Lara the loner, always the loner.

Her grandmother had provided her with the necessities of life, but none of the warmth. Her British relatives had never answered the letter she sent to them when she was a teenager. And she had never really established any close relationships with the people around her.

A strange child, her grandmother called her. Strange because she talked so little, played alone, seemed to be cautious of everyone. Her grandmother had blamed it on cultural shock and the death of her mother.

In her own mind, she was normal. She just preferred being alone. Or so she told herself. She kept herself busy, adjusting to American schools, excelling at exams, working hard at college to get accepted at law school, graduating near the top of her class in law school, and then surprising even herself by turning down a high-paying job with a corporate firm for a deputy district attorney's position in the unit prosecuting crimes against women and children.

She threw herself into her work, dealing with those around her with polite professionalism. She never went to an office party, never dropped by the "watering hole" where prosecutors, cops, and probation people met after work for "happy hour" drinks. She ate her lunches alone at her desk and didn't go to the cafeteria even for breaks.

She never had a significant personal involvement. Friends, male and female, were people she worked with. A couple of people who cared were frank enough to tell her that she shared nothing of herself, retreating into a shell every time they tried to get close.

Having gone directly from childhood to adult without stopping to be a teenager had a lot to do with it. Perhaps if her grandmother had healed the wounds, had shown love rather than tolerance.

The letter from Moscow had come at a time when she was wondering about who she was, a time when she lay awake nights and tried to put together the pieces that added up to her.

Being in the city, all alone without her work to throw herself into, had gotten her thinking not only about what happened to her mother's life, but her own.

I hate being alone, hate it hate it hate it. I've been lying to myself because I've spent my own life frightened.

She desperately wanted someone to love and someone to love her.

On the other side of the park a kiosk was selling hot tea and coffee and she stepped off the sidewalk and onto the crunchy snow on a path that led across the park.

Hands in her pockets, face down to her problems, her feet crunching snow as she walked, she looked up at the sound of yelling and laughter. Boys . . . no, young men, eighteen, nineteen years old, were shoving around an old man on the little frozen pond in the middle of the park. It took a moment for her to realize what they were doing. One would grab an arm or leg of the old man and swing him around, spinning, and then let him go, the old man sliding across the pond to one of the other young men who would spin him to the third player.

The bastards were playing hockey on the pond and using an old man for their puck.

They were street toughs wearing American-style motorcycle jackets, headbands, black pants, and black boots. There was a gang emblem on the back of their jackets but she couldn't make it out.

The poor old man was a derelict, a ragged scarecrow, his feet and one hand wrapped in pieces torn from discarded clothing, his old army coat stained filthy from nights on subway benches—or worse places. It immediately struck her that the old man had pissed off the gang-bangers in some manner, maybe trying to panhandle them or just being in the wrong place at the wrong time.

Lara looked around for help. Cars were passing on each side of the park and there were a few pedestrians, but no one was paying any attention to what was happening. And no one would be stupid enough to interfere with street toughs tormenting an old derelict.

"Stop it!" Lara yelled. She left the path and hurried across the stiff snow to the pond. One of the toughs had the old man by a leg and was spinning him, the gangbanger managing to keep his own feet under him because the ice on the pond was rough. "The police are coming, leave him alone!"

The gangbangers stopped their horseplay and looked over to her. The one spinning the old man let him go, sending him sliding on the ice, and told the others, "She wants to play, too."

Something hit her in the back, sending her flying forward, hitting the ice on her stomach with the breath knocked from her. As she rolled over on the pond she saw her assailant, a husky gangbanger wearing the same black outfit as the others. He stood above her, laughing.

The derelict scrambled away as the excited gang converged on Lara. "Fresh blood," one of them yelled.

Oh, God!

As she started up onto her feet, one of them charged her, grabbing her wrist and jerking her around. Her shoes were more slippery than the heavy boots her attacker was wearing and her feet went out from under her as he started to spin her.

He spun her around and around, her whole body leaving the ice, and then let her go. She slid and bumped across the rough ice to another player.

The gangbanger reached down to grab her foot and she kicked out with her other foot yelling, "You bastard!" Her heel hit him on the nose and sent him stumbling back, holding his nose.

He took his hands away from his nose and saw blood on them.

"Fucking bitch." He had a skinhead haircut with a pirate-style bandanna looped around his forehead, a three-day beard, gold loop earrings in both ears, and a small blue tattoo of a dagger under his right eye. His round stupid face and dark eyes were punk mean. He reached down and pulled out a buck knife from his boot. "I'm going to stomp your face into mush and cut off your fucking ears."

He came at her ready to kick—she rolled on the ice and the kick went by her head. It caught the bastard off balance and he fell on his butt as she kept moving on the ice, trying to get her feet solidly under her, hearing the crunch of the boots of the charging gangbangers as they came at her from all sides, heated up and aroused at the prospect of stomping her.

The roar of a car engine split the yelling of the men and suddenly they were scattering around her. She fell back down onto her own tush and gawked as a small red sports car plowed across the park's stiff snow and came onto the ice. The car slid on the ice, coming directly at her. It was almost on top of her before it stopped a couple of feet away and she stared at the front end of a Lamborghini.

A blond, handsome man with a medium build and a magazine-cover face got out of the car. Her first thought was that James Bond had dropped out of the sky to rescue her.

"You fucking idiot," one of them told him. Grinning, the gangbanger turned to his buddies. "He wants to give us his car."

They started converging on the blond man. He smiled at them and reached back into the car, pulling out a nasty-looking AK-47 assault rifle.

The gangbangers looked at the gun and then checked out his face.

"You're all dead meat," he told them. He turned the safety off the rifle and leveled the barrel at them. "You have three seconds . . . one . . . two . . ." They hesitated just for a second, just enough to look at each other and then start backing off. They left the pond, yelling threats and filthy insults behind them.

Lara, still on her tush, stared up at the man, the lethal weapon, and the snazzy red sports car. She started to say something but her tongue tripped in her mouth and she just stared stupidly up at Sir Galahad.

"Are you hurt?" he asked. He knelt by her.

She shook her head.

As he gave her a hand up a large popping sound erupted as the ice under the red sports car cracked.

"Your car. It's going to sink."

He tossed the assault rifle through the open window of the car and grabbed her by the hand to lead her off the pond. "It's okay, I have another."

Crunching across the snow toward the street, Lara looked back at the sports car that now was up to its frame in icy water. "Don't you think we should call—"

"No." He grinned. "The ashtray was full." He laughed, a nice open fun-loving laugh that she liked. "I heard that line in an American movie. People so rich they throw away their car when the ashtray gets full."

"Those punks looked like an American motorcycle gang from an old movie," she said. "I saw the word 'Outlaws' on the back of their jackets. Must be part of the culture of violence exported from America through Hollywood movies."

They were almost to the street as a black Mercedes skidded to a stop. Two husky men in dark suits jumped out and ran toward them. The men looked anxious.

"We lost you—"

"You're fired, both of you."

"But—"

"No buts."

He walked Lara to the passenger side door of the Mercedes and opened it for her. He came back around and got into the driver's seat. The engine was running and he put the car into gear and hit the gas, burning rubber as the car shot down the street. Lara glanced back to see the two husky men looking a little lost and forlorn and the red sports car up to its hood in the pond.

"Aren't those cars a little, uh . . ."

"Two hundred thousand."

Oh, God.

She cleared her throat. "At least you're getting a free wash."

They both laughed and she reached out and touched his right arm, squeezing it.

"Thank you."

"No problem. I drown sports cars in lakes all the time rescuing damsels in distress. Sorry about the scene with my bodyguards. But they lost me in traffic and weren't there when I needed them."

He was magazine-cover material; not the Marlboro Man type, but more like the guy in a skimpy brief staring out of a window at city lights. There was something familiar about him.

"Have we met?"

"I would have remembered you. I'm Alexei Bova."

Now she knew who he was. The enfant terrible of the new Russian rich. Probably the richest man in Russia. The most eligible bachelor in Russia. Muscovites spent their morning break recounting his latest exploits and arguing whether he should be shot or deified.

She guessed he was older than her first impression. He looked thirtyish but probably was somewhere in his forties or even early fifties. Whatever his age, he was still model material. His golden hair had just a tinge of gray in it; his tanned face was smooth and handsome with a perfectly chiseled nose and chin.

"I missed the first part of the battle," he said. "How

did you happen to get into a fight with a gang of toughs?"

She told him about the old man being tormented. "I was stupid. Maybe it was something from my childhood, being tormented once by a bunch of kids."

He stared at her a little quizzically. "You are telling a story from my own childhood. I was a sickly and cowardly child." He laughed. "But I'm making up for it by never growing up. I have to confess that today was a rare moment of courage on my part. Usually I hire people to do the fighting for me."

He glanced at his watch. "I'm afraid I have a terribly important meeting with some very boring Moscow city officials. I'm always late for these meetings, but today I am more than politely late." He pointed at the building at the end of the busy street.

She recognized it immediately: the Black Tower, one of the first high-rise office buildings constructed with private funds and the most controversial building in the country.

"Now that we have fought the enemies of derelicts side by side and defeated them," he said, "at the cost of one red dragon, we must celebrate our victory. Please have dinner with me tonight."

Have dinner with the richest and handsomest man in Russia? What an exciting and incredible opportunity. What fantastic luck.

"No, I'm sorry, but I really can't," she blurted out, her face turning pink.

"Then you must come to my party tomorrow night. At the tower. Many of the most important people in Moscow will be there."

"Well, I'm not sure . . ."

"Here's my card, Lara. Give me a call if you change your mind. Now I must drop you back at your hotel."

"No, that's all right. Let me off right here."

"Are you sure? I don't mind—"

"No, no, this is fine. I was coming down to look at these stores anyway."

He pulled the car over to the curb and she shook his hand as she got out and thanked him.

"My pleasure," he said. "Please change your mind and give me a call."

She walked away, a little dazed.

Moscow's Donald Trump had just invited her to dinner and a party with the rich and famous and she had said she was too busy.

Busy doing what? Counting the cracks in the ceiling at my dumpy hotel?

She kicked a streetlamp. Ignoring the looks of passersby, she kicked it again.

Putting her head down, she started back in the direction of her hotel. She had been too embarrassed to let him drop her off at one of the cheapest hotels in Moscow. She should have told him she was staying at the Metropole, "the place to stay this season, darling."

She had declined because she was scared and had no damn confidence in her attraction to men.

Tonight she'd have bread and soup alone in her room because she hated sitting in restaurants by herself.

Stupid stupid stupid.

In a taxi, heading back to her hotel, she stared out the back window at Alexei Bova's tower.

From newspaper accounts she knew the name came from its color, black-on-black with dark tinted windows, windows you would normally see in a sunny place like California rather than gray, overcast Moscow.

She didn't recall why the building made the front pages, but she knew it was just one of the many controversies about the man. He was the darling of the story-hungry news media. Everything he did seemed to explode into controversy. He claimed he was trying to build a new Russia; his critics claimed he was trying to *steal* the new Russia.

In the mad scramble to convert to a market economy, Alexei Bova had entered the real estate market with a vengeance, privatizing overnight major buildings and land by making deals that many people claimed were not legal.

But who knew exactly what was legal?

She recalled reading that a French fashion house had bought a Moscow building and spent millions refurbishing it, only to have the people who used to work at the location claim the building for themselves and enforce their claim by squatter's rights—setting up household in the building until the French company bought them out.

She was halfway back to her hotel when a thought struck her. He called her Lara. Did she tell him her name?

She must have told him.

But wasn't it strange that he'd risk losing a fabulously expensive car on an ice pond to rescue a perfect stranger when his bodyguards weren't far behind?

Stop it, she told herself. She was seeing plots behind every tree.

She tried to remember if she had told him her name.

IX

The peasant with his ax is coming,
Something terrible will happen.

—Russian Proverb

ONE

===

The taxi pulled up to her hotel and she sat inside a moment thinking. Returning to her room was not going to get the job done. She had to go see the truck driver.

Alone.

Why wasn't I nicer to Yuri Kirov? Why didn't I throw myself into Alexei Bova's arms and tell him I needed a little more rescue? I don't burn bridges, I dynamite them.

The address for Joseph Guk, the truck driver with the perfect driving record, was off of a major highway running west of the city. She told the taxi driver where she wanted him to take her and got an argument.

"It's a long way."

"How much is the fare for a long way?"

"The roads in that area are bad."

"How much for bad roads?"

"It's going to snow."

"How much?" she asked.

As soon as the official restraints had come off, taxi drivers were the first group in the city to throw both feet into the market economy. Almost every ride had been a memorable financial experience for her as the fare changed en route. At the airport on the day she had arrived, a taxi driver locked her luggage into the trunk of his cab and then blatantly told her a ride into Moscow was a hundred American dollars. Her willingness to yell for the airport police while she stood in front of the taxi so it couldn't move had quickly negotiated a reasonable fee.

Years of dealing with crooks, perverts, attorneys, and cops had made her tough, she thought. But that was before she tangled with a Moscow taxi driver.

After agreeing to pay double the reasonable fare, she leaned back in the seat and tried to think of a story to feed Mr. Guk.

Walking up to him and demanding to know why he had been part of a plot to create a phony accident involving the death of her mother probably would not win any points with Mr. Guk.

Half an hour later, the taxi left the main highway and groaned in and out of big potholes down a narrow road.

Lara saw no pride of ownership, none of the small, personal touches she had expected in the countryside. The area was without warmth or rustic charm. Scattered houses, shacks more than anything else, were flanked by crippled old outhouses and sheds caving in from the weight of snow. Fence posts ravaged by winterkill formed the bleached rib bones of the skeleton land. Gray and gloomy Moscow streets appeared bright and cheerful in comparison.

This is a place where people were imprisoned by the land, not fed by it, she thought. She realized there must be places like this in America, land where only snow and rocks and misery grew, but she was a city girl and those places were the stuff of news broadcasts, no more real than a flood in China or a terrorist bomb in Israel.

She shivered at the thought of living in one of the houses without indoor plumbing and having to go out and sit on an outhouse toilet during a sub-zero Russian night.

Several miles down the road a row of wooden mailboxes next to a snow-covered one-lane bridge told her that she had arrived. The numerical address she had for Guk was on one of the boxes.

The bridge spanned a small, frozen creek. On the other side of the stream were half a dozen homes on large lots, six blighted houses that neither snow nor icicle trim transposed into quaint cottages. Soiled from chimney soot, the dirty snow and icicles added to the derelict appearance of the houses.

The taxi passed the weathered corpse of an old factory before reaching the bridge. A sign wounded and scarred by time and the elements said the factory had made chemicals for fertilizer that made the Soviet Union grow.

Lara opened the taxi window and stuck her head out to get a better look at the houses. A smell of snow was in the air, a crisp dry bite to her nostrils slightly polluted by a stench that made her wonder if the chemical factory was still alive—or rotting in death.

"A swamp from factory waste," the taxi driver said about the smell, pointing to an area near the ruins of the factory. "It's almost frozen over."

An icy fog was dropping the sky around them and she could barely make out the swamp about fifty yards from the road. The abandoned factory grounds were dotted with overgrown bushes and weeds, but nothing grew near the slushy swamp, making her wonder what kind of chemicals they had used in their fertilizers.

The risk that they might have to drive out of the isolated area in a winter white-out was making the city driver unhappy.

"You know what area this is, don't you?"

"What do you mean?"

"Citizen R lived somewhere around here."

Russian criminals were referred to in the newspapers by a code name, Citizen A, B, and so forth, and it took a second for the label to register.

"Is he the one who killed children?"

"Killed children and ate their hearts. Twenty-two children they know of, probably more. Runaways they'll never trace."

Citizen R had been captured before she arrived in Moscow but the stories about him still circulated. Because of the old regime's refusal to publish horror stories for fear it would cast their "perfect" society in a bad light, Citizen R and others like him had been even harder to track down in the Soviet Union than they were in the West. A newspaper had recently estimated that most of the serial killers in Russia were still walking around free because the public was unaware of their existence.

She wondered if the driver was trying to frighten her to turn back—or increase the price again. He had tried to jack up the price on the way and her refusal had turned into a shouting match. She was tired of being ripped off. It seemed as if the whole country had been storing up greed for seven decades, just waiting for the fall of communism when they would stop being exploited and could start exploiting everyone else.

The driver's bitching had started on the outskirts of the city and had increased as they left the main highway for the bumpy road: something was going to break on his cab and he wouldn't be able to get parts to replace it; they were going to get stuck in one of the huge potholes; it was going to snow and the roads would be impassable; the overcast was dropping like a dark blanket from the sky. His final complaint was the bridge.

"I can't drive over that bridge," he told her. "It's too dangerous."

The bridge looked as if it had been sculpted from ice.

"It has a lot of ice on it, but the people over there must drive back and forth."

He twisted in the seat and glared at her. "Maybe they don't have bald tires on their cars. Do you want to end up drowned in the river?"

"I'll walk. But you have to wait. I'll need you to take me back to town."

"Pay me now. For the return trip, too."

She hesitated. "How do I know you'll wait?"

His glare went red. "How do you know the sun will rise tomorrow?"

"In Moscow, I wouldn't always bet on it." But she didn't have a choice. If she didn't pay him, he'd leave anyway. She gave him the money. "I shouldn't be long."

She got out of the taxi and swung the door closed. She had wanted the taxi to park right outside Guk's house in case she ran into any problems, but the driver would have left tire marks across her back before he left them on the bridge.

The courage and resolve she had felt in the warm, safe taxi was rapidly shrinking as the reality of actually facing Joseph Guk neared.

She knew only two things about the mysterious Mr. Guk: he was former KGB and he was somehow connected to the death of her mother.

Nervous and wary, she put one foot in front of the other and kept pushing forward. Halfway across the bridge a frigid wind lashed at her, nearly sweeping her off of her feet as her leather-soled city shoes slipped on the ice.

The wind gave her another sharp whiff of that stench from the swamp. How do people put up with it? she wondered, realizing at once the naiveté of her question. A little stink was mild in comparison to what many Russians had to put up with. Before Chernobyl, thousands of people had lived on radioactive ground because the government refused to admit accidents had occurred with nuclear reactors.

As she crossed the bridge she studied the houses on the other side. The scene looked like a black and white print of Russia before the Great Patriotic War, the Soviet countryside of the 1920s and 1930s when Stalin had forced socialism down the throats of peasants who had never read a book let alone the *Communist Manifesto*.

She prayed that the Guk house was one of the two closest to the bridge. The last couple of houses were already dark shadows in the gray mist that was quickly turning the short winter day into night. It reminded her of the tule fog generated in California's great central valley.

A dog barked from the porch of the house closest to her and a second dog, on the porch of the house across the lane, joined the chorus. She ignored them, at least to the extent of not looking at them, following advice she'd heard about not making eye contact with vicious dogs. They were big dogs, junk yard mean, not the type it would be wise to challenge.

A stout woman was getting wood from a pile next to the third house along the lane and Lara quickened her step to hail her before she went back inside.

"Hello . . . hello."

The woman ignored her and went into the house without even glancing back.

Friendly neighborhood, Lara thought.

Her nose was burning from the cold and she pulled the scarf up until it covered most of her face.

No street numbers were on the houses and she kept walking, looking for a clue to Guk's house. The dogs kept up their barking and snarling as she walked and she tried to muster the courage to barge up to one of the houses and ask where the Guks lived.

A couple of times she spotted curtains twitch and someone peek at her from inside a house.

The icy fog was falling faster. She knew she'd have to get her meeting with Joseph Guk over fast or the taxi driver wouldn't wait.

Another curtain fluttered. Go for it. At least someone in the house would know she was approaching. She started for the house when she spotted a flatbed truck parked in the rear yard of the house she had just passed.

The name Guk was painted on the side of the truck. The woman picking up wood had probably been Mrs. Guk.

Gathering courage, she resolutely walked to the gate of the Guk yard, opened it, and stepped onto the frozen pathway to the house, forcing herself to move toward it, overcoming weak knees and a faint heart.

The house was as ugly as its neighbors, unkempt and lacking any aesthetic charm—dark wooden walls and a slanted tin roof packed with dirty snow. But it was the largest house along the lane, half again as big as the others.

And she had spotted something else that set the place apart from its neighbors. In the backyard, near the parked truck, was a satellite dish. That sort of luxurious black-market item was as out of place next to the shanty as a new Mercedes would have been.

To the left of the front door was a small structure, a four-by-four square box and she wondered what it was for as she approached. She was a few feet from the box when a flap on the side of it flew open and a big dog leaped out.

She stumbled back and fell as the animal charged, snarling hoarsely and exposing lethal white fangs. It ran to the end of its chain and reared onto its hind legs a couple feet from her, snapping its jaws, bloodshot yellow eyes glaring wildly at her. She scooted backward on her rump, putting more space between her and the crazy-eyed dog.

The door to the house opened and the sour-faced wood carrier stepped out. "What do you want?"

Lara stared up at her openmouthed.

"He's chained. What do you want?"

She took a deep breath and swallowed. "Mrs. Guk?"

"I'm Mrs. Guk. What do you want?"

"I'm looking for your husband. I'm from the government," she said.

"The government?"

"We"—she swallowed again, the lie sticking in her throat—"the Ministry of Transportation, are compiling a history of the safest truck drivers in the Moscow area to be used as a, uh, an example for others. Bad drivers today, Mrs. Guk.''

''Who cares about his driving record? He's retired.''

''There may be some honors given in the, uh, form of financial reward . . .''

Mrs. Guk's vinegar expression got a little oil added to it at the mention of money. ''I'll put away the dog.''

She grabbed a club leaning next to the house and gave the dog a whack on its hindquarters. ''Get back in there.''

The dog tried to duck around the woman and fly at Lara again and Mrs. Guk hit it on the nose with the club. A couple more blows and the dog disappeared through the flap of the hut.

Lara waited until the woman had dropped the latch on the flap before she started breathing normally again.

''Come in.''

The dog pawed at the flap as Lara hurried by the hut. ''Why doesn't he bark like the other dogs?''

Mrs. Guk made a cutting motion with her hand across her throat.

The dog's voice box had been removed so the dog could attack without warning.

Charming people.

TWO

The house was furnished Soviet Utilitarian—big stuffed chairs and couches, bulky tables, big lamps, no elegance, no taste. Except for an entertainment system that took up an entire wall.

Lara's eyes widened at the sight of the big screen television, dual VCRs, and digital sound system with multiple players. There were floor-to-ceiling shelves of video cassettes, CDs, and tapes.

Boris Yeltsin's wife probably had a black and white TV and a hand-cranked record player. The retired truck driver and his wife living in shantytown had electronic equipment only available on the black market and at a price few could afford.

"Which division of the ministry do you work for?" Mrs. Guk asked.

Lara smiled and started to answer when her eye caught a picture hanging on the wall behind the woman, a photo of an older man standing beside the truck parked in the yard, with Mrs. Guk standing next to him. She was wearing a nurse's uniform.

A nurse.

"I asked you where you worked. What division?"

Lara tore her eyes away from the picture and met the woman's gaze. Her face had gone sour again as she sensed something was wrong.

Lara fought the urge to run. "My mother was Angela Patrick," she said, speaking rapidly. "She was supposedly killed twenty years ago in a head-on collision with a truck your husband was driving. I know the accident never happened. I want to find out what really happened to my mother. I'm willing to pay."

The woman's jaw slowly dropped and her eyes grew wide.

"I'm willing to pay," Lara repeated. Her right knee was shaking and she started edging back from the woman. A look akin to the mindless rage of the dog lit the woman's eyes.

Lara spun round and headed for the front door. She sensed Mrs. Guk behind her and the woman's hand grabbed at her coat as she flew out of the door.

Lara didn't look back until she was through the gate. Mrs. Guk was on the path next to the dog hut. She looked mean enough and mad enough to get down on her hands and knees and bark herself.

Lara quickened her pace for the bridge. Halfway there she suddenly stopped dead in her tracks.

The taxi was gone.

THREE

Lara crossed the bridge and started down the bumpy road leading back to the main highway. It was a good three or four miles to the highway and a gas station. A couple of hours' walk on an icy road in street shoes. She hadn't been bright enough to wear a pair of boots on a trip to the country. She hadn't been bright enough to remember Moscow taxi drivers had the ethics of Mafia hit men. Hell, there probably was no taxi ministry.

The white-out had not only obliterated everything more than fifty feet away, it had brought the temperature down to below zero, colder than anything she had experienced in the city. Her feet were already aching and she had only been walking a few minutes. She realized her feet would be frostbitten by the time she reached the main road. Her heart beat faster as she panicked and quickened her pace into a trot.

Her feet slipped out from under her and she fell hard onto her rear. She couldn't run on the damn ice. Her senses told her to go back to the houses, but she kept hurrying down the country road. No way would she go back to Guk's shantytown. She was too damn scared of his wife.

And the rest of them back there, the neighbors with their vicious dogs, the whole mess of them had probably inbred for so long she'd find a Joseph Guk and a replica of his beefy wife behind every door she knocked on.

But maybe she was the one with the genetic defects.

What else could explain her paying a Moscow taxi driver in advance? What else could explain her coming here on her own at all?

"Cold, scared, and stupid," she said aloud.

She knew her words were going nowhere, just freezing and falling to the ground as soon as they left her mouth.

Her feet began to feel hot and that caused more panic. There was no way in hell her feet were doing anything but freezing. The burning sensation must be what frostbite felt like as it froze nerves and tissue. They cut off people's toes, even their feet, from frostbite.

Knowing she'd never make it to the road without permanently damaging her feet, she decided to try for the shacks she had spotted coming in. She'd storm the first one—if she could see it in the bloody white-out.

Every inch of her face not covered by her scarf and hat was burning from the cold. She stopped and wrapped the scarf round her head, stamping her feet in place as she adjusted the scarf. Only her eyes were left exposed and they were irritated by the dry frigid air.

But it was her feet that worried her. Losing her toes or feet to frostbite. Being crippled for life because she had paid a damn taxi driver in advance.

She was focusing so much on her frozen feet she almost didn't hear the barking of dogs, the dogs back at the houses of Guk's neighbors.

Someone was leaving the settlement.

She tried to keep calm and concentrate on what she had to do but her breathing was out of control. She reached into herself to pace her breathing with her stride as if she were jogging along the beach at home. She kept glancing over her shoulder, expecting to see Guk's truck lights coming at her out of the fog, expecting to hear the sound of the engine.

And then she saw a shadowy figure in the fog and her blood ran cold. A person? A small tree?

It was a person, a dark figure with a long coat and a

nurse's hat. She was sure of it, the distinctive boxed shape of the hat.

She ran, her heart pounding in her chest, her nerves electrified, on fire with panic.

A large building barely visible in the fog was off to the left and she diverted off the road toward it. As she stumbled across the snow the acidic odor she smelled earlier grew stronger and she realized the building was the abandoned chemical factory and that she was running beside the polluted pond.

The frozen turf was slippery near the pond and she worked away from it, her breathing coming in gasps as her eyes searched the fog behind her. Wind was whipping the mist and visibility had dropped to a few dozen feet. She couldn't tell if anyone was approaching.

Turning back, she moved toward the building, anger and determination to live and fight rising in her. There might be a telephone, a caretaker, even something she could use as a weapon.

As she approached the building the dilapidation became more obvious, chipped paint, broken windows, snow-coated debris scattered in the yard. It was not a living factory but the withered ghost of one, rotting in its own putrid stench.

The only entrance in sight was a doorway large enough to drive a truck through. Double doors, enormous slabs of rusted steel, protected the entrance but one of the doors was leaning over, its top hinge broken, leaving a space large enough for her to slip through.

A loading area with a dock for trucks was before her. Just enough light came from the broken windows to cast the interior in dark shadow. She started to yell for help but stopped. She knew there was no one in the building and a yell would only draw the person stalking her closer.

She went up the steps of the loading dock. *Hide, I have to find a place to hide*.

Hurrying across the dock, she spotted an open doorway

that led deeper into the factory. She went through and pressed herself up against the wall on the other side, forcing herself to stop and listen. Closing her eyes, she slowly calmed her breathing and focused on sounds. Little noises came to her but she couldn't separate them from the creaks and groans of the old factory turning in its grave.

The room was darker than the loading area and the stench of chemicals worse. She moved slowly round huge metal tanks, some of them several times taller than she was, and what seemed like an endless and mindless array of pipes and valves.

She took each step cautiously, straining to hear behind her, looking around for something to use as a weapon. A piece of steel pipe would have been perfect but all the pipe she saw was attached.

A noise came from somewhere in the factory and she stopped and listened, her heart beating faster. She was scared, terribly scared, but the terror was mixed with anger and she knew this time she would fight back, would not stand petrified as someone attacked her. *I need a weapon, something to bash that bitch's face with.*

She moved among the maze of piping and tanks looking for a place of concealment. There had to be offices, someplace where paperwork was done, a room with a heavy door and a lock.

Another opening led into an area of open vats, some of them large enough to swim in. With each step the stench grew more noxious and she decided the room was probably some sort of mixing room where chemicals were combined before being fed to the processing tanks in the other room.

Some of the containers were set below ground level and had protective railings no more than a couple of feet high. With night closing as each moment ticked by, the factory was getting darker and darker. She couldn't wander around the vat room trying to feel her way out—some vats still contained solutions that she was sure would melt her bones.

The odor in the room was fiery, a noxious stench of long-decayed acids that made her lungs burn. With usual Soviet efficiency, the factory had probably been closed one day and left to rot the surrounding environment.

It occurred to her that there was no place safe in the old factory. She had to get back out in the open, back to the little settlement and make enough noise to let the people there know she was in danger.

The last of the daylight outside glowed dimly through a doorway at the other end of the room and she worked her way round vats and piping toward the exit. She had to hurry—she needed some light to get back to the settlement.

A couple of dozen feet from the doorway she moved cautiously around a large vat that was at ground level. Something hanging over the big vat caused her to look up.

The arm of an interior crane extended over the vat. As she stared at the object, a scream started, one she couldn't stop. It was a man, hanging upside down with his feet tied to the top of the crane. At first she thought the man was wearing a dark shirt but then she realized that his chest was covered with blood.

Lara ran out of the building and fled from the factory mindlessly, not thinking about the direction she took. Stumbling down an embankment, she fell and slid on hard snow to the bottom. She was on the road but visibility was down to almost nothing. She was totally disoriented with no idea of where the settlement was. Her mind racing with panic, she started moving down the road, going to her right for no other reason than that was the direction her feet were pointing.

She could still taste the rotted acid from the factory in her throat and her lungs burned now from the freezing cold. Her breath came in great gulps.

When she felt ready to drop, she staggered to a stop to get control of her breathing. She looked back down the road and saw something coming toward her, a small dark thing coming at her in the fog like a speeding bullet. She knew what it was and started running again. *The Guks' dog was loose.*

She slipped, falling to her knees, pain shooting up from the ice rocks that cut in. No sound, no warning was coming from the dog but she knew it would be on her at any moment. She ignored the pain in her knees and forced her feet to move again.

Plows had thrown snow against trees lining the side of the road and the embankment ran seven or eight feet high. She went up the embankment on her hands and knees, slipping back because of an icy crust of surface snow, frantically breaking through the crust with her elbows, fists, and knees to gain purchase. Almost at the top of the embankment, she heard a hoarse snarl behind her. She grabbed the lower branch of a tree for support and twisted round as the dog flew at her.

Lara screamed and kicked blindly with her feet. The dog's teeth clenched her shoe and she kicked at his face with her other foot, causing his grip to slacken. The dog slipped down, jaws snapping. She was able to pull herself up a few inches but it was back again. Still kicking blindly, she felt its teeth graze her ankle as she smashed down on the dog's nose with her free foot.

A shrill horn blared and a pair of headlights came at them from the direction of the shantytown. She kept kicking and the dog slid back down the embankment, confused by the oncoming car.

The car skidded into the embankment only a few feet from her and someone jumped out of the driver's side. A gun fired, the sound of it shattering the eerie quiet of the white-out. Patches of snow from the tree branches overhead splattered down on her.

She lay on her back on the embankment as a man walked toward her.

Yuri Kirov stopped at the foot of the embankment and looked up at her. He had a gun in his hand.

X

Russia is a riddle
wrapped in a mystery
inside an enigma.

—Winston Churchill

ONE

I was waiting up the road from the bridge when you left the Guk house," Yuri told her. He helped her into the passenger side of the car. "Take off your coat."

"I'm fre-freezing."

"The coat will keep out the warmth from the car heater." He pulled off her coat and draped it over her. "Watch yourself, I'm closing the door." He walked around to the driver's side and got in.

"There's a man, a dead man," she said.

"What are you talking about?"

"Back at the old factory. There's a dead man."

At the rear of the factory, Yuri turned off the car engine and headlights and they sat still for a moment, looking out the windows before he took a flashlight from the glove compartment.

"Wait here," he said.

"No." She opened the car door. "I'm not waiting alone."

When he came around to her side of the car, he had the flashlight in one hand and his gun in the other.

"Show me where you saw the body."

"It's near the rear door."

He led the way with the flashlight, their feet crunching on snow the only sound in the night. Near the door he whispered, "Stay back."

He turned off the flashlight and moved up to the side of the door and listened for a moment. Then, ducking low, he slipped into the factory. When she saw the flashlight go on she went in after him and stood beside him as his light swept the vat room.

"Over there," she said. "The body's over the vat on the left."

The beam of the flashlight found the vat and the arm of the crane hanging over it. She gasped at the sight of the object hanging from the crane—a piece of dirty canvas.

"It was there, the body, it was there!"

He stepped up to the vat and shone the light down into it. The fluid was dark, almost chocolate brown. He put his gun in his shoulder holster and picked up a metal rod off the floor. Standing beside the vat, he stuck the tip of the rod into the liquid. The fluid foamed and boiled. A moment later he pulled out the rod and shone the light on the end. The tip was half-eaten off.

"If a man had been dropped in here, not even the metal fillings of his teeth would be left."

"If? What do you mean if? I saw a man—"

"It was dark—"

"I'm sure I saw a man hanging there, naked and bloody. I can't believe this is happening." She was close to tears.

He dropped the rod and put his arm around her shoulder. "Calm down. Look, I believe you." He swept the room again with the flashlight. "Let's get out of here."

They returned to the car and drove down the bumpy road toward the main highway.

She leaned up against the passenger door, her head pounding. "You don't really believe me. You think I imagined it. But I didn't. There was a man."

"I'll check it out in daylight."

"Get a crime team out there—"

"I'm going to check it out personally, with my partner Stenka."

"But—"

"You don't understand. We have limited resources. We don't have enough police to handle street crime and drugs. My supervisor would slap me into a night job answering emergency calls if he caught me investigating anything about you."

"What do you mean?"

"You showed up in Moscow a couple of weeks ago and started stirring up the past. You're listed in the system as a problem foreigner. My supervisor will call it a wild goose chase and pull me into another assignment."

Her jaws tightened and anger swelled. "Everyone believes I'm running around imagining things. Fine, let's test my imagination. I'm sure that the dead man is the truck driver I came to see. He's supposed to have driven a petrol tanker truck my mother crashed into."

"Guk is the dead man?"

"I . . . I don't know what Guk looks like, but it's logical. He's not at home, he's the man I came to see, he knows about the past. Look, if you don't believe me, let's turn this car around and go back to his house. You can ask Mrs. Guk where her husband is."

"And if she doesn't know? The police have been called several times because of battles between the Guks. He has a habit of disappearing for days at a time on a drunk. When he gets back there's a row."

"We're just going to leave it like this? Ignore the fact I saw a dead body?"

"Stenka and I will make inquiries on our own."

"But—"

He reached over and touched her shoulder. "Trust me."

"I don't know what to think. I've probably got frostbite on my feet," she added inconsequentially.

He pulled the car over to the side of the road and put it

in neutral. "Give me your feet." He lifted her feet onto his lap, took off her shoes, and vigorously rubbed her toes. "They're ice."

"I'll put them by the heater."

"No, I have a better idea."

He pulled up the sweater he wore under his suit jacket and pulled his shirt out of his pants. He tucked her cold feet against his bare flesh under his shirt and sweater. As soon as her icicle toes hit his warm skin he yelped. "It's okay, just fine."

She leaned back against the passenger door as he got the car moving again toward the main highway. His strong face and dark eyes were as welcome a sight to her as an angel from heaven. Fear and anxiety were leaving her. *Maybe I did imagine the body*. And if I didn't, I have a tough cop to check it out.

"Thank you. Not just for saving my feet."

"It's all right. My job, as a matter of fact. Saving beautiful women from mad dogs."

"I'm not beautiful."

"What? Of course you are."

"No. I've never even gotten flowers from a man."

"Never?"

"Not ever."

He shrugged. "I've never had flowers from a woman."

She felt giddy, light-headed, now that the fear had passed. "You saved my life. That makes you responsible for me. It's an old Chinese custom. Chinese-American."

He swerved around potholes in the road. "There's a similar old Russian custom that says when a man warms a woman's cold feet on his chest, they will become lovers."

"I like old customs," she said. She hesitated asking an important question, not wanting to ruin the magic of the moment with a dose of reality. "How did you know where to find my cold feet?"

"I saw the taxi leave, saw you cross the bridge and head

for the main road. I waited to see if anyone followed. When the dog went by I suspected it was trouble but this classic automobile built by heroic Soviet workers decided to give me a problem starting.''

''You were following me?''

''Of course. How else would I have the opportunity to save you? Spying is another old Russian custom.''

''Did you shoot it?''

''The dog? No, it was on the other side of the car. I fired in the air to scare it off.''

''Good.''

''Good? It attacked you.''

''It wasn't the dog's fault. It's a poor animal those people turned vicious. A little like the children in some of my cases, ten-year-olds who stab other children. They weren't born crazy and mean, someone worked to make them that way.''

She played with the knob on his glove box, thinking. She really liked Yuri Kirov. But no one in Moscow seemed to be exactly who or what they said they were. Saving her life had raised a couple of interesting issues.

''How did you know the Guk name? And the fact that they fought?'' She didn't mention she had only found the name herself from secret KGB files.

She felt his belly tense against her feet.

''How did I know Guk's name?'' He turned and looked her squarely in the eye. ''Your taxi driver called in the address to his dispatcher. I had Stenka get it from the dispatcher, run it for a name, and check out the name. We do have police computers you know.''

She sighed. ''You've been following me. Do you also have the hotel staff spying on me?''

He shot her a look. ''Of course. This is Russia. Everyone has always spied on everyone else.''

''Why are you following me?''

''We still have one body for sure to account for.''

She didn't like the implication that there was only one

body, but she let it pass. "Have you found out anything more about Belkin?"

"No. And there's been no decision as to whether the cause of death was accidental or not."

She rubbed her head. "Please, give me a break. You know it wasn't accidental."

He shrugged. "Anyway, that's how I stumbled onto you."

"Did you see anyone? Back there in the fog?"

"No, just the dog. Why?"

"I'm not sure. What do you know about Guk? And his wife? I think she's a nurse." Speaking the word "nurse" made her cringe.

"Only what Stenka told me. Guk goes off for days drinking and when he comes home he fights with his wife."

Her feet were beginning to melt and she started to remove them from under his sweater. "I bet I've given your belly button frostbite."

He pushed them back against him. "Leave them. I want them hot so they can dance tonight."

"Dance?"

"I'm taking you to dinner. To a real Russian restaurant, a ruble restaurant, not one of those hard currency places with food for tourists. You'll see, it's not town food."

"I . . . I can't go dancing."

"Why?"

"I don't dance." Confessing it embarrassed her.

"You don't dance? A beautiful woman, no flowers, no dancing." He nodded his head. "Yes, now I understand your secret."

"What secret?"

"You are a nun. Or you have been in prison since you were three years old."

"Seven. I've been in prison ever since I was seven." She wanted to explain why, to bare her soul to him, but she wasn't ready. "Could we . . . could we go to dinner and not dance?"

"An excellent idea. Do you know why?"

"Why?"

"I don't dance either. Honestly."

"Amazing. You must have been raised in prison, too."

"Something like that," he murmured.

"I have to go back to my hotel and change. My hair—"

"Is beautiful. And the restaurant will be closed by the time you change. You look fine."

"But—"

"Believe me, you will be the most beautiful woman in the place."

She sighed and closed her eyes. Going to dinner with a handsome Russian cop who told her she was beautiful was the least she could do after he had saved her life.

She wiggled her toes against his stomach. Her toes were purring. She was warm, safe, and happy for the first time since she had been in Moscow.

TWO

She woke up and discovered they had been in a traffic jam on the outskirts of the city for over an hour. She went back to sleep again and awoke when they were near the restaurant. She could smell cigarette smoke. He had the driver's side window down and a cigarette hanging out of it. He tossed the cigarette and rolled up the window as she struggled into her coat.

"Sorry," he said, "bad habit."

"Cigarette smokers are addicts and cigarette manufacturers are drug pushers." She smiled to take the edge off her words. "I read that on a sign put out by the health authorities back home."

"Is cigarette smoke any worse than the air in the city?"

"Probably not. Actually, smoking is a private matter and is no one else's business." *What a hypocrite I am.* Now I'm lying about my opinions because he called me beautiful.

It was toasty warm in the car. But just looking at the cold, dark night gave her a chill. He left the driver's side window down a little for air.

She was embarrassed about her confession about never having received flowers and her lack of dancing ability. What an idiot. She had violated the first rule of dating: never tell your date your life story. Especially if it makes you sound like a nerd.

"I had this dream while you were driving," she told him. "I dreamed that I had told you I had never received flowers from a man. Actually, I receive flowers all the time from men. Big men, small, tall, short, young, old, you know, lots of men."

"I knew that. I'm a good detective. I realized a woman as beautiful and sensuous as you would be showered with flowers and jewels and furs."

There was something about Yuri she liked. A lot of somethings . . .

The restaurant called Moscow Nights had a line of two dozen people waiting in the chilly night air to get in. The lead couple was in a heated argument with the doorman. Lara couldn't hear the words as they drove by, but the body language spelled trouble. The people were trying to open the door and the doorman was leaning on it to keep it closed.

"We'll freeze waiting for a table," she said.

"There are plenty of tables. You don't understand the system at Russian restaurants."

He parked the unmarked militia car behind the restaurant and she followed him through a back door that led into the kitchen. A wave of warm and wonderful food aromas hit her as they entered.

A big man, bigger than Yuri's partner Stenka, looked up from chopping a side of beef with a meat cleaver. He wore the hat and white uniform of a head chef.

"Ah, the police. Give him the drugs and counterfeit money," he yelled to the kitchen help, "so he can go back to his dacha and leave us poor people alone."

"Offering to bribe a police officer. You are all witnesses." Yuri waved at the other workers. "Actually, I am not here about drugs and funny money. There are stories about the food. I have been sent to investigate."

The chef raised the big cleaver. "I filleted and made shish kebabs out of the last customer who criticized my food."

"The stories I am to investigate are that the food is wonderful. Which means you must be doing something illegal." That one got a laugh from everyone.

"Constantin, this is Lara Patrick, a rich American. She has promised to take me back to Texas with her and support me in a life of moral depravity."

"Ah, a woman whose heart beats with mine. Go on, take her into our fine restaurant. When she is finished with our delicious food and your boring company, send her back here and I will excite her with tales of my prowess as a lover."

"His prowess has landed him four wives and nine children," Yuri told her as he led her through swinging doors and into the restaurant, "not to mention a jail term when he neglected to divorce one wife before marrying the next."

The restaurant was huge, a wide-open area with seating for a couple of hundred people and an elevated stage for a band and entertainment. The color red dominated—red flocked wallpaper, red velvet drapes, red carpeting; a grotesque chandelier had red crystals that hung from it like teats from a rosy milk cow. Lara thought the place was wonderfully tacky.

"It's only half-occupied," she said as they selected their own table. "Does Constantin know he's losing money because the doorman is turning people away?"

"This isn't Constantin's restaurant. Like almost everything else, it is owned by all Russians, one hundred and sixty million of us. The restaurant workers get the same pay if they serve one customer or if they serve a hundred."

"So they turn away business. No profit motive. But surely that's all changing now that you're going to a market economy."

He shrugged. "Unless the Communist Party comes back into power."

"I don't think your people would permit that after communism failed so badly."

"People failed, not communism. Stalin built Russia into an industrial and military superpower with a reign of terror. Now, after forty years of peace and tranquillity, our atomic reactors explode in our laps and we have managed even to forget how to grow wheat on fertile soil."

"You're not saying you need another madman like Stalin to get the country moving, are you?"

"We need vodka and good food to get the country moving," he said. "And no more political discussions."

"Politics? No politics allowed in Moscow Nights," a waiter said. He set a bottle of frozen vodka on the table and two glasses. "By some miracle of the market economy, this bottle of fine vodka broke on the floor of a general's kitchen and yet has turned up here as if it were whole. It is of course an economic illusion and the bottle does not actually exist. Because it does not exist, it will not appear on your bill."

"Victor, I congratulate you. Your apparatchik mentality has survived the fall of the Party."

Victor bowed modestly. "I was a member of the Party

until the purge of seventy-three. What can I say? I learned from the best.''

''How's your son?''

''My boy is doing well. He has a job as a plumber. Thanks to you he is not in jail.''

''You have a good boy. I did only what was right.''

''You did only what was human.'' Victor glanced around. ''There is some caviar that also escaped from that general's kitchen.'' He slipped away to get the fugitive caviar.

''What did you do for Victor's son?'' she asked.

''Gave him good advice.''

''Just advice?''

''Maybe a little gentle persuasion. You know, before Victor became a waiter, he was a Russian count with a great estate and a thousand serfs.''

''Really? That's amazing ... Wait a minute, there haven't been Russian counts and serfs for nearly eighty years.''

Yuri grinned. ''A story waiters are using on tourists.''

He poured them each a healthy slug of the premium vodka and saluted her with his. ''Na zdorovie.'' To your health.

''Not for me, I don't—''

''This is not liquor, it is liquid platinum.''

''I don't like liquor. Even good liquor.''

''You don't like cigarettes, you don't like liquor, you don't dance, and you wear bulky clothes that cover a lovely figure.''

''How do know about my figure if it's covered with bulky clothes?''

''How do I know? Did you think I would let you dress yesterday without observing whether you hid something or had a gun?''

''You pervert, you watched through the crack of the door. You and Stenka—''

''No, I never permitted Stenka to look. Rank has certain

privileges. Besides, I wanted you all for myself.''

''I think I will take that drink.'' She took the shot of vodka and gulped it. Her throat was hit with molten lava. Her face turned red and her eyes went wide and watery. She teetered on the brink of choking and spitting it out on the table. Finally she leaned back and took a deep breath, wiping her wet eyes with her linen napkin.

''Good stuff,'' she croaked.

Black Beluga caviar made its way to their table, followed by a delicious eggplant relish, hot and tasty red cabbage borscht, chicken Kiev with a sea of garlic and butter flowing into a bed of rice. Dinner was the best she'd had since being in Moscow.

''I love the way they do the chicken. Usually you get a thin watered-down butter concoction that soaks into potatoes and makes them taste greasy. What did you mean when you said it wasn't town food?''

''There used to be restaurants and stores for the Kremlin elite and only those with special passes could enter. If you were a Chosen One, you could buy a fine pastry sculptured by a French chef. The rest of the people bought lumpy cakes at the local bakery. Kremlin food. Town food.''

She took another slug of vodka and gasped, her eyes nearly crossing as the liquid burned down her throat. When she got her breath back she leaned toward him and confided, ''I've never been drunk.''

''I guessed that.''

''Why? Do you think you can get me drunk and take advantage of me? Listen''—she poked him in the chest with her forefinger—''I may not be experienced with liquor, but I have an intellectual understanding of it. I know it can take hold of my body, but I would never surrender my mind. Do you understand? My father had a problem holding his liquor but I know it's simply mind over matter.''

''I understand perfectly . . .''

The lights went down and sparkles above their heads,

ignited by the glow of the chandeliers, turned the ceiling into a red star-clustered night sky.

The band began to play "Moscow Nights," the folk song after which the restaurant was named.

"It's also called 'Midnight in Moscow,' isn't it?"

"Yes, 'Midnight in Moscow on a starry white winter night.' " He leaned closer to her and rested his hand on her knee. "Lovers in a horse drawn sled, warm under the blankets, the stars smiling down at them, the man leans over and kisses her . . ."

His face was so close to hers, she thought he was going to kiss her but he stopped and searched her eyes.

Mesmerized by his dark, soulful eyes, she suddenly wanted to be kissed by this man, wanted to be in his arms. She leaned forward to meet his lips—

And knocked over the bottle of vodka!

"Oh, God, I'm so sorry." She grabbed at the bottle and knocked a glass of water into his lap.

"It's okay. Don't move! You almost knocked your plate off the table. Just stay where you are. Have another drink. It'll relax you. I need to dry off in the kitchen. And check in with Stenka."

Yuri left the table and she sat back and stared up at the midnight ceiling. *Why me, Lord, why is this happening to me?* She was just starting to feel good from the liquor and she had to make an ass of herself.

Onstage a troupe of wild Russian dancers gave way to a man and woman dancing a scene from *Swan Lake*. The restaurant reminded her of a 1940s American nightclub, at least the kind portrayed in movies that played on the classics channel.

Yuri came back with a long face.

Guilt-stricken and embarrassed, she said, "I'm sorry if I've caused—"

"No, it's not that."

"What's the matter?"

"Something Stenka just told me. A possible suicide. I

have to meet him at the scene of the death.''

"Oh. Well, I'm relieved that you're not mad about the vodka and the wet pants.'' She smiled and reached over to touch his arm but he leaned back in his chair and she pulled her hand away.

He took a sip of vodka and watched the ballet dancers as he spoke. "The dead woman is a schoolteacher. Apparently she became upset yesterday after a visit from one of her former students, a young American.''

The warm glow of vodka turned to ice in the pit of her stomach. "Malinovsky?"

"She fell seven stories from her apartment window.''

"Are they sure it's . . . suicide?''

"After a seven-story fall, the only thing they're sure of is that she's dead. She had a history of emotional imbalance. She was apparently very upset after you left yesterday.''

Lara controlled the tremors gripping her and spoke very softly, but firmly. "I'm not responsible for that woman's death.''

"I didn't say you were.''

"That look on your face implies it. I'm not a nut or a troublemaker. I simply asked that woman about the day I was picked up at school, the day my mother died and I was taken to the airport.''

"Why?"

"I told you, I don't believe the official version of my mother's death.'' She told him about the attack on her as a child and when she returned to St. Basil's. She suspected that he already knew the story from police records.

"You went to see Malinovsky because you suspected that a woman dressed as your mother picked you up at school when you were attacked as a child?''

"Yes. Look, I can't seem to get across to you what sort of runaround I've been given since I arrived in Moscow. And not just from the bureaucracy. The first person I went to was my mother's best friend, a woman my mother constantly mentioned in her letters home. She also taught at the university. The woman welcomed me with open arms but the moment I brought up questions about my mother's death she literally threw me out. She said I was on a witch hunt.''

''She was a KGB informer against your mother.''

''How do you know that?''

''You keep forgetting where you are. You are staying at a hotel where during the old regime every room was bugged. Every room in every hotel in Moscow was bugged. Every tourist who came to the country had an Intourist Agency guide. When I joke and say everyone in Russia was an informer it is only a little joke because there's much truth to it. Your mother was a foreigner living in Moscow. Everyone who came into contact with her would have been contacted by the KGB and questioned. Those people were not paid agents. They were average citizens. They would answer out of fear for their jobs, their families, and their lives.''

''But that's all gone, the KGB's been disbanded,'' she said.

''But the memories and the records are still here. That professor was your mother's friend, but from time to time she would have had to report your mother's activities to the KGB. Few people want to talk about that part of the past. You're causing a great deal of trouble for people for what happened long ago.''

''I'm not causing problems for anyone. Do you really think that my old teacher killed herself? That Belkin was given an accidental overdose? That I just happened to imagine Guk's dead body?''

''Those matters are still under investigation.''

''You . . . you even think I threw myself down a set of stairs because I'm crazy. I came here to clear my mother's name and people have been murdered!'' Her voice had risen and people at adjoining tables turned to stare.

''The fact that you have come to Moscow hysterical and

angry over a motherless childhood does not turn your suspicion into fact. You should go back to America before more innocent people are hurt.''

She jumped out of her chair so fast it went over backward. "You . . . you . . ." Speech was beyond her. So was reason. She reached across and flipped the plate of caviar into his lap. *"Bastard!"*

She rushed out, going back through the kitchen the way they had entered. Flying through the swinging doors to the kitchen, she snapped at Constantin, "I need a taxi. Now. If that man comes back here I'm going to use your meat cleaver on him.''

The swinging doors behind them slowly opened and Victor, the waiter, stuck his head through first and then his hand holding a pair of shoes: "Were you leaving without your shoes?''

"Give me those and keep Detective Kirov out of here.''

"Detective Kirov is busy scraping several thousand rubles' worth of caviar off his pants.''

"It'll take an hour to get a taxi,'' Constantin said.

"How far is it to the Gorky Hotel?'' she asked.

"Too far.''

"I can drop you off.''

The speaker was a woman Lara noticed for the first time, a young woman of about twenty. She dropped a cardboard box on a pile of other boxes. Each of the boxes contained the markings of the army quartermaster corps, the supply division. She wore a Russian army work uniform.

"I'm going in that direction on the way back to my unit.''

"Then get her out of here,'' Constantin said, "quickly. Before Yuri comes back here and I have a dead policeman in the restaurant.'' Constantin grabbed Lara and gave her a bear hug and a kiss. "Call me. I am between wives.''

Behind the restaurant, next to Yuri's little militia car, was a Russian army truck. Lara climbed into the passenger side less adroitly than her benefactor.

The young woman got the truck moving.

"I'm Tatyana. Constantin's my father."

"I'm Lara." She didn't ask why Tatyana was delivering army supplies in the middle of the night to the restaurant her father ran. No doubt it was more damaged goods from the general's kitchen.

"Yuri and Lara," Tatyana said. "The tragic lovers from *Dr. Zhivago*. Just like Romeo and Juliet. I love romantic tragedies, don't you?"

X I

═══

"The sun's already reached its peak," he announced.
"If it's reached its peak," said the captain reflectively,
"it's one o'clock, not noon."
"What do you mean?" Shukhov demurred. "Every old-timer
knows that the sun stands highest at dinnertime."
"Old-timers, maybe," snapped the captain, "but since
their day a new decree has been passed, and now
the sun stands highest at one."
"Who passed that decree?"
"Soviet power."

—Aleksandr Solzhenitsyn,
*One Day in the Life of Ivan
Denisovich*

ONE

===

Arriving back at the Gorky Hotel in a Russian army truck did nothing to lessen Lara's already suspect reputation with the hotel staff.

She lifted her chin high and walked across the lobby like Princess Di at a ball. The porter and night clerk stared at her with the wide-eyed diffidence reserved for presidents and ax murderers.

She passed up the unreliable elevators on the grounds that she had used up that day's luck by surviving frostbite and a crazy dog and went directly to the stairs, without giving the staff any indication that she was aware of their existence.

She stamped up the steps, imagining Yuri's face underfoot every time her shoe came down. She had made a complete fool of herself, from her silly confessions in the car while she toasted her feet on his belly to her dumb act in the restaurant.

The only thing that redeemed her from total humiliation was the fact that he was a worm.

I'll never see that bastard again.

The floor maid was outside the linen room, busily folding towels on a cart as Lara reached the top of the steps.

"Good evening, madam." The woman bowed and smiled, then bowed and smiled again.

Lara noted that she had to unfold towels before she folded them. Obviously, the woman had been told to stand in the corridor and watch for her. *Maybe they think I play with matches.*

Lara stomped by her, barely giving her a glance. Pausing to insert the key into her door, she suddenly looked back and caught the maid staring at her. The woman quickly turned back to unfolding towels.

Lara shoved open the door, flipped on the light, and stepped into her room. A couple feet into the room, she stopped and stood still.

On the dresser was a doll. Dressed as a nurse. Between the doll's legs was a fat candle shaped like a penis.

She recoiled and let out a gasp of horror. She started back toward the maid, who dropped her towels and ran.

Lara caught her at the end of the hallway. "Who's been in my room?"

"No one," the woman wailed, cowering against the wall behind her.

"Someone's been in my room. Tell me who it was."

"Nobody, I swear. Just that nurse this morning."

"What nurse?"

"Right after you left, a nurse told me to let her into your room because you had forgotten your medicine. We all know you are under medical care."

"Get the bellman up here. I'm leaving this place, now."

The Moscow Grand was big, expensive, and, she hoped, safe. The room doors could be double locked from the inside.

Her fourth-floor room, the cheapest room in the house, was located next to the whining and vibrations of the elevator shaft on one side and the rumble of ice machines on the other. There were no windows.

She could barely afford the room. The hotel catered to

German and Japanese businessmen. Her windowless room cost five times what she had paid at the Gorky for a two-window room without vibrations.

She stripped down to long underwear and burrowed under the covers. She was weary and tired but felt secure in her new room. She was fast asleep in a short time.

TWO

I n bed the next morning, she stared at Alexei Bova's card and fought with her self-respect. She just didn't know how to ask for help, but the doll had really gotten to her. It hadn't been a warning—it was a show of sadistic power, like pulling the wings off a fly to watch it suffer before killing it. Finally, admitting defeat, she picked up the telephone.

By some miracle of electronics and economics, there was actually a hotel operator who responded at the Moscow Grand when one needed to make a call. She gave the operator the number and was surprised when the woman told her to wait on the line. A moment later the operator came back on and asked her name. Then a man's voice came on.

"This is Ilya, Mr. Bova's secretary. How may I help you, Ms. Patrick?"

"Mr. . . . Mr. Bova," she stammered self-consciously, "invited me to a party—"

"Yes. That's the Western affair tonight. May I send a limo for you at eight?"

"Uh, yes, that's fine. Eight is perfect."

"Your hotel?"

"The Moscow Grand."

"Excellent. The limo will be there at precisely eight. Are you enjoying your stay at the Grand?"

She looked around her windowless room. "It's okay. I would have preferred a room with a better view than four walls, but I'm on a budget."

"I will let Mr. Bova know."

She hung up and banged her fist against the side of her head. What a mouth I have? Letting him know I can't afford a room with a window? I'll probably get a call back in an hour: "Mr. Bova regrets to inform you that he doesn't invite people to his parties who can't afford a decent hotel room."

She jumped out of bed. It was after twelve. She had less than eight hours to get a dress and accessories for tonight. From what Bova's secretary had said, there would be mostly Westerners rather than Russians at the party and that was fine with her. It would be easier raising her mother's case with Bova without Russians listening over her shoulder.

She needed a dress, but she had to be realistic about it. She couldn't afford to spend a lot of money on a dress she was only wearing one night.

Nor could she afford the Moscow Grand. Tomorrow she'd find another hotel on the budget scale of the Gorky, only in a part of the city where there were lots of people and taxis.

What does a dress cost here? she wondered. Could she find something for under a couple of hundred? It was the coat that was going to be the problem. She had no dress coat, period. And the ski jacket she wore with pants and two pairs of long underwear wasn't going to be quite the thing for a party given by Alexei Bova.

If Westerners were the main guests, there would probably be ambassadors, trade ministers, international business executives. They would dress fairly conservatively, she imagined. Simple and elegant was likely to be the dress code with some of the younger, better built women wearing less clothes and more cleavage.

Considering the state of the economy, it would be easier to make a deal for a Russian tank than an evening dress.

With no time for a luxury soak, she showered, dressed, and was out of the hotel in less than an hour. There were no strange looks from the hotel staff as she came down the stairs and crossed the lobby. Apparently her reputation at the Gorky hadn't made it over yet. Last night when she left the Gorky she had the taxi take her to the Russia Hotel, where she switched cabs; not so much to throw off pursuers as to prevent the Gorky staff from finding out where she went and calling her new hotel and telling the staff she was a nutcase.

Out on the street she walked quickly in the direction of the fashion shops she had seen in the neighborhood of Bova's Black Tower.

She had stayed in bed this morning, running every move she had made over and over again in her mind. Yuri, and her anger at him, repeatedly sneaked into her thoughts like a puppy dog craving attention. She could forgive him for tricking her about Belkin, and even his damn cigarettes, but stupidity was unforgivable.

A thought kept popping up in her mind like an itch that would not go away and finally she faced it. Yuri was not stupid. He couldn't really believe that swill he gave her. Was he protecting somebody? And what was he doing at the carnival the night Belkin was hit by the truck?

She wanted to call up Yuri, to tell him she'd had a visit from the nurse, but her pride and worse—that he might think she was making it up—stopped her.

Yuri is out of the picture, she told herself. And Alexei Bova could open doors for her. How she would approach him, she didn't know. She knew nothing about asking for help, less about networking. And she couldn't just walk up to him at the party and tell him she needed help with several unsolved murders.

THREE

The French had invaded Russian fashions and it was a French shop she tried first.

She knew from the look of the place there wouldn't be anything she could afford. But she had to have something decent. Rich people like Bova probably assumed that all women traveled with six steamer trunks, ready to whip out an outfit for any occasion.

The last evening dress she had bought, the *only* evening dress she had ever bought, was the one she got for the high school graduation dance no one had invited her to. It was still hanging snug and warm in her Pacific Heights condo with the price tag on it.

"May I help you?" a sales clerk asked.

The saleswoman was wearing a floor-length maroon dress with a slit that came up the side almost to her hip. With a long bead of pearls, a pageboy hairdo, glorious makeup, and a haughty attitude, she was perfect for Alexei's party, Lara thought. Maybe I ought to tell her to go instead of me.

"I'm just looking," she replied.

She wandered through the store, looking hungrily at the beautiful clothing, trying to appear as if she wasn't dying to try something on. She needed to find out the price range of the clothes, but was too embarrassed to ask and too self-conscious to rummage for price tags.

Something very European, a black wool suit with a white shirt, rather elegant even though it was modeled after a man's business suit, caught her eye. A 1920s gangster's hat, a white scarf thrown carelessly over the shoulders, and black patent shoes with white spats set off the outfit.

It wasn't her, much too showy, but what intrigued her

about the outfit was that she might get away without a coat. With pants, suit jacket, and scarf, she could wear two pairs of long underwear underneath and not look silly without a coat.

She walked round the outfit, trying to get a glimpse of a price tag. She found one sticking out from under the scarf. It gave the price in hard currency: $500.

A lot of money, more than she had hoped to pay, but did she have the courage to wear it? Was it too flamboyant for her? Too trendy for a conservative party?

She took a closer look. The outfit was really quite clever, very feminine, yet a bit different. It was an outfit that made a statement. The last thing she wanted was to be noticed. But she could get away without an evening coat and a decent coat would cost several times the price of a dress.

"Find something you like?" the saleswoman asked.

"Perhaps. I'm traveling and suddenly need an outfit for tonight. I'm just wondering if this outfit isn't a little too, uh, fashionable for me. Are the shoes and spats separate or are they included in the five-hundred-dollar price?"

"Madam, the five hundred dollars is for the scarf . . ."

FOUR

The Arbat is one of the oldest districts in the city and the one that holds whatever charm Moscow is said to have. The streets once housed the court artisans, the silversmiths and pastry cooks, woodworkers and glass cutters that served the gentry. Later it became a favorite place of the aristocrats, and ultimately evolved into an area of small shops and crafts.

Lara decided its present ambiance was a chemistry made

up of small shops, pickpockets, street musicians, beggars, and Beats—the 1950s variety.

After having crawled out of the third foreign fashion house, depressed and humiliated, she took a subway to Arbat Square. One could find almost anything in the area, from souvenir Soviet army flags to handmade lace.

In a small shop she found a classic black rayon dress that came with a cropped jacket. The top of the dress came all the way to her neck and had full-length sleeves. The skirt extended down to her shoes with a modest slit on one side that reached to just above her knee.

The outfit was modest and conservative, she told herself, not really old-fashioned. Its charm was that the little jacket would keep her from looking conspicuously coatless.

She already had black shoes and the right color tights. And a silver bracelet watch that looked expensive and wasn't. With the high neckline, the watch was the only jewelry she needed.

Best of all, the whole outfit was $180.

"Am I going to look like I'm wearing my mother's dress to a high fashion party?" she asked the saleswoman.

"A great ballerina wore this dress to her lover's funeral," the old woman told her.

"It's secondhand?"

"Worn only once. After the cameras captured her suffering, the ballerina gave away all her worldly goods and secluded herself in a convent in France. New, the dress would be five hundred dollars."

Lara shifted her weight from foot to foot. "The outfit seems a little conservative."

"You are in Moscow. We still preserve the dignity of our women when they attend parties."

The assistant manager intercepted her at the foot of the stairway when she got back to the hotel.

"Your room has been changed, Ms. Patrick. The night

clerk was remiss in putting you in that little room by the elevator shaft.''

Oh-oh, they've heard from the Gorky. Probably think I'm planning to bomb the place. ''The new room doesn't have padded walls, does it?''

''Padded walls? You want padded walls? I don't believe we have a room with padded walls, but I'm sure you'll enjoy the one we've moved you to. It's the best in the house available at a low level. I mean height, of course. You told the front desk last night you didn't want anything above the fourth floor.''

''I was joking about the padding,'' she said as they went into the elevator. ''You know, padded cell, crazy people.''

''Oh, yes, very humorous.'' He gave her an artificial laugh.

She looked up at the ceiling of the elevator. Time to change hotels.

They went past her old room, down to the end of the hall, and round the corner. He paused at double doors, opened one door, and stepped aside for her to enter.

She walked in, her eyes growing wide.

It wasn't a room. It was a suite.

Bouquets of flowers lined long tables on both sides of the entry. A table of hors d'oeuvres with a bottle of champagne was in the center of the sitting room. Off to the side was a bowl of fresh fruit, not a piece of which was grown within a thousand miles of Moscow in the wintertime.

A maid came out of her room and gave her a small curtsy. ''Welcome to the Tsarina Suite, madam.''

Lara had to restrain herself from laughing—they must think I'm a rich American. ''I really appreciate all this but I'm afraid there's been a mistake.''

''A mistake?'' The man almost jumped out of his pants. ''Have we done something wrong? You don't like the room? The food—''

''No, no, I'm talking about a mistake in identity. I'm

Lara Patrick. I have the room by the elevator and the rattling ice machines.''

"Lara Patrick. Exactly.''

"You don't understand. I can't afford this room.''

"Afford? The suite is compliments of Mr. Bova.''

"Alexei Bova?''

"Yes, of course.''

"Mr. Bova had all this done for me?''

"Yes.''

"Oh, well, now I know there's been a misunderstanding. I appreciate Mr. Bova's generosity, but I don't permit men to pay for my hotel rooms.''

"Mr. Bova owns the hotel.''

"Mr. Bova owns the hotel?''

She looked round the room. It was bright and cheerful. Three windows. All closed, the way she liked them. She went over and looked out. A couple of floors below was the terrace to one of the hotel restaurants. If someone threw her out she'd probably only break a leg.

Elegantly carved crown molding decorated the walls and ceiling. Instead of the dull gray-white walls of her elevator-shaft room, the suite was decorated in soft pastels. The carpeting was so thick and soft she could bury her toes in it. The bedroom was as big as the living room.

She inspected the bathroom. Oh, God, a Jacuzzi bathtub. Soaking in a hot tub full of bubbles was one of her favorite luxuries.

She kept a straight face as she held out her hand for the key, the way she thought Katharine Hepburn might handle the situation.

"Since Mr. Bova owns the hotel, I suppose we can consider me a house guest," and not a kept woman, she added silently.

"Thank you, madam.'' The assistant manager bowed all the way to the door.

The maid held her ground.

Lara lifted her eyebrows.

"I'm your personal maid," she told Lara. "Did you wish me to draw your bath?"

"Yes, yes, that would be nice."

As soon as the maid disappeared into the bathroom Lara grabbed a cracker and dipped it into caviar, kicked off her shoes and swam her feet in the thick carpeting all the way to the bed.

She flopped backward on the bed and grinned up at the ceiling.

Why would a man I had only met briefly do all this for me?

He's rich. He does wild and crazy things. Maybe he's attracted to me. Hell, maybe he's after my body. She looked round the luxurious bedroom. *I could learn to like this.*

"Just call me a slut," she told the ceiling.

FIVE

To get rid of the maid for a few minutes, Lara sent her down to buy a can of hair spray. As soon as she left, Lara picked up the telephone and asked to be connected to the United States Embassy, marveling again at the telephone efficiency when the operator told her to stay on the line.

Eric Caldwell, the embassy's legal attaché, took her call. *Probably assumed I'd be on his doorstep if he didn't,* she thought. She had been working through him to convince the Ministry of Security to reopen her mother's "accident" case. He had not been very helpful despite her calls and visits to his office. His excuse was that the Russian government was shaky enough without bringing up dirt from the past.

"Mr. Caldwell, is there any news from the ministry

about reopening the investigation into my mother's death?"

"Nothing further. It is still under study," he said curtly.

"In other words, they're waiting for my money to run out so I'll go home."

"You have to understand, Ms. Patrick . . ."

He gave her the same line he had given her a half-dozen times about how long these matters take in Russia, especially in this time of social, political, and economic turmoil.

"I had another question, more of a social one, nothing to do with my mother. I've been invited to a party and I figured it would be nice to get some background about my host. His name is Alexei Bova."

"You've been invited to one of Bova's parties?" Caldwell's voice changed from bored tolerance to envy and amazement.

"Yes. Can you tell me a little about him?"

"Everybody in Russia can tell you something about him. He gets more news coverage here than Princess Di and Donald Trump combined get from the scandal magazines in the West. His parties are something that would make a Roman emperor envious. He once served Chicago pizza at a party. Real Chicago pizza. This madman ordered a Chicago pizza parlor dismantled—ovens, booths, barrels of flour, two Italian pizza makers, the whole nine yards— and had it flown to Moscow for one of his parties."

"He sounds like one of those Depression day American millionaires who threw ostentatious parties while people starved."

"Good comparison, and if you've ever read about the Depression, you know that the exploits of those wild and crazy rich people got more publicity than the antics of today's rock stars. People loved and hated and envied them. Russians feel the same about Alexei. When they're having a hard time buying milk for their babies, they curse him for his extravagances, but most people are actually proud of his accomplishments.''

"How did he make so much money so fast? The market economy has hardly started here.''

"Wheeling, dealing, leveraging. Owns his own bank. Uses OPMs—other people's money. That big building, the one they call the Black Tower, is supposed to be an example of free enterprise at work, but Alexei stole the land from the government with a fast paper shuffle. Then millions of dollars in building material came from government factories eager for orders, orders that got filled but never paid. In other words, he built the tallest building in Moscow and it didn't cost him a dime, personally.''

"That's how many self-made American millionaires did it.''

"True, but some of them went to jail along the way. I've also heard that he had to import millions more in materials to finish the building and that money came from depositors. The government has the building tied up in the courts and no one's occupying it except Bova. You must have read about his dacha?''

"No, I didn't.''

"He grabbed a tsarist country palace that's been a museum,'' Caldwell said enthusiastically. "Bought it from the workers committee that ran it, with the workers getting more money than any of them would have earned in a lifetime. The government's suing to get it back.''

"How can someone buy something from a committee that doesn't own it?''

"Who knows who owns what in Russia today? Besides, to say he bought it is misleading. What the clever devil did was take out ninety-nine-year leases on the land and the palace. Workers committees don't have authority to sell the properties they run, but they can enter into contracts. The leasing angle was a loophole in the law that the government's trying to close in the courts.

"And one other thing of interest,'' Caldwell said. "That

Black Tower may have turned into Bova's folly. There are rumors of major structural problems created when he threw it up so fast. Moscow building inspectors won't give it a certificate of occupancy. An empty skyscraper has to be one helluva cash flow problem, especially with the people who put up the money in the first place."

After she had finished talking to Caldwell, she checked out the bath Anna had drawn for her in the Jacuzzi tub. It looked heavenly. Six inches of bubbles and a temperature you'd boil a lobster in.

She hurried into the living room and quickly prepared a tray of hors d'oeuvres, poured a tall glass of champagne, and then thinking what the hell, brought the bottle of champagne as well as the food into the bathroom.

She stripped off her clothes and slowly submerged into the luxuriously scented water. With bubbles up to her neck, she reached out and took caviar on a cracker. A few crackers later she tried the champagne. It tasted wonderful and tickled her nose. The only champagne she had ever tasted before was the $2.99 variety served at weddings. Cold champagne in a hot tub. This was really living. The life of the rich and famous.

She poured another glass. Champagne had none of the kick of vodka. Giggling to herself, she poured the rest of the bottle into the bathwater and flipped on the air jets.

She lay back and let the water massage her.

Oh, I could get used to being a kept woman . . .

XII

The great proof of madness
is the disproportion of
one's designs to one's means.

—Said by Napoleon Bonaparte,
the man who lost his army to a mean
Russian winter

ONE

===

Does Madam wish me to help her dress for the party?''
No one had helped her dress since her mother died.
Not even her grandmother had helped her dress.

"I'll be fine. But I do need an iron. One sleeve of my jacket is a little wrinkled.''

"I'll iron it for you, madam.''

"Thank you, Anna.''

Anna had that hardy Eastern European build of a peasant woman—stout and short. She also had a club foot and walked with a noticeable limp.

I'm going to have to get used to the personal service, Lara thought. At least until she turned down the "payment'' she expected Alexei would want in exchange for his rent and found herself out of the hotel. No doubt with her growing reputation with the Moscow hotel industry, her next room would be at a homeless shelter.

How can rich people stand to be waited on? She always found herself thanking the busboys in restaurants every time her water glass got topped. She'd be hoarse at the end of a day if she had a staff of servants.

Slipping into a pair of red woolly long underwear, she recalled reading somewhere that General Eisenhower's valet used to hold the general's underwear open so the general could step into it after showering. She wondered if anyone held Alexei's underwear for him . . .

Anna brought the ironed jacket into the bedroom. She stared at the long underwear as the evening dress went on.

"I don't have a warm coat," Lara explained.

Anna looked puzzled. "Everyone in Russia has a warm coat."

Lara smiled. "What I meant was I don't have a coat to go with an evening dress. I, uh, left my evening coat at home. This way I'll be able to survive without a coat. I'll roll up the legs and no one will be the wiser."

"Yes, madam."

There was nothing readable in Anna's voice or expression, but Lara could imagine what the woman was thinking. Rich Americans are strange . . .

She felt good. It surprised her that just two glasses of champagne should make her feel a tiny bit tipsy. Not a bad feeling, but a nice, warm, relaxed sensation. No wonder people drink so much in cold climates. That little glow she got from the alcohol warmed her toes and made her less apprehensive about facing dozens of strangers at the party tonight. Maybe that's why her father drank. Maybe he was so sensitive he needed liquid courage to face the world.

She looked over her outfit in the mirror.

Is it too conservative? What would ambassadors and businesspeople wear?

"Is there any more champagne?" she asked Anna.

"I put another on ice after you finished the last one, madam."

"Don't tell anyone, but most of the last one went into my bathwater. I think I'll have just a glass of the new bottle. Want to join me?"

"No thank you, madam."

"Why don't you call me Lara."

"Yes, madam."

Lara sipped champagne as she put on her makeup. The maid stood back, ready to help, but Lara couldn't think of anything for her to do.

"Have you worked for the hotel long?" Lara asked.

"I work for Mr. Bova."

For Mr. Bova personally. That was interesting. She wanted to ask why she hadn't simply been supplied a hotel maid and decided it would be impolite to ask. The woman might even take offense, perhaps think that Lara didn't want her because of the handicap.

Lara rolled up the left leg of her long underwear to above the knee. It created a bulge that showed against the dress so she unrolled it and simply pulled it up above the knee, letting the elastic hold it there. It appeared tight enough to keep from slipping down.

The top of the evening gown looked a bit silly with a shirt of woolly red underwear poking out, but once she slipped on the little jacket that went with the dress, there was no sign of the underwear.

"Well, what do you think, Anna?"

"Very nice, madam."

She didn't sound too convincing.

Lara took another sip of champagne. "Well, other than taking a gun down to the fashion district and getting a dress that way, this is what I'm stuck with."

The phone rang just then and Anna answered it.

"The driver is downstairs, madam."

Lara looked at herself in the mirror again. Not glamorous, she thought, but not a spinster schoolteacher either. About how a poor shop girl would dress wearing her stepmother's evening gown to the prince's ball. She started to giggle at the idea and clamped a hand over her mouth.

"Anna, can a couple glasses of champagne get you drunk?"

The woman shook her head. "No, madam."

"You know what," she told the blank-faced maid, "I don't really care what people think. I am what I am and if people don't like it, they can just go to hell.''

She thought about this as she went down the corridor. I don't usually think that way, she told herself, but that's the way I should think. Not worry so much about what the rest of the world thinks about me. I'm a good person. I don't hurt anyone. If this dress is what I can afford and they don't like it, that's their problem, not mine. That's what my mother and father would have said. To hell with what the world thinks.

"Liquid courage," she said, in English, in the elevator.

"Madam?" the attendant asked in Russian.

"Nothing, just talking to myself.''

She had a new attitude toward things, and it wasn't liquid courage. *Champagne doesn't affect me that much anyway.* Not like liquor affected my father. Besides, it's not like real liquor.

The uniformed limo driver was waiting in the lobby near the doors. A garment was folded over his arm. As Lara approached, he unfolded it and she realized it was a full-length black sable cape.

"May I?" he said, holding the cape to drape it round her.

Lara didn't know what to say.

"Your car coat, madam.''

"Thank you.'' She let him put the coat round her shoulders and followed him out to the limo. Inside the back of the limo she took off the cape and examined it. She had seen sable and this was no ordinary piece. It was midnight sable, the finest and most expensive. And there was one helluva lot of it. The coat had to have cost more than the limo she was in and Alexei Bova used it as a "car coat" for guests?

"Poor sables," she told them, stroking the coat. She was against wearing exotic animal skins.

The limo was a black Mercedes. She had noticed in the lobby that the driver had only one eye, perhaps a congenital defect because of the way the skin covered the other eye socket area. It struck her that Alexei seemed to go out of his way to hire people with a handicap.

The drive to the Black Tower was short and she was there before she could change her mind and tell the driver to turn around and take her back to the hotel so she could hide her head under the blankets.

A doorman opened the car door for her. Two more doormen were waiting to hold the lobby doors open.

"You forgot your coat, madam," the doorman told her.

"It's not my coat, it's the car coat."

There were two more attendants waiting at the elevators. "Good evening, Miss Patrick," one of them said.

"Good evening." She wasn't surprised that they knew her name. The driver who brought her was supposed to bring a Ms. Patrick.

She watched the lights on the elevator buttons as they went up. Forty-nine floors and then the penthouse. Usually her stomach would get a little queasy at such heights, but tonight she felt warm and glowing. Despite her glow, she worried about what was going to happen when she stepped off the elevator and confronted women in ten-thousand-dollar dresses laughing at her off-the-rack outfit.

"I'm not running home and hiding my head under the cover," she told the elevator attendant.

The man blinked. "Yes, madam."

She remembered a story from one of her college teachers, a Polish woman. When the Soviets invaded Poland in 1939, things were a little primitive in the Russian army ranks. It wasn't unusual for the occupying troops to bring women along, some carrying guns, others as camp followers. The Russians were little more than hillbillies, her teacher said, and thieves who broke into Polish homes. The women wore stolen nightgowns on the streets in the mistaken belief that the nightgowns were fancy dresses.

She got a sudden pang of fear and looked at her dress,

wondering if she had confused a nightgown for an evening dress and then laughed at her stupidity.

"Sorry," she told the attendant. "Private joke."

"Yes, madam."

The elevator stopped at the penthouse level. Lara took a deep breath and launched herself out of the elevator and into the lives of the rich and famous.

She came face-to-face with the Lone Ranger and Tonto.

TWO

Somewhere in the room a cow mooed and a horse neighed in answer.

With her eyes growing wider and her mouth slowly dropping, she watched General Custer walk by arm in arm with Sitting Bull followed by two older women whose pot-bellies were bigger than the rear bustles of the granny dresses they wore.

Across the room on an elevated stage, a pistol-packing mama was belting out the words to "Elvira" while dozens of Russian cowboys and cowgirls were shuffling, or at least making an attempt at shuffling, to the Texas Slide.

Alexei suddenly appeared in front of her. He wore all black—black hat, shirt, pants, and boots. His cowboy hat had a silver band and his silver-studded gunbelts held a pair of pearl-handled six-shooters.

"I feel like a fool," she said. "When your secretary said something about Western dress—"

"You didn't realize he meant the Old West. It's our fault entirely for not making that clear. Here's Ilya now."

A young man dressed as a riverboat gambler came hurrying up. Like most of the men in the room, he wore a pair of six-shooters.

"Ilya, this is Lara Patrick. I'm afraid you didn't make

it clear that we were having a cowboy shindig.''

Ilya was grief stricken. "I'm so sorry, Ms. Patrick.''

"No, I should have asked about the dress code.''

She held out her hand to shake his and then quickly pulled it back. He had a deformed right arm and hand that left the limb and hand much smaller than normal.

He smiled and offered his left hand. "This one works fine.''

"The mix-up is my fault,'' Alexei said. "It would have been impossible for you to find Western clothes at such short notice in Moscow anyway. I had clothiers come here from Dallas a couple of weeks ago to outfit my guests.''

"Is that where you got your band?''

"Nashville.'' Alexei grabbed her arm. "Come, I'll find you a drink.''

"Alexei, I really think I should go.''

"You can't go. Not unless you plan to leap all the way to the street. I won't let the elevators take you down. Besides, I want you to meet someone, a friend of mine who knew your parents.''

"My parents?'' She was stunned.

"Your mother was Angela Patrick, wasn't she?''

"Yes.''

"My assistant, Felix, knew her and your father.''

"Really?''

"You're staying then?''

"Staying? I'm camping out, partner.''

Alexei laughed and took her arm. "Let me introduce you to Felix. He's something of a snob, literary variety. I keep him around because he adds a little class to my peasant upbringing.''

A waiter came by with a tray of glasses containing a yellowish concoction. Alexei picked up a glass for each of them.

"You'll like this. Apricot-flavored vodka. Not unlike a brandy.''

"I'm not much of a drinker.''

"*Na zdorovie,*" he saluted.

"*Provst.*" She took a sip. "Hmmmm, it's good, sweet." It tasted as good as champagne, not at all harsh like the liquid fire she had drunk with Yuri.

In the middle of the room fenced enclosures had been set up with a cow and bales of hay in one, hay and two horses in another.

The room itself was amazing, an enormous circular cavern with a high ceiling, over thirty feet she estimated, windowed all around. On the side opposite the elevators a grand stairway led to a second level. The band stage was next to the stairway.

"It was designed to be a revolving restaurant, one of those places you go at night to watch the city lights as you dine," Alexei said. "We're revolving now."

The movement wasn't noticeable but the scenery outside had changed slightly since she entered.

"I have the system activated during parties. I fell in love with the place after it was built. Not only is it the tallest place in all of Moscow, but no one since tsarist times has had an apartment as grand as this one. I look down at the city and the entire city looks up at me." He laughed. "You only live once, Lara. If you can do it as a megalomaniac and enjoy pleasures that few have experienced, why not?"

She saluted him with her sweet-tasting vodka. "Why not?" A few more of these and she'd be ready to stand on the rooftop and yell to the poor people clamoring for bread below to eat cake.

"Felix, this is Lara Patrick."

He was tall, slender, probably in his early sixties, she guessed. He had very short, thin sandy hair and pale, thin features.

"Felix will tell you how embarrassed he is to work for me while I make sure the kitchen staff doesn't burn down the place. They're roasting a whole Texas cow over an open pit." Alexei hurried away.

"Why are you embarrassed to work for Alexei?" she asked.

"Alexei is a charmer . . . if you like spoiled children with vast amounts of money and no common sense. However, he has one redeeming feature: he has a great deal of money and I have none. It is purely for my own capitalist sense of greed during these times of economic chaos that I tolerate this madman."

Lara was saved from having to find a response to this by an eruption of screaming and shouting from the far corner of the room. She stood on tiptoes to get a peek at the action.

"A mechanical bull," she said.

"Straight from Texas. We've had one broken arm so far tonight, a deputy minister of trade."

"What, uh, is your position with Alexei's organization?"

"Everything but change his diapers, and if he could he would have me do that. Actually, my official position is senior aide. Ilya handles the mundane matters and I have the glory of doing everything from counting Alexei's losses for this Tower of Babel he built to preparing his autobiography. Hopefully his investors will permit him to live long enough to finish the book, but I assure you I'm prepared to be his biographer if he runs foul of a lynch mob."

Lara laughed hard and then took a sip of the sweet vodka. Felix had the sharp, dry sense of humor of a Mr. Chips.

Two urban cowgirls wearing skintight, low-cut silky outfits no cattle range ever saw moseyed by and gave longer than polite stares at Lara's dress.

"Don't pay any attention to them," Felix said. "Word has gotten around that Alexei sent his personal limo for you tonight and you'll find the young women in the room all have their claws out."

She took another sip. The more she drank, the less she cared about what other women thought.

"Alexei said you knew my mother and father."

"In a manner of speaking. I was not a confidant of either. However, they were part of a literary and intellectual scene of which I was also a member. It was back in the sixties, the time in America when many young people were rebelling against the Vietnam War and here in Russia writers and poets were hiding under their beds writing words that could earn them a trip to the labor camps."

He raised his glass,. extending his little finger as he drank. "I was the editor of a small literary magazine supported by the university. Obviously, we published only approved items because the switch to the printer was never turned on until the censors had stamped the copy. But I was something of a beacon for writers who sought alternative methods of getting their stories published."

"You mean underground?"

"Underground and smuggling to the West. I am proud to say that some of the best writing of dissenters against the Soviet regime was passed by me. But that is history and you are interested in your parents. I met them both on a number of occasions. They were well liked and popular, although your father's appearance in Moscow was as a shooting star. He flashed through the city and the next thing we heard was that he had been killed in Africa."

"What was he like?"

"Wild and brilliant. He was British, I seem to remember."

"Yes, from Wales."

"A poet and a revolutionary. My feeling about your father is that he was less interested in ideology than in adventure. He just loved a good fight. And romance. He was very handsome. Let's see, he must have died when you were a baby. You've seen pictures of him?"

"I have one picture."

"My best recollection of your father says a great deal

about his wild and impulsive personality. It was at a party, one of those dull university gatherings where we eggheads try to impress each other with our own brilliance. Your father, after more than adequate drinks, stood the party on its head by climbing up on the railing to the balcony and dancing on it while balancing a bottle of vodka on his head. You have to appreciate that we were on the fifth floor."

Lara laughed so hard she started choking. She stopped coughing and then hiccuped. "Oops. I'm sorry."

"That's all right."

"I'm not used to drinking."

"Really? How disappointing. I was hoping you were like your father and that after a few drinks you would stand this party on its head."

"To tell you the honest truth—*hic*—I am nothing like my father. I am extremely conservative and reserved. I've had more to drink in the last couple days than the last ten years. I discovered I really love champagne. And this flavored vodka tastes soooo good."

"You'll find out that experienced drinkers avoid sweet-tasting drinks because it's easy to drink too much without realizing it."

"I'm careful. I also have good—*hic*, sorry—control over it. People stupidly surrender themselves to the effects. I believe that while liquor can affect your body movements, it's just mind over matter. It can control my body but it will never take my mind." She held her breath to try to control the hiccups.

"That's an intellectual approach to drinking I've never heard before," Felix murmured. "But so much of life is mind over matter."

"What about my mother?" she asked eagerly, returning the stare of two more cowgirls.

"Nasty little things, aren't they?" Felix said. "Alexei is the most eligible bachelor in Russia. Every woman in this room is anxious to find her way into his bed and into his bank account. No one has yet.''

''The bed or the bank account?''

He shrugged and smiled.

Three cowgirls had grouped together nearby.

''Another one of those looks and I'm going to knock these bitches on their tush.'' She put her hand to her mouth. ''Sorry, I usually don't say things like that.'' She shook her head. ''Moscow must be giving me brain fever.''

She grabbed another drink from a passing waiter. ''Tell me about my mother.''

''As I said''—he looked at her drink—''you remind me a bit of your father. Your mother was physically like you, an attractive woman, but she was a very serious intellectual. Fiery like your father, but while he might get across his point when words failed by punching his opponent, your mother was more inclined to tear the flesh from the enemy with shearing words.''

''In America,'' Lara said, ''my mother had a reputation as a violent revolutionary, but she wasn't violent at all. I've read the news reports of the riot that turned violent and through our freedom of information laws I obtained the FBI reports on her. She wasn't militant. Things just got out of hand.''

''My recollection is that she was a woman of uncompromising opinion,'' he said. ''There was a great deal of pressure placed upon her to write anti-American pieces, but other than anti-war articles, she refused. She would not back down to anyone, not even the devil or his censors. She was a woman of great moral courage. Had what you Americans call guts. If she saw a man beating a child with a stick, she would not have called the police. She would have grabbed the stick from the man and struck him with it.''

Lara's eyes moistened and she stared down at her drink.

Alexei came up and put his arm round her shoulder. "Is Felix driving you to tears with boredom?"

"We were just discussing her parents. What do you remember about them, Alexei?"

"You know I never met them, Felix. I told you that earlier. Your memory must be getting as thin as your hair."

"Aren't you going to introduce us?"

The voice was a commanding one and the three of them turned to a woman in a bright red sequined cowboy outfit, red sequined vest, red sequined chaps, red leather pants, and silver-plated boots. The woman was Nashville *hot, hot, hot.*

"Nadia, this is Lara Patrick," Alexei said. "You probably recognize Nadia. She's an anchorwoman on the Moscow Evening News."

Lara did recognize her. A very attractive woman with classic Slavic cheekbones and dark blond hair combed back in a wet look, there was an edge of hardness to her that kept her from being beautiful. Whatever it had taken to get where she was in life, her body language said she wasn't giving up an inch of the territory without a fight.

She had nothing on under the loose-fitting vest and her breasts flashed every time she moved.

"So nice to meet you," Nadia said, amused eyes sweeping Lara's dress. Lifting her arm to taste her drink, the vest pulled away, exposing her bare breast to the nipple. "My mother would love your dress."

Lara flushed and then paled with anger.

Alexei cleared his throat. "Felix, why don't you tell Nadia about that idea we have for her own news program while I give Lara a tour of the penthouse."

He took her arm to lead her away but Lara held back and spoke to Nadia in a stage whisper. "You know, you can hide those breast implant scars with tattooing."

Nadia's jaw dropped.

Alexei pulled Lara away so fast, she stumbled beside

him. They were across the room before she realized he was laughing so hard there were tears in his eyes. As he led her up the grand stairway, he asked, "Do they really do that? Hide implant scars with tattooing?"

"It's an old trick strippers use. Most implants are put in through the areolas. A tattoo artist can turn the scars the same color as the rest of the areolas."

She couldn't believe she was having this conversation with a man she hardly knew. Don't let the liquor take control, she told herself.

"How did you know she had implants?"

"Please. Breasts that firm and perfect only exist in male imaginations and the wonderful world of silicone."

"For a woman who leaves an impression of having led a sheltered life . . ."

"I have led a sheltered life. Personally. Someone recently accused me of having been raised in a convent. But professionally I'm a big city prosecutor. I've dealt with pimps, perverts, prostitutes, murderers, and other scum, not to mention their lawyers and their victims. The Nadias of this world are a piece of cake compared to some slimy bastard who has raped and murdered a child."

"I'm impressed. You have dimensions I never suspected."

"I'm sorry, Alexei, I didn't mean to go off like that."

They stopped at the top of the stairs and looked back down at the party.

"I have the impression," he said, "there is more to Lara Patrick than I first imagined. I thought you were some sort of commercial spy and now I find out you are much more complicated."

"Commercial spy? What do you mean?"

"I thought you had been sent to Moscow by certain business interests in the United States and Western Europe who are trying to get a financial foot in Russia by gaining control of my bank."

She looked down at her drink. "I've obviously had too

much to drink. I think Scotty has beamed me up." She handed him her half-empty glass. "Keep this away from me. I've had several in short order. And champagne earlier. I'm feeling a little numb. Does that mean I'm drunk?"

"It's a start. But liquor takes a while to get into your bloodstream, so the best is yet to come. Haven't you ever been drunk?"

"Drunk? I've never even been buzzed. Now tell me about the commercial thing. Why on earth would you think I was a spy?"

He raised his eyebrows and spread his hands. "Why do you think I was following you yesterday? And then after we met, you left that terrible little hotel where it appeared you were hiding out in secret and moved into a hotel I own."

"Following me? You were following me? Why?"

"Isn't it obvious? I thought you were involved with his death."

"Whose death?"

"Nikolai Belkin's. My chief negotiator."

THREE

T he landing at the top of the staircase spread out left and right.

He guided her left, leading her to the end of the hallway. "This is a private entrance." He opened a door to an alcove with an elevator. "That elevator permits me to come and go without entering the public lobby."

She was bursting with questions but she kept her mouth shut—she needed time to think.

He opened doors in the hallway on the way back.

"Spare bedroom . . . there are three . . . gym, fully equipped. Personally, I hate exercise. It's only the fact that

I have a personal trainer with instructions to flog me if I don't cooperate that I keep in good condition.''

He gave her a brief glance at the master bedroom that was in the corridor to the right. ''Fit for a king,'' he told her. ''I'll let you see the rest of it someday but right now it would get the guests buzzing with gossip.''

''Let's talk about Belkin,'' she said. ''You dropped a bomb and we need to clear the debris.''

''Belkin was a . . . how would an American put it? He was a shit.''

''That's one way of putting it.''

The numbness was spreading in her system and her balance felt off just a hair. *Take hold of yourself.*

She started concentrating on how she walked and talked. She certainly wasn't drunk and didn't want to leave that impression.

''But a very useful shit in certain situations. He talked the same language as the old hard-liners and was very effective dealing with them. When I heard he was killed, perhaps even murdered, and that an American woman was involved, I was naturally curious. Especially after I found out you were staying at a hotel where it's unlikely an American would register.''

''I'm a poor American. Besides, I speak Russian, so I don't have to stay at a tourist hotel.''

''Well anyway, I arranged with the hotel staff to spy on you.''

''Gee, I hope they have a photocopy machine.''

''A photocopy machine?''

''With all the spying that goes on, they should mass produce their reports. I can't believe the amount of paranoia in this country. It hangs over everything like ominous clouds.''

''In Russia, paranoia is simply heightened awareness. Russians don't have to conjure up fictional enemies, not with everyone in the country ready to put a knife in everyone else's back and the rest of the world surrounding us like vultures as we struggle to get on our feet.''

She shook her head. ''I agree. I've had vultures flying overhead since I arrived in Moscow.'' Shaking her head made her mind spin a little and she decided not to do that again.

''However, I no sooner learn that the police are investigating you than the hotel security man disappears, apparently off to the country for his health.''

Lara thought about Yuri. ''Are you also paying the police to spy on me?''

''That would have been my next move, but I wanted a look at you myself. When someone from the hotel called my office to report that you had left on foot, the message was relayed to me in my car. I swung by to get a look at this mystery woman only to find myself ice skating in a sports car.'' He grinned. ''The rest is history.''

They went up a stairway and through a door that led to another hallway.

''We are on the top floor now. My office is through the door on the left and the outdoor spa is at the end of the hallway.''

His office had glass windows all along the corridor. Heavy drapes on the inside kept the office private.

He opened the door at the end of the hallway and showed her the steaming spa. ''I'm sure before the night is over some of my guests will find their way into the spa with too much to drink and not much to wear.''

He closed the spa door and Lara followed him into the office.

If the revolving structure was the crown of the skyscraper, the office was the crowning gem. Floor-to-ceiling windows gave a panoramic view of the city.

''This is my favorite room,'' he said. ''I feel like I own the city when I stand here and look down.''

She stayed back from the windows. Heights made her head spin and she already felt like a Saturn rocket ready to launch.

"I . . . I'm sorry, I don't like heights. Usually it only bothers me when I'm next to an open window, but these floor-to-ceiling windows are scary." She swayed, dizzy.

"Are you all right?"

"Yes. Perhaps we should go downstairs. I think I need some food in my stomach."

He closed the office door and led her back down the corridor. "You've had a little too much to drink."

"No, it's just a little vertigo. Sometimes I get it around heights."

They paused at the top of the stairs.

She grinned a little sillily and immediately wiped the grin off her face. *Control yourself.* With a more serious tone, she said, "You haven't asked me why I came to Moscow."

"I know why you came to Moscow." He held her arm as they went down the stairs. "Mr. Caldwell from your embassy called today. A courtesy call to let me know that you might attempt to elicit my help in a case that the Ministry of Security has already decided not to reopen."

"That bastard." Her temperature went soaring.

"I wouldn't give him that much credit. I think he was really only trying to get an invitation to the party."

"Good thing you didn't invite him. I'd kick his butt for snitching on me."

"Yes, well, let's get you some food."

She had more questions about Belkin but she had a problem getting her mind and tongue to coordinate.

At the bottom of the steps his assistant, Ilya, whispered something to him.

Alexei squeezed her hand. "I'm going to leave you in Ilya's hands for a few minutes while I deal with a crisis in the kitchen. He'll get you some food to, uh, offset the liquor."

Ilya led her to tall stools at the back of the room as a small person came onstage dressed in a cowpoke outfit and announced a Western show to be followed by a contest for best-dressed cowgirl. The announcer reminded her enough of the hustler at the carnival freak show to be his twin.

"I'll get you a plate of food," Ilya told her after he got her settled on a stool. "Will you be all right alone for a moment?"

She gave him a cockeyed grin. "All right alone? I've been alone most of my life."

"Yes, I see . . ." He backed up and then rushed for the food tables.

A waiter came by with a tray of drinks and Lara took one. She was dying of thirst. She sipped the drink and kicked her legs as a cowboy performing rope tricks entertained the audience.

Her glass was empty by the time Ilya got back.

"You shouldn't have done that. You need food in your stomach before you get totally bombed."

She leaned toward him and tapped his chest with her forefinger. "I'm not as inexperienced at these things as one might suspect. I've handled murderers and rapists. I can certainly handle a little liquor."

She leaned closer to say something else and nearly fell off her stool. "It's a matter of mind over matter," she told him, balanced once again on the stool. "Liquor enters your body and takes control, but I have a very strong mind. It will never take mine. My mind, I mean. Do you follow me?"

"I think you better have some food. That flavored vodka is deceptive. It's as potent as the clear variety."

"Don't worry, I'm in full control."

The rope artist was followed by a buckskinned Indian throwing knives at a buxom blonde. Lara clapped for each act, a bit harder than the rest of the audience, but she was feeling really good.

Ilya kept watching her out of the corner of his eye. She thought of asking him if he was the one who held General Bova's underwear in the morning and started giggling at the idea.

Then she saw Nadia and two other girls lining up at the side of the stage and her mood blackened.

That bitch. She looks like a cheap slut in that red outfit.

"The judges have cast their votes," the dwarf in cowboy duds announced, "and we have the results for the best-dressed cowgirl and the two runner-ups. The winner is Nadia Kolchak, with Katrina Dolchin and Natasha Florinsky as runner-ups."

The three women came onstage to thunderous applause.

Lara was having a little trouble keeping the women in focus but it didn't take much imagination to realize that the judges must have been all men and that the less-dressed were the best-dressed. One of the women had on a clear plastic cowboy suit—and nothing on underneath.

Nadia took the flowers offered as her prize and stepped up to the microphone a bit unsteadily. "Thank you, thank you."

"She's—*hic*—had too much to drink," Lara slurred. "Can't hold her liquor."

"Appears so," Ilya replied.

Onstage, Nadia looked around the room until she spotted Lara. "Now that we've had the best-dressed cowgirls awarded, it's time to give the award to the funniest-dressed." She pointed down to Lara. "And that award should go to our American guest in the dress that looks like something Stalin's mother wore. To her grave."

The girls onstage giggled and there were a few laughs in the audience, but not everyone was laughing. People were staring at Lara wondering what would happen next.

Lara went black with rage and a devil crawled under her skin. "And those aren't Western outfits," she yelled to the girls onstage. "Those are what *call* girls wear, not cowgirls."

Lara unbuttoned her jacket and threw it to the side. Murmurs went through the audience as she reached down and pulled her dress off. She turned to Ilya and grabbed his white cowboy hat and put it on her own head. "Give me your guns," she told him.

He started to protest so she unbuckled the gunbelts for him and put them round her own waist.

Dressed in woolly red long johns, white cowboy hat, and a pair of six-shooters, she announced, "This is how real cowgirls dress."

The audience responded with an assortment of laughter, clapping, cheers, and whistles. All the commotion made Alexei come out of the kitchen and stare in utter amazement.

Lara grinned, and strutted a little, drawing her six-shooters. "Yahoo!" she yelled, pointing the guns overhead and pulling the triggers.

The guns fired, knocking her backward. Bullets struck the huge crystal chandelier and glass rained down. It sent the audience stampeding in panic. Nadia, terrified by the shooting and the flying glass, fell off the stage trying to get under cover.

Lara sat on the floor with the two smoking six-shooters in her hands and stared up at the world openmouthed.

"I didn't know they were loaded."

FOUR

Alexei hustled her out the back corridor and down his private elevator. The limo was waiting. They climbed in and Alexei told the driver to wait, he wanted a word with Ilya before they left. He couldn't stop laughing.

"I don't know why you think it's so funny. Who would be crazy enough to have loaded guns at a party?"

"They're all loaded," he said, still laughing. "Live bullets were easier to find than blanks at the last minute so that's what I gave them."

"You are insane."

"Me?" He gawked at her red woolly underwear, white cowboy hat, and crossed gunbelts and began to laugh so hard he started choking.

She shook her head. "I just don't believe those guns could have been loaded."

He patted her knee. "You made a believer out of the rest of us." He grabbed her and gave her a big hug. "You made my party. Tomorrow this will be in every newspaper in Russia."

"Great, just what I need."

Ilya appeared at the side of the limo and Alexei got out to speak to him.

She was still buzzed, she could feel it, but the shock of shooting up the most luxurious penthouse in Russia had brought back her senses somewhat.

Embarrassed, dying of shame, devastated, were words that described how she should feel—but didn't. She realized she did have some of her father in her and that the liquor had brought out the crazy and wild side. She didn't feel one damn bit ashamed. There was just one thing that bothered her and the moment Alexei got in the car she hit him with the question.

"Are you going to sue me?"

"Am I going to what?"

"Sue me. For the damages."

"No, my dear, I'm not going to sue you."

"But that chandelier must have cost a fortune."

He patted her knee again. "Don't worry. In a manner of speaking, it was stolen."

"You forget, I'm a prosecutor in my country. A champion of law and order—"

"Enforced at gunpoint, no doubt."

"Did you ask Ilya how your guests reacted to my, uh . . ."

"A couple of the drunker ones decided to see who had the fastest draw before everyone was disarmed. And you'll be happy to know"—he chuckled—"that Nadia's injuries aren't serious. One of the guests was a doctor and he examined her. She'll be black and blue for a couple days. Here, put these on."

He handed her a pair of silver cowboy boots.

"Where did you get these?"

"I had Ilya borrow them from Nadia. She's lying down and won't miss them. They go nicely with your red underwear."

"In a manner of speaking, you might say you stole her boots."

"Exactly."

Lara struggled into the boots as the limo entered traffic. "They're a little big, but I'll survive. Why am I wearing Nadia's boots?"

"You need them where we're going."

"And that is?"

"Dancing."

"Dancing!" She collapsed back against the seat. "What is it about this country? Everybody wants to go dancing. Do you know how well I dance?"

"It doesn't matter. Where we're going dancing is merely a polite word for letting out the savage within."

"Alexei, I've had a few drinks, but I'm not drunk enough to go out in public dressed in long underwear. That wasn't me back at your party. That was the ghost of my father."

"Don't worry, at Planet X you'll be overdressed. The sable cape is yours, by the way. To keep."

"This cape cost a fortune. I can't take it." She pushed it at him.

His face fell like a little kid told he couldn't have candy. "But I want you to have the cape. It's unique, irreplaceable. It belonged to Tsar Nicholas's oldest daughter. It's been in cold storage in a musty old museum for three quarters of a century. You'll give it life."

"How did you get it?"

"I bought the museum."

"Wait a minute. Are we talking about the museum that people say you stole?"

Alexei shrugged and gave her a naughty little boy smile. "All right, I stole the museum."

She sighed. He had an amazing amount of boyish humor and charm, but she knew that was an act. From everything she had heard and read, he was a hard, tough businessman. The best in Russia, where business wasn't just war as it was in Japan, but all-out thermonuclear overkill.

"I appreciate your generosity, but I don't wear coats made from animals slaughtered so people will look good."

"You wear cow leather shoes."

"People eat cows."

"Russians eat sables. Hell, we eat people when we get hungry enough." He shoved the cape back. "You have to at least wear it tonight."

"Considering my other alternatives, okay." She grabbed his hand and squeezed it. "Alexei, you are generous. You are handsome. Fun. Best of all, rich. But I have to tell you something."

"Yes."

"I'm a terrible prude. I'm not going to sleep with you for that fancy suite. And I'm not keeping the coat, stolen or not."

He leaned over and kissed her cheek. "Lara, there are fifty women back at my penthouse who would sleep with me for a ride in this limo. And gladly murder someone for that coat. I don't expect anything from you in return because I know you really don't want anything from me. That's part of your charm." He put his fingers to her lips. "Now be quiet. We're almost there."

"There" was a semi-industrial area, small grubby-looking factories and warehouses, some of which appeared deserted.

As she stared out of the window she thought about his comment about not wanting anything in return. One thing she had learned about people who had possessions was that short of winning the lottery, people didn't usually amass great material wealth if they were generous to a fault. Alexei either didn't fit the pattern or he hid his greed nicely.

A block down the street she could see a long line of people in front of an old warehouse.

"Oh, no, no-no-no, stop the car."

Alexei gave the command to the limo driver.

"What's the matter?" he asked.

"This is one of those discos where you have to be chosen to get in, isn't it? There's a big bouncer at the door and if he thinks you look like the Beautiful People, you're let in right away, otherwise you wait hours in line."

"Lara—"

"Listen to me. I like you, so I'm going to tell you one of the terrible secrets of my life, one of those scars we women carry around."

"You're going to show me a scar? Like Nadia's—"

"Very funny. When I was a new prosecutor I had to attend an evening indoctrination lecture. After class, a couple of the girls wanted to get a drink at a disco down the street. I had driven to the class with them so I had to tag along. When we got there, the bouncer ushered in those two and told me to get in line." She cringed at the memory. "He let me in when he realized I was with them but by then I was so embarrassed I wanted to crawl under a sewer lid on the street."

"Why did he let them in and—"

"Because they had big boobs and long blond hair and I was wearing glasses and had my hair up in a bun. After that I bought contact lenses and swore never to wear another bun."

"That wasn't the reason the bouncer told you to get in line. He sent you to the back of the line because you acted like a mouse. It wasn't breasts and long hair that attracted the bouncer to the other women, it was their body language. They were there to have fun. Fun-loving people encourage other people to have fun.''

He instructed the driver to continue on. He shook his head and laughed. ''Besides, there isn't a disco in the world that would keep out a woman dressed in long underwear and packing six-guns.''

When the limo pulled up at the curb, a uniformed attendant opened the door for them. Lara stepped out first, the crowd getting a flash of her long underwear and holstered six-guns under the fabulous cape. The people in line whistled and applauded when she put on her cowboy hat.

As soon as Alexei stepped out, people up and down the line whispered his name.

Someone shouted, ''Alexei, throw the poor some money!'' The crowd broke out in laughter.

The disco doors were pulled open by a doorman who ceremoniously said, ''Welcome, Mr. Bova.''

''The next twenty people are on the house,'' he yelled to the bouncer, which brought immediate cheers from the eager crowd.

''Do you own this place?'' Lara asked when they finally made it inside.

''Of course.''

''Why doesn't that surprise me.'' She wondered who he had stolen it from.

They went down a dark stairway illuminated by red lights to another door. She thought about the reception the crowd gave her and a big grin spread across her face.

Stepping through the door at the bottom of the stairs, they were assaulted by lights, music, people, all from another planet.

The stairway continued down to a rectangular stage packed with dancers. On three sides of the dance area were tiers of small tables and chairs jammed at each plateau, sardine style. A dozen feet above the other side of the stage was a long narrow platform where professional disco performers danced.

Music blasted from a dozen speakers hanging from the ceiling. It penetrated into every pore of her body, a tidal wave of noise—no particular beat or rhythm, just violent sound waves pierced by stormy lightning created by pulsating lights.

The people were everything she expected and nothing she imagined. Roman gods danced with girls in jeans and tank tops, women in sequined evening dresses were partnered with guys wearing G-strings. Girls in G-strings and breast tassels hugged and kissed and danced with . . . girls in G-strings and breast tassels.

As an attendant with a flashlight led them down the steps, they passed a glass booth where a man and a woman were taking a shower. They were scrubbing each other and the only covering Lara could see was soap suds.

They were shown to a table chained off from the rest. Alexei's name was on the reserved sign.

"Let's dance," he said.

There was no use telling him she didn't dance. No one else in the place seemed to know how to dance, at least not in any particular style. People on the dance floor appeared to be swaying and moving arms and legs to whatever private message they received from sound effects that were probably destroying billions of brain cells every second.

As she followed Alexei down to the packed dance floor she looked up and saw a nun dancing on the small stage above. As the nun's habit swayed, the slits in her habit revealed nudity underneath and a very unnunnish penis and testicles.

A group of beautiful young men, all wearing G-strings and nothing else, separated her from Alexei as they pranced by holding on to each other's hips in a daisy chain.

Alexei was instantly swallowed by the crowd on the dance floor and she was standing by herself feeling awkward when someone grabbed her arm and spun her round.

It was Hercules, or at least a kissing cousin to Arnold

Schwarzenegger—big bronze arms and chest, raw, naked, and pumped, muscles and veins bulging from a neck the size of her upper legs, a sack between his legs overloaded and on the verge of bursting with the heavy equipment packed inside, golden thighs rippling with muscles.

He reached around her with long powerful arms and grabbed her buttocks, one huge paw per bun, and jerked her to him until her chin was almost on his chest and she was staring openmouthed up at his rock jaw.

''We dance.''

FIVE

Two hours later Lara burst out the doors of Planet X and spun in a circle, the sable cape flying.

She whipped out a six-shooter and tried shooting the night sky, but Alexei had unloaded the guns.

''Oh, damn it, Alexei, give me some bullets. I wanna shoot out the stars.''

''Get in the car, you're drunk.''

She started to argue and he pushed her into the back of the limo.

As the car started moving along the street she rolled down the window and stuck her head out and pulled the trigger of the empty gun.

''Bang-bang-bang,'' she yelled.

He pulled her back inside and rolled up the window.

''You're crazy,'' he told her.

She grabbed him and gave him a big hug. ''I feel like a little kid. I never had so much fun in my life. While other kids were out having fun I was always sulking in a corner. God, it feels good, as if I've . . . I've added pieces to my life, as if life's a bunch of little pieces and I've been missing most of them.''

He had been laughing when he shoved her into the limo and now his face was sad.

"What's the matter? Have I said something to offend you?"

He shook his head. "No, you said something to make me like you even more. People say I'm a kid who never grew up. What they don't understand is that I'm a grownup who was never a kid. You know what the mark of a great man or woman is? An unhappy childhood. You name somebody great, a Lenin or a Napoleon, a Pushkin or a Tolstoy, and I'll show you an unhappy childhood."

She leaned back in the seat with a big sigh. "I'm too tired to show you anything."

She closed her eyes and fell asleep.

"Wake up, cowgirl, we're back at your ranch."

She sat up in the seat of the limo and stretched. "I feel like I just fell asleep."

"You did."

She grabbed his arm. "Did I snore? Tell me the truth, did I snore? I always wanted to know."

"A gentleman never tells. Besides, haven't your boyfriends ever told you?"

"My boyfriends were all gentlemen."

The hotel doorman opened the limo door and she got out slowly, still a little dizzy, followed by Alexei.

He embraced her and gave her a kiss on the lips. "I have to get back and throw out the guests left over from my party. And check to see how much has been stolen. I'll call you tomorrow."

When she reached the front doors, she remembered she was still wearing the sable cape and she spun round, but it was too late, the limo was already on its way down the street.

"I'll have to return it tomorrow," she told the doorman, who gaped at her outfit. She realized she was wearing only one gun. She must have left the other one in the limo.

As she entered the almost deserted lobby, the two clerks at the front desk and the two bellmen followed her progress with wide eyes. Apparently they were not accustomed to seeing a woman wearing red woolly underwear, a six-gun, silver cowboy boots, white cowboy hat, and a sable cape that was one of the national treasures of Russia.

The elevator attendant kept his face pointed straight at the doors as the elevator rose, but she knew he was watching her out of the corner of his eye.

On the way down the corridor to her room she checked her watch. It was after two. The sable cape slipped off as she dug into her purse for the room key. Too tired to put the cape back over her shoulders, she entered her room, dragging it beside her.

Her nose was immediately assaulted by the reek of cigarette smoke and she froze in the doorway.

Yuri Kirov was sitting across the room next to an open window, a cigarette dangling from his mouth, his feet up on a coffee table, an open bottle of vodka and a glass on the table next to an overflowing ashtray.

XIII

Cigarettes were good aspirin.

—Martin Cruz Smith,
Gorky Park

ONE

He glared at her with as much arrogance and contempt as his handsome face could muster, starting with the cowboy hat, then slowly down to open buttons at the top of her long underwear that exposed her breasts, pausing at the six-shooter, and then down to the boots. He grimaced at the sable cape being dragged on the floor.

Moving from her, his eyes took in the luxury suite as if he were seeing it for the first time, the many bouquets of flowers, imported from Holland and the Far East at prices equaling their weight in gold dust; the incredible hors d'oeuvres table with the food from hours past replaced with fresh delicacies and a bottle of imported champagne on ice.

His features remained rigid and stiff as he locked eyes with her again.

"Sable," he said. "I have never even felt sable. And you get sable and all this"—he waved his hand around—"in one night."

"It's okay. It was stolen."

"You are a tramp."

He smoked too much. His suits were cheap, his shirts wrinkled. His necktie was always loose and cockeyed. He treated her rotten. And acted suspicious as hell. But as far as she was concerned, Yuri Kirov was the sexiest man in the universe.

And best of all he was jealous.

She went to him, dragging the cape of the tsar's daughter with her, letting it go when she reached the coffee table. Using her knee, she pushed the coffee table aside until his feet dropped off to the floor.

He didn't move, didn't smile.

She sank her knee into the soft cushion of the chair between his legs, pressing against his groin as she leaned down and took his face in the palms of her hands. She forced his face up so she could look into his eyes, those dark, dark Gypsy eyes.

Very slowly, tenderly, she kissed one eye closed, then the other. Kissing the tip of his nose, her lips moved around his, brushing his lips against hers, stroking his lips with the tip of her tongue until their lips melted together.

She kissed him hard and passionately. An expansion between his legs pressured her leg and fired her blood. She broke the kiss and leaned back, feeling his erection against her leg, pressing harder against it. Her desire was uncontrollable. She grabbed each side of the open top of her long johns and jerked them apart, buttons flying off, fully exposing her breasts, nipples straining against her bra.

Yuri pulled her down to him, burying his face against her breasts. "No!" he yelled. He pushed her back and she recoiled away from him, shocked, as he struggled to his feet, banging his leg against the coffee table, almost knocking over the bottle of vodka. He walked around the room like a madman trapped in a prison cell.

"It won't work, it can't happen."

Hurt and embarrassed, she grabbed the sable cape and covered her chest with it.

"What's the matter?"

"It won't work between us. I can't give you these things." He waved at the room.

"I haven't asked you for anything."

He stopped pacing and stood straight, adjusting his coat. "I am here on official business."

"Are you crazy? What're you talking about?"

"I have to warn you against Alexei Bova. He is not who you think he is. The man is . . . is a thief, he is robbing the whole country. He's dangerous."

"He's the only person in Moscow who's been decent to me."

"He's deceiving you."

"Why? What does he need from me? I have nothing."

"Did he tell you Belkin worked for him?"

"Yes."

"Did he tell you he used to be KGB?"

"Everybody in this damn country used to be KGB."

"Everything he tells you is a lie and a fraud. He is the most dangerous man in Russia. Even the government can't stop him."

"You're jealous of him."

"My feelings aren't important. Your actions are the problem. You have managed to get yourself entangled with a snake."

"I'll associate with anyone I like."

"Then you had better give him an invitation to visit you in America because you are leaving Moscow tomorrow."

"Like hell I am. I came—"

"You came to uncover a crime. But you have also committed a crime."

Her jaw dropped. "What are you talking about?"

His features were stern and unyielding as he made the accusation. "You have violated Russian law by bribing a guard to gain access to government records. If you are not on a plane back to America by tomorrow night, I will arrest you."

"I told you that in confidence."

"I'm a policeman. It's my duty to uphold the law."

"Get out of here, get out of my room!"

He turned to the door. She jerked the six-gun from her holster and threw it at him. It crashed into the wall to the right of the door and disappeared behind a chair. She grabbed the vodka bottle off the coffee table but he was out of the room before she had a target.

It was her turn to pace like a wild animal. Her blood was boiling. She had thrown herself at him and he was running her out of town under threat of arrest.

bastardbastardbastard

She hated him. How could she have ever been attracted to that bastard? And why had he suddenly changed on her?

The door across the room opened and Anna poked her head cautiously out.

"Is everything all right, madam?"

"What are you doing here?"

"I sleep in this room, madam. Is that policeman still here?"

"He's gone. For good."

Lara put down the vodka bottle and threw her cowboy hat on top of the sable cape and unbuckled the gunbelts. "Return this stuff to Mr. Bova first thing in the morning. And tell him I've left."

"You've left?"

"I'm returning to America tomorrow on the first available plane." She sat down to take off the boots and add them to the pile.

"Does Mr. Bova know you're leaving?"

"Mr. Bova knows nothing," she snapped. "Look, I'm sorry, Anna, I just got some bad news. Go to bed, please. I need to be alone."

She dumped the boots on top of the gunbelt and started to walk away when she noticed Yuri had left his pack of cigarettes on the coffee table. Not to mention an overflowing ashtray. She grabbed the cigarettes and vodka bottle and rushed to the open window.

He was standing at the curb below, getting ready to cross the street.

"Hey!" she yelled down. "You forgot something!"

She threw the pack of cigarettes. It dropped toward the street and disappeared in the dark night.

"Here's your booze."

She sent the vodka bottle flying and watched it explode on the street.

She grabbed the ashtray full of butts and threw it out, too.

Sticking her head out the window, she yelled, "Kissing you was like kissing an ashtray!"

He looked up at her, his hands in his overcoat pockets, and shook his head. As she leaned farther out to yell something nasty, the pavement came up and smacked her between the eyes. Her eyes crossed and she threw herself back, landing on the floor on her tush, her head spinning.

She was so angry at him she had forgotten about her vertigo. Crawling across the floor toward her bedroom her hand hit something lying on the floor.

A bouquet of roses.

Not the incredibly expensive long-stemmed ones that Alexei had delivered by the dozens, but a few scrawny roses, all Yuri could afford, she thought. The roses probably cost him a week's wages.

How sweet.

She clutched the roses to her bosom and tried to tell herself she hated the bastard, but the words wouldn't come.

At four o'clock in the morning the incessant jar of the telephone ringing forced her to emerge from under the blankets and fumble for the phone. The receiver fell to the floor and she snaked off the bed and onto the floor after it. Belly down on the carpet, she groaned into the phone, "Hello."

"This is Minsky," a nervous voice told her. "You must come at once. I found your mother's file."

TWO

She staggered into the bathroom and threw up. The champagne and vodka that had been so sweet on her lips had curdled in her stomach. She sat down on the toilet and leaned her head against the wall.

She wanted to die.

She was dying.

If this was the life of the rich and famous, she was ready for a farm in Kansas.

She thought about Minsky's call. She was used to his nervousness, but this time there had been a new ingredient in his voice. Fear.

A whole day had been spent away from her own fears. A day of being Somebody. Andy Warhol's fifteen minutes of fame.

As she sat on the toilet after puking out her guts, she wondered what lay in wait for her at an underground station at an hour when no one was out on Moscow's dark streets except murderers and rapists.

She stuck her head into the sink and threw up again.

The advantage of staying at a first-class hotel was that there were taxis outside twenty-four hours a day. Dressed in jeans and a ski jacket with a scarf over her head and tied under her chin, she got in a taxi and gave the cabbie the name of the metro station. The driver had been asleep at the wheel and he yawned and stretched before he got the cab moving.

Her paranoia was riding high and she watched out the back window to see if they were being followed. They had gone a block when the lights of a car that had been parked on the other side of the street about half a block from the hotel went on.

"Make a right turn," she told the driver.

"The station is—"

"I know. You'll be paid well. Just make the turn."

The car to the rear made the same turn. Certain it was Yuri's militia car, she leaned forward to talk to the taxi driver.

"Look, I've been with a friend and I think my husband is following me. Lose him and I'll pay you twenty dollars, American."

She caught a flash of the driver's teeth as he grinned. He hit the gas and spun the wheel into a sudden turn, sending her flying back against the seat.

Twenty minutes later the driver pulled up at the metro station. She had three tens ready to give him. He turned to her with a big grin and she knew she was in trouble

"One hundred dollars," he said.

"The deal was twenty. I'm giving you another ten for the fare, which is a lot more than I owe."

"One hundred dollars. I know the difference between an unmarked militia car and a husband's car. A hundred dollars or I call the militia and tell them where I dropped you."

She leaned in closer and dropped a ten-dollar bill in his lap. "Call them. When they get here I'll tell them you raped me."

She got out of the car and slammed the door. As she walked away, he stuck his head out the window and yelled, "What about my twenty dollars?"

"If you're still here to take me back to my hotel when I come out, you'll get the twenty. If you're not, I'll give it to the next driver."

She went down the steps as fast as she could take them. A trip to Wales to find out more about her father when this was all over was definitely in order. She had certainly inherited some form of madness from him.

The tea shop was closed and Minsky was nowhere in sight. Five or six derelicts, one of them a woman, had bedded down for the night on benches.

Her stomach muscles knotted. This was not a nice place for a woman alone. For anyone alone.

One of the derelicts got off a bench and walked toward her. She started to go back up the steps when he spoke to her.

"You looking for Minsky?"

He was pale and thin with an ulcer on his cheek and a grubby beard. His frame was wasted from booze or drugs or whatever his brand of devil was. He held up a folded piece of paper. "Minsky said to give this to you. He said you'd give me money."

"Where's Minsky?"

"Sick, I think. He looked real sick when he gave me the paper."

"Give it to me."

He docilely handed her the folded paper and she gave him one of the ten-dollar bills from her pocket and quickly walked away.

The taxi was waiting outside. The driver didn't even turn to look at her when she got in, he just got the cab moving in traffic toward her hotel. It was six o'clock in the morning, still pitch-dark in Moscow. She held the paper up to try to read it in the bluish glow of streetlamps they passed but couldn't make it out.

"Put on the dome light, please."

He turned on the dome light without saying a word.

The paper was a one-page KGB document titled "Report of Death of Foreign Subject." The top half contained statistical information typed into blocks: her mother's name, date of birth, address, occupation, employer, political status.

The word "Remarks" appeared on the bottom half and a statement was typed below:

SUBJECT 35-YEAR-OLD FEMALE U.S. CITIZEN DIED AT CHARSKY INSTITUTE. SUBJECT HAD BEEN TAKEN INTO PROTECTIVE PSYCHIATRIC CUSTODY FOR TREATMENT AND POSSIBLE REEDUCATION AFTER SUFFERING DANGEROUS DELUSIONS CONCERNING DEATH OF FRIEND.

SUBJECT MENTALLY UNSTABLE AT TIME OF ADMISSION.

COMMITTED SUICIDE BEFORE INSTITUTE STAFF WERE ABLE TO IMPLEMENT TREATMENT PROGRAM.

SUBJECT HAD HISTORY OF MENTAL INSTABILITY AND HAD ATTEMPTED SUICIDE IN THE PAST. TO AVOID ADVERSE FOREIGN PRESS COVERAGE, SUBJECT'S DEATH WILL BE ATTRIBUTED TO VEHICULAR ACCIDENT.

Back in her hotel suite, Lara sat in the stuffed chair next to the window and read the document over and over.
Buzz words from the report spun in her head.

DELUSIONS
DEATH OF A FRIEND
MENTAL INSTABILITY
ATTEMPTED SUICIDE IN THE PAST

The report was designed to say just enough to defame but not to explain.

It was dated the same day Lara was put on the flight back to the United States. She couldn't remember the time the flight left Moscow but she was sure it was at night. Her mother's death was listed for that same evening at 7:35.

Not one word about an attack on Lara earlier that day.

Not one word about her mother picking her up at school and taking her to St. Basil's.

The one irrefutable fact the document established was that the Soviets had lied about how her mother had died: she had not died in a crash with a petrol tanker.

A lie upon a lie.

Lara's hands shook as she read the report for the twentieth time. The dead can't defend themselves and their living champions can be crippled by clever phraseology: history of mental instability, delusions, attempted suicide in the past . . .

Someone took her mother's life.

Murdered her.

Then they covered their tracks by smearing her memory.

A perfect cover-up. Some bastard maniac kills a woman and has the power to have a psychiatric report generated that her mother was a suicide.

She understood why the "accident" story was put out instead of the "suicide" one: a suicide would be subjected to scrutiny by the foreign press and raise questions, a demand for an investigation. By the same token "suicide" would completely satisfy Soviet authorities. Generate paperwork internally that her mother committed suicide, and with the Soviet propensity for avoiding a bad foreign press, release a story that it was an accident.

Confuse and conquer, that's how insiders manipulated bureaucracies.

Minsky hadn't got the document to her out of love or money. He had been motivated by fear. Someone had put a fire under him to see to it that the paper reached her. By now Minsky was probably on his way "out of town" for his health. If he wasn't floating facedown in the Moscow River.

She had been manipulated into coming to Moscow, that was a given. Someone wanted to open up an old murder case. Or wanted her back for more sinister reasons. The report was more bait. She was now sure that the information about the truck driver had been spoon-fed to her through Minsky. That would explain why he was so damn nervous when she met him. But he was only supposed to give her the truck driver's address. Suddenly the rules changed and Minsky was ordered to give her another clue about her mother's death.

Why? What had changed?

Someone had the power to draw the document from the KGB archives and scare the wits out of the guardian of it. Scared her, too.

Someone had tried to kill her, had killed Belkin, frightened I. Malinovsky to death—or killed her—and sent Minsky and the hotel security man running for cover—or maybe even killed them.

She looked at the report again.

DANGEROUS DELUSIONS CONCERNING DEATH OF
FRIEND

She took the picture of the mutilated woman out of her purse and examined it, repulsed at having to look at it.

Who is the woman in the picture?

X I V

===

All human beings have gray little souls—
and they all want to rouge them up.

—Maxim Gorky,
The Lower Depths

ONE

Yuri was stepping out of his basement apartment as the building manager hurried to him from the boiler room down the hallway. Her name was Pinoff and she was dangerous.

The woman, a champion discus thrower in her youth, had broad shoulders, giant breasts, and a rump to match. Whenever she got near him her red face turned redder and her breathing got heavier from sexual excitement. She reminded him of a polar bear in heat.

Yuri didn't know what it was about his undersized (compared to her) body that put her into a rape mode, but whatever it was scared him—she was big enough, strong enough, and looked aroused enough to jump on him and break a few of his bones in foreplay.

Her husband, a Neanderthal, had taken an instant dislike to Yuri from the moment he moved into the basement of the building. Every time they passed each other in the hallway the man looked ready to forget the foreplay and simply rip off Yuri's arms and legs and beat him with the bloody stumps.

He had no idea why he aroused such passions in either of them. Perhaps the woman had shouted his name in some primeval fucking session with the Neanderthal.

"A man asked about you earlier."

"Who?"

Her face twisted in a scowl. "Mafia."

Mafia could mean anything, from a petty thief to the person checking the gas meter. All it really meant was that she didn't like the man.

"Did he tell you his name?"

"No."

"Did he say what he wanted?"

"No."

By the numbers—that was the way his conversations went with Pinoff. Like a two-year-old, she couldn't chew gum and walk at the same time.

"What did he say to you?"

"He asked if you were home."

"And?"

"I said, why do you want to know? He said he was a friend. I said Yuri's friends know if he is home."

Her bear face broke into a broad smile at her cleverness and Yuri grinned.

"What did he say to that?"

The scowl came back. "He said a sharp-tongued woman could get her tongue cut out and I told him to get out of the building or I would bite his balls off. He left."

I don't blame him, Yuri thought.

"What time?"

"About an hour ago."

"Why did you wait to tell me?"

"I thought you were gone. You are usually gone at this time."

She moved a little closer to him, radiating sexual heat and the smell of cabbage. "I need to check your plumbing. It is my duty."

Yuri stepped around her. "Later."

* * *

He went up the steps to street level and paused at the front door. There was no back way out of the building.

He checked his gun, cocked it, and slipped it back into his shoulder holster. He had no idea who was looking for him, but all of the probabilities were bad. Some were deadly.

He had to go out onto the streets and face whoever was there. To avoid it meant the next time he might be ambushed. At least this time he had been warned.

He kept his movements loose and casual as he stepped out, but his eyes swept up and down and across the street. He moved down the street, keeping his pace relaxed, trying not to show the rush of adrenaline surging in him.

Fifty feet ahead a man stepped out of a doorway.

It wasn't someone stepping out to pick up a pack of cigarettes at the corner kiosk. He came out and faced Yuri like a gunfighter with a challenge in his body language.

The polar bear was right—the guy was mafioso, a stupid, brute-faced, thick-necked thug who had probably been low-level KGB before the secret police organization was broken up. Now his type hired out to anyone who needed muscle—drug dealers seeking protection, drug dealers busting up other drug dealers, businessmen needing bodyguards to protect them from the shakedown racket thugs, and as thugs shaking down businessmen for protection money.

Yuri didn't know what had brought the bastard into his life, whether it was one of his cases or closer to home, but he knew the trouble wasn't going away unless he faced it, so he locked eyes with the man and went for him.

He caught a movement to his right and turned too late. A man shot out of a doorway and was on him with a gun shoved into his ribs before he could do more than flinch.

A black Volga accelerated down the street and came to a halt beside them. The thug who had been facing Yuri on the street hurried over and opened the back door. The man with the gun reached inside Yuri's coat and took Yuri's gun, then shoved him toward the car. As Yuri bent to get into the backseat area, the gunman hit him in the back of the head with the gun and gave him a push into the car. The gunman climbed in, pounded him again with the gun, and used his feet to shove Yuri down onto the floor. As the car got moving the gun-toter sat in the backseat and used him as a footrest.

TWO

No one spoke as the car raced down city streets. Volgas were still a sign of power and authority and traffic cops held traffic and waved the big car through busy intersections.

He had been a footstool for about ten minutes when the car pulled to a curb. The man in the backseat climbed out.

"Get out."

Yuri's awkward effort to crawl backward out of the car wasn't fast enough for the goons and two of them grabbed his legs and pulled him out. He caught himself with his hands to keep his head from bouncing on the sidewalk.

The gun-toter and the guy who faced him on the street jerked him to his feet and hustled him down a set of concrete stairs next to a brick building.

He recognized the area—a block of tall government buildings not far from the Kremlin.

A set of metal doors was at the bottom of the steps. One of the thugs pounded on the door with his fist and it was opened by a clone of the two manhandling him.

Yuri's mind raced not in panic but in analysis—panic was unnecessary because there wasn't anything he could do about the situation. He had already decided they were going to kill him and that he would take any opening to die fighting—but so far there had not been a chance.

It was no use asking the thugs who hired them—they would get pleasure out of not telling him, savoring the revelation for a final moment when they could torture him with the thought.

They led him down an interior stairway made of steel girders, one man in front of him, two behind, no one saying a word. The stairway went deeper and deeper and Yuri wondered if it had something to do with the subway system.

One of the thugs read his mind and answered the question about the stairway. "It's leading to hell," he said with a laugh.

They came to a landing, went through even heavier metal doors and onto a steel platform suspended over dark water.

Stepping through the doorway he was hit by warm air and the stench of decaying chemicals and gases and he knew he was somewhere in the city's sewer system, a vast network of underground channels created by diverting a dozen rivers for sewerage disposal.

He knew for certain that they were going to kill him because there was no reason to bring him down to the sewers except for easy disposal of his body. He turned on his left heel, swinging at the man directly behind him, but the punch glanced off and he went down under a barrage of fists and knees as the three piled into him.

Two of the men pinned him to the steel floor while a third clamped a handcuff around his ankle. He heard the scrape of steel chain and horror exploded in his brain.

They were weighing him down to drown him.

He could have taken a shot in the head with numb defiance but the thought of drowning, slowly suffocating as his lungs filled with water, sent a wave of horror through him.

They lifted him off the platform and threw him over the side, the handcuff on his ankle, a length of chain connected to the handcuff.

A gasp escaped him as he fell.

The length of chain suddenly ran out and he screamed in pain as his descent suddenly stopped, almost ripping his leg out of his hip socket.

He dangled upside down in midair a couple of feet over the water, spinning around, held by the handcuff on his ankle and the chain that went back up to the landing.

Blood rushed to his head and for a moment it darkened his brain. As his senses came back he heard footsteps on the platform near the water's edge.

He saw the shoes first, expensive loafers of fine Italian leather; the pants that went with the suit cost as much as a year's wages for a Moscow cop. He was dizzy and fighting back screaming from the pain but even upside down he recognized the face that went with the expensive clothes.

"My sources tell me you're a good investigator," Alexei Bova told him. "Put some of that analytical thought process to your present situation. Do you know where you are?"

Yuri's reply was a gasp of pain as he tried to twist around.

"You're in one of Zemo's Dachas." There was superiority, contempt in Bova's voice. "It was a secret in Stalin's time and it's probably not well known now."

As he talked, Bova walked around the steel platform, looking over the huge chamber that was mostly lost in dark shadow. Barrels and crates lined the walls of the landings on each side of the water.

"After the Americans dropped the bomb on Japan, Stalin was paranoid that the next target would be Moscow. The Inner Circle needed a place to hide from an A-bomb so the army's chief engineer, Zemo, constructed reinforced chambers under the Kremlin and a couple other areas. The chambers aren't very big but people like you were considered expendable."

Bova stopped near the edge of the platform.

"You know who I am. You know I have enemies trying to topple me."

Topple. The word connoted an attempt to overthrow a king, not outmaneuver a businessman.

"You're investigating the death of Nikolai Belkin, a man who worked for me. My sources tell me you're trying to turn Belkin's death into a murder case. His death has no meaning to me except that it would be an embarrassment to me at a very critical juncture if it were discovered that one of my aides was murdered.

"You're also harassing an American woman who has become my friend. Someone has suggested that you're doing it deliberately to cause me problems."

The stench was clogging Yuri's lungs and his breath came in gasps.

"I am going to give you the benefit of the doubt and assume that you're just a dumb policeman and you're not involved in intrigues against me. If I change my mind about your motives, the next time you're dropped into the sewer you won't have a lifeline."

Bova paused. "You should feel privileged, Detective Kirov. The KGB used this place to question some of their own people when the questioning was unofficial and couldn't be done at the Lubyanka. The person being interrogated was periodically dipped upside down into the crud to encourage cooperation. They usually drowned on their own vomit. Few people invited down here left alive.

"Take a vacation, Detective. The Black Sea is wonderful this time of year."

He started to leave, then stopped and looked back at Yuri.

"I forgot to tell you. The key to that handcuff is on the banister above. You'll have to pull yourself up to get it. But don't shake the railing, Detective. My men wanted to make the game sporting so they put the key right on the edge. If it falls in, you're going to be down here until your flesh rots off."

XV

The murk of night still prevails.

—Boris Pasternak,
The Poems of Yuri Zhivago

ONE

≡

Lara sat in a rental car and watched the Charsky Institute from a block down the street.

The neighborhood was a quiet avenue of small professional buildings. The institute was at the corner of the block and was the only facility with grounds. It needed a paint job and tender loving care. Wooden railings and window frames were chipped and weather-beaten. Broken windows, three observable from where she was parked, had been boarded up. The grounds, grass, bushes, and a dozen small trees were overgrown.

Something about the place didn't feel right to her and it took her a moment to realize what it was. The second-floor windows had steel shutters. Once those shutters were pulled closed and no doubt secured by a padlock inside, the rooms became as secure as prison cells.

The place was a prison in disguise.

It had an abandoned look to it, but she knew it wasn't deserted. Three people had come and gone in the two hours she had been parked down the street. It probably no longer housed inpatients, she guessed, but still had a small number of outpatients.

Darkness fell early during Moscow's winter and although it was still only dusk, lights were already being turned on in the buildings along the street. The only lights she saw at the institute were on the ground floor and those shone through windows clustered near the front entrance.

Her guess was that the institute had fallen from favor either with patients or more likely with the government that paid its bills. The Soviets had been notorious for their use and abuse of psychiatry as part of their control apparatus, an expense the new "free" Russian society couldn't afford and probably abhorred.

The brutal treatment had been based upon the premise that the Soviet system was perfect, thus anyone who disagreed with the system must have been mentally deranged. Instead of wasting money keeping dissenters cold and miserable in Siberia, clever bureaucrats and quack psychiatrists devised a plan to "cure" them. Anyone suspected of deviant thought was sent to a psych ward for "treatment" rather than being thrown in prison.

Those who didn't respond to the treatment were found to be criminally sane and were given appropriate punishment.

The thought that her mother might have been subjected to the mental torture of the brutal therapy appalled her. She was not convinced that her mother had died the day she herself was put on a plane for the West. The date of death given on the KGB report didn't have to correspond to reality. Her mother could have lived for months longer while she was battered mentally and physically.

With that terrible thought, Lara jerked open the car door and started for the institute.

She tried to think of a cover story as she walked but her mind was too tired to be creative. Too tired and too angry. She hadn't gone back to sleep after returning from the subway station. When Anna came into the room to straighten up, Lara dressed and left the hotel after arranging for a rental car. She drove around for hours, more because of the thoughts storming in her head than to throw off anyone who may have been following.

Yuri's threat of arrest no longer had any power over her. Her mother had been a woman filled with love and courage and exciting ideas. She had been killed and labeled a nut. Getting on a plane was out of the question. Not until she had cleared her mother's name and seen her mother's killer punished.

She had ended up driving by the institute in the early afternoon. Going there had been the next logical step. Her mother's file would be in the building because the Soviets never threw anything away.

Somebody wanted her to see that file.

She wanted to see it, too.

T W O

A short stone wall surrounded the institute. The pedestrian gate was open and bent back from age and abuse. As Lara got closer the building looked even more rundown than it had from the car.

She took the six steps up to the front porch slowly, gathering her strength. This was the place where her mother had died. She had to get that out of her mind and keep it out or she would not be able to function.

It's just a building, there's nothing left of my mother here.

The front door was unlocked and complained when she pushed it open. Butterflies swarmed in her stomach as she stepped into the entry hall and proceeded into the reception area. No one was about. There was a corridor to the right of the reception desk.

A stairway to the second floor appeared first in the corridor, next to that an elevator—beyond that office doors lined both sides of the hallway. To the left were waiting-room chairs, and behind the heavy curtains would be the French patio doors she had spotted from the street. French doors were not a popular architectural item in winter-bitter Moscow. Already attuned to the logic of the way the country had been run, she decided the windowed doors had been added to give the reception area a light, airy, and friendly feel, and the heavy curtains had been kept shut to make sure no one enjoyed it. Or to keep out the cold, she begrudgingly admitted.

What she sensed most in the atmosphere was hopelessness, as if all the hope had packed up and moved out, leaving the building to wither.

A call bell, the type tapped with fingers, was on the reception desk. Lara gave the bell's plunger a couple of taps and moved over to check out a directory on the wall.

The listing that caught her eye was the Medical Records Department. In the basement. She went down the corridor to see if there was a stairway. A door labeled STAIRS was on the other side of the elevator. The elevator had a pointer and three positions set out above it: basement, ground floor, and the floor above. The arrow pointed to the basement.

She heard the elevator doors slam below and the old beast began creaking its way up.

Must be the receptionist returning, she thought. She stepped over to the door marked STAIRS and opened it, coming face-to-face with a woman in a nurse's uniform.

Lara quickly stepped back. "Excuse me—"

"What do you want?" the nurse demanded. The woman had an armful of patient files and a set of keys in the other hand. She stepped past Lara and went to the reception desk. "Are you here for an appointment?"

"No, I—my mother was treated here."

"Your mother is not here. We do not have inpatients and the last patient appointment was an hour ago."

"She wasn't treated today."

"Not today? Well, what is it you want to know about your mother?"

"I need to see her file."

"Her file? Your mother would have to come in and discuss that with the doctor. Why do you want to see her file?"

"To fill out family papers. You know, family medical history."

"Why don't you ask your mother?"

"My mother's dead. She died some time ago."

"When was she a patient here?"

"Years ago. Over ten."

The woman's eyes narrowed. "You want to see a file that is over ten years old?"

"I was told you kept files that old. And older."

"We have the file for every patient since the Institute opened thirty years ago. But no one is permitted to see those files without official authorization."

"How do I get the authorization?"

"You must go to the Ministry of Public Health. They have the forms."

"Isn't there some way I can do it more quickly? The ministry will take months." Lara reached into her purse and pulled out a wad of bills. "Perhaps if I can make a donation to the institute . . ."

The woman's face went dark. "This is a medical facility, not a kiosk. We don't sell our patient files. No doubt Mr. Yeltsin wants us to sell our patients' secrets so he will not have to provide money for the institute. What little he gives us now is barely enough to keep the doors open."

Die-hard Communist, Lara thought. Flashing money was the wrong move. "Perhaps if I talked to your director, explained the circumstances."

The woman turned stiffly and marched to a door behind the reception area. She knocked, then stepped in, closing the door behind her.

Lara nervously pushed aside a section of the heavy curtains blocking the patio doors and stared out at the overgrown bushes and weeds poking out of the snow. The doors had a painted-shut look, as if they had not been opened in years. One of the door latches was half-undone and on impulse she gave it a little nudge that opened it all the way.

A moment later the nurse came back into the reception area followed by a skeleton of a man with dried brown skin stretched across his bones. Like the building, he had a look that said all hope had fled.

"I am the director. No files can be seen without permission of the Ministry of Public Health."

"That would take months."

"That is the rule." He disappeared back through the doorway.

Lara turned her back on the woman's triumphant smirk and left the building. At least she had established that her mother's file should still be in the building. And no one had asked her name.

Now she only had to do two things. Get back in her car and drive away so they would believe she had left. And come back after dark and break into the Charsky Institute.

THREE

T wo hours later she parked down the street and turned off the headlights of the car.

At the institute a dim light, just enough to make the building look a wee less than abandoned, shone from above the front door. She watched the building for over an hour and determined someone was inside. Lights went on and off in the same pattern a cleaning person might make. Or a night watchman? The way things worked, or didn't work in this country, it could also be members of the medical staff doing night duty at a time when there were no patients.

With the fall of darkness, every building on the street had been closed up, leaving behind only the empty sidewalks and an occasional light.

Dense clouds buried the moon and cast Moscow in a shadowless night. The radio had said a storm was coming and would hit the next evening.

Keeping the engine running to heat the car was not possible. It would have made her presence on the street conspicuous. Instead, she sat in the car and nearly froze to death, swearing that once she left Moscow she would never go any place again where the temperature fell below balmy.

Unable to take the cold any longer, her courage slowly worming away, she put a small flashlight and a screwdriver into her coat pockets, opened the car door, got out, slammed it, and walked with all the determination a 115-pound woman cold and scared and all alone could muster.

Earlier that morning someone had dropped the Charsky Institute in her lap. Now she was wondering if that someone would be waiting in the dark building for her.

Glancing back nervously as she neared the front gate, for the fourth time she determined there was no one else in sight. She slipped through the gate and moved off onto the snow-covered grass, her heart pounding. She quickly crossed the lawn to the side of the building where the French doors were located.

A small patio jutted out from the French doors. The one she had unlatched earlier was on the left. She took hold of the knob and pulled. The door didn't budge. She pulled a little harder. It groaned but still didn't budge. She took the flashlight and shone it at the inside latch.

The latch was closed.

Her heart rate shot up twenty beats and she nearly ran off the porch before a thought occurred to her. If they were setting a trap, they wouldn't have locked the door. Encouraging thought, but now she had to figure out another way in.

All of the other doors looked solid. A set of metal doors at the bottom of steps led into the basement on the other side of the building, but there was no chance of her getting through those without a blowtorch. She couldn't break a window and climb through—all the windows on the ground floor were at head height.

The patio doors were her only chance and a pane of glass was between her and the latch. The only tool she had was the screwdriver she had brought to use as a jimmy in case the medical records were in locked cabinets. Tapping the glass to break it with the screwdriver would make too much noise.

On impulse she hit the pane of glass with her elbow. She never even thought about it, just gave it a blow with her elbow protected by her ski jacket.

The glass broke with a sharp shattering sound. She listened breathless for a moment. Not a creature stirred. Swallowing hard, she looked over her handiwork. The glass couldn't have made much noise inside; fragments had fallen to the carpet and the heavy curtains would have smothered the sound. She hoped.

With her gloved hand, she picked and pulled at pieces of glass until she could get her hand in and open the latch.

She pulled lightly on the door. It made more noise than the glass breaking. Taking the frame with both hands, she slowly worked the door open, every creak and rusty groan adding years to her life. She stepped inside and closed the door behind her.

The reception area was dark but the adjoining hallway was lit by a dim night-light.

She moved quickly across the reception area and to the doorway labeled STAIRS.

The stairway was a black well.

A light switch was on the wall next to the door but she didn't dare put on any lights. Not knowing if there was an open doorway below, she was afraid to even use her flashlight. She slipped in, letting the door close behind her. The door shut with a clicking and she belatedly wondered whether it was self-locking. She tried the handle. *Locked.* That's why the receptionist had the keys in her hand when Lara bumped into her. It must be a patient security system from the old days.

The question was whether she was now trapped in the stairwell. Logic told her they wouldn't lock the whole stairwell, that would be too dangerous in case of fire. The top and bottom would have to be left open. If it wasn't, she'd be trapped till they opened the institute in the morning. Those heavy metal doors leading into the basement from the outside were typical fire doors.

Feeling her way cautiously, she got a handhold on the railing and took the steps one at a time. She checked out the door at the bottom of the stairwell.

Locked.

So much for her damn theories. So much for Soviet planning in case of fire.

The door was a thick, wooden one. She examined it with the flashlight. A quarter-inch gap separated the door from the frame and the lock was nothing more than a normal door-handle lock, not a dead bolt. She wiggled the screwdriver into the space, pushing back and forth and pulling on the door until it opened.

Night lighting at both ends of the room gave just enough illumination for her to see the layout. The Medical Records Department was before her—a long, long wooden counter and behind it thousands of mud-brown files on wooden shelves.

She tested the handle to the bottom stairwell door from inside the room. It turned freely. The lock only worked from the stairwell side. She closed the door and was making her way toward an opening in the counter when she heard the whine of the elevator.

The floor indicator above the elevator door was moving.

She watched, frozen in place, as the indicator slipped down to the ground-floor mark. The whine stopped.

Breathless, she got her feet moving and went round the other side of the counter. The floor indicator was still at the ground-floor mark. Either a night watchman or the cleaning people were in the building. The basement might be the next stop. She had to hurry.

She turned back to the files and shone her light on the rows. These had to be either current files or from the past few years, she thought. They certainly couldn't represent over thirty years of patient care. The old records would be archived. But where?

She found a steel door marked KEEP OUT to the rear of the shelves at the far left side of the room. It was secured with an old-fashioned lock that took a key as thick as her finger.

A key as thick as her finger was hanging on a ring to the left of the door. She tried the key in the door lock. It fitted. It didn't surprise her. There was no one to keep out anymore. Besides, most people were so obedient during the Soviet regime, the key probably hung by the door and only authorized persons used it. When a Soviet sign said keep out, people kept out.

She pointed her flashlight into the darkness before her.

The light picked up rows and rows of shelves containing file folders. More dinosaur guts. Three light switches were by the door and she tested them and found that they turned on lights in three separate areas of the room. The place was only a small fraction of the size of the KGB archives. That was encouraging.

She turned off all but the light in the far corner of the room. She was too scared to go into the place with no lights on at all, even with her flashlight. She stepped into the room, closing the door behind her, but leaving it un-locked. The door swung open half an inch. She closed it again and it slipped open slightly again. She could have solved the problem by locking the door from the inside, but no way would she lock herself in even if she had the key in her pocket. Very slowly she pushed the door shut. It stayed and she backed away.

Moving quickly down the rows of files, she tried to decipher the filing system. No labels were on the shelves. She started pulling files and found they were alphabetical by patient name and date.

It's a piece of cake, she told herself, just keep moving down the aisles, checking files, going down year after year.

Her mother's file was in the last quarter of the room, opposite where she had kept the light on. It was thin, only a few pages. She knelt down and balanced the file on her knee. With the flashlight in one hand and turning pages with the other, she quickly read the file.

Her mother had been brought to the institute the day Lara had been picked up at school. The diagnosis was "Class 3 mental derangement: delusions. The patient made anti-Soviet statements and claimed that her next-door neighbor had been murdered and the crime concealed."

She had been tranquilized and taken to a private room. A few hours later she was found dead with a hypodermic needle in her right hand and a needle mark on her left arm. There were traces of potassium in the hypodermic.

There was "evidence" that the patient had suicidal tendencies and had gained access to a medical cabinet located outside her room.

The cause of death was suicide. The time was the same as that listed in the KGB report, about seven-thirty in the evening.

Lara stared at the page and willed her mind to remember.

Standing on the landing outside their apartment, her mother giving her a kiss on the cheek when a woman in white, a nurse, stepped out of the apartment above, her mother asking if anything had happened to Vera . . .

Chills crawled over her and she started shaking.

Vera Swen. The pretty woman in the apartment above

theirs. She used to give Lara cookies and candy.

The woman in the picture, the mutilated woman, was not her mother. It was their neighbor, Vera. And her mother knew something about the killing. Lara had seen something, too.

The nurse turned around and looked down at them. The eyes—

The elevator started whining. It was coming down to the basement.

Trying to unzip her jacket with shaky fingers, Lara dropped the flashlight and it hit the floor with a bang. She grabbed it and turned it off. She fumbled with the zipper until she got the front of her coat open. She stuck her mother's file inside and rezipped the jacket.

She started to make her way back toward the door and the light switches. She was almost at the door when she heard it creak open. She froze behind a set of shelves, her breathing suspended.

The lights went on throughout the archives.

Maybe they don't know I'm in here, maybe it's a guard who thinks the day staff left the light on.

Footsteps sounded from near the door and she strained to listen. The person stopped. Then the footsteps started down the center aisle.

The person was checking each aisle.

Lara crept around the end of the shelves and tiptoed toward the door. She heard the other footsteps stop—she raced for the door. It was open. She hit the light switches, throwing the archives into darkness, and slammed the door shut. She groped for the key to lock it and it flew out of her hand. In a panic she ran, making a mad dash for the stairs.

The elevator doors were open but she flew by them, fearful the elevator took a key to operate at night. She went through the door to the stairway and paused for a moment when she remembered. The ground-floor door was locked.

She raced up the steps, turning her flashlight on as she

went, praying that the upper floor would be unlocked. There'd be no reason for a lock on that level, she told herself. They had to keep people from getting off the second floor, not onto it.

Breaking onto the upper landing, she rushed at the door. It was locked.

She heard the elevator doors slam in the basement and frantically shoved the screwdriver between the door and the jamb, using both hands to force the blade against the bolt.

The elevator whined upward.

Frantic, she jammed the screwdriver at the lock and the door sprang open. She bolted through it and ran down a corridor with the same dim lighting the lower corridor had. She stopped and stared at the elevator floor indicator.

It was almost at the upper level.

She spun round in panic. Break a window and jump and she'd probably break her neck. It was only the second floor but it was probably equivalent to three stories of a building with average ceiling heights. She ran down the hall in mindless panic and dashed into a room to her left as she heard the elevator doors opening.

From the dim light of the hallway she could make out that the room was a recreation area with chairs and card tables. A door on the other side of the room had to lead to the upper patio she had seen from the street. The door was locked from the inside with a bolt. She slid it aside and pushed the door. It swung open quietly. She stepped out onto the patio, her feet crunching on the snow. As she started to shut the door, her feet slipped out from under her and she knocked the door shut causing it to slam with a bang.

Struggling to her feet she got a glimpse of someone in a white uniform entering the recreation room. She grabbed a folded wooden chair leaning against the wall and raised the chair overhead.

A cyclone of images swirled through her mind. The

apartment building landing. A stranger in white coming out of Vera's apartment. Her mother asking if something was wrong with Vera. The person turning, looking down at them. The eyes of the woman taking her up the steps in St. Basil's.

The door opened to her right and the person stepped onto the patio. Lara got a flash of the nurse's uniform and then the face.

The truck driver's wife, the nurse.

She screamed and struck out with the chair. The woman stepped back to avoid the blow and hit the wooden railing behind her. The railing gave way with a crash and the woman fell backward off of the building.

X V I

But why rake up all that past?

Why reopen the old wounds...

Why recall all that when it is still the same today?

—Aleksandr Solzhenitsyn,
The Gulag Archipelago (II)

ONE

===

This woman is a danger to Soviet—I mean Russian society." Orlov, the Ministry of Security's liaison to foreign embassies, paused to pour water into a glass from a plastic bottle on his desk. "The violations of Russian law and the harm to the citizens of Moscow have been nothing less than staggering."

Lara sat quietly with her hands folded together. On her right was Eric Caldwell of the American Embassy. Yuri was sitting to the left.

"It is only by the most fortunate circumstances that her latest victim escaped with significant, but nonfatal injuries."

Orlov turned his attention from Lara to a woman sitting behind and slightly to the left of Yuri. Lara could feel hate glowing where the woman sat with her neck in a brace, her head bandaged, her right leg in a cast, a pair of crutches propped against the chair. Mrs. Guk had not weathered her fall well.

"I resent the statement that I'm the aggressor and this woman is a victim," Lara said. Caldwell touched her arm with his hand but she ignored it. "The woman would have killed me if I hadn't fought back. She chased me up two floors."

Orlov took a drink of water to wash down what appeared to be a bad taste in his mouth. "The woman, the unfortunate Mrs. Guk"—nodding to Mrs. Guk—"was performing her duty as the sole night staff at the institute when she discovered that someone, *you*, had broken into the institute."

"She turned a vicious dog on me."

Yuri cleared his throat. "That dog may have gotten loose by itself. I must remind the deputy minister that the day the dog incident occurred, Lara Patrick had forced her way into the Guk residence and made accusations about Mr. Guk being involved in a cover-up of her mother's death over twenty years ago."

"Yes." The deputy minister washed down more bad taste.

"And that besides breaking into the institute to steal a file, Lara Patrick was found to be in possession of documents from the archives of the former KGB that are still considered state secrets. It appears she bribed an employee of the government to give her these documents in violation of Russian law." Yuri never looked in her direction as he spoke.

Lara scooted to the edge of her chair. Caldwell put his hand on her arm as a warning to stay quiet but she jerked her arm away. "The files confirm that there was a cover-up about my mother's death and my own investigations show there is a second death related to my mother's, a young woman who lived next door."

"This ministry is not involved in a cover-up of your mother's death or any other death. The files you refer to were not given to you because they are the property of the state," the deputy minister said. "The only cover-up, as you put it, was an attempt to save your mother's reputation by keeping her suicide out of the newspapers."

"My mother didn't commit suicide."

"That's what the records reflect, Ms. Patrick."

"Which records? The ones that say she died in an auto

accident? Or the ones that say she died of an overdose of potassium? Isn't it a bit coincidental that Mr. Belkin died of an overdose of potassium, administered by a nurse, and that my mother died of the same thing at a facility with nurses."

Lara turned and met Mrs. Guk's glare. "Maybe we should find out how long Mrs. Guk has worked at the institute." Mrs. Guk began growling. It was the only sound she could make with a wired jaw. "Over twenty years, I would say. And was she—"

"Mr. Minister," Yuri interrupted, "I checked Mrs. Guk's whereabouts on the night Mr. Belkin died. She was attending a Communist Party conference. She's still a member of that organization. There are several hundred witnesses because Mrs. Guk was receiving an award for loyalty."

"That's very convenient," Lara snapped, "and what about you, Detective Kirov? You always seem to show up at the right places at the right time. Where were you the night Mr. Belkin died?"

Yuri threw his hands up in exasperation. "So far she has accused everyone in the room of plotting against her, including the ministry and the American Embassy. May I remind the deputy minister that it has been reported that this young woman recently took off her clothes and fired a gun at a party."

"You—" Lara started out of her chair toward Yuri but Caldwell got a firm hold on her arm and pulled her back down.

Yuri refused to turn to meet her eye. He kept his face straight ahead, directed at the Ministry of Security official. "As a police officer, I abhor this woman's actions and yet"—he shrugged—"I am not without sympathy. In my opinion, she has become so psychologically wound up in her mother's death she has begun to see plots and conspiracies every place she looks. My recommendation is that the government cancel her visa so she can return to the United States immediately and obtain psychiatric help."

"I'm not the one who needs their head examined—"

"Ms. Patrick, please," the deputy minister said.

"I'm tired of being pushed around by this whole damn crazy system you people have. You're all afraid of bringing up the past because the whole country has a guilty conscience. I'm not afraid of bringing up the past. If I can't get satisfaction from the government, I'll take my story public."

The deputy minister smiled but his eyes were cold. "We are trying to resolve this situation with as little inconvenience to you as possible. However, if you would like us to proceed officially . . ."

"Shut up or they'll charge you," Caldwell whispered in her ear.

She pressed her lips together and clenched her hands.

The deputy minister sighed and took a deep swallow of water. "Ms. Patrick has one major factor in her favor. One of our most influential citizens has taken an interest in her, uh, welfare, and has vouched for her. I have agreed to release her to Mr. Bova's custody—"

"I'm not a child," Lara protested.

"As opposed to putting her on the next plane out of the country."

"I'll be glad to have Mr. Bova's guidance."

"Mr. Minister, as a police officer, it's my duty—"

"The matter has already been decided, Detective Kirov. There will be no more discussion. Mr. Caldwell, I suggest you leave first with your client."

"Wait," Lara said. "Please, you have to listen, you're my last hope. They say I'm crazy and paranoid, but I have a very important question. Mrs. Guk is here, but where's Mr. Guk? What Detective Kirov hasn't told you is that the last time I saw Mr. Guk he was hanging like a piece of meat over a vat of acid." She locked eyes with the deputy minister. "Show me Mr. Guk and I'll admit that I'm crazy."

The deputy minister turned to Yuri 'and raised his eyebrows. "Detective Kirov?"

Yuri sighed and slowly rose from his chair. As he turned toward the door, Lara's heartbeat doubled. As he reached for the doorknob, her pulse started pumping in her throat. He opened the door and stood aside as his partner, Stenka, propelled an older man with disheveled clothes and a hungover face through the door.

"This is Mr. Guk," Yuri said.

TWO

I was set up." Lara moved so fast down the ministry corridor that Caldwell had to almost run to keep up with her. "And Yuri—Detective Kirov did it. There was a body. I didn't imagine it." She stopped and spun round so quickly that Caldwell almost ran into her. "And putting me in someone's custody as if I were a child."

"Better than being in police custody."

"My own government has not been any help at all since I arrived in Moscow."

"I've explained on a number of occasions the delicate balance of political and social turmoil in the country."

"But what about human beings? The Russian government and my country's own embassy are so caught up with the world of politics and the fate of nations that they've forgotten about the fate of people. Horrible injustices were done to two women and God only knows who else. And you haven't done one thing to help."

"Perhaps, madam"—the diplomat stiffly tipped his hat to her—"some of us are less human than you. *And* less imaginative.'' He marched away, a soldier wounded in pride.

She followed Caldwell out of the front door and into a chilly Moscow afternoon, the wind catching her coming out of the door and nearly blowing her back inside. She wrapped her scarf around her face and put on gloves as she came down the steps. A horn honked off to her left as a black Mercedes limo pulled up to the curb.

Alexei stuck his head out of the window. ''Need a ride, cowgirl?''

She hurried down to the limo and got in, giving Alexei a hug after she shut the door. She took off her scarf and gloves and leaned back as the limo moved in traffic. She was worn out from dealing with idiots.

''Thanks for the help. They were trying to make up their minds as to whether I should be shipped to the airport or to Siberia. Either way it would have been in chains.''

''My assistance was not a major feat. Deputy Minister Orlov has been anxious to invest in a computer opportunity.''

She shook her head. ''That's how it works, isn't it? Money talks in politics.''

''Money talks everywhere. Almost everywhere. There are a surprising number of ethical people in Russia. Mostly people over the age of forty. Raised in an atmosphere of pure communism, many people get guilt complexes just talking about money. On the other side are the hungry tigers. Russia is up for the taking and it's the tigers with the largest appetites who will get the biggest mouthfuls.''

''Are you a hungry tiger?''

He smiled. ''There is an old Russian proverb, one that long outdates communism. It's said that if you distribute all the geese in Russia evenly, giving the same number to each person, the geese will soon return to their original masters.''

''I'm sorry, Alexei.'' She laughed softly and took his

hand in hers. "I'm so wrapped up in murder I can't make head or tail out of geese at the moment."

He leaned closer and kissed her cheek. "What I love about you is your honesty. Women around me usually pretend to be fascinated by my every word."

"Including Nadia?"

"Nadia is a bitch. She's fascinated by my money and how she can get it. I give her a little and dangle more and she in turn ensures that my public image on the country's most watched news program is not muddied."

"And what am I?"

"You are . . . you are a lovely gem that's been locked away in a jewelry box in a dusty old attic."

Embarrassed, she changed the subject. "Tell me about the geese, why do they return to their owners?"

"Some people gather material wealth, others don't. Those who don't think in terms of gathering geese will soon find their birds have flown to those who do."

"You gather lots of geese, don't you?"

"I gather toys. Making the money to get the toys is just a means to an end. And it's not difficult to do. You see, it's easy to win when you don't play by the rules."

"You don't play by the rules?"

"Of course not. There are no rules in Russia. Even if there were, I wouldn't play by them and neither do most of the rich emerging from this chaos. Look at your own country. The great fortunes were founded by men who violated all the rules. The railroads that opened and united the country were built on land swindled from the government and the bones of thousands of Chinese coolies who died hammering the spikes."

He squeezed her arm. "Imagine it, Lara, there's a whole country up for grabs, a country over twice the size of your own. Out of all this chaos some of the greatest fortunes the world has ever seen will be made over the next few years. Now, I can sit around and watch my geese being stolen or I can steal everyone else's."

She turned away from him and stared out of the window.

"What's the matter?" he asked. "You don't like my bluntness."

A question nagged at her. "Alexei, why are you helping me? If you're lusting for my body, I have two surprises for you. I'm not going to sleep with you and I probably wouldn't be worth the price, anyway."

"You're wonderful. It's a rarity to find a beautiful woman who doesn't know she's beautiful. And you're right, my motives are base. You're a wonderful centerpiece for my parties. The whole country is talking about your last performance." He grinned and shrugged. "I love the attention."

"At the party you told me Belkin——"

"Stop. No more questions. Relax your mind and your suspicions. This weekend you will step back in time and share with me the glories of a past age."

She suddenly realized that they were heading out of town. "Where are we going?"

"To my dacha."

"Your dacha? Why are we going there?"

"I'm having a party there tonight. It is the biggest dacha in all of Russia, a palace no less," he said, grinning. "Seventy years ago the Bolsheviks stole the palace by murdering the prince who owned it. Now, with the stroke of a pen, I have stolen it back. An example of capitalism at its best."

"Alexei, you have done some nice things for me, a stranger, and you haven't asked for anything in return. You are good-looking and dynamic and rich and generous and crazy. I think I could learn to love you. But I don't think I could ever really like you as a fellow human being. Even with all your charm, you're just too much of a bastard."

THREE

An hour out of the city the limo pulled up to a sleigh with two horses waiting by a stone wall.

"It's a troika," Lara said. "We're going to take a sleigh ride!"

"You can't arrive at a palace built in the days of Catherine the Great in a car. What's the use of owning a palace if you can't live like a king?"

She jumped out of the limo and went directly for the horses, giving them equal attention. "Are they cold?" she asked the troika driver. The driver wore a tall hat and old-fashioned greatcoat from a past age. The only thing that separated him from the pictures in history books of an eighteenth-century nobleman's troika driver were dark blotches on his face from a skin disease. Leopard's skin is what the kids at school cruelly called a young boy with the ailment when she was a teenager.

"They're Russian horses, madam, born with an icicle between their teeth."

"I just remembered I'm not a Russian horse." She started back for the limo when Alexei stepped out holding the sable cape. "Forget something?"

"I'm just going to borrow it," she said, letting him slip it over her shoulders.

They climbed aboard the troika and let the driver cover their laps with a huge bear blanket. Lara pulled it all the way up to her chin and snuggled close to Alexei.

She kissed him on the cheek. "You make me feel like a little kid."

"You're wonderful. Everyone around me—Felix, Nadia, my business associates—all of them try to make me act my age. They want me to throw away my toys. You're the only one who wants to play with me.''

The troika went through a wide gate in the stone wall and down a snow-covered road crowded by trees heavy with snow and glistening with icicles. Sleigh bells jingled as the horses stomped and blew vapor from their nostrils.

''I can understand your friends. They've already had their childhood. What happened in your life, Alexei? What caused you to skip being a kid?''

She felt his body tense next to hers.

''I don't mean to pry.''

''No, that's all right. You're the first person I've met that I would like to share it with. I was a sickly child, the type other kids didn't want to play with. Ugly, too.''

''You can't sell me on the ugliness,'' she said.

He looked away from her as he spoke. ''Plastic surgery can do amazing things. And I was a teenager during the renaissance of Soviet science and medicine.''

As the sleigh passed a small cottage on the right a family of four, two children and their parents, stepped onto the porch and waved. The entire family was dressed in peasant costumes and the man wore a great black beard.

Alexei waved back.

''Don't tell me,'' Lara said. ''Those are peasants, serfs, and they belong to the lord of the manor.''

He chuckled and snuggled down in the blanket like a naughty little boy. ''Of course. He used to be a gunnery officer on a battleship and she was employed in a factory that made washing machines that ripped clothes. Now they're both unemployed, but they have a nice little country dacha to live in and all they have to do is wave to the prince a couple of times a month.''

''Alexei, you are not just an arrogant bastard, you are a spoiled bastard.''

''Isn't it wonderful?''

They broke out of the forest and the palace was before them, a wide, gray-stone structure with a carved frieze along the roof and tall, narrow windows. Four pillars in front flanked a short set of stairs up to the huge doors. The palace extended to two tall stories, perhaps as high as fifty feet, and was about a hundred feet left and right from the front entrance before it dropped down to one story at each end. The end wings had ground-floor balconies enclosed by a bronze balustrade.

"It's beautiful. I expected something like a castle. This is more like a French chateau."

"There's a private lake in the rear. I would have it polished for ice skating for the party tonight, but there's a storm coming in and we don't expect the party to go late."

"Why don't you delay the party if there's a storm coming?"

"Because everything has been set—costumes, musicians, servants. Besides, I don't care if my guests have to drive home on icy roads in a blizzard. It's a small sacrifice to make to be near me."

As the troika pulled up at the palace two servants in livery came down the stairway with a set of wooden steps which they placed beside the carriage. They assisted Lara and Alexei as they stepped down from the sleigh.

She had a hard time keeping a straight face as they entered the palace and Alexei assumed royal airs. The great hall was as grand as the exterior. Huge crystal chandeliers hung like pregnant diamonds from the ceiling; gold leaf trimmed the railing to dual stairways that rose to the second floor and also covered much of the elaborately carved ceiling. Between the stairways was a fireplace large enough to burn small trees in. It looked like a forest was on fire inside it.

The great hall was warm and it couldn't have been from just the fireplace across the room. "There's modern heating, isn't there?"

"No expense was spared by the previous owners, the Union of Soviet Socialist Republics. Modern heating, modern plumbing. It was on the books as a museum, but the most powerful men in the Presidium often used the place to entertain. I didn't really steal this place from the people. I took it from what you call the fat cats.''

Ilya, the assistant she had met at the Western party, came down the stairway to greet them. Lara shook his left hand.

"Ms. Patrick's room is ready. I'm afraid Nadia is a bit perturbed. She's accustomed to having the room Ms. Patrick is occupying.''

"Alexei, I don't care which room I'm in.''

"I do. I deliberately had Nadia moved down the hall and placed you closer to my suite." He grinned. "Royal prerogative. Nadia has been exceptionally bitchy lately. And the price of her friendship has gone up. This is my way of telling her to get back in line.''

"All right, but if the woman scratches my eyes out, I'll sue you.''

"The Great American pastime. In this country you'd get an award of six rubles for two eyes. Ilya, show Lara her quarters. Then I want to go over the arrangements for tonight. Is Felix here?''

"He's in his office in the west wing.''

"Do you mind if I take a walk after I check into my room?'' Lara asked.

He gave her a kiss on the cheek. "I can have you carried on a sedan chair by slaves if you wish.''

"How sweet.''

The two words dropped from the top of the stairway. Nadia glared down at them. "I hope I'm not in the way.''

"Show Lara to her room,'' Alexei told Ilya. He beat a hasty retreat toward some inner domain of the palace while Ilya led Lara up the stairs.

Nadia had disappeared by the time Lara and Ilya reached the landing.

FOUR

Grounds covered by winter's mantle extended from the back of the palace to the lake. The lake was frozen. It's too bad there's a storm coming, she thought, it would be fun to ice skate. The idea brought a vague recollection of being with her mother and skating on a frozen pond in a park near their Moscow apartment.

Storm clouds were brewing, but there was hardly a breeze, and despite her abhorrence of even the threat of getting cold, walking alone in the forest provided needed peace and quiet to do some thinking.

The thought that Yuri had popped up everywhere stuck with her as she walked. Why would a policeman investigating a chain of deaths want a key witness to get out of Moscow? That morning after viewing Belkin's body, he should have taken possession of her passport so she couldn't leave, not argued with her because she didn't want to leave. None of it added up. Neither did her feelings for him. She should just write him off as a louse but the thought of him made her heart ache. *Damn, I've fallen in love with that bastard.*

She headed back for the palace. She had thought of the first bit of help she wanted from Alexei: a background check on Detective Yuri Kirov. Most importantly, what case had he been working on the night she saw him behind the carnival tents?

The business about Belkin working for Alexei also bothered her. She needed to know more about Belkin and his activities, but she'd have to tread carefully because Alexei didn't want his fantasy weekend disrupted with reality.

As she approached the west wing of the palace she saw Felix approaching from the opposite direction. He waved and said hello. "I was also taking a walk," he said as he fell into step beside her. "What do you think of Alexei's little toy?"

"The palace? Everyone should have one. Unfortunately, if it was mine, I'd be bankrupt just paying the heating bill for a month. How long is the government going to let him keep it?"

"That is the subject of a meeting we're having tomorrow with the ministry that considers the palace within its domain."

"They're coming out here?"

"No, we will go to them. Alexei won't allow them on the property. By the way, did I tell you that I might have published one of your father's poems?"

"Really? Do you still have it?"

"I'm not sure. The thought occurred to me a moment ago as I saw you walking. It's a possibility."

"I'd love to have a copy. I don't have any of my father's works."

"I'll take a look. I don't have the actual magazines with me, but I have an index of literature that I've published over the years. It's in the office I've set up here at the dacha. Why don't we take a minute and check it? If a poem's listed, I could get you a copy in a few days."

They went up a short stairway to the balcony of the west wing and through double doors to a small, cozy library.

"Oh, I love this room," she said.

It was a stately room, but intimate, with thick carpets, a roaring fire, old but comfortable furniture, and bookshelves soaring to impossible heights. Behind a desk hand carved from Siberian rosewood were tall windows giving a view of the front of the estate. The fireplace was in the wall opposite the desk, with a large mirror above, a clever arrangement that permitted a person to sit at the desk with window light behind while the lovely grounds reflected in the mirror above the fireplace.

"It's different from the other parts of the palace I've seen. It's more . . ."

"Me, more me," Felix said. "This room was the one real luxury I've demanded from Alexei for years of faithful service. I fell in love with it the moment I walked in. It was almost bare then, just a few pieces of antique furniture and some volumes about the life of Lenin. The poor shelves probably hadn't had their fill of books since they belonged to a prince."

He walked round the room, running his fingers along the bookshelves.

"You did a wonderful job." She almost asked who Alexei stole the books and furniture from, but caught herself.

"Let's see," he said, "my index is over here. While I'm searching for your father's poetry, why don't you take a look at that stack of pictures on my desk and give me your opinion about which ones should go into Alexei's book."

"I'll look forward to reading it when it's published."

"It's sort of a horror story in a way. There are similarities between Alexei and Tsar Peter that are startling."

"That's quite a compliment." She picked up the stack of photos and started looking at them.

Felix grinned at her. "I wasn't talking about Peter the Great, my dear, but Peter the Third, the eccentric madman who used the palace guards for toy soldiers until his wife and lover had him murdered." He chuckled at his own humor and she couldn't help but join him. She enjoyed his dry, cutting wit. Alexei must have a thick skin to keep Felix around, she thought.

The first picture was of Alexei receiving some sort of medal. He was in a military-looking uniform and an older man with a general's stars was pinning a medal on his chest. Alexei looked quite a bit younger in the picture and she mentally dated it about ten or twelve years back. The next picture was a banquet scene. Her eyes scanned dozens of other men at the table in the room, but none was familiar to her except the man who had been in the general's uniform earlier. He was in civilian clothes and so were Alexei and all the rest of the men in the room. She noticed words inscribed on curtains behind the tables:

COMMITTEE OF STATE SECURITY

A chill ran through her. "Committee of State Security" was the official name of the KGB.

She held the picture in one hand and picked up the next one. Her hand began to tremble as she stared at the picture. It was a party scene, people standing around talking and laughing, drinks in hand. Three people in the foreground leaped out at her—two women holding drinks and laughing and a man bent almost double with laughter, his drink spilling from the glass he held. The woman on the right was her mother. The woman on the left was Vera, their neighbor. The man between them was Alexei.

"Lara?"

She turned slowly. Alexei had entered the room and was standing near the door.

"I see Felix has put you to work."

Felix looked up from a book and adjusted his glasses, smiling at Alexei as he said, "I thought she might give me a hand with the photos for your autobiography. You know how concerned I've been about selecting just the right ones."

"Excellent. Did you find anything?" he asked Lara.

She put the pictures back on the stack. "No."

"I'm sorry, Lara," Felix said, "but I was wrong about having published your father. I don't see anything by him listed."

"That's okay," she managed.

"Your costume has arrived," Alexei said. "You have to go upstairs for a fitting in case any alterations are needed."

"Of course." She walked by him, keeping her face neutral. As she stepped outside the room, Nadia was coming down the hall. She gave Lara a dark look and as the two passed each other, the door to Felix's office slammed so hard it startled both women.

Lara keep walking, not acknowledging Nadia's presence.

Upstairs in her room she went to the window and stared out at the frozen lake and the snow-draped forest.

Miles from town and I'm a damn prisoner, she thought.

Her door opened and she turned as a maid with a club foot entered with a costume draped over her arm.

Anna smiled.

XVII

===

Strike me dead, the track has vanished,
Well, what now? We've lost the way,
Demons have bewitched our horses,
Led us in the wilds astray.

What a number! Whither drift they?
What's the mournful dirge they sing?
Do they hail a witch's marriage
Or a goblin's burying?

—Aleksandr Pushkin

ONE

═══

S he had a plan. It wasn't perfect and it would probably get her deeper into trouble, but at least it was a plan.

A white wig, black cheek mole, powdery facial makeup, bold blue eye shadow, and a billowing pearl-colored gown that gave her the frosting and figure of a wedding cake were a perfect disguise, making her look as ridiculous as the rest of the women in the room and un-recognizable as the woman who shot up Alexei's last party.

Making her way toward the front entrance, a glass of champagne that had barely touched her lips in one hand, a fan in the other, listening to small talk as she passed people, it struck her that everyone always seemed to talk about how Alexei spent money. No one mentioned feats of financial wizardry in making money. She had heard herself mentioned as "that crazy American woman" but no one had pointed a finger at her and shouted that it was her.

Her plan was to get through the crowd and out the front entrance without being seen by Alexei, Felix, or the horde of spies that she imagined must monitor her every move. Outside, she'd make a dash for Felix's office. Then, picture in hand, or at least tucked somewhere beneath the billowing dress, she'd return to the party. As Alexei had said, the party wasn't destined to last long, the storm was already blowing arctic air and snow was expected shortly. When that happened, she'd flow out the front doors with the guests and hitch a ride into town, hopefully with a charitable-looking couple in a warm limo.

Simple and neat, she told herself. All she needed to carry it off was a miracle. What she would do when she was back in Moscow she hadn't worked out yet. Damn Yuri. She needed him.

Near the vestibule leading to the front doors she paused to check out the enemy. She hadn't spoken to Alexei or Felix since the incident in the library. At the moment Felix was engaged in a discussion with several people near the center of the room. Alexei had disappeared down the west wing hallway a moment earlier with a harried Ilya on his heels, not on his way to Felix's office, she was sure, but to do battle in the kitchen. That was her interpretation after watching Alexei lashing out at servants and Ilya scurrying behind him patching wounds. Alexei is in a foul mood, she thought, his manner toward the servants much nastier than the Old West party where he had simply harangued them to move faster.

She slipped into the vestibule. Only one attendant stood near the great doors. She could hear voices in the cloakroom off to the left.

Smiling at the doorman, she said, "I left something in the car. Be back in a moment."

"It's very cold outside, madam. I'll get it for you."

"That's all right. I love a little fresh air." Liar. She was going to freeze her tush off.

She set her fan and champagne glass on a table next to the door and smiled bravely as he held the door for her. She stepped out into the night air casually, as if she were taking a walk along the beach.

Jesus, it's cold.

As soon as the big door closed behind her she lifted her

dress and ran for the west wing. It was almost impossible to keep the wedding cake dress from dragging on the ground and there was no way to see where she was putting her feet.

Her plan was based on the premise that the palace doors didn't get locked. Lara had heard Alexei tell Ilya that doors on the ground floor should be left open so the guests could wander around and admire the place. She assumed that meant all of the doors. If the doors leading to Felix's office from the balcony were locked, her poor arms would be frozen brittle and ready to break off by the time she made it back to the front entrance.

The night wind swept inside her tent-dress and nearly lifted her off her feet as she went up the half-dozen balcony steps. Her teeth were chattering as she made it to the doors.

The door handle slid down easily and she slipped inside and shut the door, leaning back against it, so damn cold her exposed skin felt bruised. The fireplace was brightly lit and she rushed over to it, glancing up at herself in the mirror above it. Her face looked paler than even the heavy white powder made it. The powder felt frozen against her skin.

Forcing herself away from the warmth to examine Felix's desk, she found the manuscript stacked on the desk, but the pictures were not in sight. Leafing quickly through the thick manuscript to see if the pictures had been tucked inside, a movement caught her eye and she looked up at the mirror above the fireplace. A face in the frosted window behind her was peering in.

Lara spun round but the face had already disappeared.

She ran for the door leading into the west wing corridor, opened it, and flew through. At the other end of the corridor servants were busy with food tables lined up against the wall. A group of people with Felix at the head, engrossed in conversation, had started down the hallway. She opened a door to her right and darted through—and came face-to-face with a woman.

Nadia.

The Moscow Evening News anchorwoman grabbed her arm and jerked her out into the cold night. She slammed the door behind Lara and the two women stood facing each other, the bitter night air brushing their clothes and clawing at their skin.

"You're spying on me," Lara said.

"And you're spying on Felix."

"What do you want?"

"The same thing you do. Felix has something on Alexei. I heard them arguing about you and a picture after you came out of Felix's office today. What's so important about the picture?"

"Why do you want to know?"

"Don't be a fool. Alexei has money, more money than you can imagine. And it belongs to all of us."

"And you want a share."

"Just as you do." Nadia glared at her.

Lights went on in Felix's office and through a window to her right Lara saw Felix and the people from the corridor enter the office.

"I've got to get inside," she told Nadia. Her teeth had started chattering again. If she stood outside any longer, she'd be frozen in place.

Nadia spoke in an urgent tone as they hurried back toward the front door. "Alexei has plenty of wealth for all of us."

"I don't want his money," Lara said.

Nadia scoffed. "You and Felix, Felix the old-time Communist, but you've seen how he decorated his office and library. The bastard pretends he doesn't care about money, but I know he has some sort of control over Alexei. Alexei hates him, but he keeps him around. And sometimes Felix acts like he's in charge. I've seen Alexei back down to him. Oh, they do it very subtly, but I can tell when Alexei eats shit.''

Lara wanted to tell her she didn't give a damn about her greed and her plots, but it struck her that she might be able to use Nadia. The woman obviously had an inside track to whatever was going on.

Unable to stand the cold any longer, fifty feet from the front doors Lara broke into a run but stopped as Nadia grabbed her arm.

''Listen to me. We have to get our hands on that book. They're all going back into town tomorrow and returning tomorrow night. They have a big meeting at one of the ministries. I know the routine. Felix will take the book with him in that black attaché case he carries. He never goes anywhere without it. He'll lock it in his office. It's at the top of the penthouse, next to Alexei's office and the spa. I'll meet you at the back street-level entrance tomorrow at noon.''

''At the tower?''

''Yes, but you have to get the key to the elevator and the back doors.''

''Me? Why me?'' Lara's teeth were chattering so badly the words came out in chips. A light snow was falling.

Nadia grinned with malice. ''Alexei keeps a complete set of keys for everything he owns in a cabinet in his dressing-room closet. I got my hands on a set by bribing a servant, but I don't have them anymore. You can get a set tonight after he fucks you.''

''After he what?''

''Don't act innocent with me. I'm not the one with the sable cape. Hell, I've never even been in his bedroom.''

Lara turned and ran to the front doors. Blood rushed to her head and she felt faint as she hurried into the warm interior. She moved quickly past people to cross the room and get to the roaring fireplace. Standing close to the fire, she roasted each side of her body. It felt heavenly.

People were already starting to leave. She realized she

was going to have to make her move to get a ride into town, but she held her ground, staring into the fire. Nadia's proposition was tempting. All except the part about sleeping with Alexei.

Nadia was suddenly at her side holding two cups. "This will warm you inside," she told her, holding out a cup.

"I don't want anything to drink."

"There's no booze in it. I promise."

Lara took a sip of the drink and eyed the crowd moving toward the front doors. Alexei was there, saying good-bye to guests. If she was going to leave, she'd have to exit by one of the other doors and approach people outside where the cars were.

"I think I misjudged you," Nadia said.

The drink tasted good, hot and sweet. "What do you mean?"

"I saw the expression on your face when I mentioned fucking Alexei." Nadia had stepped closer and her voice was lower, huskier. "You don't understand what I've had to go through. I'm being pressured."

Lara didn't have the faintest idea what the woman was driving at. The room had started glowing brighter and then dimmer, brighter and dimmer. People and furniture got bigger, then smaller. Everything was cockeyed.

She wanted to ask Nadia what was in the drink but her lips felt much too thick to open and close properly and the words came out as baby talk.

Nadia laughed hysterically.

TWO

Nadia held on to Lara's arm tightly and helped her down the stairs to the sub-level of the palace. "You need to clear your head and sweat out some of the cold you've been exposed to," Nadia told her. "A sauna will do both."

Lara nearly fell when her foot struck the floor at the bottom of the steps and Nadia struggled to hold her up. "You sure don't have much tolerance," she said. "I just wanted to make you feel good."

A maid who had fallen asleep on a bench near the sauna woke up at the sound of the two women approaching and came forward to help.

"Is the sauna ready?" Nadia asked.

"Yes, madam."

"Help me get her clothes off," she told the maid, "in the sauna where it won't be cold."

Between the two of them they started stripping Lara of her costume. Lara tried to tell them to stop and to push them away, but her mind was swimming around her head and her hands and feet felt twice their normal size.

When Lara was naked on a sauna bench, Nadia sent the maid away and undressed. Sitting behind Lara on the bench, she pulled Lara up against her. She whispered in Lara's ear as her hands traveled up Lara's abdomen and cupped her breasts. "Ever do it with a woman? I like it both ways." She kissed Lara's neck and tickled her ear with her tongue. "Sometimes at the same time. I like to fuck a woman's cunt with my mouth while a man's pumping me doggy style," she whispered. "You ever had it at the same time?"

The door to the sauna opened and Nadia turned to tell the maid to go away.

It was Alexei, not the maid.

THREE

Lara lay awake staring up at an ornate ceiling and tried to place herself in the universe. She moved her toes and they operated. She tried her hands and arms next. It slowly came to her who she was and that her head had been stepped on by a tyrannosaurus.

She shot up in the bed, her head spinning from the sudden movement.

Where the hell am I?

It was a big room, grand, more than twice the size of the room assigned to her in the palace.

Alexei's room.

She was naked. Not a stitch of clothing on.

"Oh, no."

She crawled out of the blankets and sat on the edge of the bed, her mind taking a swim in a whirlpool for a moment before she rescued it. What happened last night? She remembered going to Felix's office. Freezing outside while Nadia talked of blackmail. Something in her drink. The sauna. She felt her bare breasts and blushed. That bitch. She drugged me. And then there was . . . Alexei.

She jumped off the bed and looked at it. Were the three of us romping on it last night?

A white terry-cloth robe was draped across a chair near the bed. The robe had a note attached to it:

DARLING, LAST NIGHT WAS THE MOST INCREDIBLE EXPERIENCE I'VE EVER HAD WITH A WOMAN. MAKING LOVE TO YOU WAS A JOURNEY TO NIRVANA.

She collapsed back down on the bed and put her head in her hands. Please God, stop the world and let me off.

Everything was wrong. Alexei. The note. The situation. *Think*, she hit her forehead with her palm, *think*. But the consequences of the note were too horrendous and puzzling for her to analyze at that moment.

They were probably all gone, back to the city. Nadia said they would be leaving. Some big meeting at a ministry. Nadia wanted to meet her at the penthouse at twelve o'clock. The ornate clock on the fireplace mantel said it was a little past ten. The palace was an hour from the city.

She could get dressed and be at the tower by twelve. If she wanted to.

Not that she had a choice. It was the tower or the airport. And she wasn't running away. She was going to get the picture and storm the American Embassy. If Caldwell looked at her cross-eyed, she would go to every foreign news bureau in Moscow and tell them about her mother, the neighbor woman, Alexei and Felix, Yuri and his penchant for hanging around places where people died, Belkin, the man at the acid bath, and, hell, being drugged and molested.

Either she'd make headlines or they'd commit her.

She put on the robe and started for the hallway to sneak down to her own room when she remembered Nadia's comment about keys. The bathroom to the suite was bigger than her room at the Gorky. Leading off from it was an even larger dressing room. She found a square metal box on the wall in the dressing room. It didn't surprise her that it wasn't locked. Hanging inside the box were a couple dozen keys, each with a little white tag that identified their purpose. Choosing a set of three marked TOWER, she slipped them into her robe.

She understood why Nadia would have had a hard time getting to the keys if she hadn't been invited to Alexei's bed—the only way in or out was back through the bedroom. But it struck her that Nadia must have had opportunities to get the keys before she fell out of favor with Alexei. She could have just snuck down from her room when no one was looking.

She opened the bedroom door and checked the corridor. It was clear. She went out and headed for her bedroom, slipping quickly inside, checking the hallway again to see if she had been seen. She quietly closed the door and turned as her bathroom door opened and Anna limped out. Lara heard running water coming from the bathroom.

"I'm running your bath, madam."

Lara forced a smile. "Still here, I see."

"Yes, madam. Everyone has gone but the servants. After the cleanup, some will return to the tower, others will stay here. I will go wherever you go."

No, you won't. "Order me a car, Anna. Now."

FOUR

Yuri parked his militia car on a side street two blocks from the Black Tower and slowly walked toward the tall building.

His leg ached from the treatment it got in Zemo's Dacha and the pain was the only strong emotion in him. He knew that what he was going to do was dangerous, that if he got caught at the very least it would destroy him—even a trip back to the sewer—but he had lived with fear for so long it had burned a hole in him and let out most of his feelings. When he discovered years ago that fear no longer inflamed him, it had bothered him like other men might be bothered by being impotent. He had lost so much—love, family, security—the loss of fear, a prime emotion, was a final blow.

Passing the front of the building, he pretended not to be checking out the guards in the lobby. The only thing he wanted to confirm was that it was the same two guards on duty and that nothing about their lazy, bored body language had changed. Something in their body language, a little tension, would have tipped him off that they had been warned that someone was going to break into the penthouse.

He walked around the block and came up to the building from the rear. As he approached the private entrance he took out the set of keys he got from Nadia.

Fighting back the impulse to look around to see if anyone was watching, he casually stepped into the alcove and unlocked an unmarked steel door.

He knew the door was alarmed, but most alarm makers assumed that if a person had a key to enter, they had a right to enter, and designed alarm systems to activate only by forced entry. A product of the brute force mentality that dominated Russian thinking.

As a cop he knew the alarm makers were not far off in their thinking—Russian burglars had no finesse and were much more likely to kick in a door than pick a lock.

Two options led up to the penthouse—a private elevator or a thousand or so steps. The guards at the public entrance might have indicator lights for the elevator, he thought. And he could be trapped in an elevator easier than a stairwell.

The worse part was that he wouldn't be able to have a cigarette to propel him up the steps because of the odor it would leave in the stairwell.

He came out of the stairway at the penthouse level and selected a likely looking key from the set to test on the rear entrance. Before turning the key he felt the reassuring bulge of the gun in his shoulder holster. Bova's men had not returned the gun they took and like all good Moscow cops, he had gone out on the street and bought a black-market replacement.

Nadia told him that Bova was too paranoid to even allow domestic staff into his residences unless he was there, preferring to have them follow him around from house to house like a king's retinue. Bova was due into the city later in the day and the penthouse would be buzzing with people. But if she was wrong—or was setting him up . . . people like Nadia who had had information squeezed from them were not the most reliable sources. He still had her in a state of terror but at some point she would turn to Bova or someone else who had the brutal resources to get rid of a pest.

Yuri cursed a little to himself as he turned the key in the lock, not knowing what or who was on the other side.

He went across the first level where Bova entertained his guests and up the stairway, following the instructions Nadia gave him. Down the corridor he'd find Bova's office, if you run into the spa you've gone too far, she told him.

A key on the ring would fit the office door.

Yuri stepped into the office and looked around. Floor-to-ceiling windows flooded the room with light.

The filing cabinets, he thought.

They were on the far wall.

He was tempted to go through the drawers, but he knew it was a waste of time. The things Bova had to hide wouldn't be found in unlocked drawers.

Kneeling by one of the cabinets, he opened the bottom drawer half an inch, just enough to give it an ajar look. Taking a glove out of his pocket, he dropped it next to the cabinet.

Having accomplished what he came for—to leave Lara's glove where Bova would find it and conclude that Lara had been spying on him—he left the penthouse the way he had come in.

FIVE

The storm had passed and left several inches of fresh snow. Gray clouds and a sharp north wind put a dull edge on the day and kept the new snow from looking fresh and white.

As she sat in the back of a Mercedes limo and whizzed past lesser mortals and their lesser cars, she rather regretted that Alexei had turned out to be a louse. It would have been nice to have a rich and famous friend—even though she had discovered that friendship in Moscow had about the same enduring quality as a game of Russian roulette, in more ways than one.

People had died around her but she was still alive. There had been plenty of opportunities for someone to kill her after the attempt failed at the cathedral. If nothing else, she had wandered around the city in the dead of night. She certainly wasn't being protected.

If she wasn't being protected, she was being used. The thought struck her and it rang true. It was as simple as that, she thought. She felt the keys in her side pocket. Why have a metal safe for keys and not lock it? No, no, don't get paranoid, she told herself. People aren't used to locking up everything in this country.

Alexei was ex-KGB. No surprise there, so was half the rest of the country. But he hid it while others, like Belkin, rather flaunted it. Why did Alexei hide his past? And what did he have to do with her mother? Could he have been the one that gave orders to . . .

To do what?

She would keep the appointment to raid Alexei's office at the penthouse. Nadia was a world-class bitch but stupidity wasn't one of her faults. Like Alexei, she knew how to steal geese. Whatever was in the manuscript of Alexei's autobiography, it was probably her last hope of getting information about her mother's death.

The thought of breaking into Alexei's penthouse spooked her even more than the psychiatric institute had. This time she felt a foreboding, as if she was taking steps laid out for her by someone else and that very soon there'd be nothing under her foot.

SIX

The limo let her off in front of her hotel. Casually walking through the lobby to the restaurant, she smiled at the maître d' and said she had forgotten something, turned round, and exited the lobby. The limo was gone. She climbed into a taxi and gave the driver directions that she thought would get her within a couple of blocks of the tower.

The taxi dropped her two blocks from the rear of the tower and she walked slowly toward it, trying not to think about the fact that she was once again in the business of breaking and entering. Actually, she was Alexei's live-in guest. There was nothing wrong with grabbing the keys to the penthouse so she could be waiting for him when he returned from his meeting. *Yeah, sure, how many times did I hear a story like that when I was prosecuting a thief?*

She had a view of the back of the building for more than a block and Nadia was not in sight. When she got to the rear door it was almost exactly twelve. Trying to look inconspicuous, she moseyed down the street a little, turned, and walked back.

Why should I wait for Nadia? The woman's a blackmailer. I'm not trying to hurt anyone, I just want that picture. And a peek at the rest of Alexei's autobiography. Without wrestling Nadia for it.

On impulse, she turned and stepped into the little alcove leading to a tall set of steel doors. She fumbled nervously with the keys before finding one that made the lock turn. In seconds, the door was closed behind her and she was in the corridor leading to Alexei's private elevator. Quiet as a crypt.

She made her way to the elevator. She pressed the button to the right of the doors. Nothing happened. She fumbled with the keys again and found a small, round cylindrical one that looked as if it should fit an elevator or alarm system. She put the key in, turned it, and the elevator doors slid open.

Scared but determined, she stepped into the elevator and faced the control panel. There were only two choices: UP and DOWN. She hit the UP and the door slid shut. The elevator gave a little lurch before it started ascending smoothly. She examined her key collection, feeling very claustrophobic in an elevator that had about fifty unoccupied floors between the two levels it served.

The night she had shot up the place Alexei had taken her from the ballroom to a corridor where the kitchen facilities were located and out a back door to the elevator. The third key on the tower ring had to be to the rear door of the penthouse.

The elevator slowed and came to a stop along with her breathing. The doors swung open. The alcove was deserted. Breathing again, she stepped out.

She went quickly to the door across from the elevators. Her nerves were going to hell and her hand was shaking as she got the key into the lock, twisted it, and opened the door. Stepping in, she quietly closed the door behind her.

The interior corridor was dark. To her left, open doors let in light from windows in the adjoining rooms. No lights on was a good sign. If people were here, they'd have the lights on. She went down the corridor unconvinced that there weren't killers hidden in every nook and cranny. Opening a door cautiously, she peered into the grand ballroom. Other than a little light coming from partially opened drapes, the place was cast in darkness and shadow.

She crept in and slowly closed the door, carefully releasing the door handle so that it didn't make a sound. Moving quickly across the ballroom, she went up the stairs leading to the second-floor landing. A couple of steps from the top she heard a noise and froze in place. She listened, trying to place it. A door shutting? She wasn't sure.

Probably nothing more than the central heating blowers kicking on, she told herself. Nothing to fear but fear itself. At the moment she couldn't remember who had said that. Fighting her instincts to turn and run, she crossed the landing to the gloomy corridor beyond.

The door at the end of the corridor was closed and didn't have a lock. She opened it and looked up at the stairway. A noise was coming from somewhere on top, the faint hum of a machine. The central air machinery, she hoped. She was at the bottom of a dark well, but there was faint light at the top of the stairs. She carefully closed the door behind her and looked up at the gray light. Her mouth was dry and her nerves on fire.

One step at a time, she told herself.

At the top of the steps she paused and looked down the dark hallway. The door to the spa was partially open and she realized the humming noise was the spa pump. Was it on its auto filtering cycle? she wondered. If someone was in the spa, they hadn't bothered to turn on any of the lights along the way. The corridor was dark and narrow. There had to be a light switch at both ends. The short stairway to the offices was immediately to the left of the spa door. Interior windows to the offices were above and no lights shone through them.

She had come too far to let what might be nothing more than machinery running cause her to turn back.

Why me, Lord? Why couldn't I have stayed home, safe with my cat and my condo?

The hum got louder as she went down the dark corridor, her eyes glued on daylight coming through the narrow opening of the door to the spa. Just the spa going through its filtering cycle, she told herself, no one would be in the spa this early.

A few feet from the door her foot kicked something. A

metallic object on the floor. She bent down to get a closer look.

A gun. A big six-shooter, like the ones from Alexei's party. A noise came from the stairwell area behind her. Picking up the gun, she held it in both hands, her heart bouncing in her throat. She listened but the noise didn't come again.

Swallowing hard, she pushed open the door to the spa, her eyes adjusting to the daylight. She stared at the spa, her mind rejecting what her eyes saw. Blood-red water bubbled and foamed in the spa. Floating facedown was a naked woman, her blond hair spread out. It had to be Nadia. She turned and ran back down the corridor, holding the gun with both hands.

Stumbling going down the dark stairwell, she reached the bottom and jerked open the door with one hand, the heavy gun in the other. When she was sure no one was waiting to jump her, she started running again, holding the gun with both hands.

Racing across the balcony, she was near the stairway down to the grand ballroom when the double doors of the ballroom burst open. She caught a flash of Yuri at the head of a group of men and guns being raised in her direction; she threw herself down, the gun flying out of her hand as gunfire exploded in the room.

A few seconds later Yuri was beside her as the other men streamed by. Stenka picked up the gun she had dropped.

"Are you all right?" Yuri asked.

She got onto her feet, her ears ringing.

"What are you doing here?" he asked.

"There's a body in the spa, on the roof. I think it's Nadia." She couldn't remember the woman's last name and she stammered, "The newswoman."

"This gun's been fired," Stenka said, holding the six-shooter with a pen stuck in the barrel.

"It's not my gun," Lara said. "I found it upstairs."

Yuri's features were stone. She suddenly realized she was surrounded by men, all staring at her.

"I didn't kill anybody. Look, I just got here. I went upstairs, saw the body, and ran."

A man shouldered one of the other officers aside. He had gray hair, an air of authority, and was dressed in a more expensive suit than the others. "We saw you running with a gun in your hand," he said.

"I know Miss Patrick," Yuri started.

"I'm handling this, Detective Kirov. You and Stenka go upstairs and make a search of the roof. Give me the gun."

Stenka grabbed Yuri's arm and pulled him away as Lara faced the man, not flinching under his hard look.

Her pulse was beating in her throat; she was hot and sick with fear.

"How did you get in here?" he asked.

"With keys."

"The elevator people say no one came up."

"I . . . I came in the back way."

"We received an anonymous call a short time ago. The caller said a woman with a gun had entered the building and a shot had been heard."

"I didn't shoot her."

"How did you know who was in the spa?"

"It was just a guess. I saw her and I thought—"

"You saw her and you shot her."

"I never shot her!"

"You came in the back way, you say."

"Yes."

"Did anyone pass you as you came in?"

"Pass me? No, no, I didn't see anyone."

"We saw no one either and we came in the front way. No one except you running with a gun in your hand." He smelled the barrel and checked the chamber. "A recently fired gun. Two bullets missing. It would be my guess that we're going to find the two bullets from this gun in the dead woman."

"You have to believe me, I never did anything. My foot kicked the gun. I picked it up, saw her in the spa, panicked, and ran. I didn't kill her."

The man held the gun up in front of her. "Have you ever seen this gun prior to today?"

"I don't know."

"You don't know?"

"There was a party. The gun looks like the six-shooters people had at the party."

"You had such a gun?"

"Yes." She stared at the gun in his hand as if it were a poisonous snake. She'd had two of the guns. One she had left in the limo. The other she had thrown at Yuri when he was leaving her hotel room.

Her mind was in such a fog she didn't catch the man's next words to her. "What did you say?"

"I said you are under arrest for the murder of Nadia Kolchak."

XVIII

To whom shall I tell my sorrow?

—From an old Russian spiritual

ONE

Nina Kerensky looked at the wall behind the woman waiting for her on the concrete bench in the courthouse corridor as she sat on the opposite side of the bench from the woman. The walls were once white but had aged ungracefully to the color of nicotine on an old man's fingers. Someone, probably a defendant waiting to be sentenced, had scribbled "Russian justice is Russian roulette" on the wall. It rather summed up her own feelings about the justice system that morning. Part of it was being at a district court that was one step below sewer workers.

The court was not a court "house" but a corridor of justice, one long hallway with four doors on each side and a courtroom behind each door, a concrete bench against the wall between the doors. The whole assembly, eight doors, eight courtrooms, six benches, and one hallway formed half the first floor of a six-story building harboring a sanitation workers union.

What bothered her was not so much that the system that administered justice was located beneath the system that administered sewers, but that some sewers were probably kept cleaner than the courthouse hallway. Coffee stains and cigarette butts littered the floors, adding to the train station ambience created by the dirty walls and graffiti. If justice couldn't clean up its own act, how could it hope defendants could clean up theirs?

More than the crusty hallway, it was her own feelings about the justice system and herself that put her into a philosophic mood that morning. She was different than most attorneys in Moscow, different than most people in Moscow, even different than most people in Russia. In a city where blondes were as common as vodka bottles, Nina had black hair. And black skin. She was Russian, but there was no question that she also had an African heritage. Her father had been African, her mother a light-skinned Russian, but the physical appearance traits Nina had gotten from the genetic lottery came from her father.

Of medium height for a woman, five-four, she had warm brown eyes and ebony skin that glowed. Her hair was long and straight, raven black. Her cheeks were arched, her nose slender, and her lips full, the lower lip pouting, the kind of lip women see on the faces of magazine cover girls and wish they, too, had the price of collagen.

Her skin, her eyes, her features, hinted at the exotic in pale Moscow, speaking of a natural beauty and grace that had its roots far beyond the Urals to the shores of Lake Tanganyika. But she didn't think of herself as a beauty, certainly didn't think of herself as exotic or anything other than simply Russian, and most people would pass over the natural beauty and see instead the big thick eyeglasses and studious countenance of a woman who took life seriously.

"Good morning, Dasya," she said to the woman on the bench. "Today you will be sentenced. Five arrests for prostitution in the past three years alone. The judge is going to make you do time, probably a year."

"I have to eat. I work to feed my babies."

Nina looked at the investigator's report. The woman was in her late forties and her children had been taken away from her twenty years ago at the same time she had been subjected to an involuntary hysterectomy by a judge who didn't want the woman to produce any more children that she could not care for. Removing the woman's reproductive organs for being a drug addict and prostitute was cruel justice, she thought, from some idiot judge who thought you could remove criminal tendencies with a surgical knife.

Nina glanced up at the woman when she saw her age. Making it to middle age on a diet of prostitution and drugs was a testimony to something about the woman . . . but times change. With AIDS the average life span of prostitutes and drug addicts was a statistic with a downward spiral. Nina had carefully seated herself at the opposite end of the bench and had not offered to shake hands with the woman. While Dasya's arms and legs were covered by heavy winter clothing, Nina knew the woman's life story was written in needle marks. She could see marks on the back of the woman's hands. Drug addicts usually go to the veins in the back of the hands last because the veins are smaller and the tracks more visible. That meant the woman probably had open sores on her arms and legs, ulcers from too many dirty needles.

"Keep away from the drug addicts," her law school professor had told her when she had announced in her final year of school that she wanted to specialize in criminal law. "Don't touch them, don't shake hands with them." AIDS phobia but good advice.

"I will speak to the judge. Fortunately Moscow jails are becoming overcrowded and there's been talk of releasing prisoners before their full term."

"The judge will give me the full term. I knew that when he said you were going to be my attorney."

Nina shuffled her notebook in her lap and pretended not to have heard what the woman said.

"I will need to know more of your background in order to present the judge with mitigating circumstances. How did you first become addicted to drugs?"

The woman stared down the corridor with a faraway look in her eyes as if she were seeing her past being reenacted by people at the other end of the corridor.

"I knew your mother."

I knew your mother. The words were hot and ugly, words Nina knew she would hear someday in a courthouse hallway. Keeping her head down, she kept her shaking hand moving her pencil across the page. Intending to write the word "mitigation," she wrote "mother" instead.

"I will tell—"

"We worked on the same street, for the same pimp. It was a long time ago. I was pretty then." She brushed hair off of her forehead. "I could make as much in one night as I make in a week today. I don't have the regulars anymore. Men still stop for me but who can blame them for not coming back now that my breasts hang down to my belly."

"I will tell the judge"—Nina scratched out the word "mother" and wrote in "mitigation"—"that you were exploited by criminals as a young woman, a victim of the prior system's failure to protect citizens from being exploited by criminals."

"Karlov, that was his name. We worked for Karlov. He had six, maybe seven girls. It was a lot for those days."

"You were young and innocent when you were victimized," Nina wrote as she spoke. "Instead of officials of the State helping you—"

"Word was on the street that your mother had given birth to a monkey."

Stop it! Don't do this to me, you crazy bitch.

"That's what Karlov said, that your mother had been a factory girl and had given birth to a little black monkey. That's how she ended up working the streets. They threw her out of the factory because she laid on her back for one of those students they brought in from Africa."

Nina's eyes watered and her notes on the paper went out of focus, but she kept writing, her voice firm and professional. "When you became addicted, rather than receiving treatment for a medical problem, the government categorized you as a criminal."

"They found the student on the railroad tracks. I remember that. They said he got drunk and passed out with a train coming but Karlov said the girl's father and brothers beat him to death." The woman suddenly looked to Nina. "I knew I would get the maximum when they appointed you as my attorney. I am a worthless piece of shit. Can I go to Kalinin prison? I hear the food is good there and they don't work you very much."

After Dasya was sentenced to a year at Kalinin, Nina asked the court clerk if she could speak privately with the judge after the session was over. She waited in the courtroom as the judge continued to handle cases.

Judge Popov was quick, pushing one case through after another, almost all of them a quick plea to guilty. It was universally understood that Popov did not tolerate any meritless defenses in his courtroom—if you were guilty, or it sounded to him like you should be guilty, you pled guilty at an early stage of the proceeding or took the risk of a stiffer sentence after he went through the motions of justice. Next to Popov, one on each side, were the temporary judges called "assessors," citizens chosen to sit as judges for a couple of weeks a year.

In theory the assessors held the same power as the judge, but many judges treated the assessors as if they were there only to underwrite the judge's decisions. Popov was known as one of the worst offenders, making snap decisions without consulting with the two assessors, already on to the next case even if an assessor was trying to get out a question about the last case.

As Nina watched him administering justice with a firm but intimidating hand, she thought about an article she had read comparing the Russian system of three judges with the jury system used in most of the English-speaking countries. The Russian criminal code was based upon the old

Roman law and French Napoleonic Code even though the first taste of French justice the Russians experienced was Napoleon's invasion. Of course, under the Russian version, two of the three judges were citizen-assessors. Very democratic. If you steal a bottle of milk from your neighbor, you might see your trash man or the woman behind the bakery counter as one of the judges deciding your case.

She did not know how the jury system actually worked, didn't know if having twelve citizens chosen at random cured the abuses of judges like Popov or if the jury system added more abuses of its own.

She had been appointed to another case that morning, another drugged-out prostitute, and as she sat in the courtroom waiting to talk to the judge she hand-copied the arrest and criminal history information about the woman from the court file. A photocopy machine was located in the labor union's offices but they charged for using it. Nina was paid so little on the petty cases she was appointed to handle that she could not afford the luxury of paying the union for copies.

In some of the larger courthouses the courts had photocopy machines and court-appointed attorneys could use them, but traditionally defense attorneys had hand-copied entire files, even in major murder cases. Hand-copying was one way the Soviet system had reflected its lack of respect for defense lawyers. The new system was more talk than action.

It was almost time for the midday break when Popov had hustled through the last case on the morning calendar, well pleased with himself that all but two defendants had pled guilty at the arraignment process—one was a case of rape and battery that would be sent to the next higher court, the City Court; the other, a man who beat his wife and refused to plead guilty because he claimed she started it and beat him worse, would remain in the People's Court and be tried at another time.

"Will the judge see me now?" Nina asked the clerk after the judge left the bench and the courtroom was clearing.

"Come back a few minutes before the afternoon session. He will see you then."

That meant she would be late for the afternoon calendar at another courthouse. She could almost make it if she took a taxi, but a lawyer who couldn't afford photocopies couldn't afford a taxi. But she also couldn't afford to be late and take the ire of the judge who wanted to appoint her to the cases no one else wanted, so she would use a week's subway fare to take one short taxi ride.

As she left the courtroom, the other prostitute she had been appointed that morning to represent was waiting for her in the corridor. The woman was a younger, thinner version of Dasya, little more than a girl, maybe in her late teens or early twenties, younger than herself. Coatless and shaking in the courthouse hallway, her dress was short-sleeved, revealing that her right arm was infected and swollen. A dirty needle.

"If I am to come to your office to discuss my case, I will need your address, attorney."

Nina shook her head. "Just meet me here in front of the courtroom an hour before your next court appearance and we will discuss your case. By that time I will have analyzed your defenses and prepared to plead the mitigating circumstances to the court." It was her boilerplate reply to the whores and druggies. There was no use coming to her office because the only office she had was a mail drop at another attorney's office. The attorney permitted her to use his office after hours at a fair price but there was little need and less money for it. She knew the woman's story and could have mimicked to her the damnation and sentence the judge would pass.

"Where is your coat?" Nina asked.

"They took me out of the bathroom in a bar. My coat was on my chair."

Probably arrested in the men's room, Nina thought. "It's freezing outside. Do you have money for the subway?"

The woman shook her head. Almost groaning aloud, Nina dug money out of her purse. "Take a taxi," she told the woman. "You'll freeze to death getting to the subway."

Nina cursed herself for wasting the money as she went down the stairs to the labor union's cafeteria in the basement. The woman wouldn't use the money for a taxi. She'd get frostbite to make it to the creep that supplied her with drugs.

Inside the cafeteria she paid for a tea bag and a cup of hot water and selected a small table in a corner of the room. From her briefcase she took out her lunch, a cheese sandwich and an apple.

As she ate she pretended to be studying the reports she had copied earlier in the courtroom but she was not really concentrating on the papers but sneaking glances at a long table across the room where judges and attorneys had gathered at their regular table. She could have joined them at the table. None of them would have given any indication that she was not welcome, but it was her own feelings that kept her apart. Deep down, she didn't believe that they respected her and that if she joined them at the table the welcome would be one generated by politeness. She didn't feel qualified to join and believed that if she could get better cases and build up a reputation as a fine attorney, she would earn a seat at the table.

Over sixty, with dark, short hair, Judge Popov had eyebrows so big and bushy they could hide thoughts. His face was narrow, pinched into a thin nose, sunken cheeks, and pointed jaw. Unusual for a skinny man, he had a loose piece of skin hanging under his chin, creating the impression that his face was slipping down. His lips were thin and purple, his teeth an unhealthy-looking yellow. On his desk an ashtray overflowed with cigarette butts, which explained the heavy odor of stale cigarette smoke in the room. Another overflowing ashtray sat on the top of his judge's bench in the courtroom along with his coffee mug. Besides his cavalier attitude toward the citizen judges and defendants, and smoking while administering justice, Popov was known for being abrupt to attorneys, cutting them off in midsentence and making a snap decision before he heard all of the evidence.

"Thank you for seeing me," Nina said.

"I am sure you will not waste my time." He glanced at his watch. "I must start court in a few minutes."

"I am grateful for the appointments I receive from you and the other judges," she said. "A new attorney in criminal law cannot get started without being appointed to cases and building up skills and reputation." It was coming out as a speech because she had rehearsed it before getting up the nerve to approach him.

"Yes, yes, well, that is how we all got started."

She moved a little more onto the edge of her chair. "But I have now been a lawyer nearly two years and I am still getting the same cases . . . prostitutes and drug addicts, prostitutes who are drug addicts, drug addicts who are prostitutes—"

"Yes, yes, it's sad, isn't it? When I was a young attorney there were few cases of drug abuse in the courts. Selling drugs could bring the death penalty. Now criminals get richer and richer and our jails are crowded from the fools who use their drugs."

"I've handled so many drug addict and prostitution cases," Nina said, "that the people and cases are becoming a blur. It was good to have learned the basics of my profession from these petty cases, but now it's time for me to learn more. I am capable of handling—"

"You must have patience, Attorney Kerensky. You will

handle more important cases. They will come when you are ready.''

"I'm ready now. Most of my classmates are already handling major criminal cases. I'm the only one still dealing with only petty offenses."

"Well, you know, we have a market economy now. You may handle any case in which you are retained."

"I can't get retained because I don't have the reputation for handling serious cases. My classmates didn't get started with retained—"

He glanced at his watch. "I must open the court session. You should take this up with the Collegium of Advocates. It is they—"

"I went to the Collegium and spoke to the appointment coordinator. She told me that I am qualified to handle more serious cases but it is up to the judge to appoint me."

"Yes, I see, well, we will see. I must of course take into consideration your abilities and while the defendant does not have a choice in who I appoint, I must also not offend—I mean, I must insure that the defendant gets the best representation available for the nature of the offense."

She had already heard the speech from other judges: she couldn't get appointed to more serious cases because she lacked experience. She couldn't get the experience because she didn't have the experience to get appointed to better cases. Go talk to the Collegium. At the Collegium they told her to go talk to the judge.

What was the real reason she wasn't getting appointed to serious cases? Because the defendants would object and their families would complain. She was getting the dredges of society because, like Dasya, they were so low they thought they deserved her.

There was one thing for certain: Nina Kerensky was going to have to make it on her own with no help from anyone.

She straightened her shoulders as she walked down the courthouse corridor.

She had to do it and she would.

TWO

*S*urvive survive survive!

The word spun around and around in Lara's mind.

At the Moscow City Jail a man took each of her hands and roughly forced them onto an ink pad and rolled her prints on paper, each finger, palm side of the hand. Exemplars, the prints were called, to be compared with the latent prints lifted from the scene of the crime.

Staring down at the prints, she realized that she had seen so many fingerprint cards as a prosecutor that fingerprints and criminals went together in her mind like meat and potatoes. Now they were her prints, her marks on the justice system.

Booking photos came next, front and back and each side. She stared at the camera, as she had at the fingerprint cards, a perplexed expression on her face. *This couldn't be happening.*

After booking, she sat in a chair for nearly four hours before a husky matron, spiritual sister of the truck driver's wife, came into the room.

"Prisoner, stand up."

Lara stood up.

"Turn to your left and walk to the second door on your right."

The room on the right was a bare concrete box without windows. A long wooden table sat in the middle of the room. A gray smock had been tossed on the table. A pair of rubber slip-on shoes were on the floor.

"Take off your clothes," the matron told her.

"Shut the door, please." The voice didn't sound like her own. The words came from some far and distant place where her mind had retreated.

The woman shut the door and Lara took off her shoes and slowly stripped until she was in panties and bra. She picked up the gray smock to put it on.

"Not yet. Take off the rest of your clothes."

Lara turned and looked at her. The matron was holding a gynecological instrument.

"Prisoners are searched for weapons and contraband."

Lara lay back on the table and stared up at the cracked concrete ceiling.

Survive survive survive!

THREE

Holding on to a single blanket, clutching it tightly against her, Lara followed the matron down a cell-block corridor. She had lost track of time and knew only that it was late evening. A line of naked bulbs down the center of the cell block cast just enough light to leave the cells on each side deep in shadow.

Her feet were flopping in the ill-fitting rubber shoes, her legs were cold, but her heart was no longer pounding, her nerves were no longer on fire. Icy calm gripped her. She felt like a seven-year-old girl being led to an airplane after-having been assaulted.

Women in cells on both sides stirred as she was marched through. A voice snickered out they had a newcomer, someone to take advantage of. Prostitutes and thieves smoked cigarettes and watched her with hard eyes as she went by. From another direction a woman cried for her baby and someone else yelled, "Shut up, you crazy bitch, you killed your baby."

Stopping at a cell door at the end of the block, the matron opened it and gestured for Lara to go inside. It was a small cubbyhole, the size of a walk-in closet. Cement walls

on all three sides, no window, steel bars facing the cell
block.

Lara stepped inside and stood, clutching the blanket, her
back to the matron as the woman closed and locked the
door.

"Murderers get private cells. We don't want to expose
our whores and thieves to them."

Lara went to the rear of the cell and sat down with her
back against the cold concrete wall. Wrapping herself in
the blanket, she buried her head in her arms. She thought
the matron had left but the woman's voice came to her as
a sound from the grave.

"We execute murderers. One shot in the head. And if
they're still alive, we tape their nose and mouth shut so
we don't have to waste another bullet."

Down the cell block a woman laughed hysterically,
while another shouted, "Shut up, you crazy bitch."

FOUR

Eric Caldwell of the American Embassy took two days
to make his way across town for a jail visit with her.
He was sitting in the attorney visiting room when she
was brought in.

"Miss Patrick, how are you?"

They would send the dumbest bastard in the diplomatic
corps in her time of need. Through tight jaws she told him,
"I'm cold, unbathed, charged with a crime I didn't commit, and suicidal."

"Yes, well, I'm here to help."

"Yes, well, I need help," she mimicked. "I didn't murder that woman. I need my government to—"

Caldwell's head shook "no" so hard it threatened to
swivel off its base. "The United States government cannot

get involved in your case in any manner. Criminal matters are entirely in the sovereign jurisdiction of the Russian government.''

''I can understand that, but I need money. Everything I have is tied up in a condo in San Francisco.''

''The United States government cannot assist you financially.''

''I need an attorney, Mr. Caldwell, a good one.''

''The United States government cannot—''

''What can you do? You said you're here to help.''

''We can pass a message to your friends or relatives Stateside and let them know you are in need of assistance.''

''That's all? That's all you can do for me? Lick some stamps?''

''You have got yourself into trouble in a foreign country, Miss Patrick. We have no authority here.''

''This country is asking for billions in aid from us and my representative can't pick up the phone and ask for a review of my case? That's all I'm asking. For my government to ensure that I am not being held on trumped up charges.''

''If you had been arrested for a political crime we might be able to give assistance, but this is a murder case. The Russian government will appoint you a defense lawyer—''

''A Russian defense lawyer is a contradiction in terms. This country had been under dictatorship for over seventy years. Attorneys here have been trained to help the government convict their clients.''

''There is one thing wrong with your reasoning, Miss Patrick.''

''What?''

He smacked his lips with satisfaction. ''There is only one kind of attorney in Russia—*Russian* attorneys. You weren't expecting Perry Mason, were you?''

She bent closer to him, causing him to lean back. ''No,

Mr. Caldwell, I'm not expecting Perry Mason. I'm a little more practical than that. I am an attorney, I know my way around a courtroom in a system I can trust. The Russians are still operating under the old Soviet criminal justice system which has almost no safeguards for due process. The police work is primitive and the judicial system is barbaric. I need to find one attorney out there with the same sense of being an advocate that I have.''

"I am also an attorney, Miss Patrick. The justice system here is different from our own, certainly, but I'm sure adequate counsel will be provided to guide you through the system.''

"I don't want *adequate* counsel. I'm facing a murder charge in a country that uses capital punishment. Hell, they used to shoot drunk drivers here. I need money and help. We send the whole damn army and navy to Kuwait to help some fat little sheik who lives like a king while his people starve and—''

"You have a very unrealistic view of world events. And of your own situation. I speak both as an attorney and a diplomat. Frankly, your situation is somewhat of a diplomatic embarrassment to your government at a time when we are trying to restructure the world community after the end of the Cold War—''

"Restructure the world community? A diplomatic embarrassment?'' She got to her feet and came the closest she had ever come in her life to punching someone. "You jerk. Don't call yourself an attorney. A law degree doesn't make you an attorney any more than boxing gloves makes a fighter. You're not a lawyer until you've been in a courtroom and fought for truth and justice. You'll never see a courtroom because trial lawyers have heart and guts . . .''

FIVE

She rested her head on her folded arms on the table as she waited for the matron to take her back to the cell. Caldwell had fled, angry and speechless after her outburst.

She had focused her anger on him and felt no real remorse for doing so. The world seemed to be full of Caldwells, people who appeared to go effortlessly through life without ever once getting punished by God or whomever for never reaching out and giving a helping hand to their fellow man.

The door to the interview room opened and she looked up, tired and dragging, thinking it was the matron.

Yuri stood in the doorway. His features were grave. He slowly stepped in, closing the door behind him. Taking the seat across from her that Caldwell had left vacant, he looked around the room for a moment before he met her eye.

"I just spoke to your embassy man. He was upset."

"I clawed him for being stupid, but I was the stupid one. I should have sat on his lap instead. I don't have a talent for tact."

She studied his face, trying to read his secrets. "Did you come to finish the job of killing me?"

"What?"

"You people came through that door shooting to kill. If I hadn't thrown myself to the floor—"

"I never fired at you. I'm in trouble because I spoiled my supervisor's aim when he fired. He believes I'm too emotionally involved in your case."

"Very convenient, having the police rushing into the room as I was running through the place in a panic."

"There was an anonymous call."

"That's convenient, too."

"I told you to stay away from Alexei. You were seduced by his money and glamour."

"That's a lie. I turned to Alexei because I had nowhere else to go. I tried to get your help and you drove me away."

For a moment she was sure she saw a flash of pain in his face and he looked away. When he met her eye again, his features were neutral. "It may be better for you to be in jail. It's safer. You would have been dead soon if you'd kept wandering around Moscow sticking your nose in the past."

"Better in jail? Facing a murder charge? Are we on the same planet?"

"Tell me what happened."

She ran her hands through her hair. "I look like hell, don't I? You need money for everything in here, even for soap and a comb."

"I'll leave money for you."

"No, thank you. I just have to get to my purse."

"You have a hard time taking help, don't you?"

"I . . . yes, all right, but, Yuri, don't . . ."

"Don't what?"

She almost sobbed but held it back. "Don't betray me."

He looked away again as she started talking, beginning with being taken to the palace by Alexei after leaving the ministry.

"When I returned from my walk, Felix invited . . . I guess lured me in is more accurate." She led him through seeing the picture of her mother and the neighbor with Alexei, the party that night, being intercepted by Nadia.

"She asked you to meet her the next day at the tower so she could gather evidence to blackmail Alexei?"

"Yes."

"But she never told you what she suspected?"

"No, only that Felix must have a hold on Alexei."

"What happened after you spoke to Nadia?"

Too embarrassed to tell him about the sauna scene with Nadia and waking up in Alexei's bed, she said, "I had something to drink and passed out. I . . . I'm sure I was drugged."

"What happened next?"

"Everyone had already returned to town by the time I woke up. I got dressed, took the key . . ." She described the key safe, returning to the city, going to the tower, finding the gun.

"You had returned the guns you wore at the party to Alexei?"

"Yes—no, I left one gun in the limo the night of the Western party. I threw the other gun at you as you were leaving my hotel room. It hit the wall by the door and that's the last I saw of it. I . . . I don't know if it was the same gun as the one I found near the spa. Most of the guns at the party looked the same."

"So you had access to the gun that killed Nadia."

"It might have been—" A terrible, ugly feeling suddenly overwhelmed her, choking off her words. "You asked that question as if you were doing it for the record. Are you . . ."

He turned away, refusing to meet her eye.

She leaned across the table and jerked open his suit coat. A transmitter was clipped to his shirt pocket with a line of wire going to his coat.

"You're recording me!" She hit him with her fists. "How could you! How could you!"

The door flew open and a man rushed into the room, followed by Stenka. The man grabbed her, spun her round, and jerked her arm into a hammer lock so hard she cried out.

"Don't hurt her!" Yuri grabbed the man's arm and the man shook him off.

"Back off," he told Yuri. He slammed Lara into her chair and then turned to Yuri and Stenka.

"Detective Kirov, Detective Stenka, you may leave. This case is now in the exclusive jurisdiction of the Moscow City Prosecutor's office."

Yuri stepped closer to him. The man was not much taller than Lara but was broad, a shaved head on an eight-ply body giving him the appearance of a blunt-nosed artillery shell.

Yuri tapped his chest. "Don't . . . touch . . . her, Vulko. Question her, do your job, but touch her and I'll be back."

"You are dismissed, Detective Kirov."

As he left the room with Stenka, Yuri gave her a shamefaced glance.

Vulko sat on the edge of the table and stared down at her, his look a mixture of amusement and contempt. The dim light in the room cast shadows in the pockets of his rough face. He lit a cigarette, a brown thing almost like a cigar, and blew out foul-smelling smoke.

"You have got to Detective Kirov's heart, I see. Inside his pants, no doubt, too. I'll report the matter to his supervisor and he will be reassigned to walking a patrol."

"Who are you?" she demanded.

"Nikolai Vulko, chief investigator, Moscow City Prosecutor's office."

"What do you want?"

"I am here to question you about the crime you have committed."

"I haven't committed a crime. I want an attorney present. And an official from the American Embassy."

He chuckled, a hoarse rasp. His pin-striped suit was baggy and wrinkled, his white shirt open at the collar with salt and pepper chest hair poking out like a bunny's tail. She noticed he had no eyebrows, not even the residue of having shaved them.

"You have no right to have an attorney present, you have no right to have a representative from your embassy present. Your only right is to answer the questions I ask. Do you understand?"

"No, I don't understand a legal system where I have no rights."

"We are not in a debate about legal theory. You are in jail, not the marble halls of a law university. Let me explain so you will understand. I am a chief investigator for the prosecutor's office. The police arrest the criminal and gather the evidence at the scene of the crime. At that point an investigator for the prosecutor's office takes over the investigation. We prepare the case for trial, uncovering all the facts and evidence and putting it in an orderly fashion for the court."

"Are you here to twist around everything I say or to look at the facts objectively and help me out of this terrible mess?"

"I know the facts. I am here to listen to your confession and to see if there are any mitigating factors to what appears to be a crime of intentional murder with aggravating circumstances."

She tried to word her response carefully. She knew what a prosecutor's investigator was, at least in the context of an American courtroom. They took a second look at the evidence gathered by the police and in the right case they could make a recommendation that would result in charges being dropped.

"I did not kill Nadia. I went to Bova's penthouse and found her dead. I found the gun on the floor, panicked, and ran."

He chuckled hoarsely again, a cancerous throat rasp, and shook his head.

"No, you misunderstand. This is not America, we do not play legal games. There is one path, the path of justice, and in this case there is a fork in the road: if you explain your actions, show repentance for the terrible deed you have done, and offer explanations in mitigation, you take a path to murder without aggravating circumstances. If you fail to repent and offer satisfactory explanations, you take the path to murder with aggravating circumstances. It is as simple as that.''

''You're not listening to me,'' Lara said. ''I didn't kill anyone. I can't confess to a crime I didn't commit.''

He reached out and roughly took her chin in the cup of his hand. ''You are the one not listening. You must tell me the truth. Admit that you fired two shots and took the life of Nadia Kolchak.''

Lara struggled out of his grip and fell backward off her chair. She scrambled to her feet, nearly in tears. ''Don't touch me. I'll report you to my embassy.''

He blew out laughter and smoke and raised his shoulders and hairless eyebrows. ''Do you think we Russians care about a report to your embassy?''

''Maybe you'll care if it's reported in newspapers around the world that an American woman has been manhandled in a Russian jail by a Russian investigator. Maybe my congressional representative back home might want some questions answered before they vote on aid for Russia. Maybe your own career—''

''Prisoner, your threats do not bother me. You have totally misunderstood the situation because you are ignorant of Russian legal procedures. We have more than sufficient evidence of your crime. I am here to accept your offer of repentance and mitigation to place before the prosecutor.'' He blew more foul smoke from the brown cigarette. ''So, I ask you the question again. Why did you kill Nadia Kolchak?''

''I . . . did . . . not . . . kill Nadia.''

He chuckled and dropped his cigarette on the floor, then got off the table and stamped the cigarette out.

''You have made, shall we say, a *fatal* mistake.'' He paused at the door to the room. ''Perhaps no one has told you. Murder with mitigating circumstances is punished by up to ten years in prison.'' He grinned. ''Murder with aggravating circumstances is punished with death.''

He opened the door, but turned back to her again. ''Russian death sentences do not stay around the courts for years with appeals. Justice is sure and swift.''

She heard his last comment as he was shutting the door. ''You've chosen the bullet.''

Back in her cell she curled up in a corner and covered herself with the blanket.

Anger helped steady her nerves. She had been betrayed again. There wouldn't be another opportunity for betrayal because she would never allow herself to be tricked again. Or allow herself to get emotionally attached. She had trusted Yuri. And cared for him.

For the first time she understood the emotions that turn love to hate and hate to murder. Now she wished she had a gun to kill him. Not for being a smart cop, but for the hurt he gave her heart.

And she'd put another bullet in that bastard with a polished head and no eyebrows.

X.IX

___

My holy of holies is the human body,
health, intelligence, talent, inspiration,
love, and absolute freedom——
freedom from violence and falsehood,
no matter how the last two manifest themselves.

—Anton Chekhov

ONE

The next morning Lara stood in line with other women waiting to go into a courtroom. Women were being called in one by one, some for pleas and sentencing, others for the appointment of an attorney. She was weak and queasy. She had not had the courage to go to breakfast with the other prisoners. Two days in jail and she had not eaten. It wasn't a hunger strike, she just did not have the fortitude to march in line to the mess hall and eat with the other prisoners. Other than the one trip to the visitors' room, she had not left her cell day or night, not even for a shower. She didn't know how much weight she had lost—the smock she wore was designed for an elephant.

A hole in the corner of her cell was her toilet. A trickle of water could be directed into the hole from a rusty tap a couple of feet above. The water was bitter with an iodine taste but so far it hadn't killed her. The cell had a dirty mattress with a sheet stained from God knows what. She used a corner of the sheet to wash herself under the tap.

Eventually she would have to break down and join the other prisoners for food and showers. Being forced into line with them for the court appearance had broken some of the ice for her. She knew from hearing the other prisoners talk and some taunts directed at her that she was a celebrity prisoner—the news media was full of the "love triangle murder."

Her hair was in knots, her face a wreck, the smock she wore would have embarrassed a pregnant cow, but her mind was still functioning and she tried to think as a lawyer, running the facts over and over in her mind. The case was based on circumstantial evidence. No one actually saw the killing, but when you're caught red-handed by police officers with a smoking gun in your hand, it was almost as strong as a case with eyewitnesses. In her courtroom in San Francisco it would have been a no plea bargain case—the evidence was too strong to offer a lesser offense. Premeditated murder without special circumstances meant a life sentence without possibility of parole back home, a bullet in the brain in Moscow. She would rather have the bullet than spend the rest of her life in prison.

A matron grabbed her arm and pulled her out of line.

"Prisoner, your lawyer is here."

She followed the woman, wondering what was going on. Lawyers were being appointed in the courtroom.

The man waiting for her in the attorney interview room was about forty years old with dark, slicked-back hair tied in a ponytail, a narrow face, and a patrician nose. He wore an expensive pin-striped, double-breasted Italian suit, hand-painted silk tie, and Bally loafers with tassels.

He introduced himself. "Viktor Rykoff. I'm the best lawyer in Moscow."

Smart, successful, high-priced big city lawyer—she recognized the type. Some of them really were actually the best but a lot more were better at promoting themselves outside the courtroom than performing their dance steps in it. If Russian lawyers were developing along the lines of their American counterparts, "best" probably meant the most financially successful. Many a household legal name in America got famous handling high-profile cases that they lost.

"Who sent you?" she asked.

"The gods, American and Russian, are smiling on you. Even the dead Communist ones. Your case is getting great media attention. For over seventy years there have been no crimes of passion in Russia—at least none that were allowed to be so well reported. Because you are making history, I am here to help."

He was telling her he wanted to share the limelight. She had no problem with that—if he was good and if he could be trusted. But there was something about him . . . he reminded her of the type of lawyers defendants call "dump trucks" because they drive the case all the way to the day of trial with their bullshit and dump the client when it's time to perform.

"You're the best lawyer in Moscow. I'm the most frightened defendant in the city. And I don't have any money."

He winced. "A rich American . . ."

She shook her head. "Poor American. I have a condo in San Francisco with equity in it. That's all."

"San Francisco. That's halfway around the world."

"I thought you wanted to share these historical moments with me."

He spread his hands and smiled. "Sharing is so much more palatable when there is money on the table."

Except for poets and crazies, she hated ponytails on middle-aged men. She got up. "Well, I'll be—"

"No, no, please sit down. I won't let money get in the way of our date with destiny."

"Can you get paid by the court?" she asked.

"Not enough to feed my BMW."

"What do you know about my case?"

He shrugged. "You killed one of Russia's most popular women in a heat of passion over one of the country's most famous men."

"I see. And how does heat of passion line up as a defense in Russia?"

"It's not a defense. The crime of murder is punishable by death. If the judges believe there are mitigating circumstances for your actions, you can be spared the bullet. In this case, there will be great pressure on the court. Your case is the first of its kind to get this type of attention in the country. The whole nation will be watching."

She thought for a moment. "Something bothers me. You indicated you'd take my case, but you haven't asked me anything about it. You haven't even asked if I'm guilty."

He shrugged again. "This is Russia. Your case will be won or lost in the judge's chambers by the pressures that are applied, not by the actual facts. We may even have to create facts." He leaned toward her. "Do you have jewelry? Perhaps something Bova gave you?"

"For your fee? No, nothing of any value."

"A pity. The more money, the more justice. Just like America," he said with a laugh.

What a pig.

He got serious again. "Don't worry, I will still take your case. Our strategy will be to stall the case for a long time, long enough for the newspeople and the public to get bored with it. That will take pressure off the judge."

Panic welled up in her. "I . . . I don't want the case stalled. I need to have it forced to trial as soon as possible. I can't stand jail. Besides, my instincts tell me that the criminal justice system here is a slow-moving bureaucracy, a fat cow. If we push hard it's likely neither the police nor the prosecutor will be ready for trial."

He frowned. "We have to get one matter settled immediately. I am the lawyer, you are the prisoner. It is my instincts that we will be following. And my instincts are to delay the trial until the right moment and when that moment comes, we move in for a kill." He made a chopping gesture with his hand.

"But—"

"We do it my way or you can go inside and take your

chances with a court-appointed lawyer. Has anyone told you about court-appointed lawyers? They are still practicing Soviet justice. They sit on you while the prosecutor beats a confession out of you.''

She stared down at the table. Her instincts were screaming against it but he was the only game in town.

''Today the judge will order your case to the City Courts.''

''I don't understand.''

''This court is the People's Court. It does not handle death penalty cases. You are being sent to the next higher court.''

''I'm not entitled to any sort of hearing before being sent to a higher court?'' she asked. ''A hearing to establish that there is enough evidence to bind me to a higher court? No hearing on being let out on bail?''

''You had the hearing. Chief Investigator Vulko came and spoke with you. You refused a statement. He made a decision to move your case to the City Court for trial as a death penalty matter.''

''He made the decision? He's just an investigator for the prosecution!''

''The case is prepared by the prosecutor's office. It is the prosecutor's decision to make it a death penalty case, but a chief investigator's opinion would rarely be ignored.''

''How about the court's opinion? Doesn't the People's Court judge look into the case to see if it has any merit?''

He became a little exasperated. ''Theories, theories, those are theories. I am telling you what happens in the real world.''

''I'm sorry. Where I come from we call those rights, not theories.''

''Next time kill someone in America.'' He held up his hand. ''A joke. Listen to me, the important thing is that I am taking care of your case. You made a serious error when you refused to speak to Vulko last night and offer mitigation. There will be no more mistakes.''

''He said I didn't have a right to have an attorney present.''

''He was speaking the truth. But there are ways of handling this matter without antagonizing the chief investigator on the case. Leave it to me. I will take care of everything.''

When she returned to the line of prisoners, the woman in front of her asked, ''Is Rykoff your attorney?''

''Yes. Is he good?''

''He's wonderful. He was my sister's attorney when she was charged with stabbing her boyfriend.''

''Did he get your sister off?''

''Get her off? Of course not. She stabbed her boyfriend.''

''Then why do you think he's such a good attorney.''

''He said nice things about my sister to the judge.''

''Did the things he say get her a lighter sentence?''

The woman shook her head in wonderment at Lara's ignorance. ''Of course not. Everyone gets equal justice. But not all lawyers say nice things about their clients.''

Wonderful, Lara thought. I've got a lawyer who can give a nice eulogy when they put a bullet in my head.

''What are you charged with?'' Lara asked.

''Stolen boots.''

''Boots?''

The woman shrugged. ''I worked in a boot factory. Each day I wore to work a pair of rubber shoes I could fold and put in my purse and wore a new pair of boots out. I did it to feed my baby. That is my mitigating circumstance. I did it to feed my baby because my boyfriend stole my money.''

She gestured as she talked and Lara saw track marks on her arm. Her ''baby'' came in a hypodermic needle.

The door to the courtroom opened and the woman with the sister who stabbed her boyfriend stepped into the courtroom. As the door was swinging shut, Lara got a flash of two men huddled together in the courtroom.

Yuri and Rykoff.

"What's the matter with you?" the door guard asked.

"What?"

"Are you ill?"

"I'm all right."

"You're next," he said.

Betrayal upon betrayal. Yuri wasn't going to be satisfied until she was dead. Or insane.

The guard was talking to her again.

"Move, prisoner. Into the courtroom."

She forced her shoulders back and held her head high as she stepped into the courtroom. The lighting in the courtroom was much brighter than the holding area and she cringed at how awful she must look, but she was determined not to let her chin drop.

The courtroom was packed and a stir went through the gallery as she entered. A metal railing ran a dozen feet into the room and she walked along it into the prisoner's dock, a wooden box with a step to elevate her, making her visible to the whole courtroom. It was hot and stuffy in the room and the heat was gagging.

She ignored a hundred pairs of eyes and found Yuri's. He was standing at the back of the room. She locked eyes with him for a moment and then deliberately looked at Rykoff. The attorney smiled and nodded. Without changing her expression she looked back at Yuri. She wanted to let him know she wasn't falling for his trick.

As she listened to the judge stating her name, the case number, and the charges, thoughts of herself in court, at the prosecutor's table, shuffling files as the cases were called flashed through her mind. The courtroom was designed like those in America, the judge's bench at one end of the room, the exit doors on the other side of the room, the spectator gallery taking up about half of the portion closest to the exit door, a railing called the "bar" cutting off the spectators from the counsel tables, clerk's desk, witness box, and the dock.

The most obvious difference was the lack of a jury box and the presence of three people on the judicial bench. The judge was dressed in a suit and wore a white shirt and a tie. On each side of him were the assessors chosen to sit in on cases with him. Lara was not certain what the exact role of the two assessors was, whether they had equal power as the judge or were just courtroom decoration.

The judge was smoking a cigarette and the ashtray in front of him was nearly overflowing and smoldering from butts not quite extinguished. Just beyond the ashtray were bottles of soda pop, mineral water, and coffee cups.

The assessor to the right of the judge was a thin, sickly looking woman, whose eyes were half-closed. She was leaning away from the judge as if she were being blown away by the smoke.

The assessor sitting on the judge's left was an older man dressed in heavy woolen workman's clothes. He, too, looked barely awake, and Lara could see sweat on his face.

On the wall opposite her was a poster of Lenin, as mandatory in Russian public buildings as images of Christ in Christian churches. Cracked and faded, the picture gave a sinister cast to the revolutionary's otherwise distinguished features. The dark, stern features and goatee reminded her of a faded old movie poster of the count from Transylvania.

The judicial atmosphere was not as dignified as she was accustomed to, but she reminded herself that the Communists had deliberately tried to make the justice system available to the common man.

Viktor Rykoff stood up at the counsel table. "I will be representing the prisoner."

"No he will not, Your Honor." She said "Your Honor" out of habit, having no idea of the proper way to address a Russian judge. "I have discovered that Mr. Rykoff has a conflict of interest. He will not be representing me in this matter."

A buzz went through the audience. Rykoff's jaw

dropped. He swung round and looked at Yuri who shrugged his shoulders and shook his head.

The judge stared at her as if she were a candidate for a mental competency hearing. The two assessors even perked up. "You don't want Mr. Rykoff for your attorney?" It was more an echo than a question.

"We have a conflict of interest."

"Mr. Rykoff is one of the best attorneys in Moscow," the judge said.

A conflict of interest apparently didn't mean much in a Russian courtroom. A surge of strength went through her— she was in a courtroom, thinking on her feet.

"I believe, Your Honor, that Mr. Rykoff is associated with one of the police officers in this matter. I would like to inquire as to his relationship with that officer and why he would offer to represent me free."

"This is ridiculous!" Rykoff exploded. "The woman is a mental case. She needs a doctor." He turned and stamped out of the courtroom, jerking open one of the double doors with such force it banged against the wall.

The judge peered down at her above the rim of glasses riding his nose. "I will give you time to hire an attorney."

"I don't have the money for an attorney. I need to have one appointed by the court."

He gaped at her. "You don't want Rykoff and you want me to appoint you an attorney?"

"Yes."

The judge shook his head. "This is a free country," he told the audience. She didn't know if he was joking but a titter went through the audience. "She doesn't want Rykoff and wants me to appoint her an attorney." The titter turned into a buzz.

He adjusted his glasses and consulted papers in front of him for a long moment, finally looking up and calling a name.

"Ninochka Kerensky."

There was complete silence in the courtroom for a moment and then a young woman stood up and came forward.

Several things instantly struck Lara about her. She was young, a little younger than Lara, perhaps twenty-five or twenty-six. She was Afro-Russian, a very uncommon racial mixture, one of the few people of African heritage Lara had seen in Moscow other than tourists in Red Square. And she was very scared.

"Attorney Kerensky," she told the judge in a nervous voice.

The judge pulled his glasses down his nose and grinned at Lara as he spoke. "Ninochka Kerensky, member of the Collegium of Law, I appoint you as attorney for the prisoner."

Nina looked frightened enough to crawl under the counsel table.

TWO

Ten minutes later Lara and Nina stared at each other across the table in the attorney interview room like two does coming face-to-face in a burning forest.

"I've never handled a serious criminal case before," she told Lara.

"Never? Not one?" Lara tried to control her voice but the words squeaked.

"Cases of prostitution. A man who beat his wife. A case of theft—a watch."

"A watch." Lara nodded.

"A cheap watch," Nina said. "Plastic. He gave it to me as a fee."

Rykoff had a BMW and Nina had a plastic watch.

"Have you won any trials?"

"I've never had a trial."

"Great." Lara dropped her head into her hands. She felt

like taking off her head and bouncing it on the table.

"The judge was mad at you. I was to be appointed to a prostitution case. He appointed me to your case to punish you."

"Jesus Christ." It was the most complex thought she could muster.

"Mr. Rykoff is one of the best attorneys in Moscow," Nina said. "I can beg the judge to—"

Lara looked up at her. "Has he ever gotten anyone off?"

By the confused look on Nina's face she could have guessed the answer.

"Has Rykoff won any cases? Walked his client out of a courtroom? Had a not guilty verdict?"

"Not guilty? Criminals are almost always found guilty. They wouldn't be on trial if they weren't guilty."

"God help me."

Nina stood up. "I'm going to talk to the judge." She turned to leave.

"Wait, please," Lara said.

Nina shook her head. "I can't represent you. You need a more experienced lawyer. The judge expects you to apologize for refusing Mr. Rykoff."

It was Lara's turn to shake her head.

"I'm black," Nina said.

Lara understood. Blacks and Mafia were favorite Russian scapegoats for everything and anything that went wrong. "A black woman in a white male-dominated system," she said. It was a thought, but she expressed it aloud.

Nina's chin went up a notch. "I have had to fight."

"It must be tough for you."

"It's been hell. I have to work twice as hard as anyone else and do three times better."

Fight and win, Lara thought, every step of the way. One thing about Nina had struck her from the moment the young woman had turned to her wide-eyed in the courtroom: she was without guile. She had clear, honest eyes. No plots, no intrigue, no hidden agendas.

"When the August coup was attempted and people manned the barricades to face off the KGB and tanks, where were you?"

Her chin went up another inch. "At the barricades."

"That's what I thought."

"I will go and talk to the judge now."

"Wait. You're embarrassed, aren't you? Because you lack experience."

"Embarrassed? I'm terrified."

Good, Lara thought, I fight best with my back to the wall. "Before you go back to the judge, may I ask you a question?"

"Yes."

"A moment ago you said all people charged with crimes are guilty. Do you really believe that?"

"Most people charged with crimes are guilty," Nina said. "All the people I have represented have been guilty of what they were charged with. But the police make mistakes. They make many mistakes, not just from stupidity, but from malice. You're a prosecutor. Have you ever prosecuted an innocent person?"

"I hope not. I chose not to prosecute some people because after reviewing the evidence I didn't believe that they were guilty."

"From what I've heard about your case, the facts all point to your guilt. But I haven't heard all the facts. I haven't heard your side."

"What if I am guilty? If you were my attorney, how would you handle my case?"

Nina thought for a moment. "In America, attorneys are gladiators who go into a courtroom to advocate their client's position. That's not how attorneys in Russia have practiced."

"The question is how you practice," Lara said.

"I'm going to be a gladiator, not a sheep. I did not

become an attorney to handle traffic tickets,'' Nina said.

"Going to be?

"Why are we having this conversation? I can't handle your case. I'm not experienced. In Russia—''

"They have the death penalty. That's what frightens you, isn't it?''

Nina looked away and then met Lara's eye. "If I handled your case, even if you were found guilty and executed, I would be famous. If I represented you and you were found not guilty, I would probably be made the president of Russia. After I changed my color and sex, of course.''

Lara smiled.

"No, don't smile. This is not a matter to joke about. Yes, I am terrified that I could make a mistake and have your blood on my hands. But I am not as frightened as you must be. For you it must be a living hell.''

Neither woman spoke for a moment. Nina kept her position by the door and Lara rubbed her face with her hands. Finally, she asked Nina, "Is Rykoff a good lawyer? Tell me the truth.''

"He is smart and rich. He has a fancy German car. And he says nice things about his clients.''

"And?''

"He has no heart, no feelings. If he gets paid enough, he makes deals in the judge's office. Sometimes the judge gets paid, too.''

In other words, he can be bought. And I would be the lowest bidder, she thought. "Assume I'm innocent, that I didn't kill Nadia Kolchak. What would it take to win my case? You've heard the facts, I'm supposed to have killed this woman in jealousy.''

"The news reports say that the police caught you with the murder weapon in your hand.''

"What would it take to win if I'm innocent?''

"Nadia Kolchak was very well known. Because of her exposure on television, she was one of the most popular women in Russia. The public is interested in the case.''

"What would it take to win?"

"The truth," Nina said.

Lara smiled. She was weary and weak, but she had gotten the response she was after. "Nina, it may just be delirium from lack of food or insanity from being in this mess, but if you are willing to stay on the case, I want you to be my attorney."

Nina stared at her. "Do you understand that criminal trials in Russia begin with a confession by the accused? If you don't confess, the judge will give you the maximum penalty. That's death in this case."

"You're telling me that I have to stand up in court and tell the judge I'm guilty or he will give me the death penalty?"

"Yes. That's how the system works. If you don't confess, then you are not repentant and will be punished severely."

"I have no intention of confessing to something I didn't do. This trial isn't going to start or finish with me being repentant for a crime I didn't commit. I'm going in to fight for my life with everything I have."

Nina shook her head. "You don't understand Russian trials. The chief investigator prepares the case for the court and the rest is mostly just procedural."

"You aren't describing a justice system, but a court system that—" Lara stopped and took a deep breath. "I have to stop thinking like an American. But in any court system the truth must win out."

Nina came back to the table and slowly sat down across from her. "You will need more than truth to win this case," she told Lara. "If you don't confess to the crime, before the court will show you mercy you'll have to enter the courtroom walking on water." She suddenly grinned. "You're a smart lawyer," she said, "but you forgot to ask me one thing."

"What?"

"Which side of the barricades I was on."

XX

In the carriages of the past,
you can't go anywhere.

—Maxim Gorky,
The Lower Depths

ONE

They returned to the courtroom and the court called the case of Lara Patrick.

"I will be representing the accused," Nina said.

The judge didn't look happy and the two assessors both turned to him, three heads with one mouth. "I believe I made a mistake, Attorney Kerensky. This is a very serious case and your name was not next on the list for an appointment."

"I am satisfied with Ninochka Kerensky as my attorney," Lara said.

"So be it," he snapped. "Case transferred to City Court."

Classic example of a judge throwing a hot potato into someone else's lap, Lara thought.

"The defendant objects to a transfer to City Court," Nina said assertively to the surprise of everyone, including Lara. They had discussed making an objection and Nina had told her it would be useless. "The defendant denies guilt in this case. Even if one is to believe the rumors circulated by the news media that this was an affair of passion, the crime would be that of an unintentional killing in a state of great emotional excitement. Thus this matter can stay in the People's Court."

An expression of deep distaste spread across the judge's face.

"Case transferred to City Court."

TWO

Braced by the fact that she had an attorney she trusted and liked, Lara got up the courage to go to lunch with the other women. No one bothered her, but the sour cabbage soup and piece of black bread attacked her stomach with a vengeance and she ended up heaving her guts into her toilet hole.

She met briefly with Nina before the lunch break and returned to the attorney conference room early in the afternoon. Nina was waiting for her with police reports stacked in the center of the table. A writing pad with a freshly sharpened pencil was placed on each side of the table.

"How is jail food?" Nina asked.

"Rotten cabbage in sewer water."

A paper bag hit her leg. Nina was bending down, her arm under the table. Lara took the bag and opened it on her lap. A wonderful aroma hit her nostrils, sending a sensation of pure joy shivering down her spine.

A Big Mac from McDonald's.

Lara started to say something and Nina said, "Whisper."

"It must have cost you a week's wages."

Nina giggled. "My friend works there. He smuggled it to me. I don't have a week's wages to spend."

A stolen Big Mac. Somehow that made it even more delicious.

Nina said in a normal voice, "I want to have some money put in your jail account so you can buy snacks and necessities with it but I discovered someone named Kirov had already put money in. That's the name of one of the policemen who arrested you."

"I don't want his money. Have some money from my purse put in my jail account. And take the rest for yourself."

"No, I won't do that. Now we must get to work."

Lara dropped the subject rather than embarrass her.

Nina dropped her voice back to a whisper. "Let's talk about the past. When we met earlier you told me about your suspicions concerning what the man Belkin had said to you about a young boy being charged with a mutilation killing."

"Yes, after I realized that the woman in the photograph I was sent wasn't my mother, it occurred to me that Belkin wasn't just making conversation, that there might be a connection with the death of our neighbor."

"You were correct. I reviewed court records for that time. A young man, actually a boy of seventeen named Alexander Zurin whose address was the same building as the one you gave me for the apartment you shared with—"

"Pasha," Lara interrupted her. "Pasha is the familiar name for Alexander."

"Yes."

"I remember a boy in our building who used to tease me, a nice boy, his name was Pasha. Was he the one charged with Vera Swen's murder?"

"Charged, convicted, the death penalty stayed because of his age, and sentenced to life imprisonment."

"Is he still in prison?"

"No. He volunteered to do roadwork in Afghanistan during the fighting there and was killed."

"He was innocent."

"You say that without knowing any of the facts? I compliment you, you have become an expert on Russian jurisprudence."

"I remember him vaguely. Not his features, just his presence at the building. He called me Little Kosca." Little cat. "I remember my mother liked him."

"The court records say that the woman lured the boy to her room to seduce him. The police theory is that he failed to perform sexually, she mocked his manhood, and he killed her in a rage."

"He confessed, didn't he?"

"How did you know?"

"Because he didn't get the bullet."

Nina grinned. "You're right. He foolishly denied the crime at first but then confessed. He received a life sentence because of the heinous nature of the offense. He probably would have been sentenced to death even with the confession, but his age kept him from the executioner's bullet." She shuffled papers in front of her. "But enough of the past, we must go through the police reports. Because of the importance of the case, the coverage in the news media, the police have been more active than usual. They have found witnesses against you."

"Nina, the secret to my case is in the past. Tell me what else you learned about Pasha's case."

"That's all. Court summaries of the records."

"Can you get to the actual police reports?"

She hesitated. "I'm not sure."

Lara stared at her. "You're avoiding telling me something."

"I . . . I already tried to look at the police reports. The police file on the case is missing."

"You mean stolen."

"I don't know."

"I do. Whoever took that file sent me one of the crime scene photos from it."

"Lara, I know how important it is for you to piece together the past, but you're charged with a murder now, not twenty years ago. We must focus on that.''

''All right, but . . .'' She clenched her teeth. ''All right, you mentioned witnesses the police found. Witnesses to what?''

''Your violent and irrational nature.''

''My . . . oh, yes, the party. Nina, I have to explain that to you.''

''I don't think you'll be able to come up with a rational explanation for shooting up a party in your underwear with half the new gentry of Russia watching.'' There was awe in Nina's voice.

''I was drunk. For the first time in my life I was drunk. I didn't know what I was doing.''

''There are more witnesses, people interviewed when this man Belkin was hit by the truck.''

''I had nothing to do with that. He was injured at the park and later given an overdose in the hospital.''

''In the police reports, an elderly couple states that a young woman, a foreigner who spoke Russian with little accent, was acting strange. You are the person Detective Kirov identified as the irrational woman.''

''That's nonsense.''

''Lara, I don't understand. It's not just the Nadia Kolchak death that these reports mention. There's a schoolteacher who died after she talked to you. School officials believe you're responsible for her death because the woman was screaming and distraught after you spoke to her. There are interviews with the staff at the Gorky Hotel who say you appeared to be irrational much of the time. A hospital report of falling down steps—''

''Falling while being chased by a maniac.''

''And an ambulance record of fainting in Red Square.''

Lara turned pink. ''That one's true. But you have to understand, everything is being bent out of shape. None of it has anything to do with the charges against me. It's all speculation, hearsay, and innuendo.''

"It's all proper evidence in our courtrooms."

"That's ridiculous."

Nina shuffled the papers in front of her again. Lara could tell she was disturbed.

"You're wondering what you've gotten yourself into, aren't you?" she said.

"For myself, I don't wonder. I'll be famous. My telephone will not stop ringing. But I wonder how things will go for you. I believe you're a good person, but some of these things . . ."

Lara laid her hands on the table, spreading her fingers. "I understand. So let's start from the beginning. I was born in Moscow. My mother was . . ."

For an hour she related every move she had made since arriving in Moscow and everything she remembered from those days as a child in the city.

Nina started to make notes and then as the story grabbed her attention more and more, she put down her pencil, leaned forward in her chair, propped her chin in her hands, and listened.

After Lara had finished her tale, both women remained silent for a moment before Nina picked up her pencil and started writing and talking.

"Point one: two women died twenty years ago. One by alleged suicide, the other by an act of insane violence. Point two: you have been lured to Moscow by someone connected to these deaths."

"Connected or has knowledge of," Lara interjected.

"Either way, it certainly wasn't by the teenage boy, he is dead."

"Get me anything you can on his death. So far about everything I've read in official documents has been a lie. So who knows?"

Nina made a note. "Next point: something is going on today that is connected to the people from the past."

Lara started to say something and Nina motioned her to whisper.

"Nadia believed that Felix was blackmailing Alexei. I'm not sure I accept that, but I know something is going on between them besides the normal work relationship. I told you about the picture. Alexei lied when he said he didn't know my mother. He knew her and the neighbor woman."

Nina shrugged. "Knew or attended the same party once. You believe Alexei was ex-KGB. Both women, as foreigners, would have had a KGB agent assigned to them. Alexei may have been that agent, or the supervising agent."

"All right. But that's a little too simple. Bova is not just a person from the past. In this cast of characters, he has to be a star performer," Lara said.

"I accept that. Point four: Alexei Bova is hiding something. Five: Detective Yuri Kirov is hiding something."

"Felix is hiding something, too. Nadia was trying to dig it all out—for profit."

"So, what occurred in the past is important today. When it all erupted, you ended up taking a fall for Nadia's death. Intentional or accidental?" Nina wrote.

"Good question. How would anyone know that I would be sure to take the keys and go to the penthouse?"

"Well, that hardly required second sight. Since you arrived in Moscow you've bribed your way into secret KGB archives and broken into a renowned psychiatric institute, never mind shooting up the Black Tower. What's breaking and entering into the penthouse of the richest man in Russia after all that?"

"Oh, God." Lara hid her face in her hands.

"Let's discuss the crime in hand. Nadia was killed by two wounds made by a .38 caliber weapon. The bullets are being compared to ones taken from the ceiling that you fired during the party. I haven't seen the reports yet."

"They'll match up. Whoever set this up would be that thorough. Alexei, Felix, Ilya, any one of that group could have taken the gun I left in the limo. But the one I threw at the wall in my hotel room, I never saw it again. It could have ended up in anyone's hands. Even Yuri could have come back for it. What about the maid, Anna? Have the police interviewed her?''

''She's not available.''

''What does that mean?''

Nina shrugged. ''A quote from the police report. It could mean anything from deceased to vacationing at a Black Sea resort.''

The two women were quiet for a moment before Lara asked, ''Were any other marks found on Nadia's body? I'd like to see the autopsy reports.''

''I'll have everything copied for you. The report mentions only the two bullet wounds.''

''But did the pathologist examine the body for other marks?''

''The autopsy was limited to an examination of the two wounds.''

''That's not a full autopsy!''

''That's a Russian autopsy. Things you take for granted in your country such as disinfecting chemicals and rubber gloves are not in good supply in Russia.''

''Nina, that body has to be examined. We need to have an independent pathologist appointed to do our own autopsy. We're also going to need an investigator who can track down—''

Nina reached across and put her hands over Lara's. ''The court isn't going to appoint a pathologist or any other expert for you. You have to share the prosecutor's experts. And its investigator, Vulko.''

''That's insane. Experts are loyal to the side that pays them. And it's not just a question of loyalty. Opinions differ, especially expert ones.''

''You don't have to convince me. But it is the Russian way. Experts are neutral because we were a classless society.''

"But it didn't work under your Communist society. Why would it work now?"

"I didn't say it worked. I said it was the Russian way. And the economy makes it worse. With the bad economic conditions, the court will not pay for experts for a person charged with a crime."

"Great," Lara said. "Okay then, tell me about courtroom procedure. Start at the beginning and take me step by step through a trial."

Nina was about to answer when a thought struck Lara and she asked, "Are we being recorded?"

"I believe so." Nina shrugged. "That was often the custom under the Soviet regime. It's hard to break old habits. Now, you understand there are no jury trials."

Nina didn't seem intimidated by the possible eavesdropping and Lara mentally shrugged it off as par for the course. She was trying to get herself in tune to the Russian criminal justice system. Thinking like an American could be fatal.

"Right. A judge and two lay persons decide the case."

"Yes. Two citizens will be appointed by the court. But don't let the presence of three people fool you. The decision will be made by the judge."

"The citizens don't have equal voting rights with the judge?"

"Possessing a right," Nina said, "and using it are two different things. The idea of having citizens share a judge's authority, reducing the power of the judge, is good Marxist-Leninist theory. But except on rare occasions the citizens merely rubber stamp the judge's decision. They would not be chosen to serve as lay judges if they weren't the type to follow the judge's lead."

"Your rules of evidence, the rules governing oral testimony and other written and physical evidence, what are they?"

"The rules are what the judge says the rules are."

"Do you understand the concept of hearsay," Lara asked.

"Yes. Unsworn testimony, things people heard and said out of court. That is all admissible in a Russian trial."

"That would mean matters of speculation, what people believe or imagine can be admitted."

"The judge can exclude evidence, but the favored policy is for everyone to have their day in court."

"Everyone? I thought this was the defendant's day in court."

"Not in Russia. In America you have two sides in a criminal case, the prosecution and the defendant."

"True."

"In Russia there are usually more than two sides to a criminal case," Nina said. "The first thing that happens after the judge calls the case is that the defendant is told to step forward and explain why he or she committed the crime. You are expected to confess. You have no right to remain silent, no right to refuse to testify."

"No right against self-incrimination. Confession is good for the soul."

"Exactly. After the criminal steps forward and explains the reason for committing the crime or, less often, denies the crime, the judge asks the criminal questions about how the crime was committed and the person's motives."

"We call that cross-examination," Lara said, "and it's conducted by attorneys, not judges, in America."

"Yes. After the judge examines the accused, the prosecutor asks more questions. If the judge has been very thorough, the prosecutor may not ask any questions."

"The purpose must be to fill in things the judge missed."

"Yes. Now, after the judge and the prosecutor ask questions—"

"The defense attorney—"

"No, I told you, there are more than two sides to a Russian criminal case. At this point questions might be asked by another interested party, let's say a psychiatrist if the accused's sanity is questioned. This psychiatrist or psychologist may simply be used as an expert by the prosecution or he may take a full part in the proceedings as a party. Next, a lawyer representing the victim's interest can question—''

''Wait. Are you telling me that the victim or the victim's family are a party in the courtroom? They can have an attorney who asks questions and participates in the trial?''

''Yes, the victim's family or employer can hire an attorney or ask questions themselves.''

''I don't believe this. First the defendant is called forward and asked to confess. Then the judge cross-examines, followed by the prosecutor, experts, and any other interested party, including the victim in person.''

Nina nodded.

''Is Nadia's family getting a lawyer?''

''They already have one. I saw him on television when I was waiting for the clerk to give me records. The lawyer told the nation that he would work to ensure that Nadia's killer is punished, that she deserves the bullet.''

''Wonderful. Is this guy any good?''

''He's one of the best lawyers in Moscow.''

''Sounds familiar.'' Lara stared at Nina. ''You're not telling me it's Viktor Rykoff.''

''The very one. He said very nice things about Nadia. And cried.''

Lara wanted to scream. ''How can the man talk to me about my case and then represent an adverse party? That's a conflict of interest.''

''The goal of the Russian judicial system is to seek the truth. What you tell an attorney can also be used against you.''

''That destroys the attorney-client relationship.''

''That relationship hasn't been important in our society. It's important to me and to attorneys like me who are thinking in new ways. But, Lara, you have to accept that good or bad, right or wrong, the Russian system is the one we are dealing with.''

"I'm sorry, Nina. I just . . . tell me, is there a time when the defense attorney gets to ask questions?''

"Yes, of course. After the judge, the prosecutor, the victim, and any other interested party, the defense attorney may ask questions. And after the defense attorney has finished, the defendant is allowed to speak again and to question witnesses.''

"You mean the defendant and the defendant's attorney can both question witnesses?''

"Yes. It's very democratic.''

"More like a circus,'' Lara said. "It's just for show, especially if the case starts off with a confession. To me, a trial is like a chess game—it's about making the right moves, taking apart your opponent piece by piece, marching in experts to defeat your opponent's experts, putting on critical evidence at well-timed moments to capture just the right effect with the jury. In America trials are battlefields. Russian trials sound more like bureaucratic hearings.''

"You're probably right. They are not battlefields, certainly. I haven't told you the worst part. When you begin a trial with a confession—''

"Which would stop an American trial.''

"Exactly. In your country, once the accused admits guilt, there is no trial. Here, we usually start the trial with an admission of guilt. If you start with the concept that the accused is guilty, the rest is just a formality.''

"So you have been telling me.''

"But you have to understand how the Russian system actually operates. The judge has before him a person accused, a person who usually has confessed. The judge will thereafter go through the facts of the case. In your country, these facts would be presented to him by the prosecution through witnesses and evidence in open court. In Russia, the judge has been given a statement of the case prepared by the prosecution's investigator and the judge will use that as a road map. From that road map he will call witnesses he wants to hear from and ask to see evidence that interests him.''

"But that's all from the prosecution's side," Lara said. "By the time the case is called, the judge will be totally prejudiced against the defendant."

"Now you understand the role of prosecutors and people like Chief Investigator Vulko. They provide the judge with a direction and the judge follows it. But there is one fundamental right that no judge would deny a defendant."

"What? To be found guilty?"

Nina smiled. "They have that right, too. No, the right I'm speaking of is the last word."

"The last word?"

"Yes. After everyone else has spoken, after all the evidence has been put forward, after everyone—the prosecution, the defendant, the victim, or the victim's family and employer—has had the opportunity to ask questions and testify, there comes the grand finale''—Nina waved her hands dramatically—''and the judge turns to the defendant and says, 'Give us your final word.' ''

"*Help*, that's the word I'd choose. I'm sorry, what's the purpose of the last word?"

"To throw yourself at the mercy of the court. To explain why the crime was committed."

"The first word is a confession, the last word is a plea for mercy. I'm not sure there's much justice in between. How did you ever become an attorney in this crazy system? No, that's a stupid question. You were born in this system."

"I'm very proud to be an attorney."

"Of course you are. And so am I. I worked hard to get a law degree and pass the bar exam. And I know that there must be tremendous prejudices and obstacles put in your way. Were your parents like mine? Foreigners living in Russia?''

"Is that a polite way of asking why my skin is black? My father was a student from the Sudan. He . . . he left my mother pregnant."

"We have something in common. My father went off to Africa to fight a war and left my mother pregnant. He got himself killed."

"It's . . . it's been hard getting started. Defendants don't want a black lawyer." She stared down at the papers in front of her. "Judge Popov was punishing you for refusing Rykoff."

Lara leaned forward and put her hands on Nina's and whispered, "Then he made a mistake, my friend, because you and I are going into that courtroom ready for combat while the rest of them are only prepared to put on a show trial."

"You don't understand," Nina whispered. "The prosecutor and Rykoff will get together with the judge and limit what we can do."

"They're not going to limit us. You said that the case was getting incredible news attention. Russia's anxious to show its democratic face to the world. We're going to go in there and open our mouths, Nina. We're going to say things that are going to be repeated around the world."

"The judge will shut you up."

"American lawyers are shut up all the time. All we do is turn around and say the same thing in another way. You're not a good lawyer until you've been held in contempt at least a couple of times."

Nina shook her fists. "I'm so excited," she whispered. "New ideas, new approaches. We'll turn the Moscow court system on its ear. You just tell me what to do, how to win." Another thought occurred to her. "How many cases have you defended?" she asked.

"Defended? I'm a prosecutor. This will be the first."

THREE

T he police reports told them little of any value in terms of constructing a defense: while sitting naked in the spa, Nadia had been shot twice, once through the chest and what appeared to be a coup de grace in the back of the head.

The hot circulating water made it difficult to pin down an exact time of death. Despite the autopsy report acknowledging the fact that the hot water made it difficult to gauge an exact time of death, the pathologist who did the report set the time of death at one minute before Lara was captured.

The pathologist's logic took Lara a while to grasp. She finally realized it was the tail wagging the dog. Time of death was a required entry on the death form. The time of death could not be determined precisely because of the hot water, so the pathologist provided a time based upon the officer's statement as to when Lara was captured. If Lara had done the killing, it was a reasonable conclusion.

"But do you see the mentality?" she demanded of Nina. "I'm arrested, thus I am guilty, thus the pathologist doesn't have to waste his time using his training and equipment to determine the time of death when he can go by what a policeman told him."

"They're shorthanded at the morgue."

"Not as shorthanded as my whole life seems to have become. The police say they received an anonymous tip that a woman carrying a gun had entered the tower and a shot was heard. I want the tape of that anonymous call," Lara said.

"What tape? If they have a tape, they won't give it to us. And if they don't have a tape, they won't tell us they don't have it. I'll find out what I can about the call. But don't expect a tape recording. The report says no one in the area of the tower reported hearing shots.''

''That's in my favor, no one heard the shots.''

''There was heavy construction down the block.''

''But the anonymous caller claims to have heard a shot. Don't you find it interesting that Yuri Kirov and his group of officers were the ones who responded to the anonymous call? There are thousands of police officers in Moscow and the one who responds is the same guy I've been tripping over every time I turn around.''

''The building is in the control area of those officers.''

''But the report says Yuri joined the cops in the lobby. I want to know everything about that call. If the call wasn't taped, I want to know the exact time it was received, who received it, who that person reported to, when the officers left the police station, how long it took them to get to the building, up the elevators, and through the penthouse doors. That's another thing—did they break in the door or have a key or were they let in by someone?''

''Do you also want to know their brand of cigarettes? An officer will testify about the call at the trial. Perhaps not the officer who received it, but—''

''No, we don't wait for trial to find out about the call. You never ask a question during a trial you don't already know the answer to because the answer might just sink your case. We need to know everything that will help us and everything that will damage us before we enter the courtroom. Keep reminding yourself that you're not an administrator of justice in the old system—you're a gladiator fighting to the death in the new one.''

''I keep reminding myself that I am a gladiator,'' Nina said, ''and a voice keeps whispering in my ear that I'm really a mouse.''

''Then be Mighty Mouse. Listen to me, Nina. I'm being framed. To frame a person for a crime like this everything has to run like clockwork. What we need to do is to uncover the inconsistencies. Remember that word, glue it to your brain, *inconsistencies*. What's an inconsistency? I arrived in the penthouse only a minute or two before the police came crashing in. That means that the call to the police had already been made before I entered. I was probably being watched on the street and when I approached the building the call was made.''

"If the call was made before you even entered, perhaps a shopkeeper spotted you entering and can pinpoint the time. If you can prove through a witness the time you entered—''

"You're getting it. We need an investigator to go door-to-door and find people who heard the shots. I might be able to establish I was still at the dacha or on my way into town when the shots were fired. The investigator can track down the maid Anna and talk to her. She would know what happened to the gun I left at the hotel.''

"It's the same bullet,'' Nina said. "I was told the report was not finished but here it is. One of the two bullets removed from the ceiling matches a bullet in Nadia.''

"Wait. You say a ceiling bullet matches one of the bullets that killed Nadia. Was she shot by two different guns?''

"Both slugs were fired from a .38, but one of the bullets was too damaged to analyze.''

"We need a ballistics expert to go over the results and personally examine each bullet. If Moscow police ballistics are as scientific as their autopsies, we'll probably find one bullet came from a cannon and the other from a pea-shooter.''

"But the ballistics expert says—''

"Nina, that's *their* ballistics expert. Our expert might find it was fired from an entirely different gun. Ballistics experts render opinions based upon evidence and many times the evidence is subject to more than one interpretation. Remember, question, question—''

"Question everything. My boyfriend has a friend in the

army who is a ballistics expert. He'll probably help.''

"Good." Lara continued talking as Nina took notes. "Let's assume it's the same gun, the gun I carried back to the hotel from the party. Yuri, Detective Kirov, knew I had it—hell, I threw it at him. He could have come back later and got it. Alexei, or perhaps his staff, people like Ilya and Felix, would have known about it if Anna returned the gun to one of them.

"If Anna didn't pick up the gun, another maid could have found it and turned it over to anyone in the world, especially in a country where everyone is still spying on everyone else." Lara ran her hands through her hair and pulled. "God, I don't know what to think. It's all too complicated."

Nina looked up from her writing. "You were the last one seen with the gun and the one caught with it. How do you explain that under American jurisprudence." ·

"You punt."

"Punt?"

"It's a joke. An American football term. When the other team's got your back to the wall you kick the ball to get out of it. Meaning you take a gamble or do something brilliant . . . or you just close your eyes and jump."

"What is our brilliant explanation?"

"I was framed. We'll know more after we get an investigator. You said the court won't help with that."

"Don't worry, I have friends who will help."

"Nina, I'm so glad you're my attorney."

The young Russian attorney grinned. "I still can't believe it either. I'll wake up tomorrow morning and pinch myself."

"I already did a reality check myself and found out the nightmare was real," Lara said. "Did they test the gun for fingerprints?"

Nina took a minute to skim through the reports. "Fingerprint tests were unnecessary because the police had observed you holding the gun."

"But what about other people who held the gun before me?"

"Your prints would have wiped out those."

"No, absolutely not. I only grabbed the gun by the handle. I don't even remember touching the barrel. That's sloppy police work. Even if I smudged some prints, there might be others." Lara got to her feet, her voice rising. "We have to have the gun tested for prints."

"Not so loud."

Lara sat wearily back down and whispered, "Sorry. I keep forgetting we're probably being bugged. We need a fingerprint expert appointed by the court immediately and an order to the Moscow police to turn over the gun for examination forthwith. And crime scene pictures, not photocopies of pictures, I want duplicate prints. Make sure they turn over all prints, not just selected ones. And besides checking for witnesses and searching for Anna, your people should interview the people on the prosecutor's witness list.

"And we'll need background checks on all the key players, Alexei, Felix, Ilya, Belkin, Nadia, and don't forget Detective Yuri Kirov. And Gropski, the security man at the Gorky who turned me onto Belkin, we need to locate him. He dropped out of sight after Belkin was killed."

Nina wrote frantically. "We'll need to enlist the Russian army to act as investigators."

"Try to find us a pathologist. We have to conduct our own autopsy."

When she was through writing, Nina looked up and asked, "Is this how criminal cases are fought in your country? With an army of experts?"

"The toughest case I ever prosecuted involved a teenage girl who had been strangled. The defense attorney not only got the court to appoint a defense pathologist to do another autopsy on the body, he watched the autopsy."

"The defense attorney won the case?"

"No, I was there, too, handing his pathologist forceps

and scalpels. The second autopsy came up with a critical piece of evidence—the young woman had been strangled from behind by a left-handed person. That was deduced by the fact that the tissue was more severely damaged on the right side of the victim's neck than the left side. If I hadn't been standing by, that information would never have been revealed.''

''So the defendant was left-handed?''

''Yes.''

''I really admire you. I have never heard of an attorney attending an autopsy.''

''Don't admire me. I was sick for a week afterward. Once, in a moment of temporary insanity, I had the pathologist lead me through an autopsy on a Jane Doe, an unidentified body, with a knife wound. Our theory was that the defendant stabbed her in the stomach. The defense position was that the wound was self-inflicted, hari-kari style. By participating in the autopsy, by observing the position her body had to be in for the holes in the layers of flesh and organs to line up, I was able to explain how the murder occurred.''

Nina's mouth had dropped.

Lara took a deep breath. ''I hated every moment of it but I told myself I was doing it for a woman who had lost so much she didn't even have a name for a grave marker. She had been pretty, too, but . . .'' Lara choked up.

''Now I know what you mean about being a good lawyer. You have to be a doctor, a detective, and a scientist.''

''Don't forget being an actor, psychologist, and occasionally avenging angel.''

Nina's face suddenly twisted with a surge of emotion and she burst into tears. It was Lara's turn to gape as the young lawyer hid her face in her hands and wept.

''Nina, what's wrong?''

''There will be no experts, no tests,'' she said, sobbing. ''They'll convict you and you will die because I can never be the lawyer you need.''

Lara got out of her chair and went around to the other side of the table. She put her hands on Nina's shoulders and squeezed. "I feel like a fool," she told Nina, "telling you what a great attorney I was back in the States. The truth is I always had a team of investigators and experts at my beck and call because I had the power of the government behind me. This is the first time I've had to wing it."

"Lara, the court will never appoint experts. No fingerprint expert, no pathologist, no investigators. I told you, I can get friends to help to knock on doors, someone to look at the bullets—"

"Just do what you can. If we can't have our own pathologist, get as much information as you can from theirs. The only thing I ask is that you try, and that you shake off the mentality that a defense lawyer is an arm of the government. You're young and tough and part of the new Russia, Nina. Don't let the old ways"—she almost said "kill me"—"make us lose."

She pointed a finger down at the young attorney. "Stop crying. We can do it."

Nina wiped away her tears. "Right. We're tough, we don't cry. I don't know what to do, I can't get you the things you need. If you had money . . . I thought all—"

"Don't say it, don't call me a rich American. If I hear that phrase one more time I'm going to run screaming into the night. Or at least back to my cell."

Lara suddenly thought about Nina's other clients. "What about the rest of your law practice? How busy does it keep you?"

Nina laughed. "The rest of my law practice takes a few hours a week."

"Take the money in my purse. It'll help with taxi fare and food while you run around."

Nina waved away the offer. "I take the metro and pack my lunch. I don't know a pathologist, but I have my own doctor who can answer medical questions."

"It won't help." Lara shook her head.

Nina looked as if she was going to cry again. "Lara, I can't get a pathologist to let me conduct an autopsy. That just isn't done in Russia."

"Don't worry about autopsies. I'll go through the pathologist's report and see what we need to have filled in. When you don't have your own experts you try to get enough out of the opposing experts to add to your case or impeach the expert at trial."

"I can't do anything about background checks. That would violate the privacy of our citizens," Nina said out loud, then leaned closer to Lara and whispered, "My boyfriend works in the military records division of the army. Most of the men we're investigating should have military records. Even if they didn't serve, there will be background checks."

"Great."

Lara stood up and gave Nina a big hug. Nina put her own arms around Lara and squeezed.

"We're going to win this one," Lara told her.

Nina gave her a high five. "Right on, sister." She giggled. "I saw that in an American movie."

It was late afternoon before they decided to call it quits. They hugged again before Nina left.

Lara sat wearily at the counsel table, waiting for the matron to return from letting Nina out.

The woman unlocked the conference door and gestured for Lara to come out. Lara waited while the woman relocked the door. The woman spoke to her as they walked back toward the cell block.

"You are making a mistake," she told Lara.

"A mistake?"

"The black girl, she's no good."

"Why do you say that?"

The matron glared at her. "Are you stupid? She's black. If she was good, she'd be white."

Jesus.

"No one will listen to her in court."

"I hope that's not true," Lara murmured.

"What did she tell you about herself? Did she tell you her father was an African king?" The matron laughed. "Everyone in the courts knows about her. Her mother was a whore, a prostitute and a drug addict. That's why they give her the prostitution cases. They say it's in her blood."

Lara didn't speak and the look on her face annoyed the guard. "Didn't you hear what I told you, prisoner?"

"I heard you. I must have one hell of a lawyer. A woman who could crawl out of the gutter and make it all the way to the Moscow courts by the time she's twenty-five must be one tough lady. I'm glad she's on my side."

The matron gave her a shove. "Move, prisoner."

FOUR

Lara kept her mouth shut the rest of the way back to the cell.

The matron opened the cell door and as Lara started to step into the black hole she realized someone was there.

"Shhh. Don't make a sound." It was Alexei.

In the next cell a woman started whining about the noise and the matron told her to shut up or she'd take away her food privileges.

Alexei pulled her into the cell.

"I can only stay a minute. I paid my way in." He laughed, an almost girlish giggle. "Imagine paying your way into jail."

She didn't say a word.

"I know this is hell for you. But it's just for a short time. I can't get you out yet, but I will. There's too much publicity about the case right now. When the publicity dies down I'll buy your way out."

"I'm charged with murder, Alexei, not shoplifting."

"Everything is for sale, but it's too soon. I even had to leave the penthouse in disguise today just to come over here. Camera crews and reporters have the tower staked out twenty-four hours a day. Darling, at the right time I'll grease the right palms."

She hated the way he called her darling. A melodramatic ring came with it. There was melodrama to everything about him right now, as if being the prisoner's savior was another role to play, riding up to the gallows at the last moment and cutting away the hangman's noose with his sword.

"You've made me famous all over the world," he told her. "Our love affair and you killing Nadia is getting more news play than Princess Di."

Anger blew the roof off her emotions. She grabbed him by the lapels. "How dare you say I killed Nadia. I never touched Nadia."

"Shhh, calm down."

"I never touched her."

"Then who killed her?"

"Why don't you tell me?"

"Me? I never killed her. I was getting tired of the bitch, and she was a bitch even if I shouldn't speak harshly of the dead. I was tired of her constant demands for money and frankly bored with her as a lover, but that's hardly a reason to kill her. I was already distancing myself from her when I brought you into my life."

"Nadia was trying to blackmail you. She knows Felix has something on you."

"What did she tell you?"

"Exactly that. What does Felix have on you? And what does it have to do with that picture of you with my mother and our neighbor?"

"Felix isn't blackmailing me."

Something about his voice told her he was telling the truth. It was the way he tossed aside the idea, as if blackmail was insignificant compared to what was really going on between him and Felix.

"You're right about the picture. I didn't even realize the picture existed. I don't remember your mother or the other woman. Apparently there was a party at Felix's apartment, I was there, pictures were taken. When you showed up at my cowboy party, it struck a chord with Felix. He found the picture and used it."

"Used it for what? You said he isn't blackmailing you."

"I can't explain."

"I'm facing a murder charge. I think I deserve some explanations."

"It has nothing to do with Nadia or the charges against you. Felix is part of my past."

"What part of the past?"

"Nothing to do with your mother. I . . . I used to be KGB."

"You and half the other people in this country. What does that have to do with anything that's happening now?"

"I can't explain. You'll just have to trust me."

"Trust you? I'm accused of murdering your girlfriend who was hot to blackmail you and you want me to trust you?"

"What were you doing at the penthouse? Searching for the picture?"

"Yes. Nadia was to meet me. By the time I arrived someone had put two bullets in her. If you want me to trust you, answer a question honestly. Anna returned my cowboy outfit to you, the hat and boots. Did she return a gun, too?"

"Who's Anna?"

"The damn maid you had spying on me."

"Oh, yes, the one with the club foot. I don't know what she returned. She would have given the stuff to Ilya. If he wasn't there, Felix probably would have taken it. Is one of the guns supposed to be the gun that killed Nadia?"

"That's what they say."

"The police were digging holes in the ceiling. They must have been looking for a bullet to match."

"They were and they did. The murder weapon was one of the guns I fired that night."

"That's bad."

"Bad?" She laughed, a harsh grate in her throat. "It's worse than bad. I feel like my life's been thrown in front of a runaway train. I need to talk to Anna. Or at least have my lawyer talk to her."

"I don't know where she is. I'll ask Ilya to locate her."

"If you want to help me, find her. If she can testify she returned the gun—"

He was shaking her head. "I remember now. Ilya mentioned that the maid had returned your outfit but not the gun. You left one gun in the limo. He wanted me to ask you about the other."

She shivered listening to him. "I don't believe this."

"Is it important she returned the gun?"

"Of course it's important. That would get the murder weapon out of my hands and into someone else's. It's the difference between being convicted of murder and having a fighting chance."

"Don't worry. I'll have Anna found and she'll testify that you returned both guns. It's as simple as that."

"That's perjury."

"It's only perjury when you get caught."

She shook her head. "No, no, you can't do that. Find Anna so my attorney can talk to her."

He suddenly looked as if he had eaten something that left a bad taste. "I've heard about your attorney. You have to get rid of her. I'll get you the best attorney in Moscow."

"I've already fired the best attorney in Moscow. I'm keeping the one I've got."

"That's insane. Do you know her background?"

The matron came back to the cell. "You have to leave. It's time to change shifts. Hurry."

Alexei took hold of Lara. She held her arms against her chest so she wouldn't touch him intimately.

"I'll get you out of this," he said. "You must have faith and trust me."

He was back to his role-playing.

"That night when we made love . . ."

She tensed against him.

"It was . . . it was the first time any woman has satisfied me. Nadia was nothing."

"Hurry," the matron hissed.

Alexei tried to kiss her on the lips but she turned her head to give her cheek.

"Find Anna," she told him.

He left and she sank in a dark corner of her cell and wrapped her blanket around her.

The adrenaline rush she had earlier had drained her and she was exhausted. She tried to put some of the things Alexei had said into a sensible order, but the thoughts kept melting away, all except one: Felix wasn't blackmailing Alexei. She told herself she shouldn't believe that statement but she intuitively knew it was true. And it raised an interesting question.

Why would two men who obviously had nothing but contempt for each other, two men who were drastically different in temperament and ambitions, two men who had nothing in common, stay together as . . . as what?

Just before she fell into a deep sleep another thought slipped into her mind like a snake slithering under the threshold of a door.

Alexei wasn't rich and eccentric. He was rich and crazy.

XXI

"I believe you said yesterday you would like
to question me...about my acquaintance
with the murdered woman...I believe it's
a sort of legal rule, a sort of legal tradition
——for all investigating lawyers——to begin
their attack from afar, with a trivial...
to divert the man who they are cross examining,
to disarm his caution and then all at once to
give him an unexpected knock down blow with
some fatal question. Isn't that so? It's
a sacred tradition, mentioned, I fancy, in all
the manuals of the art?"

—The murderer Raskolnikov,
Crime and Punishment,
Fyodor Dostoyevsky

O N E

The shock of being Lara's defender was still with Nina as she came down the public corridor at the jail with terror and elation elbowing for space in her mind. I'm going to be the most famous attorney in Russia!

She felt an unpleasant damp chill under her arms and realized she'd been in a nervous sweat talking to Lara. What have I gotten myself into? A life in my hands!

Handling the case would get her respect—no, not respect, she would be envied. Perhaps even her fellow lawyers, her colleagues is how she thought of them although she knew the camaraderie wasn't reciprocal, would treat her as an equal instead of a "girl," a black girl, who had a license to practice law but was relegated to representing legal lepers.

Still deep in thought, she pushed through the front door and was caught flat-footed by blinding flashes of light.

"What did your client tell you?"

"Why did she kill Nadia?"

"Is it true she shows no remorse?"

Television and newspaper reporters were a blur behind a flash of bulbs and glare of lights. Not knowing what to say, what to do, she simply put her head down and forged forward, plowing into shouted questions and a dizzy blaze of lights.

A stinging rain, tiny bits of ice needles, pricked at her face along with the questions as she hurried down the steps. Almost to street level, she realized with horror that she had planned to catch a bus.

I can't get on a bus!

The thought was mortifying. The lawyer on the most sensational murder case in Russia being televised around the world climbing onto a bus. Several taxis were lined up at the curb and she headed for one.

A woman jumped in front of her and poked a microphone at her face. "Tell the people why this foreigner killed our Nadia."

Nina knew she had seen the woman somewhere before, probably on the Moscow television news.

Running away like a scared rabbit was not going to help Lara's case—or her own public image. Summoning her courage and a deep breath, she stopped next to the rear door of the taxi and turned to face the media hounds.

She lifted her chin with pride and said in a strong, clear voice, "Lara Patrick has declared her innocence to me. The evidence will support the fact that my client was simply in the wrong place at the wrong time and a terrible mistake has been made in arresting her for a crime she did not commit."

As she turned to open the rear door of the taxi, someone shouted, "With a gun in her hand?"

Before she could get in the taxi the Moscow News woman was back in her face, this time without the microphone. "Good they made you her lawyer," she hissed, "she'll die faster."

Nina's briefcase strap tangled on the inside door handle as she got into the cab and she clumsily slammed the door with the strap still caught.

Her sudden elation had been deflated by the bitch's remark. She stared straight ahead, ignoring the newspeople

shouting questions at the taxi window as the driver moved
the cab away from the curb and into traffic. The driver
asked where she wanted to go.

"What? Where? Uh, take me to—" No! Damn. She
didn't have the money for a taxi. She only had bus fare
and snack money on her. A taxi ride cost more than a week
of taking buses.

"Turn left here."

After the taxi made the turn she checked out the back
window to make sure there were no newspeople following.
The coast was clear and she told the driver, "Pull over
here."

She threw what she considered to be a reasonable fare
onto the front seat and bailed out of the taxi with the annoyed driver grabbing the bills and checking the denomi-
nations in the dimming light. Still afraid she'd be spotted
by newspeople, she walked several blocks before boarding
a bus.

The bus was crowded with home-bound workers. With
standing room only, she wrapped her arm around a post
and leaned wearily against the post as nervous energy
oozed out of her.

Some international celebrity, she thought. The world
news media will have the courthouse staked out each day
of trial. She would provide a fine impression arriving each
day in a city bus!

The most famous attorney in all Russia rode home today
on a metro bus, she mocked herself with an imaginary
headline, a fine example of communism in the age of the
market economy.

She had heard that in the West attorneys, like doctors,
were a privileged class who made great sums of money.
Attorneys had certainly not been a privileged class under
communism, at least not criminal defense attorneys who
were at the bottom of the legal pay scale.

Legal services were supposed to have been free under

communism, but even before the Fall defense attorneys had to supplement their meager income with "gifts" from clients—small payments from clients who wanted the attorney to put in an "extra" effort on the case.

Not only was she too wide-eyed innocent and idealistic for under-the-table payments, her clients were the bottom of the barrel—people with both feet in the gutter and a revolving door to jail.

She loved the freedoms that came with the collapse of communism, but economically she was still a Communist and wondered if she would survive in the market economy. Dealing with people about money embarrassed and frustrated her.

People who came to lawyers had problems. Hurts. It made her mad that she was now expected to put a price tag on each problem, to price out a legal problem like a three-piece outfit. "Let's see, Boris punched you in the jaw and broke it, Ivana. That was before you grabbed the vodka bottle and smashed it across his head. That's twenty thousand rubles to defend you for inflicting a serious head injury on Boris, but I'll discount that five thousand because he broke your jaw first.

"Of course this price assumes Boris will someday regain consciousness. And after the criminal trial, there will be the divorce. The price of the divorce will depend upon the number of children and whether you own an interest in that apartment you have been sharing with Boris's parents for the past ten years, and who gets custody of the dog and the Medal of Lenin."

Doctors and hospitals had jumped enthusiastically into the market economy. Not only was there a fee for the doctor to cut out your appendix, a hundred more charges went with it, from a cost for the gurney you lay on, for every stitch that closed the wound, for the bandage over the wound, for *everything*.

She could understand how one could price out a piece of merchandise, how the price of a car depended on the size, power of the engine, quality of the paint and interior, and dozens of other features. But how do you put a price on pain and justice? Justice and medicine should not know social or economic boundaries.

A child, a golden-haired boy about five leaning against his mother's knee, stared at her from across the aisle. The boy was fascinated by her dark skin color. It may have been the first time the boy had seen a person with ebony skin.

Moscow was a city of eight million and the people with an African-Russian heritage would probably fit in one apartment building, she thought. Not that blacks wouldn't be visible among tourists and personnel of foreign embassies milling around Red Square and the Kremlin compound. During a trip to a community east of the city, she discovered that many Russians living in rural areas had never seen an ebony-skinned person other than on a television screen.

The boy had the naive, wide-eyed curiosity about her that she had found among rural people.

She wished other people in the city regarded her with such innocence instead of attributing characteristics to her based upon ill-conceived notions about people of African heritage. Even though ninety-nine percent of Muscovites had never had any personal interaction with a person of black skin, an ugly form of racism had reared in the city since the fall of communism.

It had always been there, she thought, the racial superiority that light-skinned Russians felt toward people with darker skin, but like so many other emotions, racism had not officially existed under the Soviet Union.

When the regime fell and the non-Russians to the south, people of Turkish, Mongolian, Armenian, and other ancestry, broke away from Russian predominance, many Russians became embittered and contemptuous of persons with darker skin. And she had *very* dark skin.

The resentment was characterized by the Russians calling anyone, or anything, they didn't like "black" or "mafioso" and usually as both.

The new social attitude made its way into billy clubs police carried. A few weeks ago she saw police converge on unlicensed street vendors and order them to pack up their goods and move on. The pale-skinned vendors were given tongue lashings—although a dark-skinned vendor was beaten by the officers.

Her foster mother, a tall, flaxen-haired Russian woman of great compassion, had raised Nina to be proud of her ebony skin, had told her that being the only child of African heritage in her school, in the neighborhood, in the whole world for all Nina knew as a child, was a matter of pride, not inferiority.

"Most Russian children are colorless," her pale-skinned foster mother told her, "but you were made special."

Now as a small boy on a bus stared at her in wonderment Nina felt her pride bristling and she straightened a little against the weariness.

Her eye caught someone else staring at her. To the boy's left a man, a fiftyish Russian brute with a low brow and wide, flat, vodka-reddened nose, was grinning at her.

She was about to smile at the man but then she realized that he was leering at her as he massaged something in his pants—a sausage shape bulging in his crotch.

An African's skin turns black from burning with sexual excitement, an idiot neighbor man had once told her foster mother in Nina's presence. That the remark was jaw-dropping ignorance didn't excuse it any more than the neighbor's leering at a teenage Nina. It was the mentality of some Russian men. When a Russian man was a pig, he was a world-class pig.

Her pride balled up and choked her throat. Tears burned her eyes as she turned away from the swine. Why did the color of her skin have to make her different. Her heart and soul were the same color as everyone else's.

* * *

The bus dropped her two blocks from her apartment and the "world famous attorney" walked wearily home, lugging her briefcase and the heavy thoughts that ached at her. The comment from the newswoman had undermined her confidence—and the old pervert on the bus had reminded her that she was different.

As a child, she had never thought of herself as anything but Russian. Now she was more conscious of the fact that even though she thought of herself only as Russian there were others who thought of her as something different. Worse, as something *less*.

In her early teens, she had read a story about a Russian astronaut who visited a planet where everyone had four arms and four legs and eyes all around their head. They put the astronaut in a zoo cage because they thought he was a freak. She had imagined herself as being like that astronaut, a visitor to a strange planet populated by people with all the color bleached out of their skin.

Her foster mother had told her that she was different in a special way and she had grown up with the belief that standing out from the crowd was better than being just another anonymous face in an ocean of similar faces.

She still hung on to that belief but began weathering stormy assaults on it when she entered a pristine world of white lawyers and found many treated her as something less than the other young lawyers who had had lower grades than her at the university and displayed less knowledge in the courtroom.

One of the blacks at her university, a South African exchange student, had told her that the feeling of alienation was driving him crazy, that he felt like a fly in a sugar bowl, that everywhere he turned he saw white faces and he never saw faces that looked like his.

There was a difference between her and the student. She was color blind when it came to races. She never really thought of people as Russians, Armenians, Ukrainians, or Azerbaijanis, but simply as people.

He told her that she had buried her head so she wouldn't see the racism all around her and feel the hurt. He was probably right. Racism was an ugly side to life that was there every day, like trash in the gutters and graffiti on walls.

But she ignored it and fought it, savoring the friends she had made who didn't think of her in racist terms. In her mind, if she allowed herself to think in racial terms she was becoming a racist herself and separating herself mentally from others.

Yuri pulled his unmarked militia car over to the curb and lit a cigarette as Nina got off the bus. He rolled down his window and let some of the smoke escape as he watched her cross the street, dodging cars in a city where pedestrians were fair game. The needle-rain had stopped and the chill that came with the fall of night turned the air thick.

She's a complication, he thought. That stupid judge had upset his plan when he threw the young lawyer at Lara as a joke.

When he calculated Nina had gone halfway up the block, he steered the car back into traffic and turned onto the street where she was walking.

TWO

Nina lived six flights up a blunt concrete structure built pre-Great Patriotic War-Stalinist style to repel bombs and grace. An elevator shaft went all of the way up to the tenth floor but no one had ever seen the elevator, not even old-timers who had lived in the building since it was built.

The manager claimed the shaft had been constructed to accommodate an innovative new elevator car but that the factory that was going to produce them turned out anti-tank guns instead.

She was dragging by the time she reached her apartment building. As with most Soviet architecture, the building had no esthetic value, no ambiance other than utilitarian, a ten-story concrete gray hulk wedged between two other concrete hulks. Graffiti on the wall next to the entrance door, a scrabble unintelligible to anyone but the spray-can artist, added a post-Soviet touch.

She hung her briefcase on her back before she tackled the stairs. In a foreign magazine she had seen a clever leather briefcase that converted from hand-carry to back-pack and she had sewn similar straps on her own briefcase so she could comfortably tote it miles across the city.

Being particularly poor in Moscow, as opposed to simply being poor like most people, was healthy—walking to and from bus stops and up six flights to her apartment kept her in decent physical shape.

She was proud of her body, having lost her baby fat in the first year of college when she participated in sports and boys and now kept it off by just being poor and walking a lot.

The smell of food in the hallway, trapped by walls that could repel bombs, made her stomach juices gurgle and reminded her that she hadn't eaten lunch.

As she lugged herself up six flights of stairs after the most hectic day of her life—save perhaps the day she was born—she grinned to herself and decided to hell with eco-nomic equality, just give me enough money so I can have an apartment with an elevator and the price of taxis in the winter.

There was no number or name on the apartment door but the metal door to her apartment was easy to describe to friends who came to visit. "It's the one with dents in the door." The dents were put in it by a prior tenant who tried to kick it in after his wife locked him out for drinking too much.

A crazy jumble of locks were on the door but only one of them worked and she used her key for that one.

She didn't know if the three unused locks had been put on by prior tenants over the years or if the old locks came with the door. Maybe the factory that made the keys for the locks was converted to making hand grenades before it got around to making the keys.

The entryway into the apartment was dim, lit only by a dull night-light plugged into an outlet near the floor. She smelled meat soup as she entered and heard the sound of children.

Her roommates were an older woman who occupied one bedroom and a married couple who had the other bedroom. The older woman worked the night shift and took care of her daughter's two kids in the afternoon until the day-shift daughter got off work.

Nina's private living space was the dining room to the right off the hallway. Directly across from the dining room was the kitchen, then the living room and hallway that led to the bathroom and two bedrooms. The living room, kitchen, and bathroom were communal.

Three unrelated sets of people sharing one small apartment only worked because the people were forced to cooperate with each other—there was a bathroom schedule, a cooking schedule. The only area not scheduled was the small living room and it was more a "lobby" that people passed through to get to their rooms than a real living area. It was used more for entertaining visitors and the older woman's grandchildren to romp in than for anything else.

It was too early for the married couple to be home from work and she was grateful for that because it meant she had the bathroom to herself for a while.

She slipped between the heavy curtains that partitioned off her room from the hallway, leaving the curtains open a bit so some of the light that flowed into the hallway from the living room took the edge off of the darkness. Everything was expensive on her small income, even electricity.

Nina didn't have a TV and usually didn't miss it, but tonight she wanted to see if she was on the news. Later she'd go with her boyfriend to the apartment he shared with three army buddies and watch the evening news.

She hurriedly took off her clothes and grabbed a heavy cotton robe and towel off of the end of the bed and a basket from a small table that sat just inside the curtains. The basket was a portable bathroom cabinet for her bath items and makeup.

In a society that knew only extremes it was to be expected that hot shower water would come either lukewarm or hot enough to boil eggs. The water in their building was of the boiling variety and the cold water supply only came in cranky spurts that left her alternating between being just scalded and a threat that her skin would peel off.

Wrapped in her heavy robe, she left the steamy bathroom and hurried down the cool hallway to her room. Slipping through the curtains, her hand fumbled for the light switch when a man's voice caused her to freeze.

"Don't turn around," a raspy voice said. "Put down the basket."

She set the basket on the table. As she straightened, the man behind her grabbed her robe by the back and pulled it off of her.

"You slut, you've been fucking with the wrong people. We're going to teach you a lesson."

The curtain was open a crack and cold air from the hallway seeped in and wrapped around her ankles, moving up her legs, leaving goose bumps in its wake.

The man shifted on his feet and moved closer to her. "We know what you are."

She could feel his breath on the back of her neck.

"We know what you want," he whispered.

A shiver raced down her spine.

"We're going to give it to you."

He shifted behind her again and the draft shivered her.

"My friend says you like two cocks at the same time," he whispered. A few feet in front of her, across from the foot of her bed, a male figure was barely visible in the darkness.

"He's going to fuck your teats," the voice behind her said.

She shut her eyes and swallowed slowly. Her breath was becoming shallow at the same time her pulse was racing with excitement. In her mind's eye she saw a man's penis against her naked chest, rubbing between her breasts, sliding over the mound, the head of the penis pressing against her nipple. Her nipples rose, hardening against the imagined penis.

"After he fucks your breasts he's going to stick his cock in your mouth. He's going to fuck your mouth, slipping it in deeper and deeper," the man behind her said.

In her imagination she felt the penis warm and soft, pushing by her lips, slowly sliding in, pulsating, growing larger and harder, until it had swollen to fill her whole mouth, her tongue pressing against it, tasting its maleness.

"While he's fucking your mouth I'm going to bend you over and spread your legs," the voice rasped.

She moved her feet apart.

"I'm going to slip my cock between your legs."

The man shifted again, touching the curtains, and a cold draft came in, brushing the back of her thighs, tickling the dampness between her legs. She felt her breasts, cupping one in each hand, lifting them, feeling a surge of pleasure from her nipples to her clitoris.

"As he's fucking your mouth I'm going to slip my cock between your legs and rub it against your cunt."

The goose bumps were gone, melted by her rising desire. Her legs spread farther apart and she swayed a little.

"We know what you are, we checked you out," he rasped, "you're not the innocent little girl you act like, you're a slut. While he fucks your mouth, I'm going to—"

She spun around and grabbed him, pressing her moist bare flesh against his, hungrily attacking his lips, pushing her tongue into his mouth.

From the living room came the sound of the television going on and the rousing sound of a military march as he entered her from the front, the two of them doing a dance of love as he lifted her from the floor with the power of his male part and took her to the bed, entering deep into her as he laid her on the bed.

"I love you," she whispered.

THREE

Mikhail Ivanovich Raskdikof, Misha to Nina, had the sweet face of an angel and the soft brown eyes of a doe. He should have been a priest, she told him, because of his angelic features, but he made a better devil when he whispered naughty things in her ear when they made love.

They were naked in bed. Nina's robe lay sideways across them, covering their private parts. She had the robe pulled up nearly to her chin to hide her bare breasts. Sitting side by side, they were two stripes of a zebra.

"You're famous. You'll be rich. Let's get married tomorrow. My father told me it was better to marry an ugly woman with many pigs than a beauty with none."

Nina dropped her spoon in the warm borscht he had brought for dinner and gave him an elbow in the shoulder.

"Your father works in a tire factory. He has never been on a farm or seen a live pig."

Misha grinned and slurped borscht.

"The borscht is good," she said.

"I made it last night. I told my friends we'd be there by eight and I knew after hearing about you all afternoon on the radio that you would be too busy and important to make dinner.''

She giggled with girlish pleasure. "This morning I was the least busy and least important lawyer in Moscow, in all Russia. Tonight I am too busy and important.''

"I can't believe you're handling the most sensational murder case in the country and getting no money. From an American!''

"She has no money. I guess Americans are the same as everyone else. Poor and not poor. I'm so scared, Misha. What if I fail? What if I do something stupid?''

"You won't fail and you're not stupid.''

"I've never handled a punch in the nose. This is a *murder* case.''

He shrugged. "It's all the same law, all the same procedures. You have to do what all the other attorneys do—act like you know something.''

Placing the bowl on the side table, she snuggled against him. His army uniform was neatly draped over the railing at the foot of her bed. He had come directly from his job as a computer specialist in the Moscow Area Military Command.

His cohort, the other "rapist," was on the table next to the foot of the bed. He was the upper half of the lifesize statute of Yezhov, the notorious NKVD leader at the time of the show trials of the Great Terror in the 1930s. Yezhov used to hold shooting contests in which NKVD marksmen competed to see who could kill the most prisoners with a single bullet. The marksmen obtained the best results by lining the prisoners up so they could be shot sideways.

Yezhov had been toppled from his perch in the hallowed halls at the university during the August demonstrations that swept communism out of power. Nina rescued him from a trash heap, his right ear broken, his nose flattened, from the beating he took at the hands of students.

"It's hard to pretend you know something when you've never seen good lawyering in action. Most of our legal history has involved prosecuting people because they dared to question the horrible system they had to live under.'' She threw a pillow at Yezhov and it plopped against him.

''Why did you do that?''

''He was leering at me.''

Misha shook his head. ''Famous two hours and you're already crazy.''

''Oh, Misha. When I think about the case I'm on, I feel exhilarated, like an explorer going down a path no one else has ever set foot upon. Then I think about Lara's life in my hands and I panic. It's my life, too. If I make a fool of myself and harm her case, I'll kill myself.''

She hid her head against his chest.

''You won't fail.'' He put his arms around her and squeezed her to him. ''If the case is lost, it will be because no one else could have won it. Besides, in my eyes you are not a success or a failure, you are the woman I love and am going to marry.''

''I don't know, Misha. I may fail exactly because of who I am. A news reporter said today that Lara Patrick will die sooner because I'm her lawyer.''

''That's stupid.''

''That's life. And you joke about your father's advice about marriage but you don't dare even take me to your parents and tell them you plan to marry and that their grandchild will be the color of those expensive Italian coffee drinks being sold in espresso bars.''

She told him about the little boy and the old pervert on the bus.

''I wish I had been there. I would have—''

''Would have what? Started trouble on a public bus with an old crazy? Got arrested? Maybe the old man would have a heart attack and you'd be charged with murder.'' She tapped him on the chest. ''If you can't turn your back and walk away from racial insults, we won't survive. You can't fight the whole world. The next insult may come from a gang of men who beat us to death if we say anything back.''

"It's not that bad.''

"Not if you're white.''

He shook his head. "I don't understand how so much ignorance can happen in so big a country. There aren't enough blacks in all Russia to generate prejudice.''

"It's always been there. White-skinned Russians have always been prejudiced against anyone with skin darker than theirs. How many people on the street know that Pushkin's grandfather, Hannibal, was an African who Peter the Great made a general? And that his black sons and their offspring served Russia as writers and doctors and engineers?''

"Only you,'' he said. "I tried to explain to my unit commander that there is a long history of people of African descent in Russia and he laughed at me.''

"Did you tell him about the villages in the Caucasian Mountains where blacks with an African heritage have lived for hundreds of years?''

"He laughed. He said the Caucasians is a white region, that's why they call it *Caucasian*. He claims the only blacks in Russia are the ones imported from America so that our leaders could have their pictures taken with them to impress the world with how well blacks live under communism.''

"Your commander needs lessons. You know, in a way Lara Patrick and I have similar backgrounds. Neither of us met our fathers, my mother died when I was three, her mother died when she was seven.''

"You orphans are better off. You don't have to worry about whether your parents will like the person you marry.''

They were dozing when a woman's hand poked through the curtain and dropped an envelope.

"It was on the doorstep when I came home,'' the

woman watching her daughter's children said.

Nina slipped off the bed and retrieved the envelope from the floor. She opened it and read the letter inside before turning wide-eyed to Misha.

"I've been summoned to appear before the Collegium of Advocates. To answer charges."

FOUR

The Collegium of Advocates was supposed to be an egalitarian association of lawyers but like everything else bitten by communism, it was a great theory but in practice a small, self-perpetuating group of bureaucrats ran the show and followed the dictates of the Kremlin leaders. And like everything else in Russia, the organization was reeling from having its feet kicked out from under it as law became just another commodity in a market economy.

Lara doesn't understand, Nina thought as she walked down the entry hall of the Collegium. These people give me my license and can take it away for breaking the rules.

But who knows what the rules are now?

Could they take her off the case because she was an embarrassment to the whole country?

In the "old days" one had to have permission of the Collegium to take a case. The Collegium controlled not only who took cases but on a case that was politically sensitive, would deny an attorney the right to represent a dissenter if it believed the attorney would be too strong an advocate.

The Collegium was heavily influenced by the prosecutor's office that maintained only the most shallow pretense at not interfering with the defense bar. Trial in a criminal case, in fact, amounted to little more than an appeal from the decision of the prosecutor.

In the past a defense attorney could not even see a jailed client except in the presence of an investigator from the prosecutor's office. The attorney usually didn't even get a file containing investigative reports on a murder case until shortly before the trial unless the attorney was willing to hand-copy the court file.

One certainty about defense attorneys was that they would only put up as much "defense" as the state permitted because an attorney wasn't just taken off a case— the attorney could easily be barred from practicing, period, if he or she didn't cooperate.

How many of the old rules were still in effect, she didn't know, but one thing was certain: the Collegium still had the power to remove her from a case in which the state was paying the attorney.

The morning news was filled with reports about her and the case. She was probably the most famous attorney in the country, although it seemed like half of the attorneys in the city were jumping in front of television cameras to give their "expert" opinion about the case. The question of her lack of qualifications to handle the case was mentioned repeatedly in the interviews.

I am the lowest attorney in all Russia, she thought. I shouldn't be handling the most sensational murder case in modern Russian history.

The walls and floors of the Collegium were of rich, dark hardwood paneling. It was an old building, a rare survivor of tsarist days. Even the air in the hallway smelled venerable. It made her knees tremble. She felt as if she were on her way to hear sentencing on the trial of her own life.

Trying to get her courage up, she told herself that the Collegium did not have a proud history, it hadn't been a true college of advocates but a front for Communist oppression, that it was her generation that helped ring in freedom and would ultimately have to defend it to keep Russia free.

She was not going to be intimidated. This was a new era, with fresh new thinking.

I'm not some street cleaner to be called in because of a broken broom, she told herself. I'm an attorney, licensed to practice and sworn to defend truth and justice.

Her mental courage did not keep her knees from trembling so much they nearly banged together.

The chairperson was a woman, an old bureaucrat with a face like wilted cabbage. Flanking her were two ball-less apparatchiks who Nina thought should be speaking at funerals and not in courtrooms.

The woman stared coldly down at her.

"You are not qualified."

Nina didn't need to be told what she was not qualified for but to hear it so bluntly was jarring.

Something a law professor told her about dealing with an opponent rang in her mind: kick their feet out from under them right from the start. That's what the chairperson was doing to her. Attacking her straight out.

Nina lifted her chin and met the woman eye to eye. "My license qualifies me for all cases."

"Your experience does not qualify you for a murder case."

There was a little quiver in Nina's first words but anger took its place. "What does my experience qualify me for? To handle prostitutes and people whose brains have been burned out by drugs?"

"That is where new attorneys start."

"I have been an attorney for two years and I still am given the same cases, the ones no one else wants. Is it my experience that lacks qualification—or my skin color?"

The three stared down at her in a mixture of horror. Her bluntness made them speechless. Attorneys didn't talk that way to the Collegium members.

The chairperson took a quick evaluation of Nina and changed tack.

"Perhaps there has been an injustice. Perhaps Soviet justice was not as blind as we thought. Now there is new thinking, new ways. You will be assigned to a better class of case."

"Lara Patrick chose me to handle her case."

"And I told you that you are not qualified. This Collegium still controls the qualification of attorneys."

"The client believes I am qualified and she is an attorney in her own country. A prosecuting attorney. She even rejected Viktor Rykoff in my favor."

"The woman is insane, that is why she's on trial. She is also an ignorant foreigner. It is your ethical duty not to mislead her into believing you are capable of handling her case when you are not. She is facing the death penalty. She must be given the best legal services possible. The whole world is watching this trial."

"But she doesn't want me to resign."

"You must not take advantage of her ignorance. She is in no condition to make a rational choice. Would she have murdered Nadia Kolchak if she was rational?"

"She says she is innocent."

The chairperson waved her hand, brushing away innocence as if it were a pesty fly.

"You are too young and inexperienced to understand these things. The woman says she is innocent and you accept those words as evidence. The evidence is that she was caught fleeing the murder scene with the murder weapon in her hand. You cannot win the case. An experienced attorney will be assigned to the case and ensure that the foreign press does not make a mockery of our new system."

"Madame Chairperson, you are not listening to me. I tell you Lara Patrick says she is innocent. She is a person of integrity and will not compromise her ideals even to save her life. All that she asks for is justice."

The chairperson looked down at her with something akin to pity. "Justice? Guilt? Innocence? These are absolutes only in textbooks. Lara Patrick will be convicted. The evidence is all against her. She needs an attorney who knows how to work the system to keep her from being executed."

"I don't believe that. Lara Patrick has courage and is willing to fight for the truth. I believe that if she fights for her rights the truth will ultimately prevail."

The woman's voice became firmer, a mother scolding a small child. "You must make room in your heart for the plight of this poor woman and permit us to provide her the best legal defense possible. Alexei Bova is one of the richest men in Russia and he is willing to provide her a team of the finest attorneys in the whole country. These attorneys are much older and more experienced in the system—"

The chairperson noticed a change in Nina's expression and tapered off her lecture.

Nina's eyes swept the face of the chairperson and the two funeral crows. "Lara Patrick stands convicted by you based merely upon what you have heard in the news media. The fact that she has been arrested is enough for you to say she is guilty. Lara is a very bright woman and she knows this mentality, that's why she wants to have a say in her own defense."

"Experienced attorneys will be—"

"And where were these mighty defenders of justice when dissenters were being given show trials and murdered by the KGB or sent off to the labor camps? When I was on the barricades with President Yeltsin, I didn't recall seeing any of my older and wiser colleagues beside me."

XXII

Today there's law and order in everything.
You can't beat anybody for nothing.
If you do beat anyone,
It's got to be for the sake of order.

—Maxim Gorky,
The Lower Depths

ONE

___

Nina was waiting for Lara in the attorney conference room the next morning.

"A City Court judge has been appointed to handle the trial. He's going to take me off the case."

"What? Why?"

"Because of the publicity. I don't photograph well. Sorry, I don't mean that. The real reason is a good one. I'm not qualified. The Collegium of Advocates has decreed that I should be replaced by an attorney experienced in murder cases."

"We've already been through this. The attorneys experienced enough to have handled murder cases are all products of the Soviet era. Rykoff was probably a lawyer at least a decade before Gorbachev took power. I don't want that type of lawyer. Nina, I don't want you as my lawyer because I like you, I want you because you're fresh and smart and your mind isn't totally polluted with outdated ideas."

"Telling the judge that the best lawyers in Moscow are dinosaurs practicing outdated Marxist-Leninist theories is not going to win you any favors."

"This is the actual trial judge?"

"Yes."

"How was he selected?"

"Selected? You mean by chance or deliberately?" She leaned close to Lara and whispered, "Judge Rurik was probably selected because he looks good on television. As you pointed out, this case is a chance for the new Russian justice system to show the world its face and he looks distinguished."

"Does he have any brains?"

Nina thought for a moment. "He's probably not the worst judge for your case. I've heard that he's honest."

"Has a prosecutor been assigned?"

"We'll know this morning. We're going into court in a few minutes. They say the chief prosecutor himself might handle the case. What are we going to do?"

"I don't know. I guess we'll have to punt."

T W O

For the first time since Lara had been in jail she got to see the corridor of the courthouse. She was taken down the public corridor to a meeting in the judge's temporary office.

"Judge Rurik's courtroom and chambers are being painted," Nina told her. Two jail matrons accompanied them.

"A color that will look pretty on camera?" Lara murmured.

A sideways look from Nina was her answer.

High-profile cases were the worst, Lara thought. Everyone involved, from the judge and lawyers to witnesses, start performing for the camera. She hated it when the press invaded the cases she was handling back in San Francisco. It wasn't the fact that the press covered the story.

What bugged her was the news-hungry, sensation-hungry media trying the case on television and in the newspapers rather than letting justice take its natural course in the courtroom.

They paused in front of a door and one of the matrons knocked on the door. It was opened a moment later by a woman who told them to wait for the prosecutor to arrive.

"Have you seen the chief prosecutor in trial?" Lara asked. "Is he any good?"

"I've never seen him. I'm not sure if—" She stopped as the elevator down the corridor opened to reveal three people. They stepped forward with military precision, a woman in a navy-blue uniform at the leading edge, a step behind her two middle-aged men, both carrying briefcases.

Lara recognized one of the men: Chief Inspector Vulko, who had almost snapped off her chin. He was shorter than the woman or the other man, but if his bulky frame were stretched out, his bald head would have gone through the ceiling.

She turned to say something to Nina about Vulko and was stopped by Nina's expression. She was staring wide-eyed at the three people coming up the hallway.

"Stalin's Breath," she whispered.

"What?"

"That's what they call her, Stalin's Breath. Her name is Svetlana Petroff. She's a senior prosecutor, the toughest in Moscow. She once attended an execution of a murderer to see what it was like."

She looked at Lara with a mixture of horror and dismay on her face. "She didn't get hands-on experience with a corpse in an operating room like you did. She pulled the trigger at the execution herself."

Stalin's Breath marched down the center of the corridor with people veering out of her way like waters parting for Moses. The snap of the steel caps on her heels echoed off the walls like small arms fire. Her bearing was pure military, her dark blue uniform with gold stripe as crisp as a general's. Her hair was blond, short, and combed straight back, her jaw rock, her eyes stone. She was all woman, but Lara had the impression of a pumped body under the uniform, a female Schwarzenegger.

The woman stopped abruptly, dismissing Nina with a cursory glance that said Nina didn't even qualify for her contempt, and took a long, drawn-out look at Lara, a fighter sizing up an opponent.

Nina suddenly shot forward and stuck out her hand. "Good morning, Prosecutor Petroff. I am Ninochka Kerensky, attorney for the accused. It gives me great pleasure that a prosecutor of your stature is on the case."

Svetlana Petroff flinched, hesitated, and then shook hands. "Good morning, Attorney Kerensky."

She quickly disengaged her hand from Nina's and opened the door to the judge's chambers without knocking. As Nina and Lara waited for the prosecutor and her two shadows to pass through the doorway, Nina shot Lara a grin.

They had already discovered one chink in Svetlana's armor: the most feared prosecutor in Moscow might not be able to handle a curve ball. She had been caught off guard by Nina's warm handshake.

She's a machine, Lara thought, she'll mow down everything in her path. To beat her I'll have to sneak up behind and hit her over the head.

Vulko gave them what he no doubt considered to be a pleasant smile as he passed by. Following the procession, Lara and Nina, with the two guards to the rear, entered an outer office and walked past a secretarial desk into the judge's chambers.

Judge Rurik sat behind his desk and waited for them to trail in. He looked a little like Boris Yeltsin, thick, prematurely white hair capping a large head and broad ruddy face.

Nina was right. He would look very judicial on camera.

With the two matrons behind Lara the room was crowded and Lara had to edge back to keep from rubbing shoulders with Vulko.

"I am relieving you as attorney," the judge told Nina. "I have no doubt that you are a fine attorney with a strong commitment to justice, but it is premature for you to handle this type of case. It was an error of the People's Court judge to appoint you to a complex case involving the death penalty."

"My client does not want to relieve me," Nina said.

"Your client does not have a choice in selection of counsel. The government is paying, the government decides who shall be the defendant's attorney." He gave Lara a look that invited her to challenge his remark.

He was right, Lara thought, defendants weren't given the right to choose appointed counsel in the States either. She was about to argue that she wanted Nina to remain, her only leverage being that she would take her case to the news media, when Nina punted.

"I'm remaining as counsel for Lara Patrick. She is paying me. I am no longer appointed, but privately retained."

The judge's eyes shot to the prosecutor.

One could almost see the wheels turning in Svetlana's mind as she analyzed the situation: was the defendant setting her up by having an inexperienced attorney so she could later claim her attorney had not been competent?

Lara remembered what Nina had told her about Soviet prosecutors—they had power in some situations to overrule even a judge.

"There is an easy solution," Svetlana told the judge. "She can keep Ninochka Kerensky as her attorney. But in view of the complexity of the case and the potential penalty, we will appoint an attorney to assist her retained attorney."

Lara and Nina exchanged looks, both with the same thought: two attorneys might be better than one. That's usually how it's done in the States with death penalty cases, Lara thought.

"Who would the court appoint?" Nina asked.

Stalin's Breath answered, "Mr. Venrenko." She nodded at the man to her right. "He came today prepared to take over the entire case."

Venrenko was a short, skinny man with a receding hairline and large black mustache. His clothing was neat, his shirt starched stiff, his shoes and briefcase polished.

"Venrenko is a prosecutor!" Nina said.

"No, as of last week he went into the private practice of law." Svetlana gave him a small smile. He did not return it, remaining stiffly at attention. "His desire to acquire expensive foreign cars, a fancy dacha, and the other trappings of capitalism is stronger than his loyalty to me after many years as my assistant."

"Your assistant!" Lara exploded. "You want your assistant appointed as my attorney?"

Nina grabbed her arm.

"This is Russia," Svetlana told her, speaking as to a child. "We seek justice. Our courtrooms are not theatres in which attorneys compete for top billing. Mr. Venrenko has been a prosecutor for nearly thirty years. He will bring his fine skills and sense of justice to your case."

Lara looked at him but he didn't return her gaze. "If he's been around that long administering justice, I suppose he was a prosecutor back during the days when writers and poets were tried for thinking and sent off to mental wards and forced labor camps."

Nina audibly groaned beside her and Lara suffered instant regret, realizing the judge was probably around then, too.

Svetlana was about to say something but Lara cut her short by addressing the judge. "Your honor, I'm not taking Mr. Venrenko as my attorney. There are already two attorneys on my case—Miss Kerensky and myself. I'm an experienced attorney."

"You are not experienced in Russian law."

"I have chosen Miss Kerensky as my attorney. I'm satisfied with her."

"So be it," Svetlana snapped. "Let's get a transcriber in here. The defendant's wishes will be placed on the record and she will sign it. I will have the statement distributed to the news media. We will also add that this course of action is against the advice of the court and the Moscow City Prosecutor's office."

Mr. Venrenko remained silent.

THREE

W hy do they call her Stalin's Breath?" Lara asked. They were back in the conference room.

"It's the scent she wears, a cheap perfume. I've heard it smells like the afterburn of an artillery shell. No doubt it gets its burnt smell from her personality."

"Is that story about her firing the executioner's gun true?"

Nina avoided her eyes. "It's not a rumor. I heard Svetlana tell the story to one of my law school professors when she was at the university to give a speech." Nina looked up. Her eyes had misted up. "You . . . you're not aware of how most executions are carried out. In many districts volunteer executioners are used."

"Volunteers? You mean ordinary citizens?"

"Yes."

"But they must . . . they must botch some of the jobs."

"Some of the volunteers have had a lot of practice. During a recent hunt for a serial killer the chief investigator did background checks on the citizens who volunteered to perform executions. He discovered his killer among them."

"All right, let's drop it. I don't want to talk about it." Lara spread the police reports on the table.

Nina reached down and picked up a paper bag. Lara had seen one of the matrons give Nina the bag on the way in.

"Your purse," Nina said, handing it to her. "I had it brought in from the property room. I can't leave it with you, but you said the picture that caused you to come to Moscow is in it."

Lara opened the purse. "My money's gone."

"I have a receipt for it."

"I insist you take it all," Lara told her. "Just leave me twenty American dollars for soap and toilet paper. You can't refuse this time. You're going to need it now that you're not getting paid."

"If I get desperate, I'll take a little. I've spent most of my life in a Communist country. I get embarrassed even talking about money."

Lara found the picture of the mutilated woman. "This is it. I'm not surprised it's still here considering the police work on my case. I'm certain that the woman is the neighbor upstairs at the apartment building where my mother and I lived. You can only see about half of her hair, but it's the same cut as the woman in the party picture Felix dropped on me."

Nina's face twisted in revulsion. "Poor woman. Some really crazy bastard did this. It's the work of a madman."

"I had our forensic people back in San Francisco examine the photo before I came to Moscow. We have a large data bank on killers in the States. The nature of the wounds, the high number of them, the fact that they cover so much of the body, that both breasts and the sex organs have been mutilated, the appearance of depth to the wounds, it all points to a killer in an insane but methodical rage rather than, say, a lover who grabbed a kitchen knife during an argument and attacked in the heat of the moment. They counted forty-six wounds.

"The type of killer who would inflict this sort of mutilation is a sexual psychopath who is liable to kill again. And again. There's a seventy-eight percent probability that sometime before or after this attack, there was at least one other similar act of violence by the person."

"You're saying this is the work of a serial killer."

"A high probability is the best that forensics would come up with. This type of person tends to kill more than once, so yes, it's probably the work of a serial killer. But there is a small possibility that it only happened once."

Nina shook her head. "No, I think this person has killed more than once. No one could be that crazy only once in a lifetime."

"That's how I feel. But I've never found a way to trace another killing. Sick crimes like this weren't reported publicly under the Soviet regime. So it's not a matter of going down to the library and looking through past editions of *Pravda*. Another problem is the lack of a signature."

"A signature?"

"Serial killers, either intentionally or unintentionally, often leave a clue linking them to the crime. It can get pretty bizarre—we've had men who kill only strawberry blondes or people born on Fridays or tall people or short people, some cut in a certain way or a particular pattern.

"In this case our forensic people weren't able to find a distinguishing feature. The crazed slashing seemed to be purely random although of course sexual. The killer was right-handed, but so are most people."

"What about the cross?"

"What cross?"

Nina pointed to a mark on the woman's right hand. Lara leaned down closer to get a better look. A vertical line intersected by a horizontal line was in the area between the woman's right thumb and index finger.

"The crossbar is a bit high up," Lara said.

"That's a common design here in Russia."

Lara still wasn't convinced. "There's another, smaller crossbar nearer the top of the vertical line."

"Russian crosses usually have that. Haven't you ever looked at the crosses at St. Basil's?"

Lara took her hand off the picture. She met Nina's eye and held it for a long moment. "It's possible," she said quietly. "The marks do look like a Russian cross. But they might also be wounds inflicted when she raised her hand to protect herself. It's a natural spot for such wounds. Other than the crosslike shape, there's nothing about the marks to give them any other significance."

"Not to someone in San Francisco, perhaps, but there is to me," Nina said.

"What do you mean?"

"You've heard of Ivan the Terrible?"

"Of course. Fifteenth century—"

"Sixteenth century," Nina said.

"Russian ruler. Mad as a hatter."

"Also very cunning. Made Stalin look like a monk when it came to insane violence. Stalin drove his wife and son to kill themselves, the son by alcohol. Ivan killed his own son. Ivan also founded the Oprichnina, a secret police that made the KGB look like circus clowns in comparison. Ivan had them slaughter whole cities when he felt like it. Anyway, Ivan was also a religious maniac with a rather Dark Ages view of the world."

"He had St. Basil's built," Lara said. Speaking of the church made her throat tighten.

"True. And he had an obsession about freaks."

"What do you mean?"

"People with deformities. He believed that deformities, like a hunchback, a twisted limb, things of that sort, were marks of the devil, a sure sign that the devil had played a role in the person's creation. Ivan was told that devils could be driven away with the sign of the cross, so he sent his black-robed Oprichnina riding through the country looking for freaks. Whenever they found any, Ivan's men scarred the person's hand."

"With the sign of the cross," Lara said.

"Between the thumb and the index finger," Nina told her.

"Belkin said something to me about a freak. I wasn't really listening at the time, I thought it was just small talk. He said he knows a freak, or knew a freak, something like that."

The two women stared at each other for a moment before Lara examined the picture again. She didn't see any visible deformity on the woman.

"She doesn't look like a freak."

"Maybe she wasn't a freak," Nina said. "Maybe it's the killer who is."

FOUR

A week passed with growing madness for her as she fought trapped animal sickness, imagining fires in which the flames and smoke attacked her while she was locked in her cell, going through out-of-body experiences that took her onto a plane bound for home.

Nina visited her at least once every day, and it helped, but the worst times were at night after lockdown when sounds of anger and fear, women loving women, women beating women, or just plain insanity and viciousness, robbed her of sleep. She lost more weight from her already slim frame.

Lara had never experienced life in jail before, although she had been inside a number of them because of her job. Now she questioned whether she could go back to being a prosecutor—assuming she survived Russian justice. It wasn't that she believed the women trapped behind the bars didn't deserve the punishment—most of them spoke freely of their crimes and their only regret was that they had been caught. But now that she had experienced the hell, she didn't think she could live with its knowledge. Her feelings were something akin to a person supporting the death penalty for heinous crimes but not wanting to be the executioner.

Much of her time was spent going through the police reports and outlining tactical moves for the case, tactics she went over with Nina. The two often locked horns. Nina's points were usually well taken. Lara was approaching the trial in the American fashion, strategic combat between two opposing sides. The advocacy system of justice. It was based upon the concept that the state was a powerful force and unless opposed would rob people of their liberty.

"Your system gives more rights to criminals than victims," Nina snapped during one of their arguments.

"Wrong, we give equal rights to everyone. You're presumed innocent and the state must prove the charges against them beyond a reasonable doubt. Not to protect the guilty, but to protect the innocent. When criminals have less rights than other citizens, a government can take away the rights of good citizens simply by labeling them criminals. That's what happened here in Russia."

"But look at what happened to the crime rate when controls were taken off," Nina said. "Before the fall of the Soviet regime, we could walk the streets day or night safely. Now criminals are taking over the streets."

"The people have also taken over the streets from an oppressive government. There's always a certain percentage of criminals in any society," Lara argued, "just as there is a percentage of people with mental disorders and ones with red hair. Liberty doesn't encourage crime, poverty and poor police protection does. And even if it did, I'd rather be free and have to worry about an occasional mugger than live in a totalitarian regime with a soldier on every corner and my neighbors spying on me."

Lara understood the mentality about jury trials and rules of evidence. The only exposure Russians had to the American justice system was media accounts of the O. J. and other high profile trials that left an impression that criminal prosecutions were strangled and criminals had more rights than victims. Trying to explain to Nina that the O. J. trial was a media circus rather than a classic example of American jurisprudence didn't do any good.

"If big money and notoriety can pervert the system, then the system's flawed," Nina told her.

"The system's not perfect but it's far superior to the system in Russia and Europe where politically appointed judges can be influenced."

But Nina was right about the fact that there can be a price for justice—money talks. And who wouldn't trade their pocketbook for their life? She'd like to have millions for defense to pay a staff of lawyers and experts rather than betting her life on one terrified defendant and an almost equally scared young attorney.

The arguments were therapeutic for both of them, allowing them to let off steam. And they served another purpose: Lara gained more insight into the Russian legal system and Nina learned more about the American one. Somewhere in between was the right strategy to carry the day in a Russian courtroom where no one knew exactly what the law and procedure was because the old establishment had fallen and rules were being implemented and discarded almost daily.

Lara pointed out over and over again, to drive home the point and to stir Nina's gray matter, that the police and the coroner had done inadequate jobs investigating Nadia's death. The autopsy report was a prime example: the pathologist tracked the bullet into Nadia's chest and the one in the back of her head, establishing the cause of death from gunfire wounds. But because the pathologist had not approached the autopsy objectively and had merely set out to confirm the police theory that Lara had shot the woman, he had not thoroughly examined Nadia's body.

"I tried to see the chief pathologist twice. He's avoiding me. What does it matter about the rest of her body when they're certain the gunshot wounds killed her?'' Nina had asked.

Lara felt like banging her head on the table out of pure frustration. ''We already went over this three times. What if she had been drugged and taken to the spa? No blood tests were done. What if she had been grabbed and physically forced into the spa? There was no examination for bruises or marks besides the entry wounds on her body. She was naked in the spa. What clothes did the police find? When did they find them? Had she had sex before being killed? Was there water in her lungs? She might have been killed somewhere else and put in the spa to entrap me.

''And what about keys? There's no mention of the police having found keys among Nadia's personal effects. How did she get into the penthouse? Did she come in the public entrance? What time? Was anyone with her? Can the elevator attendants set a time? If she undressed and got into the spa, she had to have been there for a while before I arrived. Not to mention the time it takes for the spa to heat up.''

''I spoke to the elevator attendants,'' Nina said. ''They had already given statements to the police. They claim Nadia didn't enter by the front.''

''Then how did she get into the penthouse? I had the key to the rear entrance.''

''That is exactly the point the police make . . .''

FIVE

The next evening when Nina returned she was dragging at the heels. ''I was at the morgue standing in front of the chief pathologist's office when he arrived for work this morning. He said he was too busy to see me right then. After three hours of waiting I realized he would be too busy until one of us died from old age. I went away and returned after five o'clock when I was sure he had left the office. I persuaded an assistant pathologist into letting me view Nadia's body.''

"Terrific. I'm proud of you.''

"Don't pin the Order of Lenin on me yet. When he slid the body out of the cooler, the smell and appearance were . . . not pleasant.''

"Not just the smell, but to think that the person on the slab was a living, feeling human being a short while ago,'' Lara said.

"It was awful. But at least the assistant was kind enough to examine the body for me. There were marks on both of Nadia's upper arms that could be bruises and a scrape in the scalp under the hairline. It's possible that someone held her arms prior to death, that she was hit on the head. But . . .''

"All right, but what?''

"But the scrape on the head could have been caused by hitting her head in the spa after the first shot. Because of the hot water, it's hard to tell when she got the scrape.''

"And the arm bruises?''

"He didn't find them particularly important. He said if Nadia bruised easily, she could have got them while making love.''

"But from what you've told me, it's possible that she was treated roughly before she was killed.''

"Yes, but a dozen other inferences are also possible.''

"Were you able to learn anything about the key?''

"No key was found in Nadia's effects.''

"People on the street, the neighborhood?''

"My friend and I combed the neighborhood for witnesses. None jumped out and bit us.'' She sounded very tired.

"Thank you.''

"For what? I've done nothing to help the case.''

"You've done a great deal. We're narrowing down the

evidence. You've discovered that there were signs of violence on Nadia's body. I'm really grateful for what you're doing.''

Nina's tired frame swelled with pride. ''Tomorrow I'll talk to the judge and demand that he provide funds for experts of our own. The old ways are gone and the new ways must increase the rights of the individual. We can no longer be at the mercy of the government.'' She slammed her fist on the table.

After Nina had left, the matron told Lara to stay in the room, she had another visitor.

A moment later Yuri entered the room.

Lara stood up and turned her back on him. She knocked on the door for the matron.

''I'm ready to go back,'' Lara told her.

The matron looked to Yuri for direction. It was a moment before he answered, ''Not yet.'' The woman shut the door in Lara's face.

Lara swung round to Yuri. ''What do you want?''

He took out a cigarette, lit it, and took a long drag. He appeared worn and haggard. The eyes that had fascinated her were now tired and weary. ''I've been trying to help you.''

''Trying to help me? You came in here before with a body-wire and taped me—''

''Vulko ordered me to do it. If I had refused, I would have been jerked off the case immediately. Luckily, my supervisor's given me some leeway to continue to investigate despite the fact Vulko's taken over.''

''Why should I believe you? We're probably being taped right now.''

''You have to believe me. I'm the one who lined up Rykoff for you. I had a little thing on him.'' Yuri shrugged. ''He wanted your case anyway. He's supposed to be a good lawyer.''

''I've got a good lawyer.''

"You have to get rid of her. You don't understand the system. She won't get respect in court. She's too young, inexperienced . . . and the wrong color. It's an old boys' network and she's not a member."

"I'm sticking with her. She has one quality that I haven't seen in anyone else in this whole damn city—honesty."

"Lara, I'm sorry, I'm . . . really sorry. But in some ways it's not as bad as it seems. You're—"

"Are you crazy? I'm in jail charged with murder. I'm facing execution. The only consolation is that I might be lucky enough to die of food poisoning or freeze to death in my cell before trial."

"You're alive. I kept trying to get you out of the city, back to America. And you kept fighting it, going back out onto the streets at night. You should be dead. You're safer in jail, protected, until I can get to the bottom of things."

She sat down and crossed her arms and legs and stared up at him. He was a wreck.

"You look worse than I do."

"I haven't been sleeping."

"What are you worried about?"

"You think I want you in jail?"

She stood and moved around the room, her adrenaline pumping, her arms still folded across her chest, drilling holes in him with her eyes. "You don't make sense to me, Yuri. You wear a different face every time we meet. You showed up at my hotel room claiming to be investigating Belkin's death, but I saw you the night before at the carnival. What were you doing at the carnival?"

"I was conducting an investigation."

"What kind of investigation were you conducting behind a fortune-teller's tent and a freak show?"

"I can't reveal that. It's police business."

"Funny thing, that freak show you were hanging around. Nina thinks freaks have some sort of connection to the killings. She's checking it out. Anything you want to tell me?''

"I don't know what you're talking about."

"And you knew nothing about me, no name, no nationality, that night at the carnival. I was just a woman walking with Belkin?"

"Yes."

"Yet within hours of Belkin's death you were at my hotel room. How did you know I was staying at a hotel? How did you find the hotel so fast? Moscow has seven or eight million people and dozens of hotels. You were banging on my door early the next morning."

He followed her with tired eyes as she walked round the room. "I told you we found your name on Belkin."

"And something else happened that morning that makes me wonder about you. We had coffee together and got into an argument because you wanted me to leave Moscow. Why would a police officer investigating a murder want a material witness to take the first flight out of the country?"

She stopped and moved closer to him, keeping her eyes locked with his. "Every time I made a move, you were right on my heels. Every time something bad was happening, you always seemed to pop up. And every time we spoke, you tried to get me to leave the country."

She started pacing again, rolling ideas off her tongue. "A policeman trying to get rid of a witness? That doesn't compute. Unless the policeman has something to hide himself. Now that's an interesting premise, isn't it?"

If Yuri found the premise interesting, he did nothing to reveal it in his expression. He continued to meet her fierce gaze with tired, half-closed eyes.

"That led me to some conclusions. You said you spotted Belkin and started following him. What if instead of Belkin you were following me? You see me with Belkin and Belkin gets hit by a truck. I tell you about the archives and the next thing I know Minsky has disappeared. I pay a visit to the truck driver and you're there, too. I was really grateful to you for saving me from that dog, but I find it hard to believe that you followed my taxi down that long, straight, almost deserted road without me spotting your car. You know what? I wonder if you didn't arrive there before me.''

''Your imagination has been infected by the mental diseases that float in the air around this place,'' he said.

''Being in jail has one benefit. It gives you time to think. Hours and days and nights of sitting in a damn cell all alone with your whole life passing before your eyes.''

''You're in this jail because you refused to follow my warnings. I told you Bova was trouble.''

She changed tactics, realizing she would get nothing out of him with a frontal attack. ''Tell me about Bova.''

''What did you find out about him?''

''I asked you the question. I know he's rich and he's crazy. That Nadia was killed in his spa. It strikes me as unlikely that he killed her. It doesn't make much sense to kill her in his own penthouse when he had the largest country in the world to do it in.''

''Don't assume a criminal will act logically,'' he said. ''Especially if he's crazy to begin with. And I don't know how rich he will remain. The government is locked in battle with him because he's stolen everything from oil fields to fishing boats. Most of his gains went into that tower, a monument to himself. The government's keeping it empty by refusing to issue the occupancy permits. There are rumors that he will collapse financially at any moment. When that happens, there'll be trouble.''

''What kind of trouble?''

''The kind that gets people killed. It's not his money that went into the tower, the dacha, his fancy cars, or anything else. The money belonged to others.''

''The news media claims he is some sort of financial wizard.''

He shrugged. ''One hundred and sixty million of us Russians don't understand moneymaking. Market economy is a phrase we hear, but don't know the workings of. I've done a great deal of checking on Bova. He seems to lose money on everything. The things he stole, like the oil wells, bring in no income—the government has seen to that. It's more like a game he plays for fun rather than for profit. He owns a bank and the bank makes investments. But before he ran into trouble with the tower he seemed to lose two dollars for every dollar he invested and yet still he made a profit. Being an economically ignorant ex-Communist, I don't understand how he does it.''

"Money laundering," she said. "It's the only business in the world where you can lose money and still make a profit. The very nature of the game is that for every dirty dollar you handle you'll lose half of it, but the remaining half is clean and it's straight profit.''

Yuri nodded. His eyes were veiled and she couldn't read his face. "I've suspected money laundering, but we don't have the resources to track such activities. Banks and other businesses conduct themselves as they want because the government agencies are incapable of monitoring them.''

"Is Bova involved in drugs? Money laundering for drugs?''

"He's not involved in drugs, I'm certain of that.''

"Then what is it?''

"The matter is still under investigation.''

"When's the investigation going to be concluded? About the time I'm being executed? Don't give me that investigation nonsense. I'm in jail and facing charges now. I need answers. Nadia knew something about Alexei. She suspected that Felix was blackmailing Alexei. What does Felix have on Alexei? Is it money laundering?''

"Felix and Alexei go back a long way.''

"What does that mean?''

"I'm investigating their affairs.''

She stepped close to him, her eyes searching his face. "Why are you doing this to me? What are you hiding? Something tells me that I've been caught up in something more than a fight over dirty money. My instincts are screaming that if I knew who was behind my mother's death and that of our neighbor woman I would know who put me in this jail.''

He grabbed her arms and squeezed tightly. "You fool," he whispered. "You stumble around with your eyes closed, stepping on poisonous snakes, trying to find out who slashed Vera Swen without any idea what you're sticking your nose into. The only reason you're alive is because you're in jail.''

She slowly drew back from him until he dropped the hold on her arms.

She rubbed her arms where he had grabbed her. "Nadia had bruises on her arms where someone grabbed her before she was killed. Did you give her a lecture, too? Right before she died?''

SIX

Nina brought someone with her when she returned the next evening.

"This is Vladimir Andreevich Dzhunkovsky.'' She smiled. "We call him Vlad.''

Vlad was a tall, thin, gangling young man, at least six feet three, Lara estimated, with a thick bushel of wheat hair. The glasses he wore were thick, the type kids at school used to call Coke bottles.

"Vlad is an expert on guns and bullets.''

"Ballistics,'' Vlad corrected. "More precisely, I am knowledgeable about projectiles ranging from small arms ammo to artillery shells. My rank in the army is lieutenant.''

This was the ballistics expert Nina had mentioned. With two bullets as the obvious cause of Nadia's death and little doubt in her mind that the bullets came from the six-shooter she had handled, a ballistics expert didn't offer much hope but at least it was another straw to clutch.

"What exactly do you do with, uh, projectiles?"

"My unit tests the efficiency and accuracy of ammunition. We fire thousands of rounds from dozens of different types of weapons. We change the amount of charge in the shell, the size and shape of bullets, and sometimes even the length or rifling of barrels. We have the most advanced technology in the world for tracking small arms fire with lasers," he said with pride.

"Sounds impressive." But how the hell would it help me? Lara wondered. "Are you also qualified to compare the rifling marks on bullets to determine whether they were fired by the same gun?".

He grimaced and waved away the question as if it was beneath his dignity. "Child's play. I have used the comparison microscopes and periphery cameras required for such examinations many times, usually after a training accident when we are sent the bullets to determine which weapon fired the shot. But my special expertise is tracking the path of bullets. Except at very short range, a bullet fired from a gun does not follow a straight line. I employ lasers to trace the paths. From those studies, we improve the effectiveness of ammunition."

"In this case, we have a very short range," she said. "Have you looked at the photos of the bullet that struck Nadia in the chest and the bullet they dug out of the ceiling? The prosecution's ballistics expert says that they come from the same gun."

"He hasn't seen them because I left my copy with you," Nina said. She was shifting through the stack of reports as she spoke.

"You'll see from the reports that there were two shots," Lara said. "Nadia was sitting in the spa, facing the door to the interior, her back to the spa rim when she was shot. The bullet went through her chest and out of her back, embedding in the rubber liner of the spa. She was then shot again, probably while floating facedown in the spa. That bullet went into the back of her head. It was also recovered. A third bullet recovered from the ceiling of the penthouse matches one of the bullets that killed Nadia. I, uh, allegedly fired that one into the ceiling a few days earlier.''

Vlad smiled a little shyly. ''I heard about it. It was on television.''

''Here.'' Nina handed the ballistics report to Vlad.

''I could make a more accurate comparison by doing my own examination of the bullets, but we can start with the police laboratory report.''

While he read the report, Lara asked, ''Any success on getting the judge to appoint a pathologist?''

Nina's lips pressed. ''No pathologist, no investigators, no fingerprint analyst, no experts at all. Vlad is my friend and the best friend of my boyfriend, who is also in the army. He will assist us for nothing.''

''That's kind of him. I appreciate it.''

Nina shook her head. ''I know that he may not be able to help. But . . .''

Lara smiled. ''In this case a ballistics expert is a shot in the dark.''

Nina laughed.

Lara liked the sound of her laughter. It was spontaneous and honest, a reflection of her personality.

Nina's pretty face became serious again. ''I spoke to the judge and the prosecutor. Svetlana telephoned me this morning and instructed me to appear within the hour for a conference with the judge.''

''A conference with the judge? Without me?''

''I think Svetlana planned it that way. She told the judge that you intend to make your mother's death an issue at the trial.''

''Of course I'll make it an issue. It is the issue in this case. I was lured to Moscow because of my mother's death and I'm sure her death has something to do with Nadia's."

"The judge will not permit you to raise the subject during the trial."

"Why not?"

Nina spoke fast, mimicking Svetlana's military tones. "We are a struggling nation trying to build a new Russia from the ashes of the old. To keep our people united we must bury the past and look to the future. The defendant will attempt to make this case into a political trial to divert attention away from her heinous crime."

Lara's face went crimson with anger and frustration. "She's trying to destroy the only defense I have. If we can't mention my investigation into my mother's death, nothing else will make sense. How can I explain what I was doing with Belkin when he was hit by a truck? The schoolteacher? The institute? Breaking into Bova's penthouse? It all goes back to my mother's death."

"I know how you feel," Nina said. "But the judge did ask me one good question and I had no answer for it. He asked me to list the evidence that linked your mother's death to Nadia's death."

"Belkin was murdered, the schoolteacher is dead, the murder of Vera Swen—"

"Those are events. What physical evidence links them to Nadia's death? The prosecution theory is that you and Nadia were conspiring to blackmail Alexei and that you killed Nadia because you wanted Alexei and his money for yourself."

"The picture," Lara said. "Both pictures. The one sent to me in San Francisco and the picture of Alexei with my mother and Vera. The picture with Alexei Bova in it was my motive for going to the penthouse, for dealing with Nadia. It proves he lied to me about knowing my mother and it shows a connection between the past and to someone alive and involved today. Nina, we need that picture."

"I have requested the picture through the police, but

what chance is there that Felix will admit to having it and turn it over to the police?''

Lara shook her head in frustration. "No chance."

"How do we explain the glove found at the scene?"

"It was planted. I have two pairs, someone stole one and planted it."

Nina sighed and shuffled papers for a moment. "My boyfriend did some of those background checks you asked for. The army's central records department came up with some interesting and puzzling things about your friends Felix and Alexei."

"What do you mean?"

"Felix's file was coded for special handling."

"Which means?"

"There are different reasons a file might be marked special. The person may have risen to political or military prominence or be the son of someone prominent. Or they could be KGB. The higher the rank, the more special and inaccessible the file."

Nina shot a sideways glance at Vlad. He was engrossed in the pictures of the bullets and the crime scene report. She indicated with a movement of her head that she wanted to speak to Lara off to the side. The two women got up and moved away from the table and spoke in low whispers.

"Vlad is very trustworthy," Nina said, "but I don't want him to overhear things that might get him or my boyfriend into trouble."

"I understand."

"My boyfriend is a computer genius. He loves to play with computer programs and has managed to gain access to secret files. The regular file on Felix contained what you would learn by being his next-door neighbor. But my boyfriend peeked into the secret file the army maintains on Felix." Nina grinned. "The army and KGB were very competitive. Each maintains secret files on anyone of importance in the other's service."

"I wasn't sure Felix had been KGB," Lara said. "But that didn't seem very important. So many people in this country are either ex-KGB or were KGB informers."

"He was KGB," Nina says, "but not just KGB. He reported directly to the head of the Finance Directorate."

"What's the Finance Directorate?"

"The department that handled the money to pay not only a million or so internal agents but KGB agents all over the world. It was answerable directly to the chairman of the KGB himself."

Lara nodded. "Alexei is rolling in money. Felix handled finances. Probably trillions of rubles, worth a lot more then, before hyper-inflation started. Money was probably funneled out of the KGB during the Gorbachev years when the upper echelon knew the system was heading for collapse."

"Exactly," Nina said. "But Felix's government position wasn't the most important thing my boyfriend discovered about him. Something about the secret file makes my boyfriend believe it's a dummy file. He suspects Felix's job at the KGB was a cover for something else. Whatever it was, it had to have been big. To have a dummy army file is one thing, to have a dummy secret file means you are very important."

"Important to whom?"

Nina shrugged. "To the KGB. There aren't many other choices. You understand what I'm saying, a great effort was made to make Felix appear innocuous."

"Alexei has a lot of money."

"Not that kind of money. Nobody had it in the Soviet Union. This sort of thing is not arranged with money anyway, but with power."

"Why do you think it was done?"

"Why, I can't tell you." A big grin spread across her face. "But I can tell you what his file originally contained."

"How?"

"Erased files can be retrieved if there are no special programs blocking it. The top-secret file storage system has a retrieval program for erased files." She grinned again. "It's the old Soviet mentality showing itself again."

"Nina, what did the damn file say?"

"Back in the sixties and seventies, your mother's era in Moscow, Felix was the editor of a literary magazine. He rubbed shoulders with all kinds of writers, ones who wrote pieces the government approved and ones who wrote pieces that had to get smuggled out of the country to be published under anonymous names."

"And he turned them over to the KGB," Lara said, making a guess. "He told me he was a beacon for people with literary aspirations and bragged about how he assisted dissenters. No doubt he helped them right to forced labor camps."

"Exactly what the secret report says. But eventually there were dirty rumors about him on the street and in the mid-seventies he became employed directly by the KGB's finance department."

"Why finance if he came out of a literary background?"

"My guess, knowing how the KGB operated, he knew someone at a high level, probably the finance director himself. When I speak of the KGB finance director, I'm speaking of one of the great power players in the Soviet Union. The KGB was not just a spy organization, it was an army with a gigantic bureaucracy which employed over a million people. The finance director had direct access to the chairman of the KGB. Felix had a staff job at the Finance Directorate as an assistant to the director until March 1985."

"What happened in March of 1985?"

"Gorbachev came to power."

"The beginning of the end," Lara said. "They had to have seen it coming, all the old boys at the KGB. The economy was going to pieces, there had already been serious food shortages, and the man selected to lead the country was crying out for new thinking. A fortune in rubles no doubt was flowing through the KGB coffers. Probably even more significant was the hoard of gold, gems, and art the KGB unofficially confiscated over the years. I bet a bunch of fat old boys got together to make sure their feet would stay warm during the long Russian winters to come.''

Vlad interrupted their conversation. ''May I see the crime scene pictures mentioned in the reports?''

''What did you think of the prosecution's ballistics report?'' Lara asked as Nina dug out the pictures for him.

''Very accurate. Obviously the same gun.''

''Wonderful,'' Lara said.

''How tall are you?'' Vlad asked.

''About five feet six inches. In meters, centimeters . . .''

''I'll work it out,'' he told her.

Nina gave him the pictures and came back to the corner to continue the whispering huddle with Lara.

''You're going to tell me that your boyfriend ran Alexei, found a regular file and a secret file that had been edited.''

''Wrong. Bova's record is stranger than that. There was no file, period.'' Nina's voice rose with excitement. ''Do you understand the significance of that? Bova is male, Russian, and a resident of Moscow. If you weren't born in Moscow, you needed a special permit to even visit the city, let alone live here. The Soviet government apparatus kept track not just of every baby born, but every paper clip manufactured. It's impossible not to have a military record, even if it was just for being rejected for service. Not to have an army file, not even a secret one, is to sit on the knee of Lenin.''

''Something like the right hand of God,'' Lara murmured.

''Whatever. Lenin's knee is an old Russian expression I just made up.'' Nina chuckled. ''My boyfriend was so fascinated, he used a military program to access other government files and found no reference to Bova prior to six or seven years ago. If Alexei Bova doesn't exist on paper in this country, Alexei Bova doesn't exist, period.''

Lara was stunned. "That doesn't make any sense. You're talking about one of the most famous men in the country. He has to have been put under a microscope and examined by everyone.''

"You're thinking like an American again. We've only had a free market economy a short time. No one had heard of Bova until he suddenly appeared as an entrepreneur who founded one of the new banks. There was nothing unusual about that, most of the new capitalists popped out of nowhere. One day a friend of mine worked behind a computer in a city office. The next day she became an importer of computers.''

"But there has to be background material on Bova. The news media must have investigated his whole life.''

"No, there's no way they could. We don't have a data base on social matters. We didn't even have telephone books. I know someone who works for one of Moscow's new scandal magazines, the kind that are always showing pictures of three-headed babies born to farm girls who were raped by Martians. She took a look at Alexei's background material in her magazine's file. It's the most mundane file imaginable. He's supposed to have worked in the accounting office of a very small company that imported raw material for government factories.''

"A private company?''

"I don't know. The company went out of business in 1985 and all the files were lost in a fire. The strange part is that all the employees died in the fire.''

"But I saw a picture of Alexei Bova at a party, a party that took place over twenty years ago.''

"You saw a picture of a man. Who says his name was Alexei Bova back then?''

"You're right,'' Lara said. "And we're back to 1985 again. Let's imagine for a moment that there was a scheme to put together a nest egg for KGB inner circle members and that Felix was part of that scheme. Alexei was another part."

"The most important part," Nina said. "The man who would handle the money."

"Money that needed to be laundered."

"What do you mean by laundered?"

"Dirty money, that is money earned illegally, comes in the form of cash. People don't usually buy drugs, fence stolen goods, take bribes, or conduct any other criminal activity except with cash. Major drug traffickers end up with millions of dollars in cash. But our society doesn't operate on a cash basis and they can't deposit it in a bank because questions would be asked about where it came from. So it's laundered, sanitized by being carefully fed to banks through dummy businesses. If you happen to own a bank, laundering naturally gets much easier."

"May I see the pathologist's report, please," Vlad asked.

When Nina returned to the corner, Lara asked her if her boyfriend had come up with anything on Yuri.

"One thing of interest, but I don't know how to tie it up. He has an extensive army file because he was a military policeman before entering the Moscow police department. His military service was honorable."

"That's what I was afraid of. Having a solid background is worse than no background. At least with Alexei we have grounds for suspicion. What's the one thing of interest in Yuri's background?"

Nina pursed her lips. "He was seriously wounded in Afghanistan and cited for extraordinary performance of duty. He had followed an escaped prisoner into the desert, a murderer, my boyfriend said, who had been brought in from a Siberian prison camp to do roadwork."

"Why would they bring a prisoner from Siberia to Afghanistan?"

"Afghanistan was the Soviet Vietnam. You couldn't get ordinary citizens to build roads across the desert, so the government brought in forced labor crews.''

"Even murderers?''

"If the man had been in prison a long time. I don't know the background of the man. Yuri Kirov was wounded in 1984.''

Lara looked at her. "The neighbor boy convicted of the murder of Vera Swen died while a prisoner in 1984. Did your boyfriend give you the name of the prisoner?''

"No, but I can ask him. It's sure to be in the file.''

"Find out for me.''

"You think that there's a connection between Detective Kirov and the neighbor boy?''

"I don't know what to think. My head is spinning.''

"I'll ask my boyfriend tomorrow. Keep your fingers crossed. The one thing we haven't been able to tie in with the case against you is the death of your mother and this Vera person years ago.''

"Except for the picture with Alexei in it.''

"Except for the picture. I don't think the judge would give much weight to such a picture especially since it will never be turned over. There must be evidence with a link to the crime,'' Nina said. "I've thought about the cross on the hand that might be the mark of a serial killer. I don't know how to research it. I've talked to a couple of lawyer friends and one of them knows someone who works with court records, but it all turned out negative. The court doesn't keep records of such things. If the police do, they're not saying anything.''

"In America you'd go to the news morgue,'' Lara said.

"What is a news morgue?''

"The place where past editions of a newspaper are stored. The sort of gruesome killings generated by serial killers would make front-page news. You just go back to year one and start forward, skimming the headlines for stories.''

"That doesn't work in a country where the stories never

made the news because the government kept them from the public,'' Nina said.

''Yes it does.''

The statement came from Vlad and caught them both by surprise. They hadn't realized they had been talking loud enough to be heard by him.

''The stories were obtained by the press,'' Vlad said, ''but were never printed because the censors cut them. All the rejected news stories for the past several decades are available to researchers. I read about the archive in the newspaper. The censored stories have been gathered at Moscow University's School of Journalism. The archive is open to scholars.''

''I'll go there tomorrow,'' Nina said, ''after my day in court. I'm still taking classes at the university and have a student card. I can say I'm doing legal research into old cases.''

''Good. Thank you,'' Lara said. Then to Vlad, ''Were you able to come up with anything that will help?''

He shook his head. ''I'll have to conduct an actual experiment using models, but I'm not hopeful.'' The tall youth stood up, grimacing in frustration. ''I can't see any way I can prove that you didn't fire the second shot, the one to the head. The entry wound is not clean.''

It took a moment for both woman to digest this remark and it was Nina who asked the obvious question.

''What about the first shot?''

He raised his eyebrows. ''But of course Lara couldn't have fired the first shot.''

Lara and Nina slowly looked at each other and then at Vlad.

Lara's voice trembled as she asked, ''Why couldn't I have fired the first shot?''

''You're too short.''

XXIII

═══

When people get accustomed to horrors,
these form the foundation for good style.

—Boris Pasternak,
Safe Conduct

ONE

N ina stopped by the university to check out the archive
of censored news stories after she finished at court
early in the afternoon. She discovered the archive was
not at the university, but in an annex a few blocks away,
a three-story building that once housed a student affairs
department. At the annex she got into a line for admission.
A notice pinned to the wall announced the cost of a ticket
to spend two hours in the archive.

When Nina's turn came, she stepped forward to the
counter and gave the clerk her identification, showing her
university permit and her identification as a member of the
Moscow Collegium of Lawyers.

The clerk examined the law membership and looked up
at Nina with contempt. Nina knew what she was thinking—what was this black girl doing with a law degree
when good ''Russian'' women were sweeping the streets?

''We have sold the quota of tickets for today. You will
have to come back another day.''

''Tomorrow?'' Nina asked.

''You can return tomorrow if you like.''

''May I buy the tickets for tomorrow now?''

''All the tickets for tomorrow are sold.''

Lara would scream at this mentality, she thought, but she understood what was really being said.

She dug into her purse and pulled out a British pound coin, less than two dollars, but worth nearly two thousand rubles at the current exchange rate. The coin had been a gift from an exchange student from Glasgow and she had been saving the money for Misha's birthday.

She made sure the woman saw her slip the coin between the ruble notes necessary for admission for the rest of the day and evening.

"It's a matter of great urgency for me to obtain access to some reports immediately. An important legal case depends upon it. You appear to be a person of some importance in this facility," she told the dull-eyed, stupid-looking bitch she would have preferred punching on the nose, "and I appeal to your authority."

The money was whisked off the counter and a stamped ticket pushed across at her.

"Next," the woman said to the person in line behind Nina.

Nina took her ticket and headed for the elevators, mentally grumbling about the system. The market economy has come to the university, she thought. Pay for services, bribe the employees, what next? she wondered. Will they start charging for attending college?

Another notice said that reports of crime were on the second floor. Someone had penciled in the words "THAT NEVER HAPPENED" after the word "CRIME" on the sign.

Students hung around the lobby, willing to assist with research for a small fee, but the cost of the ticket had already used up her money for dinner that night and lunch the next day. She still had some money left but maybe she wouldn't need the help.

When she got off the elevator on the second floor she experienced instant regret that the Soviets never threw anything away. Gray bins, hundreds of them, were on tables spread over the entire second floor. Another notice tacked to the wall told her that the censored press releases went back to the end of the Second World War, nearly fifty years ago. Rows were by year and each bin contained approximately one week of reports, the sign said.

She examined the contents of the closest bin. The news stories that were never released were printed on standard government-issue typing paper. Each release was a summary of a crime, usually a page or two in length.

Probably thousands of reports for the three decades she had to cover. She needed information only on women brutally killed but the reports were not categorized other than by date.

She spent a few minutes leafing through the bins for the year prior to Lara's mother's death and realized the chore would take her a couple of days by herself. She went down to the first floor and hired two students to help. It cost her food money for a week, but she knew Misha would understand and help out.

"I'm looking for crimes of insane violence, mutilations particularly," she told the young man and woman, "especially anything in which a mark resembling a religious cross was found on the victim."

She sent the male researcher to start at reports that began ten years ago, instructing him to move forward, the young woman to start ten years back from him. She began another ten years back, so in total they would cover the past thirty years. They spread out and went to work.

Nina had expected to find only serious crimes in the bins. To her surprise, most of the crimes reported on the sheets in the bins were commonplace—simple muggings, thefts, indecent exposure, prostitution, and the like. In order to arrive at the correct statistical results for the crime rate in general, the censors had barred the publication of tens of thousands of common crimes. Buried among reports of the theft of a coat on a metro and pilfered widgets from a factory was an occasional violent crime.

The reports were quite detailed. Often a simple theft

occupied a couple of typed, single-spaced sheets. After reading for a while, Nina decided the reports on lesser crimes were probably word for word duplicates of the actual police reports, while major crimes, a rape or murder, were summaries.

Her fingers flew through the reports, eyes scanning the short summary paragraph at the top of each one. Unless it involved the murder of a woman, she quickly skipped the rest, resisting the temptation to read on because she had limited time. There was no way she could pay her way back into the news morgue without asking for money from Lara and she was determined that Lara's little nest egg stay untouched. She had a dreadful feeling Lara was going to spend a long time in a Russian prison, and the money would help her survive.

Skimming through the bins, she decided that Russians had no criminal finesse. Thieves seemed to be stupid, stealing whatever was handy rather than what was most valuable. Killings tended to be impulsive and particularly bloody because, once again, the typical Russian murderer grabbed whatever weapon was handy, like the husband who beat his wife to death with an empty vodka bottle after an argument about his drinking. Police work was just as primitive; if the culprit wasn't caught red-handed and confessed, a little beating was amazingly soul cleansing.

A nagging worry ate at her: what if she came across an arrest report of her mother? She didn't remember how old she was when she found out her mother had been a prostitute. The knowledge had just always been there, perhaps first coming as a taunt from other children at school.

Nina had worked harder than anyone else she knew, unconsciously feeling that getting high marks and the certificates of accomplishment that came with them made up for her mother's background. She had gone into law because of a comment a friend had made. Lawyers were not a highly paid and influential class of professionals under the Communist system, despite the fact that Lenin himself had been a lawyer. But, a friend told her one night while drinking beer in a café near the university, lawyers know the law. They know what their rights are.

Having spent her short lifetime feeling that others considered her somewhat less than a Russian, somewhat less than a citizen, sometimes even somewhat less than human if the taunts of children and stares of adults were any clue, knowing her rights was a concept that appealed to her.

Ninety minutes before closing time Nina reached the end of her ten-year search with hands that were empty but soiled from the dusty records. Her hired help was still buried in the bins. She took a break to wash her hands before rounding up the two researchers. Both had papers in their hands.

"I found nothing," she told them. "Did either of you come up with anything?"

"I found one," the woman told her, holding up a sheet of paper. "About twelve years ago. A man was killed, a derelict."

"Same here," the young male student said. "About five years ago, a male pervert with a history of hanging around men's toilets."

"I told you I wanted reports of women mutilated," Nina said.

The two researchers exchanged looks. "No, you didn't," the woman told her. "You said you wanted violent crimes involving mutilation, especially if they mentioned crosses. The one I found was a man whose penis and testicles were cut off. Slashes on the man's right hand resembled a cross."

"Mine was the same," the male student said. "Penis and testicles cut off, a couple of slash marks on the right hand between the thumb and index finger. The report didn't mention any connection between the death and any others. No serial killer stuff."

"Mine didn't either," the woman said.

Nina was stunned. There was a serial killer leaving the

mark of Ivan the Terrible's cross on men, not women.

"You're right," she told the students, "how stupid of me. I was only looking for deaths of women. So we'll have to go over my section again as well as finish both of yours." She checked her watch. "You two carry on. I have to make a phone call."

From the lobby pay phone she called Misha's apartment to tell him to have dinner without her. "Lara and I have been focusing on the wrong type of killer," she told him. "I don't know what it means or how it all fits into the scheme of things, but the killer has gone after at least two men. Add in a woman victim and you have a killer that does not select his victims based upon sex. Something else sets the killer off. I'll bet we come up with something when we go through my section again. I wasn't looking for male victims."

After she hung up she turned to leave and noticed that another woman had left her purse on the shelf under the telephone next to her.

"Excuse me," Nina called to the woman walking away. "You forgot your purse."

The woman turned around and took the purse from Nina and smiled her thanks.

You would think a nurse would be more careful about things, Nina thought as she headed for the elevator.

T W O

Nina and her two researchers raced through the bins, covering almost a thirty-year period by closing time. Nina turned up another male victim in her section. The mark of a cross had been found on his hand and his sex organs had been mutilated.

Other than mutilation by knife and the mark of Ivan the

Terrible, none of the cases had anything in common.

It wasn't difficult to understand why no one had made a connection between the killings. The long time span between them, the fact that each killing took place in a different Moscow police district, the lack of public disclosure, would all make linking up the killings difficult. But the most crucial reason was the nature of the Soviet bureaucratic mentality. No official wanted to be the bearer of bad tidings by coming out and saying that there was a maniac loose on the streets of Moscow.

One killing was written off as the work of a foreign visitor of homosexual tendencies despite the fact that the victim was not identified as a homosexual. Homosexuality was simply a good scapegoat in a country where gays who came out of the closet went straight to prison. The report stated that the KGB had taken over the case. That was standard procedure—crimes involving foreigners were always investigated by the KGB, not the local police. But other than speculation, there was nothing to link a foreigner to the killing. The KGB was just as good at tossing back hot potatoes as the rest of the bureaucratic machinery and could have done so in this instance—unless the case was taken by the KGB in order to simply bury it.

Nina thought about that point. The KGB could monitor any murder case and a phone call to a supervisor at the local police station would get the investigation transferred to the KGB with no questions asked and a big sigh of relief from the police.

If we're able to find three in the censored news morgue, how many more occurred that never made it this far? Nina wondered. Lara came to Moscow to unravel one murder and stumbled onto a series of killings.

At closing time she gave the two researchers an extra bonus and left the annex. Her generosity had robbed her of even the metro fare and she set out with a quick pace for the twenty-minute walk to Misha's apartment. She was too excited to go home. She wanted to share her discoveries with Misha, perhaps get him and his buddies to hold a "think tank" session.

She pulled up her coat collar and put her head down against the wind. She reached a street corner and waited for a break in the traffic before crossing. A horn honked and a car pulled up beside her. The electric window went down on the passenger side and Nina leaned down to see who was in the car.

It was the nurse, the woman whose purse she had found, returning the favor by offering her a ride. Nina welcomed the thought of not having to make the long walk in the cold.

"You're a life saver," she told the woman as she slipped into the warm car.

XXIV

A single death is a tragedy,
A million deaths is a statistic.

—Stalin

ONE

At four o'clock in the morning Lara was awakened by the sound of her cell door being unlocked. She shot up from the mattress on the floor.

"Who's there?"

In the dim light she could see the outline of a man.

"It's me," Yuri said.

She stood up, clutching the blanket to her. "Why are you here?"

"Your lawyer is gone."

She heard his words but they had no meaning to her. "What do you mean? What are you talking about?"

"Your lawyer has disappeared."

She ran from the words, retreating back into a corner of the cell. "You're trying to scare me. I don't believe you."

He stepped closer to her. "Nina Kerensky has disappeared."

"What do mean, disappeared?"

"She was seen leaving a university research facility at closing time. She was supposed to meet her boyfriend and never reached there. The boyfriend got worried and called the police."

"No, dear God, no . . ." She swayed dizzily.

He reached out with his hand but she recoiled from him, stumbling on the mattress and crashing against the wall.

"Oh, God, this can't be." She slid down onto the floor, clutching the blanket. "There's something else, something you're not telling me. I can hear it in your voice."

Yuri's tired voice came to her from the darkness.

"Her purse was found. In Gorky Park. There was . . . blood on it. A mugging."

He sounded like an electronic voice in an elevator calling off floor numbers.

"A mugging? There was no mugging!" she screamed. "It's a lie, another lie."

Curses came from down the cell block. A matron standing behind Yuri said to Lara, "Keep your voice down, prisoner."

"Get out of here," Yuri told the matron.

The woman stepped out of the cell and Yuri closed the door. He sat down on the mattress. A match flared in the darkness and for a moment she saw the profile of his face, grim and hard. The match went out and the smell of tobacco filled the air.

"Poor Nina." A clammy cold gripped her body and she trembled. "She wanted to help. She wanted to be a good lawyer. She was a good lawyer."

"There was a ticket in her pocket for admission into the censored press release archive. Was she working on something for you?"

"Working on something for me?" A fog had seeped into her head. She heard his question, repeated the words, but the meaning was lost on her. She leaned back and put her head against the wall of the cell. She wished she were dead. It was her fault, her damn fault, sending her out onto the street.

"You were right," she told Yuri, "I'm safe in here. And I sent Nina out to be killed."

He took a long drag on his cigarette and blew out smoke. He smoked for a while, then stubbed out the cigarette and lit another. She watched the outline of his face for a second time.

"I should have returned home," she said. "I should have left Moscow. She'd be alive now if I hadn't been a fool."

"It's too late for should haves," he told her. "Tell me what she was working on, why she went to the archive."

"She was working on my case." She knew that was a stupid answer, but it was hard for her to think. "She went to the archive to find reports of women with crosses on their hand." She shook her head, trying to shake out some of the fog. "Nina noticed that Vera Swen had a mark on her hand, a cross that Nina said was the mark of Ivan the Terrible, a scar he used to put on the hands of freaks to ward off the devil."

"The mark of Ivan the Terrible," he murmured. "I remember that from school. Deformed people were infected by the devil and the cross would drive the devil out."

"She thought it might be the signature of a serial killer. She went to the censored news archive to look up stories kept out of the newspapers during the Soviet era."

"This was her first trip?"

"Yes."

"So you don't know what she found. Would she have told anyone else? A roommate, a boyfriend?"

"She might have told her boyfriend. He's in the army. Works in the records department."

"What else was Nina working on?"

"My case."

"Be specific."

She was quiet for a moment and then said, "No, I'm not going to tell you anything else. Tell me everything about Nina, tell me what you know."

He took another deep drag of his cigarette and slowly exhaled it. "I told you, her purse was found with blood on it. The lab will check the blood type. The police have put it down to a mugging."

A horrible taste of bile clogged her throat as she listened. She wanted to scream and run and cry but she sat with her back to the wall, a prisoner to the terror.

"My gut feeling is that she was killed in a car," Yuri continued, "but the local militia station commander is calling it a street mugging. They suspect the killer broke a hole in the river ice and slipped her body in to hide it. The hole would freeze up in a couple of hours and the body won't be found until the spring thaw."

"Muggers don't go through that much trouble. There's something you're not telling me."

"I went to the university annex and spoke to the guard. He had come on duty about closing time and saw Nina leave. There aren't that many black people in Moscow, so he had no problem remembering her."

"What else?"

"He remembered another woman leaving about the same time. He remembered her because of the uniform."

"It was a nurse, wasn't it? Tell me, was it a nurse?"

"The guard remembered a woman in a white uniform leaving about the same time."

"Get out of here. *Get out!*"

Tears welled up inside her and she began to cry. She buried her face in her arms as he got up and left.

A moment later she realized someone had reentered the cell and she looked up. The matron had returned after letting Yuri out and was glaring down at her. It was the same jail attendant that had let Yuri in the first time he came and who had let Alexei sneak in. "Foreign bitch. Your noise can get me into trouble." The woman kicked her, then turned to leave.

Lara launched up from the floor in a rage, screaming, "You've been spying on me! How many people are paying you?"

The woman snapped the door shut and left her in darkness.

Lara cried for the first time since she was a child. Cried

for the loss of her mother. For the loss of her youth. For
the loss of hope. And most of all she cried for Nina.

"She's dead," she said, sobbing, "it's my fault she's
dead."

From down the cell block a woman whined, "She's
dead, my baby's dead."

TWO

V lad came to see her two days later.
Lara was red-eyed and haggard. She had hardly
slept since Yuri had awakened her with the news about
Nina. Her eyes were swollen and pain never left her head.

"Nina had called Misha's apartment from the news
morgue," Vlad told her. "We tracked down the two students who helped her do research. They had already talked
to a policeman named Kirov. There's no news about her.
We don't expect any." He choked on his words. "Not
until the thaw."

He got control of his voice and told her about Nina's
discoveries at the archives—three men killed, their sex organs mutilated, the sign of the cross slashed between
thumb and index finger.

"Three men? Not women?"

"Three men," Vlad told her, "a doctor, a derelict, and
a pervert."

"What kind of pervert?"

"A guy with an arrest history of hanging around men's
toilets in parks and soliciting other men for sex. He was
fairly young, twenty-seven years old. He would follow a
man into a rest room and try to enter the same stall as if
by accident. If the man in the stall wasn't disturbed by the
sudden intrusion . . ." Vlad shrugged his shoulders.

"One day he followed the wrong person. How did the other two die?"

"The derelict, a man in his fifties with a history of arrest for being drunk in public, was also found in a public rest room, this time at a metro station. The doctor didn't fit the pattern. He was killed by someone waiting in his car, probably crouched down in the backseat. He had been giving an evening lecture at a university hospital."

"What kind of doctor was he?"

"A noted elderly surgeon who taught at the medical university. He was something of a pioneer in Soviet plastic surgery back in the forties and fifties, exciting decades for Soviet medicine—"

"And Soviet witchcraft," she interjected.

"Yes, things are starting to come out about that era, not just what happened in mental hospitals. Some of the medical practices were as bad as those for industry and agriculture. They say some Soviet doctors did experiments that would have made Hitler's quack doctors blush. Anyway, this doctor had retired from full-time teaching and now only taught an occasional class on plastic surgery."

Pain swirled in her head. "It doesn't make any sense, none of it. Only two of the victims had anything in common—killed in a public rest room. The doctor's killing doesn't fit in with the others. Neither does age, occupation, social milieu. And there's no common element with the murder of Vera Swen."

"How about opportunity?"

"What do you mean?"

"Just that. Perhaps those are the people the killer had an opportunity to kill so he killed."

"Opportunity is always a factor, but it's the trigger that's not obvious. The killer gets opportunity probably every day to kill someone, but the act isn't triggered. The two toilet killings fit the mode, but the doctor and Vera Swen . . . those killings might have been more premeditated for a reason."

"The killer planned them."

"Exactly. If they're not the type of person the killer usually goes after, then he might have had some reason beyond just his psychosis to kill them."

"They knew something about him."

"Or her. Did Nina say anything to her boyfriend about a nurse?"

Vlad shook his head.

"The person who's been stalking me is a nurse. Nina was last seen with the nurse."

The nurse at the top of the landing coming out of Vera's apartment, the woman who took her out of school and tried to kill her at St. Basil's, a nurse at the bedside of Belkin as he lay injured on a hospital bed, the nurse who left the news morgue at about the same time as Nina . . .

The nurse, the nurse, the nurse.

"There had to be a nurse mentioned in the reports. Or a woman at least."

"The researchers didn't say anything about a nurse. Or a woman. Of course, when the doctor was killed a nurse's presence might not have been considered significant since the killing took place at a hospital."

"That's a connection I didn't consider," Lara said.

"What connection?"

"Doctor-nurse. A doctor was killed, a nurse has been involved all along the line." She could see she lost Vlad. "Were any of the crimes solved?"

"In the doctor's case, a man who had been treated at the hospital for a mental condition and who had previously served a prison term for a knife attack was suspected of the crime. He was found dead, a suicide, when the police arrived to arrest him. The police listed him as the assailant and closed the case.

"The case of the pervert was similarly 'solved,' " Vlad said. "A man who was arrested with him a few years before, someone caught in the act with him, was picked up by the police. He had a heart attack and died under police

464 / JUNIUS PODRUG

interrogation. The police report mentions a confession, but the reference to the confession was so vague one can't be sure exactly to what the man had confessed.''

''And the derelict?''

''Attributed to a foreign homosexual. The toilet was in a tourist area. No arrest and the case was referred to the KGB because a foreigner was suspected of being involved.''

''It could only happen in a secret society,'' Lara said, not keeping the disgust from her voice. ''A free society with the news media watching the police and lawyers exposing police malfeasance in courtrooms would never permit these crimes to be swept under the rug.''

''Besides the bad system,'' Vlad said, ''there was a long lapse between the killings, five or six years, and the fact that the killings were not centered in a single Moscow neighborhood.''

''It's no excuse. We're not talking about bad police work, we're dealing with corruption. Someone with power pulled strings that caused each investigation to go astray.''

Lara shook her head again, trying to get her brain to process the data into a neat and orderly pattern but it wouldn't cooperate. ''There's really no pattern to the killings at all.''

''Of course there is. The same mark, the killer's trademark, is on each body.''

''You're right. And I keep looking for something about the dead people that makes them freaks and forgetting about Nina's comment that maybe the killer is a freak.''

She thought about the power and ruthlessness it would take to cover the tracks of the killer and a wave of fear for Vlad swept her. She reached across the table and grabbed his hands.

''Vlad, you have to leave Moscow until my trial is over. Go to Siberia, the Black Sea, anywhere, just get out of Moscow until it's over.''

"Your trial won't start for months. You must get a new attorney. The court will delay the trial."

"No, I'm not getting another attorney. I'm defending myself. In court this morning I signed away my right to an attorney. The judge was ready to appoint a former prosecutor, a hack who would hold my arms while that bitch Svetlana stepped on my face. I'm pushing the case to trial."

"You shouldn't do that. You will need a lawyer."

"Vlad, I am a lawyer. Not a Russian one, but Nina was the only Russian lawyer I could trust. It's my life on the line and I'm the only person I trust with my life." She squeezed his hands. "I'm worried about you. And Nina's boyfriend."

Vlad shook his head. "I'm not leaving. I will be at the trial, in the courtroom, so when you turn around you will see a face that you know and who supports you."

"I can't let you—"

"Don't worry about me. My father was also a firearms expert and I've been playing with guns since I was seven years old. I can protect myself. I came here in a car with Misha and another friend. They're waiting outside for me—with enough firepower to take on the whole Mafia. I'm going to help you at the trial, not just for you, but for Nina."

"Vlad—"

"It's all arranged. I've made models. We can establish the angle of the shot to the victim's chest by the powder burns on the door frame and the bullet embedded in the spa liner. That angle shows that a person several inches taller than you fired the shot. I can't do anything about the second shot, the one to the back of her head. It was apparently fired while the body floated in the spa and I can't determine the angle. But once we eliminate you as the author of shot number one, the other doesn't matter."

Lara looked away and said nothing. Vlad was her only hope now but there was something that bothered her about his theory. It sounded logical. Too pat, too easy. There had to be a catch and right now her mind wasn't capable of tracking the progress of a fly on a wall let alone the path of a speeding bullet.

She was also terribly afraid for the young man's safety.

"I trust you, Vlad. I know you'll do what you can. And I hate to admit it, but you're my only hope. But I'm worried.".

"Worry about preparing for your trial. I'll do my part. I'm not running. Nina was my friend."

"Mine, too," Lara said. "Mine, too."

They were silent for a moment. Lara was drained, emotionally and physically.

"I have that other information you asked for," Vlad said.

"Other information? I'm sorry, Vlad, I don't even remember what I asked for."

"You wanted to find out from Nina's boyfriend the name of the prisoner who was killed trying to escape when Detective Yuri Kirov was wounded in Afghanistan. The prisoner's name was Alexander Zurin."

"Alexander Zurin."

She stared blankly at Vlad, trying to get an incomprehensible piece of information to fit a puzzle that kept changing shape. "Pasha."

"Yes, Pasha is the familiar name for Alexander," Vlad said. "From the expression on your face, it seems this information means something to you."

"Yes, it means something to me. Pasha Zurin was the boy next door who was convicted of killing our neighbor."

"The woman Vera? I don't understand."

Her mind reeled—her head was spinning on her shoulders for all she knew. Images flashed of a picture sent from Moscow that lured her back to investigate a two-decades-old killing and of a police officer who was Johnny-on-the-spot everywhere she turned.

"I don't understand, either. Yuri Kirov is one of the

links," she told the mystified Vlad. "There's a chain that extends back over twenty years and Yuri is a link on the chain."

"A chain?"

"A chain of murder and deceit," she told him.

THREE

S even days passed, each day filled with growing anxiety and mounting impatience before Lara was brought into the courtroom for her trial. For the first time she was not put in the prisoner's dock, but taken to a counsel table.

There were two other counsel tables, one for the prosecution, the other for that strange creature of Soviet-Russian law, the *obhchestvenni*—representatives of the victim's family and employer.

At the pretrial conference she had been told that Rykoff would be present with Nadia's sister and that a representative of Nadia's employer, Moscow News, would also be at the table.

Svetlana had not made her appearance yet. No doubt she was waiting for exactly the right dramatic moment, Lara thought. The presence of Lenin on the wall—signing something, a death warrant? she wondered—and the heavily armed soldiers created a feeling that she was not just in a foreign country, but an earlier era.

And she felt something else, an undercurrent from the audience that she had never sensed in an American courtroom where stern-faced bailiffs ensure that spectators sit quietly and do not interrupt the proceedings. The body language of the spectators, they way they walked into the courtroom and talked as if it was home ground, the appraising stares she got from them, created a feeling in her that she was experiencing a vulgar sort of democracy, an arrogance almost, as if they, too, were arbiters of the justice that would be handed down.

She wondered if this was Judge Rurik's regular courtroom or if it had been selected because it was large and impressive-looking—a visual display for the foreign and local press of Russian justice in action. The courtroom was old and venerable, with heavy wood tables and benches, and wood paneling on the walls.

The gallery was full when she was brought in, with standing room only at the back. The smell of damp wool was in the air and she could see wet footprints down the center aisle. Two rows at the front had been set aside for the press.

She had already decided that with every word she said, every move she made, she would keep the press in mind because an informed press was the only thing that could keep her fighting on her feet if the system decided to railroad her to the nearest prison.

Yuri was at the back of the courtroom, leaning against the wall to the left of the big double doors leading out of the courtroom, a raincoat folded over one arm, an umbrella in the other hand. She let her eyes touch his for a moment before she scanned the rest of the gallery.

Alexei stood on the other side of the doors, resplendent in a double-breasted Italian suit and hand-painted silk tie. Media people pressed close to him no doubt so they could report having been ''in touch'' with the great man.

Nina had warned her that unlike an American courtroom where a spectator who shouted something was likely to be arrested or at least thrown out, grumbling from the audience was more likely to be tolerated. Perhaps the judge counted thumbs-up and-down. It was a silly thought, but there were a lot of strange thoughts circulating in her head.

The double doors at the rear of the courtroom snapped opened and Stalin's Breath entered at the head of her troops. She wore her military-style uniform. Vulko followed on her heels along with a harried-looking young man who closely resembled Svetlana's previous assistant, the one she had tried to palm off on Lara.

Before taking a seat at the counsel table, Svetlana paused and gave Lara a formal nod—quite different from the look of contempt Lara got from Vulko. For some reason he disliked her personally. It wasn't just a matter of police versus criminal suspect, she thought, her personality didn't mix well with his—he was a swine.

Svetlana nodded to another person in the courtroom and Lara turned in her chair to see who the person was—a well-dressed gentleman in his early sixties with a closely trimmed beard, conservative but well-tailored suit, and stiff white shirt with striped tie. He gave the impression of a professional man, perhaps a doctor, and possibly the pathologist who did the autopsy since that was the only doctor in the case. Maybe an observer sent from the Foreign Ministry because of the attention the case was getting from the foreign media.

The audience stirred as the judge and two assessors entered the courtroom.

It was time to start the trial. The trial of her life.

For her life.

FOUR

This was the first time Lara had seen the two assessors. She studied them as they took their seats while the judge shuffled papers and called the case.

The one on the judge's left was a short, heavy woman of about forty-five or fifty, a foreman at a brake-lining factory. The woman could have been the sister to the beefy wife of Guk the truck driver.

The other assessor was male, early sixties, thick glasses, and chubby. The information sheet said he was an administrator with the street department. His job description and the appearance of the man told her he was not a high-level apparatchik.

The first thing she had to do was to create a path of empathy between her and the assessors. To do that she had to reach across and tap something in them that caused them if not to understand her, at least feel what it's like to be in her shoes.

The female assessor was a hardworking, divorced parent with two kids. She had a management-type job, but was more blue collar than white collar. Other than their sex, Lara had almost nothing in common with the woman. Worse, Lara's professional background might create negative vibes with the woman.

Digging deep for ideas that would cast her in a light that the woman might understand who and what she was—that she was a person perhaps worth saving—Lara had come up with two common denominators: like the woman, she had worked hard at her job, in her own way, probably harder than the woman assessor had done because there were thousands of hours of "overtime" that were not compensated for when pursuing a professional career. The second tie was children. Lara didn't have a child, but in her mind the case she was on trial for started when she was seven years old. The woman might relate to that.

The male assessor was a harder nut to crack. She could think of nothing she had in common with him. Watching his body language as he leaned toward the judge like a faithful dog to hear some whispered comment, she realized he would be easily swayed by the judge's authoritative position.

She perceived him as petty and stupid, the type who would be a tyrant at home and at work to anyone beneath him, but a bootlicker to his superiors. He probably believed he was the only efficient employee in the entire country. Casting herself as a victim of government inefficiency, while carefully noting that there are many fine examples of efficient . . .

Forget it. It was hopeless. The only way she'd get the man to relate to her was if God were her co-counsel. And even in a post-Communist society, that might not do it.

The judge was the most important, perhaps the only true trier of fact, and he was a professional and had no doubt seen about everything there was to see in a courtroom. He would be the hardest to sway with courtroom tactics.

Judge Rurik called the case and briefly, for the record and no doubt the press, introduced the participants in the courtroom, starting with Svetlana and her staff, moving to Rykoff and Nadia's sister, then to the representative from Moscow News, a young woman with thick glasses and short blond hair whom Lara was certain she had seen as an anchorwoman on the news program.

"I have read the investigation reports and they appear to be complete and in good order," the judge said, nodding at Vulko, who rose slightly to give the judge a small bow. Lara couldn't help but imagine him snapping his heels and giving a Nazi salute.

The judge went on briefly to summarize the facts set forth in the report: the call to the police from a "concerned but anonymous citizen" reporting a woman entering the tower with a gun, the police rushing in, Lara seen with a gun, Nadia, a prominent news media personality, found dead—

"My sister was loved by all in Russia," Nadia's sister cried out. From the audience came a chorus of muttered sympathies.

"I watched her show every night," Rykoff said.

"A great loss for our country," the judge said. "A wrong that we are here to punish."

The circus has started, Lara thought.

Judges in America would not have permitted such theatrics. Nina had warned her but she was still taken aback that people could make totally irrelevant and inflammatory remarks in a courtroom.

It was a moment before she realized the judge had spoken to her.

''Lara Patrick, come forward and tell us what you know about this matter.''

You have no right to remain silent, Nina said, no right to refuse to testify. The court will call you as the first witness and you will be expected to confess your sins. Confession is good for the soul . . .

XXV

It is true that liberty is precious—
so precious that it must be rationed.

—Lenin

ONE

L ara stood at the counsel table. She cleared her throat and looked up at the judge and the two assessors in a display of more confidence than she felt.

"What do I know about the crime? I know a young woman lost her life. I know I stand accused. And . . . I know I am innocent." She took a deep breath. "Nadia Kolchak's life was taken not because of anything I did, but because of a failure of the Soviet regime to protect—"

"Miss Patrick," the judge interrupted. "We are not here for a history lesson about the failings of the Soviet justice system. This is the time and place for you to take responsibility for your acts. Tell us about how you came to take the life of Nadia Kolchak. Tell us about the blackmail Nadia Kolchak proposed, about the jealousy between you and Nadia over Alexei Bova, and how you felt driven to take Nadia Kolchak's life in a sudden rage of anger and passion."

Tell us mitigating circumstances and you won't die from a bullet was what he was implying.

She was at the fork in the road.

Her right knee trembled and she leaned against the table

to steady herself. Her eyes met the judge and in a strong, clear voice she said, "This case didn't begin with the death of Nadia Kolchak. The events that led up to the death of Nadia began—"

"My apologies." Svetlana rose at the prosecutor's table. "If the judge will permit, I need a few minutes to investigate a matter of importance."

The judge frowned. "It is a bit unusual, Madam Prosecutor, but if it is a matter that recently arose . . ."

"Yes. I need ten or fifteen minutes."

"The court will be in recess for fifteen minutes."

The judge and assessors left the courtroom and Svetlana followed them through the door that led to the judge's chambers and the holding tank for prisoners farther down the corridor.

A few moments later, Lara was ordered to follow one of the courtroom guards. She would have preferred to stay at the counsel table with her papers rather than be put in the holding tank for the fifteen-minute break, but she didn't bother trying to argue. She got up and was escorted by the guard to the rear door of the courtroom.

In the rear corridor she automatically turned in the direction of the holding cell but the guard caught her arm. "This way," he said. He took her in the opposite direction, pausing at the office to the judge's office. He knocked on the door, opened it, and stood aside as Lara entered, and then shut the door.

At the other end of the room Svetlana stood at a window, smoke from her cigarette surrounding her. She turned slowly, the dull gray light from the window making the smoke a glowing halo around her, creating not so much an angelic impression as that of an avenging angel.

"Do you want to live?"

Lara stared at her, at a loss for words. "Do I want to live? Is that a question or a threat?"

Svetlana chuckled, an almost manly rasp. She moved away from the window, leaving a trail of smoke in her wake as she stood and looked at the law books lining the wall behind the judge's desk.

"This is a very bad time for Russia," Svetlana told her. Lara wasn't sure if the woman was talking to her or just thinking aloud. "Not since the Great Patriotic War has there been such fear. For my entire career it has been a crime to make a profit from the sale of goods or services. Suddenly, people are told that if they do not make a profit, they will no longer have homes and their children will starve.

"As a prosecutor, I have been privy to reports of madness in rural areas where the supplies of food and fuel have been the lowest, stories of atrocities that I did not believe possible for good Russians to commit."

Lara stood silently, wondering why she was getting the economics lesson. Svetlana put out her cigarette in an ashtray and sat on the edge of the desk.

"Did you make deals with criminals when you were a prosecutor?" she asked Lara.

Lara thought about the question and answered it honestly. "I treated people fairly. If the defendant had evidence that rebutted or mitigated the crime, I wasn't afraid to dismiss charges or be lenient. But I never made deals in the sense that I offered anything less than what the evidence showed the person deserved."

"I never make deals," Svetlana said. "I have been a prosecutor for twelve years. In every case I have handled the criminal was found guilty of the charge that I originally filed. There is no compromise with me. Justice is not blind to me as it is in the West."

"Justice is blindfolded to make her impartial," Lara said, "not to make her ignorant."

"I am offering you a . . . what do you call it, a plea bargain?" The words came out in a rush as if Svetlana were spitting out something foul.

Nerves fluttered up Lara's throat from the tight knots in her stomach. "What exactly are you offering?"

"Your life."

"I see. And what do I have to do for my life?"

Svetlana slipped off the edge of the table and returned to the window, her back to Lara, speaking to the gray day outside. "This is a new day in Russia. New rules. The prosecutor general has received calls from the Foreign Ministry and the Economics Ministry. The bureaucrats in those departments know nothing about this case except what they read in the newspapers, nothing about the process of administering justice, but they fear the publicity being generated by putting a woman on trial who has blood ties to both America and Britain at a time when Russia is looking to the West for loans."

"It's not only me, is it?" Lara said. "It's the other killings. You don't want that to come into the public eye. My mother's death, our neighbor, all the others."

"You are barred from mentioning those deaths in court because they are not relevant to this case."

"You'll have to gag me. That would look pretty for the foreign press, wouldn't it? An example of the justice system of the new Russia at work."

Svetlana waved her hand as if she was shooing away a pesty insect. "It doesn't matter. There will be no trial. My instructions are to give you back your life."

"In exchange for what?"

"You will plead guilty to killing Nadia Kolchak with mitigating circumstances. You and Nadia were competitive lovers for Alexei Bova. We can leave out your mutual greed for his money. In the heat of the moment, overwhelmed by your emotions and sexual rage, you murdered Nadia."

Lara kept her voice calm as she answered, "I already told Vulko, I am not going to prison for something I didn't do."

"There is another part to the deal. You will have to serve only one year. After that, you will be released and

immediately shipped out of the country. The excuse will
be that some close relative is gravely ill.''

''I have no close relatives.''

''Then you can have one of mine. Don't talk nonsense
when you are witnessing a miracle.''

''I'm not accepting the offer.''

''What?''

''I'm not pleading guilty to something I didn't do.''

''You are a fool.''

''I am innocent. I don't think that means anything to
you. You say every case that came before you in twelve
years was black and white. I was a prosecutor and I learned
that there are some innocent people in this world. That's
where your system fails. Justice isn't just blind in Russia—
she had her eyes gouged by people like you.''

Svetlana stepped close to her, close enough for Lara to
smell her perfume, the acrid scent of spent gunpowder,
close enough for Lara to feel the heat of her anger and
contempt.

''Put the past on trial,'' Svetlana whispered, ''and you
put Russia on trial.''

She suddenly realized Svetlana had a small caliber automatic only inches from her stomach. She stared at Svetlana, wondering if the cold bitch had lost her mind, unable
to believe her own eyes as Svetlana's grip tightened on
the gun, the trigger finger slowly contracting, drawing back
the trigger . . .

A flame popped up from the top of the gun.

Svetlana smiled and slowly raised the lighter to her cigarette. She blew smoke in Lara's face.

''Put Russia on trial and I will pull the trigger myself
at your execution.''

TWO

When Lara was returned to the courtroom by the guard, Svetlana was standing at the railing to the gallery talking to a man on the other side, the distinguished-looking individual Lara had noticed earlier.

Svetlana took her place at the prosecutor's table after Lara was seated.

The judge and the assessors returned to the bench and the judge nodded down at Svetlana.

"The defendant has denied the crime," he said. "You may proceed with your evidence."

Lara flinched and rose at the counsel table. "Your Honor, I'm not through with my statement."

"You have denied the crime. That is sufficient. If you do not wish to admit your guilt, there is no use wasting the court's time. We will proceed with the evidence."

"But I want the court to know—"

He waved away her objection. "A trial in Russia is not a melodrama in which those accused of crimes give speeches. You are entitled to cross-examine witnesses, present your own witnesses, and at the end of the trial you will be given the last word." He nodded at Svetlana again. "Proceed."

"My first witness is Chief Investigator Vulko of the Moscow City Prosecutor's office."

The chief investigator gave a simple, straightforward narration of the results of the police investigation. He began with the anonymous phone call and moved forward chronologically. "When officers arrived at the Bova penthouse and entered the front door, the first person they saw was the accused. She ran across the landing at the top of the stairway. She was holding a gun. Fearful for their lives, the officers began to fire their own weapons."

Vulko went on to describe the scene of the crime, showing the murder weapon "taken from the defendant's hand," describing Nadia found dead in the spa, two gunshot wounds, two empty cartridges in the gun Lara had been caught with.

"A glove belonging to the defendant was found in Mr. Bova's office. It was found beside a filing cabinet that had been tampered with."

Vulko wasn't there, she thought. It's all hearsay, every word of it. Multiple levels of hearsay as he testified to what one officer told another officer who told him . . .

She realized with a start that the prosecutor had no intention of calling the other police witnesses: Vulko was it. What he said would convict her without her being able to poke holes in the story. It would be impossible to cross-examine him effectively when everything he testified to was told to him by other people.

He then expanded his testimony into the subsequent police investigation, including the taped conversation between Lara and Yuri in the jail.

"Is it your conclusion, then," Svetlana asked, "that the accused was involved in a scheme to blackmail Alexei Bova and that she murdered Nadia Kolchak after Miss Kolchak discovered the scheme?"

"Objection." Lara jumped to her feet. "There is no foundation for the question."

"No foundation?" the judge asked.

"There is not one shred of evidence in this case that I was involved in any manner with blackmailing Mr. Bova. On the contrary, the only evidence concerning blackmail are my statements that it was Miss Kolchak who was planning to blackmail Mr. Bova."

"Objection overruled."

"But, Your Honor—"

"That is not the correct way to address a Russian judge."

"Your . . . Judge, Mr. Vulko has testified to the truthfulness of facts he has no personal knowledge of. Now he has drawn a conclusion from those facts that the facts themselves don't support. It's pure speculation on his part."

"Madam, you are in a Russian courtroom. I am a Russian judge. You are not a Russian attorney. You were given the opportunity to accept a Russian attorney for this trial—"

"My attorney—"

"Sit down! Do not interrupt me again." He pointed his finger at her.

She sat down, her jaws tight. It wasn't an argument she was going to win. If she opened her mouth they would probably have her cuffed and gagged.

"Under Russian law," he told her, his tone more neutral, "the chief investigator is allowed to draw inferences from his investigation which he believes are warranted. He is only permitted to draw reasonable inferences, but we are not bound by the rigid legal rules of the American system of justice. The chief investigator is given great latitude under our system," he said, obviously to the gallery and the news media people, "but so is the defendant. Miss Patrick will be given great leeway in presenting her defense. No rigid rules of evidence will hackle her. She will be given every opportunity to present her case without restraint from artificial rules that keep the truth from the courtroom."

There's one thing wrong with your analysis, she wanted to say. The chief investigator wasn't propounding the "truth" but rather a conclusion drawn from thin air. Those "artificial rules" of evidence used in American courtrooms were not designed to keep the truth from the courtroom but to keep people like Vulko from making groundless accusations. She kept her thoughts to herself, careful to keep her features blank. She wasn't going to improve her position by mouthing off and giving the judge an excuse to gag her.

Vulko elaborated on the blackmail scheme and then Svetlana announced, "No more questions."

Lara started to rise to ask questions as the judge said, "Mr. Rykoff, it is your turn."

She sat back down. She had forgotten. The representative of the victim's family was next. And then Nadia's employer, the news station, would have a shot.

Rykoff stood up, reintroduced himself to the court and the gallery.

The knowledge that he had discussed the case with her and then had turned around and offered his services to an adverse party infuriated her. So did his body language. He was there to get attention for himself and not justice for the victim's family.

"Chief Investigator Vulko," he said, "Nadia Kolchak was a great asset to the new Russia, was she not?"

"Objection. No foundation. No evidence has been admitted establishing that Mr. Vulko had any knowledge of Miss Kolchak prior to her death."

Before the judge ruled, Rykoff held up his hands. "No, no, it is all right, Judge. I withdraw the question." Rykoff shot a look at the audience and then, in a pandering tone of voice, asked, "Chief Investigator Vulko, have you ever watched the Moscow News on television?"

As the gallery roared with laughter, Lara sat back and folded her arms, her face burning.

Rykoff stopped the pretense of asking questions and began making a speech to the court and audience, feeding maudlin "facts" about Nadia's past life, starting with her childhood. As Rykoff talked about the flower of Russian youth, portraying Nadia as something of a cross between Joan of Arc and Mother Teresa, Lara closed him out of her mind and thought about the Nadia she knew.

Whatever Nadia was, and she certainly wasn't a saint, she didn't deserve to be brutally murdered.

As Rykoff droned on about the loss to Nadia's family and to all Russia, Nadia's sister sobbed beside him. Lara didn't know if the woman's tears flowed from her sense of loss or the melodramatic atmosphere that Rykoff had created. In the States she would have asked for a "sidebar" to object to the testimony out of hearing of the jury, but there was no jury and she wasn't in the States.

Half an hour later Rykoff took his seat and the Moscow News representative stood up.

"Mr. Rykoff has presented to the court the great loss to the family and to all Russia. What Mr. Rykoff has said is true. We at Moscow News . . ."

Her mind wandered and she was startled a few minutes later by the judge addressing her.

"The defendant may question the witness."

Lara stood up, rustled her papers for a moment, and then met Vulko's eye.

"Let's go back to the scene of the crime, Chief Investigator. My recollection of your testimony is that you were not present when I came into contact with Moscow police officers at the penthouse, is that correct?"

"It is not required under Russian law that I be present in order to testify. I am permitted to conduct an investigation in which I question police officers and the defendant and testify as to the results." He looked at the prosecutor and then at the judge, both of whom gave nodding confirmation.

"So everything you know about what occurred at the scene of the crime you learned from other officers."

"I am permitted to do so."

"I am not asking whether what you did was permissible, Chief Investigator, I am asking about the procedure you followed. What you know about the scene of the crime you learned from other officers. Isn't that true?"

"Yes."

"And it's true that you did not personally observe any of the activities."

"Under Russian law—"

"And, Chief Investigator, in testifying to those things that others told you, you have not left out any of the important facts that should be before this court, is that correct?"

"Of course. I placed all the facts before the court."

"But not having been at the scene, you did not pick up all the . . . the little details, things like"—she shrugged—"well, whether my hair was in a bun or hanging loose."

He grinned. "I don't know whether you combed your hair." Laughter came from the gallery.

"Or the expression on my face."

"Or the expression on your face." His grin widened.

"If you don't know the expression on my face when I first contacted the officers, you cannot know if I was running in terror from the real killer, can you?"

"I don't understand what you are getting at. I—"

"You testified for the prosecutor that I came running onto the landing with a gun, but you don't know what my demeanor was, you don't know if I was running in terror."

"You were running in terror. You were terrified because the police were confronting you."

"Excuse me, but you just testified that you knew nothing about my demeanor. Going back over your previous testimony, you mentioned the fingerprint tests the criminalist took at the scene of the crime. The criminalist told you about all the results, and you testified about all of them, didn't you?"

Smelling another trap, Vulko's eyes narrowed and he sat upright in the witness chair.

Lara's eyebrows went up. "Why don't you tell us now which of the results you failed to tell us about?"

Vulko hesitated, knowing he was being set up but not knowing which way to turn. He exchanged looks with Svetlana. "I testified about all of the results."

Good, she thought. The idea was to commit him completely to his prior testimony or get him to expand upon it.

"Now, Officer—excuse me, Chief Investigator, no fingerprint tests were done of the gun that has been identified as the murder weapon. Is that correct?"

"No fingerprint tests were done of the murder weapon," he repeated slowly, seeing if any of the words bit back. "No, there were no fingerprint tests done of the murder weapon because—"

"Because it was found in my hand, isn't that correct?"

"Yes, that's correct."

"In my statement to the officers at the scene, I said I had found the gun on the floor and had picked it up just before they entered, isn't that correct?"

"That was your statement. They—"

"And despite—"

"Judge, she is cutting off the witness," Svetlana objected.

"I apologize," Lara said, not meaning it. She was deliberately cutting him off to keep him from justifying every negative response.

"Let the witness finish his answers," the judge instructed.

Sure. "You mentioned that a glove purportedly belonging to me was found next to a filing cabinet."

"It was your glove," he said. "It matched one we found in your hotel room."

"Were any tests done on the gloves to determine whether they were in fact my gloves?"

"Yes," he snapped. "I looked at the two gloves, held them up to the light, and my eyes told me they were the same."

"But you didn't do any scientific tests, no analysis of hand cream residue, makeup, hair, nothing of that sort to link me with the glove." She was taking a risk. It was her glove and they could still do the tests, but it was too good an issue to pass up.

"No, it wasn't necessary."

"And the theory is that I dropped the glove at the crime scene when I went there and killed Nadia."

"Yes."

"Please take a look at the police report and tell me how many gloves were taken from my person at the scene."

He shuffled through papers and looked up, glaring at her.

"Two."

"Let's see, that's two found on me and one found on the floor. Chief Inspector, use those good eyes of yours and tell me how many hands I have to put gloves on." She held up her two hands.

"I don't know how that glove got there," he snapped.

"Exactly. *Neither of us do!* Now, Chief Investigator, if someone had handled the gun before I did, I would not have necessarily smeared all their prints, would I?"

"I can't say—"

"Isn't it true that you can't say whether someone else handled the gun before me, someone who might have shot and killed Nadia Kolchak and dropped the gun on the floor? And isn't it true that person would now be on trial instead of me if the police criminalist had simply done a fingerprint test of the murder weapon?"

"Objection," Svetlana shouted. "She is asking multiple questions and not giving the witness a chance to answer."

"She has made her point," the judge told Svetlana.

"It is also true, is it not, that no paraffin test was conducted to see if I had fired a weapon?"

Vulko thought about the question, his jaws noticeably tighter, his eyes narrower, than when he strutted up to the witness stand. *You're not getting the respect you get from Russian lawyers, are you, you chrome-headed bastard.* She knew she had created another dilemma for him. A paraffin test, applying wax to a suspect's gun hand and testing the wax for gunpowder residue, sometimes established that the suspect had fired a gun. The tests were not completely accurate but police agencies all over the world still used them.

Vulko's dilemma was that if he damned paraffin tests as being inaccurate or unnecessary, the testimony would be repeated in the news media and would come back to haunt him in cases in which the police relied on the tests.

"A paraffin test was unnecessary because you had the murder weapon in your hand when you were captured."

Relief flowed through her. He thought he had avoided the trap but that was the answer she wanted. "No paraffin test was done to see if I fired a weapon because I was seen with the weapon in hand. No fingerprint test was done because I was seen with the murder weapon. Is that your testimony?"

"Yes," he said stubbornly.

"No one saw me pick up the gun, did they? It's my word alone that I found it on the floor, isn't it?"

"Your word alone."

"And no one saw me shoot Nadia Kolchak, did they? It's my word alone that I did not shoot her, isn't it?"

"It's your word alone."

"It's my word alone," her voice rose, "because the police failed to conduct tests that would have cleared me, isn't that true?"

"Objection! Objection!"

Lara sat down while Svetlana voiced her objections. She had finally managed to wake up the two assessors. She glanced behind her to the audience and noted that the news media people were writing frantically. Her eyes swept Yuri's and Alexei's faces. Both men gave her a smile of encouragement, but there was something in the expression of each of them that disturbed her. It was as if they knew something that she didn't know. Their looks made her uneasy and she wondered if she had forgotten some critical issue.

The judge ruled in Svetlana's favor and threw out the

question, but as he had noted previously, Lara had made her point.

''Ask your next question,'' he told Lara.

Trials combined the subtlety of chess moves with guerrilla war tactics and it was time for her next move. She could keep on tearing apart the police investigation—the officers had not even bothered to question potential witnesses at business establishments near the back entrance to the penthouse—but she decided that this was a good time to leave Vulko alone. She had made several major points and didn't want to obscure them by going on to make smaller points.

''No further questions,'' she said with a sense of dread that she had forgotten some vital fact.

THREE

T he court called a noon recess. Lara sat alone in the holding tank behind the courtroom, unable to eat the sandwich of rancid beef and stale bread provided for prisoners in trial. The feeling she got from the people watching the proceedings bugged her—she didn't understand what they knew that she didn't. Things were pretty bad when the spectators were better informed than the defense attorney.

Returning to the courtroom, she briefly met Svetlana's eye and the woman gave her a small smile.

The bitch is up to something.

Vulko was just the opposite. He gave Lara a look that told her he'd like an opportunity to give her a good old-fashioned police ''attitude adjustment.''

The judge and assessors took the bench and the judge ordered Svetlana to call her next witness. She rose from her seat at the prosecutor's table. "The prosecution calls Dr. Zubov of the Petroff Institute."

The announcement sent a shock through Lara as she turned and watched the distinguished-looking man Svetlana had spoken to earlier rise from his seat in the gallery and proceed into the arena of the courtroom.

The Petroff Institute. In her mind the name was identified with KGB psychiatrists who certified intellectuals and dissenters insane while helping them turn that way with "treatment." To most Russians it was a prestigious name, the most prominent psychiatric organization in the country.

She glanced at Yuri, staked out in his place at the back of the room. His features were solemn. When she glanced over to Svetlana, the woman's usual intense glare had folded into a smirk.

Dr. Zubov took the stand, bowed slightly to the judge and assessors, and adjusted his glasses before he turned to face Svetlana.

"Dr. Zubov, please tell the court your professional background."

Zubov adjusted his glasses again and looked up at the judge and assessors as he spoke. "I am a graduate of Moscow University and have served . . ." He went on to detail forty years in the service of Russian psychiatry, over twenty-five of it at Petroff.

Lara did some quick calculations as he talked. Forty years of service would make him a young psychiatrist back in the fifties, the last days of Stalin and Beria, the rise of Khrushchev.

Zubov, she decided, would have been about thirty-five or forty during the trials of the intellectuals in the late sixties. Just about the right age in his profession to have been a major player in the institute's destruction of some of the finest minds in the country.

"Dr. Zubov," Svetlana said, "are you familiar with the psychiatric case of a woman named Angela Patrick?"

Lara gave an involuntary start at the mention of her mother's name.

"Very much so," the psychiatrist said, "although I was not directly involved in the patient's treatment. I practiced at the Petroff Institute at the time and the woman was a patient at the Charsky Institute. However, it was my responsibility to review certain patients at other institutions. One of those was Angela Patrick. Dr. Komoson, my colleague at the Charsky, was the principal doctor assigned to the case and we had discussions concerning Angela Patrick's condition. As you may recall, this was over twenty years ago. Dr. Komoson passed away ten years ago."

"Doctor, have you also recently had the opportunity to review the psychiatric file of Angela Patrick that is maintained by the Charsky Institute?"

"Yes. As recently as yesterday."

"What was the course of treatment for Angela Patrick at the institute during the period she was treated there?"

"I should mention that Miss Patrick was only briefly treated at the institute. Sadly, she was in a very advanced state of mental deterioration at the time of admission."

"Could you define what you mean by an advanced state of mental deterioration?"

"The woman was suffering from severe paranoia, untreated paranoia. Her mental condition had degenerated to the point where she was having delusions and was suicidal. Unfortunately, because she had not been treated at the institute before her admission, though the paranoia was easy to diagnose, her suicidal tendencies were not immediately recognized. As a result, no suicide watch was placed upon her. In retrospect, this was an error because she took her own life shortly after admission."

"Doctor, what exactly is paranoia?"

"Paranoia is a psychotic disorder characterized by delusions of persecution or grandeur. In general, it involves an extreme distrust or fear of others."

"Is paranoia a hereditary condition?"

A shock wave went through Lara.

Svetlana slowly turned toward her and stared at her, thus focusing the attention of everyone in the courtroom on Lara. The good doctor peered at Lara over his glasses, the judge and assessors stared down from their lofty thrones, every head in the audience turned toward her.

Lara started to rise to object to the question but sat back down. It was a setup and she couldn't win with an objection.

"There is certainly some evidence that paranoia, like other mental conditions, has a hereditary factor, but even more important than that is conditioning or what you might call the behavioral factor. Children, for example, commonly adopt the behavior pattern of the parent or parents that raise them. The child's attitude toward other people, work ethic, even politics and the family dog, is very much molded by the behavior patterns consciously and subconsciously taught to them by their parents. A person raised by a parent suffering from psychotic paranoia tends to have paranoid characteristics to one extent or another. Sadly, some succumb completely to the disease."

Svetlana turned and gave Lara another long look.

Her face red, Lara struggled to maintain her composure, to keep anger and fear under control, forcing herself to take careful notes of what the man said when she really wanted to leap to her feet and call him a quack.

"Doctor, have you had the opportunity to examine the defendant in this case, Lara Patrick?"

"Yes, I have."

"That's a lie!" Lara leaped to her feet. "I've never seen this man before he appeared in court today."

Svetlana smiled tolerantly. "If Miss Patrick could be persuaded to take her seat, we will explain."

Lara sat down. The woman had tricked her into jumping on command and making herself look foolish.

"Please explain, Doctor, about the examination."

"I did not examine her in my office. Such examinations

are of little clinical value. The most valuable are those in which the patient is examined without knowing she or he is being watched. Those are the type of observations I conducted in this case."

"Go on, tell us about the examinations."

"Miss Patrick was observed while she was in jail—in her cell, in the corridors, and in the interview room. There were several hours of observations."

"What did you conclude from these observations?"

"Objection, Your Honor," Lara told the judge. "There is no foundation for any of this testimony. We haven't been told who made the observations, when they were made, what was observed—"

"Miss Patrick is correct," Svetlana interjected. "Doctor, please tell us how these observations were made."

She had stepped into it again.

"I can show you," the psychiatrist said. He reached into his briefcase and took out a videotape. "Miss Patrick was videotaped on a number of occasions. I have selected portions that illustrate the reasons for my conclusions."

On cue, the door to the rear of the courtroom opened and a guard came in pushing a television-VCR combination unit. As the guard was plugging in the set, Svetlana asked, "In regard to your opinion concerning Miss Patrick's psychiatric state, perhaps you can give us that opinion before we see the tape. That way, we might better understand why you arrived at your conclusions."

Dr. Zubov adjusted his glasses and cleared his throat. "It is my opinion that Miss Patrick suffers from the same sort of psychotic paranoia that her mother suffered from."

"Are you saying that Miss Patrick is insane, Doctor?"

"The word 'insane' has a psychiatric and a legal definition. From a psychiatric point of view, my opinion is that Lara Patrick's mental state caused her to falsely interpret the acts of those around her, to imagine conspiracies, to interpret innocent behavior as threatening behavior. For example, the matter in which she reacted to what she believed was the Guk woman's intention to harm her. That imagined threat generated fear within her and she struck out, nearly killing the woman.

"Thus, I find Lara Patrick, from a clinical point of view, to be a very dangerous woman due to mental disturbance. However, in a legal sense, no disorders of the nervous system appear present. She appears to be neurologically intact. I have no doubt that the killing of Nadia Kolchak was in some ways triggered by the defendant's paranoia, but the killing was motivated by profit, not from a mental defect in the defendant."

"What you are telling us, Doctor, is that the defendant is a disturbed and dangerous woman who could kill out of imagined fears, but in the case of Nadia Kolchak, the defendant killed out of a sense of greed."

"Yes—"

"This isn't psychiatry!" Lara yelled. "It's witchcraft!"

"Silence!" the judge snapped. "If you disturb the proceedings I'll have you gagged."

"Doctor, shall we show the tape."

Svetlana used a remote control to start the VCR playing.

A burst of static was followed by a scene of a jail matron backing away from Lara in a cell. Lara's hair was wild, her face was twisted with rage. "You've been spying on me! How many people are paying you to watch me?"

The next scene was of her in the interview room, screaming at Yuri, attacking him with her fists as she accused him of plotting against her.

Lara shrank down in her chair at the counsel table.

In the video she looked crazy. And dangerous.

FOUR

Her turn to question the psychiatrist came and she approached the task with dread. She wanted to rip the bastard's lying tongue out but she had to keep cool and professional, do and say nothing that would support his allegation that she was paranoid.

She slowly stood up at the counsel table, pushing her chair back to get a little room to be nervous in. She sensed the guards closing in on her from the rear and the judge shook his head, indicating that she could have the freedom to move a little when she asked questions. An encouraging sign from the judge after a psychiatrist had just labeled her a dangerous nut.

"Dr. Zubov, you mentioned mental conditions. Isn't it true that a physical condition can also affect a person's mental state?"

He thought about the question for a moment. He had been in the courtroom when Vulko testified and he was wary of traps. "Yes, certainly, being physically ill with a disease, for example, might bring about depression."

"Did my mother's limp in any way affect her mental condition?"

"Her limp? Well, a limp . . . a limp does not cause paranoia—"

"But isn't it true that her limp . . ." she paused. "You did say you actually saw my mother in person, didn't you?"

"Yes, many years ago, of course."

Lying bastard. "And you recall the limp?"

Hesitation. "Yes."

"Which leg was lame, Doctor?"

"Which leg?" He smiled and shook his head, a schoolteacher gently scolding a naughty child. "It's so long ago, I don't remember which leg."

"That's good, Doctor. In fact, that's about the only truthful statement you've made in this court, isn't it?"

"I object—" Svetlana started.

"There was no limp, Your Honor, I made that up. I just wanted to see how far he would go to lie for the prosecution."

A stir went through the audience. The judge started to say something and then withdrew.

"I should tell the court—" Zubov began.

"Excuse me, Doctor, but there is no question before you. Now, tell me—"

"Madam," the judge said sternly, "if a witness wishes to explain an answer, he has the right to do so and you have no right to restrict that answer. Dr. Zubov, what were you about to say?"

"The defendant is correct, I do not recall a limp. However, the reason was not that I was lying, but that it was so many years ago. I simply accepted that the suggestion made by the defendant about her own mother was correct."

"Thank you, Doctor. The court is well aware of your high qualifications and, certainly, it was a long time ago. You may proceed, Miss Patrick."

She shifted gears, knowing that to continue to impeach him about what he didn't remember was not going to work.

"Have you ever been falsely accused of murder?" she asked Zubov.

"Accused of murder? Of course not."

"Ever been held prisoner in the Moscow jail?"

"No, of course not."

"Would being falsely accused of murder, stripped naked, enduring an intimate body search, and being held prisoner in a cold, brutal jail tend to affect one's mental state, Doctor?"

"Yes, certainly. And if one were suffering from a mental disease such as paranoia, such deprivations would aggravate the condition."

"Your opinion is based upon my actions in the video, is that correct?"

"You say video as if it were a movie. My opinion is based upon your actions recorded on videotape."

"Thank you, Doctor. You were not present, you did not witness the events, did you?"

"No, of course not."

"And you personally do not know whether this jail matron had been paid by someone to spy on me in jail, do you?"

He floundered for a moment, trying to avoid the obvious. "Miss Patrick, my opinion—"

"Dr. Zubov, I asked a simple question. You do not know from your own knowledge whether this woman was being paid to spy on me. Isn't that true?"

He smiled. "Of course she's being paid to spy on you. She's a jail matron. That's her job."

A ripple of laughter went through the audience.

"Exactly. She's paid by the government to spy on prisoners, true?"

"I would imagine that is one of her functions although I don't claim to be an expert on jail procedures."

"But you know enough about jail procedures to know it would be a crime for a jail matron to take money from a private party to spy on an inmate. Isn't that correct?"

He hesitated, trying to step around the trap.

"I'll take your silence as an affirmative response, Doctor. And since you have no knowledge as to whether this woman was corrupt and had violated her sworn oath of office, you don't know whether my accusations against her were paranoid delusions—or frustration at having been mistreated, do you?"

"I have heard no evidence that she was a paid spy, but

I have witnessed your behavior and that convinces me that your reaction to her was one of paranoia.''

''Tell me, was the disappearance and probable murder of my attorney also a product of paranoid delusions on my part? Did I imagine her death, did I imagine she had been murdered?''

''From what I understand you have not imagined her disappearance. Whether it was at the hands of another or for other reasons has not been determined. But it is not the situation that is created by paranoia, it is the interpretation of the situation. Men and women are being murdered with increasing frequency here in Moscow, crimes that were unheard of in the past. Your interpretation is that your lawyer was murdered as part of a grand conspiracy against you. My interpretation is the one accepted by police—that she was the victim of a random act of violence.''

''Was the death of our next-door neighbor when I was a child also imagined?''

He shrugged. ''People die all the time. Every day, in every part of the world. Some violently.''

''And some murdered,'' she said.

''And some only murdered in one's imagination.''

More chuckles came from the audience behind her.

''Tell me, Doctor, when you 'examined' my mother, were you wearing your KGB uniform?''

''Objection!'' Svetlana snapped. ''KGB affairs are a matter of State secrecy. There is no KGB issue in this matter.''

''The question is stricken,'' the judge said. ''Ask your next question.''

''My next questions concern the KGB and this doctor's involvement. Is the court telling me that I cannot ask these questions?''

''You heard my ruling.''

''Then I have no more questions.''

She sat down, satisfied with the ruling. There was probably nothing to be gained with a KGB line of questioning, so being foreclosed from asking was better than falling on her face. At the end of the trial, when the witness was gone from the courtroom, she'd accuse the witness and the prosecution of being involved in a KGB cover-up.

As Svetlana started to ask a question, Lara stood up again. It occurred to her that if the judge wasn't going to let the doctor answer any questions about the KGB, she might do more damage without shooting herself in the foot.

"Just one last question, Doctor. As I recall, you mentioned you have been with the Petroff Institute for nearly three decades. How many of Russia's bright minds, how many intellectuals—"

"Objection!"

"Were destroyed by your diagnosis of mental illness to keep them from telling the world the truth?"

"That question is stricken!" the judge shouted. "Miss Patrick, you are out of order. You are attempting to create a political cause out of a simple murder trial. I will not permit it."

"It goes toward impeachment, Your Honor," she snapped back. "If this man has used his medical degree as a tool to suppress dissent in the past, I should be allowed to inquire whether he is doing it again."

"You have heard my ruling. And stop addressing me as 'Your Honor.' That is a form of addressing used in a society where the classes are divided. In Soviet . . . uh, Russian courts, all are equal." He nodded to Svetlana. "Does Madam Prosecutor have any more questions?"

Svetlana glared at Lara. It was obvious she didn't enjoy having to resort to the judge to keep Lara from damaging her witness.

"Yes, just one. Doctor, you have now had a face-to-face exchange with Miss Patrick. Has that in any way affected your opinion of her mental state?"

"Yes." He stared directly at Lara. "The defendant's line of questioning leads me to conclude that the mental disease she is suffering from has deteriorated. The conspiracies she imagines now include not just those in direct contact with her, such as the victim, Nadia Kolchak, and the jail matron, but persons such as myself and members of the court.''

Lara looked away and said nothing. She had made points, but an accusation of being crazy was like one of child molesting—the accusation didn't have to be proven, it was enough that the charge had been made.

Svetlana had beaten her. She had turned down an offer to spend one year in prison and now she was facing the death penalty, or at the very least the rest of her life in a Russian prison. Deep in a haze of frightening thoughts, she heard the judge ask if Svetlana had any more witnesses and the prosecutor replied that she would call the pathologist to the stand briefly to elaborate upon the cause of death.

"But I will have to call her later because she is not available at present," Svetlana said. She looked to Lara.

"This would be the time for the defendant to put forward a defense. If she has one."

Lara struggled to her feet. "I call . . ." She paused and looked to the rear where Vlad was pushing the double doors into the courtroom open with his back.

Yuri was standing nearby and he grabbed one door and held it as Vlad backed in, pulling a hand truck loaded with cartons.

"I call Vladimir Andreevich Dzhunkovsky."

Judge Rurik frowned. "What is the purpose of this testimony?"

"Mr. Dzhunkovsky is an army ballistics expert. He will be testifying regarding ballistics."

"We already had Chief Investigator Vulko testify as to the ballistics expert's findings," the judge said.

"That was the prosecution's evidence. I am presenting evidence as to the defense ballistics findings."

"The prosecution has no objection to this testimony," Svetlana said.

The hair on the back of Lara's neck rose. It was something in Svetlana's voice. Why would the woman not object when it was obvious that the judge was willing to bar the testimony as redundant?

XXVI

What people usually ask for
when they pray to God is
that two and two may not make four.

—Russian proverb

ONE

===

Lara held the gate to the arena area of the courtroom open for Vlad to back through. He was grinning—and very nervous with beads of sweat running down the sides of his face and neck. First time in court and the whole world was watching.

As she watched Vlad set up, she snuck a glance at Svetlana. There was no emotion displayed on the prosecutor's face. If anything, her features were placid and neutral. Vulko was casually leafing through a report, not paying any attention to Vlad setting up his equipment.

Fear fanned the hairs on the back of Lara's neck again. Something was wrong. She looked back to the audience and met Yuri's eye. He looked worried.

She focused back on Vlad and on the equipment he was arranging. He had set up his laser device in the open area of the courtroom, between the elevated position of the judge and assessors and the counsel table, the ''well'' in American courtrooms. The laser had a base of about a foot square that appeared to be heavy. Lara assumed it was the source of the beam. A framework of metal tubing came vertically out of the base and extended up four or five feet. At the top of the tubing a pipe extended out horizontally.

At the end of the horizontal pipe a real pistol had been attached. The gun had been modified so that the laser pipe became part of the gun barrel.

Clever, she thought. The beam will go through the pistol. Vlad had showmanship in him.

The rest of the display appeared to be a cardboard "mock-up" of a section of the spa. To her surprise, he unfolded the upper half of a cardboard "woman" and set it on the spa display. The cardboard torso had a bullet wound in the chest.

After Vlad finished setting up the display, the judge looked at it as if he were a theatre owner and the equipment were the props to a play that couldn't pay the rent.

Lara began her questioning of Vlad by laying a foundation for his expertise, his training, education, and experience. After getting specifics, she asked him about his laser work. He explained the operation of lasers and how lasers were utilized in his work.

"Projectiles fired from weapons, whether we're talking about small arms such as handguns and rifles, or artillery pieces, will soon divert from a straight line after they leave the barrel. The lasers we use for the distances involved are able to maintain a steady line. By comparing laser paths with the paths of projectiles, we are able to determine the best way to make bullets and artillery projectiles more accurate. That involves adjustments and experimentation with the chemical composition of the charge, the size, shape, and weight of the actual projectile, barrel length, and many other factors."

"Thank you. Now, please explain to the court the purpose for the equipment you have set up."

"This is a laser device that emits a beam. I have modified a pistol so the beam passes through the pistol's barrel. For purposes of this demonstration, you can think of the modified pistol as the murder weapon."

He pointed at the cardboard contraption at the other side of the room. "That assembly is the exact size, shape, and height of the spa. The mock-up of a woman is based upon the size of the victim, Nadia Kolchak. That wound in the chest is exactly where the shot struck the victim.'' He walked over to the display and lifted up the cardboard torso so the rim of the ''spa'' to the rear was visible. ''This hole in the spa rim was made by the bullet after it passed through the victim's chest and exited her back. The criminalist removed the bullet from the hole and stated in his report that he was able to do so without enlarging the original hole. He did that by taking apart the rim rather than digging out the bullet.''

''Have you studied the criminalist's report and the pathology report in this matter?''

''Yes.''

''And did those reports reveal anything else in regard to your study?''

''Two shots struck the victim. The first shot struck her in the chest while she was sitting in the spa facing the door from the interior of the penthouse. The second shot was to the back of the head. The only gunpowder residue was found on the door frame at the entrance to the spa. Because no residue was found farther up the hallway, the criminalist concluded, and I agree, that the shooter fired the first shot standing in the doorway.''

''How would gunpowder residue get on the door frame?''

''When a gun is fired a spray of gunpowder follows the projectile—the slug—out of the chamber. This fast-moving 'dust' can stick to nearby objects. In this case the criminalist conducted tests that showed such residue struck the door frame. From the residue, he concluded and I concur that only one shot was fired from that position.''

''Does the gunpowder residue tell you anything about the shooter?''

''Only within narrow limits. The residue provides a clue as to where the shooter was standing when the trigger was pulled, but it tells me little else other than the shooter was of adult height. Not a child or a dwarf.''

Vulko guffawed. ''Well, that eliminates a few suspects.''

Loud laughter burst from the audience. Lara ignored it and plunged on. ''And you determined which shot was fired first from—?''

''The pathologist report. The pathologist said the first bullet entered the chest. And from the general description of the crime scene found in the criminalist's report, it appears the distance from the shooter to the victim was about twenty feet. The shot struck the victim in the chest, made a clean path through the body—''

''What do you mean by a 'clean path.' ''

''Bullets are often deflected from a straight line by bone or cartilage in the body. This bullet passed entirely through soft tissue and exited, burying itself in the rubber rim of the spa at the victim's back.''

''And what about the second shot?''

''It's hard to tell anything about the second shot because it hit the victim in the back of the skull at one of the thickest points of the skull. The bullet shattered the skull and veered from a straight path. From the other facts, I concluded that the victim's body convulsed in the spa after being hit by the first shot, that the killer approached the spa and, at a point when the body was facedown, shot the victim at close range.''

Lara couldn't help herself—she glanced again at Svetlana, but the prosecutor's face revealed nothing. Its very neutralness sent Lara's paranoia boiling. Svetlana's silence felt like crosshairs of a telescopic lens aimed at the back of her neck.

''Did you conduct any examinations of evidence or perform any tests in this matter?'' Lara asked.

Vlad nodded. ''Yes. I visited the scene of the crime. Mr. Bova was kind enough to allow me in.'' He nodded at Alexei standing near the back of the courtroom. ''And in my laboratory I fired a pistol of the same caliber and type as the murder weapon to determine a number of factors about it, including how far the weapon spread gunpowder residue, what distance the projectile pushed forward in a straight line, and the range of recoil. By recoil I'm referring to the 'kick' of the gun when fired by people with different grip strength.

"I also conducted a number of tests involving shooting stances, specifically in regard to how people of various heights and strengths would hold a weapon when firing at an object of the victim's size at a range of twenty feet."

"From your study of the reports and findings of the police, pathologist, and criminalist, your examination of the murder scene and the tests you conducted, did you arrive at any conclusion about who fired the fatal shot?"

"Well . . . no."

"No?" Lara froze.

The audience, the judge, the assessors, all froze with her. The testimony had been followed closely in the courtroom and everyone seemed caught by surprise.

Vlad cleared his throat nervously. "I don't know who fired the shot. But I know you could not have fired the shot."

A wave of relief washed through her and her knees went weak. "I'm sorry, that's what I meant to ask. Please tell the court how you arrived at the conclusion that I could not have fired the fatal shot."

"May I demonstrate?"

"Yes, go right ahead."

Vlad turned on the laser mechanism. He went to the dummy torso and made adjustments back and forth. When he finished, a laser beam funneled through the pistol barrel struck the chest of the cardboard torso where the "bullet hole" had entered the chest. Standing next to his equipment, he spoke up to the judge and assessors.

"Besides making adjustments for variables such as recoil and shooting stance, I needed two critical pieces of information about the shot. First, I had to know the exact angle that the bullet entered the victim. In this case that angle was possible to determine only from the chest wound. From that angle I drew a straight line back, initially on paper and later with the laser. That line was the path the bullet followed from the gun to the victim.

"The second critical factor was where the shooter was standing. If I didn't have this information I wouldn't know where along the bullet's path to place the gun. Where the gun was placed along the path determined the height the gun was held when it was fired.

"Thus by knowing the path the bullet followed, as determined by the angle of entry and where the shooter stood, and making adjustments for other variables, I was able to reach a conclusion about the height of the shooter."

"And that conclusion?"

"That the gun"—he pointed at the pistol superimposed on the laser—"was held at this height and angle at the time the shot was fired."

"The height and angle that you presently have your demonstrative weapon adjusted to?"

"Yes."

"And how did that tell you that I did not fire the shot?"

"Would you step over here, please."

Lara came to where Vlad was standing by the machine.

"Stand beside the laser equipment . . . that's right, now put your hand in the grip of the pistol."

A murmur swept through the audience and the judge and assessors straightened in their chairs as Lara reached up to grasp the pistol butt. It was obvious that she would have to be much taller in order to hold the pistol in a natural firing position.

The judge's eyes went to Svetlana and the chief investigator at the prosecution's table. Svetlana lifted her eyebrows but revealed no other expression.

"That's all the questions I have," Lara said.

She walked back to the counsel table with wobbly knees.

"No questions from the prosecution," Svetlana said.

Lara bumped into her chair as she swung around to stare at Svetlana. A "no questions" response was impossible. To leave the testimony uncontroverted would result in an acquittal.

"No questions?" the judge asked. "Are you telling me the prosecution has no questions?"

"That's correct," Svetlana said.

The judge looked to Vlad. "You are trained by the army? This demonstration, it is something your commanders would approve of?"

"My commanding officer helped me construct the model," Vlad said.

"And it is your conclusion that Miss Patrick could not have fired the shot to the victim's chest, the first shot, because the angle of the shot demonstrates that it was done by a taller person?"

"Yes."

"Your model shows the exact height of the shooter?"

Vlad hesitated. "Not the exact height but a midrange representing the height within a couple of inches either way. I can't calculate the exact height because of variables such as grip strength and weapon handling experience, but I established a range of height and determined that the shooter was considerably taller than Miss Patrick, at least five or six inches taller."

The judge turned to Svetlana. "You have heard this testimony and you have no questions?"

"No questions," Svetlana said.

Another stir went through the audience. Lara sat rigidly in her chair, ready to break into pieces from the tension. *Something's wrong. I've missed something, I've missed something critical.*

"However," Svetlana said, "as soon as this . . . this person"—she gestured at Vlad—"clears away his toys, we have another witness to call.'' She turned and smiled at Lara.

It was the same smile she had given Lara when she pointed the pistol at her in the judge's chambers.

TWO

The prosecution calls Dr. Uspensky.''

Lara's mind swirled. Another psychiatrist? Were they going to try and prove Vlad was crazy, too?

The name sounded familiar to her but she could not place it.

A mousy little woman, wearing a heavy wool jacket and shirt that looked more' like a military uniform than street clothes, made her way to the witness stand.

The woman could have been thirty or sixty—her ill-fitting clothes and stringy hair looked the latter. With droopy eyes, fat round cheeks, and unhealthy pale skin, she reminded Lara of an albino salamander that hadn't seen the light of day for ages.

Svetlana rose to address the witness. ''Dr. Uspensky, please state your occupation.''

''Pathologist,'' the woman said.

Pathologist? Who the hell is she? She didn't write the pathology report, Lara thought.

''And by whom are you employed?''

''Moscow City Office of Pathology.''

''And did you examine the body of Nadia Kolchak, the victim in this matter?''

''Wait.'' Lara got to her feet. ''I'm being sandbagged,'' she told the judge.

He scowled at her. ''Sandbagged?''

''It's an American legal expression. This witness has been withheld from me and is now being called to give some sort of surprise testimony that wasn't revealed to me in the reports I was given.''

''Has the defendant received any information about this witness?'' the judge asked Svetlana.

''Of course she has. Dr. Uspensky is the pathologist who did the autopsy on the victim. I believe the defendant's confusion is that the chief pathologist signed the reports. However, he did so in his function as Dr. Uspensky's supervisor. The chief pathologist never actually examined the body.''

''But I assumed that the person preparing the report was the person who performed the autopsy.''

The judge's scowl grew. ''It is for that sort of reason you were asked over and over again to take a lawyer who understood Russian procedures. It is common practice for a chief pathologist to sign a report. Who signed the report makes no difference, anyway. This witness did the autopsy, she can testify about it.''

''This is unfair, I should have been told about this witness for my preparation.''

''You don't need to prepare for the truth. The truth is simply there. You keep raising the sort of technical objections that the American justice system is based upon. We are not interested in technicalities, but in the truth.

''If you believe the witness does not speak the truth, you may question her, but this is not a game we are playing where the truth is excluded because no one told you about it. Or because you didn't ask.''

''But I should be able to prepare for the testimony of this witness. I don't know the nature of the testimony that will be offered.''

''Sit down and we shall both find out,'' the judge said.

Lara sat down, anxiety crawling over her like a bad case of hives.

''Dr. Uspensky, you performed the autopsy on the victim, Nadia Kolchak, is that correct?''

''Yes.''

"And what were your findings in regard to the cause of her death?"

"She was shot twice, once in the chest, once in the back of the head."

"From your examination of the deceased, were you able to determine which shot struck her *first*."

"Yes," the pathologist said.

Lara felt the trap opening beneath her feet. They had had her bugged and videotaped. Svetlana knew everything she and Vlad had talked about. They knew exactly what Vlad's theory was, what he was going to testify to, and had been ready for it.

"And which shot struck her first?"

"The shot to the head."

A sense of horror sent goose bumps creeping up the back of Lara's legs and into the small of her back.

"And how do you know the head wound preceded the chest wound?"

"The occipital artery was severed as a result of the head wound, creating hemorrhaging. In order to have hemorrhaging to the extent I observed in the surrounding tissue, the heart must have still been pumping."

"How do you know that the chest wound was not inflicted prior to the head wound?"

"A comparison of the hemorrhaging. There was almost no hemorrhaging in the chest area. That means that the fatal shot, the shot that killed the victim, was the first shot, the shot to the head. The victim didn't die immediately, and was again shot, this time in the chest, perhaps only a few seconds later, but in those seconds the victim died. However, also in those seconds before the heart stopped, it had pumped out enough blood to create hemorrhaging."

"Hemorrhaging in the head wound, the *first* wound," Svetlana emphasized. She shuffled papers in front of her. "I noticed that in the pathology report, the one signed by the chief pathologist, reference is made to, and I quote the report, 'the first gunshot wound, a wound to the chest.'

You are familiar with the passage I am referring to?''

''Yes, but the reference is not to the first shot that struck the victim, but to the first gunshot wound that I examined. I started by examining the chest wound and then turned the body over and examined the head wound.''

She paused and glared at Lara. ''No one asked me which shot I thought struck the body first,'' she said defensively. ''What did it matter anyway? Either shot was fatal. The victim was shot in the back of the head from the doorway. The impact of the bullet would have pushed the body forward, across the spa, even causing it to turn over and convulse violently from death throes. The killer moved in closer and fired the shot that struck the victim's chest, probably to insure the victim was dead.''

Hell boiled at Lara's feet.

Vlad's reconstruction of the killing was based upon the premise that the first shot was fired from the doorway and created the chest wound.

He couldn't reconstruct the flight of the bullet that had created the head wound because that wound did not have a clean entry and exit.

Vlad's entire laser demonstration was meaningless.

XXVII

Even a pig does not shit where it eats.

—Denunication by KGB head
of Boris Pasternak for
writing *Doctor Zhivago*, as quoted in
Andrew and Gordievsky,
KGB: The Inside Story

ONE

===

A reception committee was waiting for Yuri as he came down the broad stairway in front of the courthouse— two of his friends from the sewer. One of them, the gun-toter who liked to hit people, nodded at a black Mercedes limo waiting at the curb.

Keeping his face expressionless and his right hand in his overcoat pocket he veered for the limo, hoping that the two thugs who fell in beside him would wonder if he had his finger on a trigger. He kept his eye on the limo, not looking over at a very big man climbing out of a small militia car parked several car lengths behind the limo.

A dozen feet from the Mercedes Yuri paused and using his left hand only shook out a cigarette and lit it. The pause allowed the big man time to reach the limo.

The two goons escorting Yuri suddenly woke up to the fact that something not in their plan was coming down.

Yuri could barely keep a grin from breaking out as he approached the limo.

Stenka was carrying his overcoat in his hands and the coat had a suspicious bulge. As Stenka stopped by the car's rear window and pointed one end of the overcoat at the window, Alexei Bova found himself staring at the lethal end of a sawed-off riot gun, the kind issued to police in a society where rioters were expected to be shoveled into meat wagons after they had their say.

Yuri knew that Stenka's finger would be on the trigger and Bova had to realize he was a fraction of an inch from having the window blown away, along with the upper half of his own body.

As Yuri stepped up to the window, the two goons stood around awkwardly, shifting on their feet, not knowing what to do. Stenka was big enough to rip their heads off even without the riot gun.

The back window came down and Bova made eye contact with Yuri. Seeing Bova in a sable-lined overcoat and hand-woven cashmere scarf instantly made Yuri feel like a sow's ear in his cheap overcoat.

"You constantly surprise me, Detective Kirov."

"Sometimes I surprise myself."

"I should have—but never mind, I ignored all the fine training the KGB provided. I've been civilized by all this democracy erupting around me. In the old days I would have put a bullet in your head and cut the chain."

"You don't look like you've left the old days behind. You're still surrounded by sable and thugs. The only difference now is that you ride around in a foreign import."

"You're right, Detective, you're smart enough to realize that the old days are still with us. I'm going to give you some advice that a smart man would take—get out of Moscow. There are opportunities in the Urals for smart men. Perhaps I'll even give you one of the iron mines I've come into possession of there. You can be a rich, smart man in the Urals . . . instead of a dead one in Moscow."

Yuri shook his head. "I'm not as smart as you give me credit for. I'm so un-smart that I think I'm going to put a bullet in your head before you put one in mine."

"This isn't about a personal vendetta, Detective. If it was you'd be dead already. I let you have some rein because I thought you might be able to help Lara after she was arrested. I was wrong, you've done nothing but raise her paranoia to where she trusts no one, not even me. You try to help, but you think small like most Russians raised under communism. I can buy Lara all the law she needs. If it wasn't for all of the publicity, she'd already be out of jail.

"But there have been arrangements. She'll be found guilty to satisfy the public. In a year when interest in the case is gone, the appeals court will reduce her sentence and I'll have her on a plane the next day. I need you to stay out of it, to stop blundering around with your detective's badge and your small plans."

Yuri took a drag on his cigarette and blew the smoke above the car. "Where does justice fall into your plan?"

Alexei stared at him, his jaw dropping. He laughed hysterically as the electric window went up.

The two goons got in the limo as Yuri and Stenka walked to the militia car.

Yuri, red-faced, told Stenka, "He's right, I am dumb."

XXVIII

───────

I shall laugh my bitter laugh.

—Epitaph on
Nikolai Gogol's tombstone

ONE

Lara walked beside the matron in a weary, unsteady daze.

News of the court proceedings had spread through the cell block. The women behind the bars, whores and thieves who had stabbed their husbands and lovers, stood in their cells and jeered at the fallen prima donna as she walked by, the foreign celebrity prisoner who starred on the nightly news.

"Got your ass kicked in court today, bitch."

"Stalin's Breath is coming for you."

"Hey, give the executioner a blow job and he'll grease the bullet for you."

The jeers and taunts didn't affect her. She was cold and dead inside.

Locked in her cell, she curled up in a corner with the dirty blanket wrapped around her, hoping it would help the trembling fear she had because she didn't have the strength to fight it.

Svetlana had ripped open her chest and tore her heart out.

Fatal error. I committed a fatal error. I thought and acted like an American attorney.

Nina had warned her, told her the prosecution would eavesdrop on conversations in the visitors' room. The warning hadn't penetrated because spying on a defendant's trial preparations was too outrageous.

A Russian attorney, *any* Russian attorney, would have heeded the warning, never would have made such an amateurish mistake. She and Vlad had openly planned her "surprise" defense while Svetlana and Vulko listened at the keyhole and laughed.

Dumb American mentality, raised on a diet of truth, justice, and the American way, she had been clobbered in a courtroom by people who had survived by manipulation and deceit. Even Rykoff, shit that he is, would not have fallen into the trap.

Svetlana had led her around by the nose and she should have seen it coming. The tip-off had been when Svetlana had not called the pathologist in logical trial order—I should have seen the curve ball coming, she thought. Svetlana ran a trial like a general doing battle—she would never have permitted a key witness to testify out of order.

The last word.

That's what it had come down to.

She barely heard anything Svetlana had said in her closing statement as the prosecutor demanded the death penalty and had turned herself off completely while Rykoff went on and on about the flower lost to Russia while Nadia's sister cried and screamed out "a life for a life."

When it was Lara's time to speak, the judge had looked down on her, a little pity showing in his distinguished features. "You have the right to the last word" the judge told her. Then he mercifully adjourned the trial until the next morning.

She had thought of the "last word" as being analogous to the closing argument by a defense attorney. But that was thinking as an American again. This was Russia—brutal, harsh, cold, tough, lean, and mean.

The last word was a plea for mercy, a plea for one's

life, to an omnipotent system that was accustomed to going to the extreme.

There was nothing to argue in her last word anyway. She hadn't presented an iota of evidence that had any credibility. No clever phrases, no winning legal strategies came to mind.

She was expected to go before the court on bended knee and beg for mercy. At the moment she was so tired and beaten she didn't have the energy to do anything but crawl up to the judge's bench and cry.

"Lara."

He was at the door to her cell. She recognized the voice and the figure.

"Hurry," Yuri whispered, "I don't have much time."

She got up and went to the cell door, taking the blanket with her.

"What do—"

"Shhh. We have to talk quickly. I had to bribe my way in. The guards have orders from Vulko not to admit anyone."

"What is this? Another trick? Haven't you done enough already?"

"Listen to me, the trial has gone badly."

She started to laugh but her jaws were too tight and it came out as a choke.

"You have to turn things around tomorrow. It's your only chance."

"Do you think I haven't thought of that? I have no chance. It's finished."

"You focused on the wrong thing during the trial. You tried to prove your innocence, that you didn't do it."

"What was I supposed to do? Provide old-fashioned Russian confession?"

"There's a critical piece missing. Who did it?"

Her mind wasn't working on all fours and she stared at him a little stupidly. "Who did what?"

"Who killed Nadia? Why was she killed? You tried to

prove your innocence. It's easy to prove guilt with circumstantial evidence. Your only hope is to prove someone else did it.''

"I have no proof someone else did it. But I've got plenty of candidates.''

"You have to think it out.''

"Are you crazy? The trial's over, I'm finished.''

"Think it out. It's your only chance. There's a chain. It started with your mother and Vera Swen and ended with Nadia.''

"Nadia was trying to blackmail Alexei.''

"And being blackmailed herself. You have to put together the chain of evidence. You have all the pieces, you just don't have them in the right order.''

The door to the cell block clanged open.

"I've got to go,'' Yuri whispered. He reached through the bars and squeezed her arm. "Good luck, Kosca.''

Yuri disappeared down the dark hallway and Lara faded back into her cell, back to her corner.

She tried to make sense out of what Yuri had said, but her mind was too fatigued, too numb to kick into gear. Something gnawed at her, something Yuri had said, and she fell into a troubled sleep with that thought hanging over her.

She awoke with a start in the middle of the night, all of the pieces of the puzzle in place.

She realized who had killed Nadia.

And how it was linked to the death of her mother's neighbor.

TWO

What is your final word?''

Lara rose and looked to the rear of the courtroom before turning to face the judge.

As usual, the courtroom was packed, every seat filled, with people standing at the rear near the double doors leading to the outer corridor. Today the audience had a mean look. They had come for a lynching, not a hand slap.

Alexei stood to the left of the doors, smiling with false hope. Felix, stoic, was beside him. Both men were holding raincoats. The courtroom again smelled of wet wool.

Yuri was to the right of the doors, wearing the cheap raincoat he had had on the night he spied on her from behind Gypsy tents. The shoulders of the raincoat were wet and he held a long black umbrella, tapping it in the palm of his hand as if it were a club he was getting ready to use.

Her eyes held Yuri's for a moment. His face was impassive. No messages were passed in the look they exchanged, but her heart pounded and her throat tightened—with fear, with crushed passion.

She turned to the judge and assessors.

''There is an American expression that an attorney who represents herself has a fool for a client. I am one of those fools. And because I am a fool, I lost this trial. The prosecutor beat me—not because I am guilty, but because she played the game better than I did.''

The judge shot a glance at Svetlana.

Lara continued. ''In America we have adopted the British system of jurisprudence, the advocacy system in which attorneys are gladiators who battle in the pit of the courtroom. The message that has been hammered at me by this court is that the advocacy system is a bad system because so much depends upon the skill of the attorney and trial tactics.

"After the experience I have had in this courtroom, I reject the argument because we have one thing that is fundamental to the American system and which I have seen no sign of in the Russian system: fair play."

Svetlana started out of her chair but the judge waved her back down. "This is the defendant's last word. Let her speak her mind."

"Thank you," Lara said. "I am not going into great detail about all the deviations from fair play and reasonable trial procedures. Put simply, I was set up.

"The prosecutor spied on my strategy meeting, withheld evidence and a witness, all to lead me into providing a defense she could sweep away with one grand gesture. In other words, the prosecutor played the role of Western advocate and the role of Soviet prosecutor who could break all the rules of fair play because the rules only applied to those who believe in them.

"You said that the truth never hurts," she said, locking eyes with the judge. "The truth hurts when it's been withheld from you, when it's used against you as a weapon of surprise.

"I thought I was the best lawyer for the job because in my country I am a good lawyer. But that doesn't count in a system where the rules can be broken by the state. I was an easy mark for the prosecutor's list of dirty tricks.

"I'm not asking for the court's sympathy or even its mercy. Just its understanding. I did nothing for which I should be on my knees. I did not kill Nadia Kolchak. More significantly, it was never proven in this courtroom that I killed Nadia.

"What was proven was that the woman died, violently, at the hand of another, and sometime after her death, police officers observed me in a panic holding the murder weapon. That scenario, coupled with an alleged blackmail scheme, led to my arrest.

"The evidence was circumstantial because no one saw the crime. The evidence was damning because I was at the murder scene with the murder weapon in hand. The court did not permit me to rebut the evidence by going into the past and showing that Nadia's death was just one death in a chain of violence that began when I was a child. While the court was limiting me on what I could present, the prosecutor and her cohorts were spying on me and withholding crucial evidence."

She left her position behind the counsel table and moved in front of it, the judge and assessors before her, the rest of the courtroom to the rear. She was in the well, the area lawyers and defendants in American courtrooms are forbidden to enter during trial because it brought them too close to the throat of the judge.

"I am accused of trying to blackmail Alexei Bova, one of the richest men in Russia. I, too, thought there was a blackmail motive, not on my part, but an attempt by Nadia to blackmail Alexei. But Nadia was not trying to blackmail Alexei—Nadia herself was being manipulated by a blackmailer."

She stopped and poured a glass of water from the pitcher on the counsel table. Her hand shook and she spilled some on the table. The courtroom was filled with an aching silence, as if it was preparing for a cry of outrage or triumph at any moment.

"In order to understand what brought me to stand over Nadia with the murder weapon in my hand, we have to go back, back before I returned to Moscow a few months ago, back to when I lived here as a child."

"Miss Patrick—" the judge started.

"You said this court is interested in the truth, so I want to bring it all out. The first truth is that a woman, a woman who lived next door to my mother and me, died over twenty years ago. Her name was Vera Swen and she was probably Scandinavian, at least that's what a man named Belkin told me. She died violently and was mutilated. That is a fact, not the delusion of a paranoid mind.''

Her voice quivered and she took a deep breath to still her nerves.

''The second truth is that my mother believed the woman had been murdered and that there had been a cover-up. That is a fact.''

She held up her hand as the judge started to interrupt her. ''Oh, yes, I was in the courtroom when a psychiatrist was paraded in to tell the world that my mother and I were both paranoid nutcases. A psychiatrist who never examined either of us and who made his name during a shameful era of Russian quack psychiatry. Anybody in this courtroom who believed that man needs their common sense overhauled. Leaving aside questions of his credibility, we still have something very significant that we haven't dealt with: a trail of bodies going back over twenty years.

''My mother and Vera Swen both died violently. All the psychiatric mumbo jumbo in the world isn't going to change that. I spoke to Nikolai Belkin. Belkin ended up dead within hours. I spoke to my old schoolteacher. She died. I arranged to speak to Nadia Kolchak and she was murdered. My own attorney was murdered while I was being held in a jail cell.''

The judge shifted uneasily in his chair. ''Miss Patrick, I have tried to give you great latitude because of the seriousness of the charges and the ultimate punishment you are facing, but you have done nothing but relate events. You have not managed in any way, other than your own relationship with people who died, to link those people in the past to the deaths in the present.

''Tell me,'' he said, ''tell the assessors, tell all of us how the death of Nadia Kolchak is in any manner connected to the past or to any of the other deaths you mentioned.''

"First," Lara said, "we have to deal with one more fact. Belkin was selling me access to KGB files, but he hated doing it and wasn't interested in the money I offered him. Why? Because he was being forced to do it. Belkin was being blackmailed, too.

"I've since discovered"—she turned and found Yuri's eyes at the back of the courtroom—"that Belkin had a police record for being a pervert. I don't know why Nadia was being blackmailed, perhaps it was linked to her past before her success, perhaps even to Belkin's criminal activity—"

"Lies! Lies! The bitch defames the dead!"

The outcry came from Nadia's sister.

"Give her the bullet!" someone shouted and a grumbling of approval swept through the gallery.

Rykoff patted Nadia's sister on the shoulder and told her in a stage whisper loud enough to be heard all over the courtroom, "Let her speak. By showing no remorse she's pointing the executioner's pistol at her head."

Lara took another sip of water. Silence returned to the courtroom, but she could see from the sullen faces in the audience that they had already passed judgment upon her and that their verdict was guilty.

"Who was blackmailing Nadia and Belkin? And why? The person blackmailing them had a link to the past because I was sent a picture of a mutilated woman from a two-decades-old police file. That picture lured me to Moscow to reexamine the facts surrounding my mother's death. The idea was to get me to Moscow and force Belkin and Nadia to lead me to where the blackmailer wanted me.

"The blackmailer had access to old police files, access to more recent information on Belkin and Nadia, and had probably even checked me out and discovered that I was a prosecuting attorney in America."

Lara looked back to Yuri again. He stood stiffly next to the door, his face still expressionless.

"A Moscow police lieutenant has access to the type of

information that I've mentioned. Someone like Detective Yuri Kirov.''

Heads in the audience turned from her to Yuri like spectators at a tennis match.

''Detective Kirov was present, hiding in the background, that night I first met Belkin. He knew Belkin was a sex offender. Rather conveniently, he was the investigating officer when Belkin died. Every step I took, every time I turned around, he was there, telling me to leave Moscow, telling me I was imagining things.''

Lara kept her eyes on Yuri as she slowly walked toward the railing separating the gallery from the arena. Tension was building up in the audience.

''Detective Kirov, always there. He was even with the police officers who charged into Alexei's penthouse and saw me with the gun. But isn't it strange that the police report says he met the other officers in the lobby.''

''Miss Patrick,'' the judge said, ''you will not find favor with this court making a groundless accusation against a Moscow police officer. We have only heard words. No evidence has been put before us.''

''You want a connection to the past killings and the present ones? The link is a teenage boy who was convicted of the murder of Vera Swen. His name was Alexander Zurin. He was our neighbor when I went to school here in Moscow.

''Detective Kirov's military record indicates that he was on duty in Afghanistan in 1984 when Alexander Zurin escaped from a work crew there. Another coincidence?'' she asked the judge.

''That is speculation, not evidence,'' the judge said, but his voice carried a note of uncertainty in it that she had not heard during the entire trial.

She swung around and glared at Yuri, tears blurring her eyes.

''If you want evidence, get a fingerprint expert into this room and take Yuri's fingerprints. I believe it was Alexander Zurin who survived terrible wounds in Afghanistan, not the military policeman sent to bring him back. Alexander Zurin came to Moscow using the identity of Yuri Kirov and ultimately sent for me as part of a blackmail scheme to—''

Yuri shoved a man out of the way and burst through the double doors to the outer corridor.

No one moved in the courtroom for a frozen moment.

''Get him!'' the judge screamed at the guards.

''He's jammed the outside handles,'' a guard pushing at the doors yelled back to the judge.

''Break down the damn doors,'' Svetlana snapped.

XXIX

Owing to certain circumstances
I was forced this very day
to choose such an hour
to come and tell you
that they may murder you.

—Fyodor Dostoyevsky,
The Possessed

ONE

M oscow was cold and gray and drizzling when Lara came out of the jail. Darkness was falling, twisting the already taut city in its icy grip. Within a few hours the rain would turn to snow, covering the city's secrets with a false blanket of purity.

No one was waiting for her. The crowd of gawkers, the newshounds, and Alexei's limo were all at the front of the building. She had bribed a jailer to let her out the back. She was sick of crowds, sick of living in a cage where she had to hear other women's body functions, sick of notoriety. She felt tabloid dirty, victim of the sort of notoriety that goes along with Elvis sightings and two-headed babies.

Her brain was muddy. Drained physically and mentally, she didn't want to see anyone, talk to anyone. Yuri had fled the courtroom, leaving her innocence in his wake, but instead of being exhilarated, she was an emotional zombie, the thrill of being free chilled by exhaustion and heartbreak.

A sharp breeze cut through her clothes as she went down the steps to the street, but she didn't care—wind symbolized freedom. In jail you didn't have the choice to be warm or cold but had to take whatever was given. Her baggy clothes whipped in the wind. The clothes were the same as she had worn into the confinement, but she had lost pounds as well as a piece of her soul.

Hailing a taxi, Lara told the driver to take her to the Grand Hotel. Alexei had sent a message that he would be outside the jail waiting with the limo to take her back to the hotel where her belongings still occupied her old suite. She wondered if Anna would be there, spying for Alexei as she limped around the room.

Her plans were to pick up her luggage and take the first flight out of Moscow, going anywhere, preferably home, but if necessary she'd take a flight to Mongolia to escape the city. Her credit cards and nearly a thousand dollars were in her purse, to her surprise. She had expected the jailers to rob her but nothing had been taken.

Even as her common sense told her she had to get out of Moscow immediately, she knew she wouldn't leave the city until she had looked into the police investigation about Nina.

As the taxi pulled up at the hotel, the doorman approached with a professional smile that turned into a gawk as he recognized her. He flew over to open the front doors for her, whispering, "Congratulations, you're on all the news."

Walking across the lobby caused a sensation as people stopped and stared. She kept her eyes averted, occupying herself with fumbling in her purse for her room key as she headed for the elevators. She wasn't ready for stardom— or freakdom—better yet what role the public would cast her in.

Alone in the elevator, some of the energy created by tension oozed out of her and she was dragging as she went down the corridor to her room. If Anna was there she was going to order the woman out, barricade the door, unplug the phone, soak the stink of jail out of her with a champagne bubble bath, crawl into a real bed with clean sheets . . .

No! She'd pack up and head for the airport.

She unlocked the door to the suite and stepped in, turning on the light and swinging the door shut. As it closed, a hand flew around her face and clamped over her mouth.

"Don't scream," Yuri whispered in her ear.

He let her go and she stumbled forward before spinning around to face him. "You're insane, what are you doing here?"

He grinned without humor at her. "Hello, Little Kosca."

She wanted to scream, to rush for the door, but her feet were glued to the floor. "Why, Yuri, why?"

"You're in danger," he told her. He moved closer and she backed away from him.

"Stay away or I'll scream."

"Don't be stupid."

"You're a murderer."

"I've never murdered anyone."

"You confessed to killing Vera Swen."

"I was a terrified seventeen-year-old kid in the hands of a sadistic cop who beat the hell out of me. He took me into Vera's apartment and had me touch things so my fingerprints would be all over the murder scene.

"Then he said my mother would be arrested as an accomplice if I didn't say I did it. My mother was sick, it would have killed her. Hell, my arrest did kill her. Think about it."

He jabbed his finger at his temple. "Use your brains. I wasn't the one responsible for killing your mother and covering it up through the KGB. I was only seventeen years old. That sadistic cop who grabbed me for Vera's killing saved my life. If he hadn't coerced a confession out of me I would have been found hanging in my cell with a suicide note confessing the crime."

"The real Yuri Kirov—"

"I escaped during a firefight in Afghanistan and tried to cross the desert. Kirov was a military policeman in charge of the prison detail. A guy about my size and build, not a bad person at all. He caught up with me in a Jeep. It was cold and he had me wearing one of his coats on the way back when a mortar round hit. Hell, I didn't even know they thought I was Kirov until I woke up from a coma with half my body reconstructed."

"I . . . I don't understand." Weak-kneed, she stumbled to the couch and sat down. He sat down beside her as she hid her face in her hands. "It's too much, it's too damn much."

"You were right about most of it," he said. "I was blackmailing Belkin and Nadia. I knew there was something rotten about Alexei and his crowd and that they knew Vera and your mother. Belkin was a scum who liked to hurt women. I zeroed in on him as the killer and squeezed him with a sex offense charge. He swore he didn't kill Vera but thought he knew who did.

"Belkin's the one who gave me background on Nadia's past that I used to rope her in with. And I had checked you out, found out you were a prosecutor, and lured you to Moscow with the picture of Vera Swen."

"But why me?"

"To try and shake the killer out of the trees. Belkin had two candidates—Alexei and Felix. Both knew the women, both are a bit weird. My days as Detective Yuri Kirov were numbered. If I didn't bump into someone from the past, I was sure some routine check of fingerprints would someday trip me up. I had to find out who killed Vera. I lured you to Moscow for bait to draw out the killer."

"Last night you deliberately exposed yourself to me. You knew I would use it against you in court today."

He grinned again, and this time there was a trace of hard humor in it. "That's why I stationed myself by the door with the umbrella to jam the doors with on my way out. I even had a friend's motor scooter parked on the street. The only thing I wasn't sure of was whether you would pick up on me calling you 'Kosca' or if I'd have to reveal my identity in open court and make a dash for the door."

She bolted off the couch and he followed, the two of them circling in the room like a couple of jungle beasts getting ready to fight.

"Do you think you did me a favor?" she asked. "You lured me to Moscow, nearly got me killed, got me charged for murder, and left me in jail to rot."

"You were safer there."

"Fine. Let's call the police so they can tuck you in a nice safe cell."

"Don't be a fool. I wouldn't survive a night in jail. Money would pass hands and I'd be found hanging in my cell the next morning, a 'suicide.' "

"What about me?"

"I paid jail matrons to watch over you."

"You framed me with a glove. It was you, wasn't it?"

"I left the glove so Alexei would be suspicious of you. He'd cut his ties and you'd be forced back to America."

"Did Alexei kill Vera Swen?"

That stopped him and they stood and faced each other.

"I don't know. I haven't put it all together. There is something strange about Alexei, something I can't put my finger on. He was KGB. Protected, super-protected. He had a strange relationship with the head of the KGB's Finance Directorate. An old KGB agent I got to know told me that Alexei was the director's 'woman.' "

"His woman? Alexei's gay?"

"That's the rub. I've checked him inside out. If he's gay, he hides it incredibly well. And there's another crazy thing about Alexei."

"I know. He doesn't exist. On paper."

"I spoke to families of the people killed in the small factory where Alexei was supposed to have worked. His name was not familiar to any of them."

"What about the KGB finance director? Where does he fit in?"

"He died a few years ago. He was one of the most powerful men in the Soviet Union. I'm sure that he was responsible for diverting KGB controlled assets into a secret hoard. I think Alexei inherited control when the director died. I suppose he was chosen because of his ability to make money."

"Alexei doesn't know how to make money, he knows how to spend money. He told me a proverb about Russian geese returning to their owners. Alexei would have roasted all his geese with one big banquet."

He stared at her bewildered. "Geese?"

She swept the question away with her hand. "Never mind. Yuri . . . Pasha . . . hell, I don't know what to call you."

"Lara, I'm sorry for everything I put you through, for dragging you into this. That's why I kept trying to get you to go back to America, because I . . . I cared for you. I don't want anything to happen to you. Stuff a bag with a change of clothes and head for the airport."

"Oh, God, Yuri." She went to him and they hugged each other in silent desperation. "What's going to happen to you?"

"Russia's the largest country in the world. There has to be a tree somewhere I can hide under."

Pounding on the door startled them.

"Alexander Zurin, you were seen entering the hotel, we know you are in there. Give yourself up."

The command came from Yuri's police department supervisor. Yuri jerked away from her and drew a gun from the back of his waistband.

Lara clutched at the gun. "No! They'll kill you!"

"Get down!" He grabbed her arm and spun her away from him, but lost his balance and stumbled back as the door to the room crashed open.

Gunfire exploded in the room and Lara watched Yuri

fall against the window, his body crashing through.

She stood frozen in the center of the room, dazed and stunned, staring helplessly at the window as police poured into the room.

She couldn't move, couldn't think. An image of Yuri's shattered body on the street below flashed in her eyes and then a dark cloud soaked into her brain and the image was gone.

Someone took her arm. She turned and stared at Alexei with a brain-dead expression.

"I have to get you out of here," Alexei said. With a firm grip on her arm, he led her through the doorway and out into the corridor.

TWO

Alexei propelled her down the corridor to the elevator. A police officer with a walkie-talkie blocked their way into the elevator.

"Call your supervisor," Alexei told him.

At that moment the police supervisor stuck his head out the door of the room and yelled, "Get down the stairway to the first floor."

"These people—"

"Let them go. Get down the stairs."

Alexei pulled her into the elevator and the doors closed behind them. Lara stared blankly at the two doors. He put his arm around her shoulder and whispered something but her mind didn't hear him.

She was remembering . . .

A cold winter day, a schoolday. Her teacher saying her mother had come to pick her up.

Walking toward the cathedral with a woman wearing her mother's coat and scarf.

She had a sudden flash of Yuri crashing through the window and she cried out in pain.

"What's the matter?" Alexei asked.

"Yuri . . ." She knew she should focus on the here and now, that there was something about Yuri, something about Alexei, that she should focus on but when she tried to concentrate, the thoughts retreated into the dark corner of her brain where the terrible secrets of the past had been locked since she was a child.

Alexei led her out of the elevator, his arm still around her shoulder.

She was as catatonic as she had been that same day policemen walked her across an airport terminal to a plane when she was seven years old.

Stenka, Yuri's big Cossack partner, was standing near the first-floor elevators, walkie-talkie in hand, and he quickly moved in front of Alexei, concern narrowing his eyes as he observed Lara's state of shock.

"Nobody's allowed to leave the hotel."

"I'm not nobody, you fool. Get out of my way."

Stenka's broad forehead creased with a heavy frown and his fists clenched. The police supervisor's voice erupted from his walkie-talkie and Stenka answered the call.

"Get out and cover the front of the hotel," the supervisor said.

"What about Bova and—"

"The hell with them. Cover the front."

Stenka reluctantly let them pass, following the richest man in Russia as he steered Lara across the lobby.

In front of the hotel Alexei ushered her into the waiting limo.

Stenka stood on the curb and watched the limo move down the street as he radioed his supervisor. He kept his voice neutral, hiding his emotions as he asked, "Did you find Yuri?"

"No, damn it. He dropped only two stories and hit the restaurant balcony. There's blood up here, he's wounded or bleeding from the fall, but he's nowhere on this damn balcony. He might have already made it outside. I've called in a city-wide alert . . ."

Something caught the big Cossack's eye as he was listening to the radio call. A white handkerchief was on the street. He hadn't noticed it before because it was near where the limo had been parked.

He stepped into the street and bent down and examined the handkerchief. It was stained with blood.

He straightened and stepped back, leaving the handkerchief where it was.

About where it would be if it had dropped out of the limo's driver door, he thought. Why would a limo driver have a bloody handkerchief? And drop it?

He looked up at the hotel. The hotel balcony was at the next level but it was too far to jump without breaking a leg. Of course, someone could have fallen onto the balcony, come down the inside stairway, out the side entrance to the hotel to the street, saw the limo waiting nearby . . .

He stared at the limo disappearing in the distance, a thought burrowing its way into his thick skull.

THREE

Night had closed in on the city as the limo pushed its way through heavy traffic along the Moscow River embankment. The drizzle had turned to light snow and Lara stared at the flakes hitting the window beside her.

Focus focus focus. The word kept bouncing around in her mind but it didn't land anywhere. She knew she was in the limo, knew she was with Alexei, but her mind had locked up on her with the horrible knowledge that she had again lost someone she loved and was once more alone.

Alexei rambled on and on beside her, talking mostly to himself because she was only catching a word here and there as he gloated and laughed about how she had been the final blow to his house of cards.

"It's all tumbling down," he told her. "That bastard Yeltsin has sent in armed guards to take over the tower and the palace. They've seized my bank and are doing an audit. My, uh, investors, as you might call them, are dangerously annoyed. They lost everything they worked so hard to steal while they were in the KGB and they will no doubt soon be arrested."

He laughed again. "They made that fool Felix my controller, but he never had any control. The money passed to me and they were never able to get it back. They never understood that I wasn't really one of them. I used the money for what it would buy me, not what it would make them. Felix thinks I still have millions hidden. He's right. How does Brazil sound, my darling? Hot beaches, hot music, and bright colors. Have you noticed how everything in Moscow is gray? In Brazil there are greens and blues and reds . . ."

Grays, Moscow was winter gray again.

It had been a gray day when it all began. Snow had started falling when she left the school with the person dressed in her mother's brown coat and red scarf.

The woman had kept a tight grip on her little hand. A couple of times she had tried to jerk her hand loose and had told her mother that she was holding her hand too tightly, but the pressure of the grip remained.

They entered the cathedral and started up the stairs, the woman pulling her up the steps as she became frightened and hung back.

The woman looked at her and Lara saw eyes that

weren't her mother's.
  In the room at the top of the stairs the
woman had gestured to her . . .

"Come closer."

"What?" Lara snapped out of the grip of memory. "What did you say?"

"I asked you about Brazil, whether we should go there."

"No you didn't. You told me to come closer."

"No, darling, I'm afraid you're hearing voices in your head. I was talking about Bra—"

"*You're lying!*"

"Lara—"

"I know what you said. You're playing a mind game with me."

"Control yourself, darling." He reached out for her and she batted away his hand. "Dr. Zubov said you had a bit of—"

"You knew my mother."

He leaned back in the seat and sighed.. "The picture taken at the party. Yes, I knew your mother. I knew a lot of people. I was at that party because Felix was having an affair with Vera Swen—"

"I'm not interested in Felix."

He shrugged and grinned with boyish charm and innocence. "All right, I didn't want to tell you this because I thought it would drive you away. I had an affair with your mother—"

"That's not true. You never had an affair with my mother or Vera Swen, and you never slept with Nadia."

The Venetian blind on the window that separated the passenger area from the limo driver was down and half-closed enough that only a vague outline of the driver's head and hat could be seen. Alexei closed the blind even tighter before he turned back to her, his face red and stiff with anger.

"You seem to have become privy to my sex life, even that part of it that occurred when you were a child. Have you suddenly developed psychic powers?"

"You made a major mistake, Alexei. You bragged about what great sex we had the night I passed out at the palace. You knew I was too drugged to know what really happened."

His features suddenly turned stricken with grief. "Don't say it, Lara. I really like you. I love you and that's the truth. You're the first woman I've ever really loved, the only person I've loved in my whole life. It was your innocence, your freshness, your purity . . ."

"It's strange, but I believe you really do care for me. But I can't live a lie. And I can't take any more nightmares. You never made love to me, Alexei. I think you've never made love to any woman."

"You can't say that—"

"Yes, I can. You made a blunder when you claimed you made love to me. Alexei, listen to me. *I'm the oldest virgin left in the world.* I know I never made love to you. I passed out a virgin and woke up a virgin."

He laughed with an edge of hysteria. "And you think I'm the crazy one."

"It was important to you, wasn't it? To make me believe you had made love to me. That's why you kept changing girlfriends, why women like Nadia were so frustrated. You never made love to any of them, did you?"

"You don't understand. I was used, always used. The director used me as a . . . a . . ."

"As a woman," she said. "When I met Belkin in the park he talked about a freak he knew. That was you he was referring to. Now I realize he was testing me, to see how I would react when he dropped the hint."

"A freak," he said.

"You were out there that night, too, dressed as a nurse. That's what you do, isn't it? Dress up as a woman? As a nurse. You killed him because you thought he was selling your secret to me. What is it about you? What is it about deformed people?''

''Deformed people?''

One part of her wanted to reach out and touch him and tell him everything would be all right. She cared for him, but she knew he was sick and needed help.

''It's too late for lies. You surround yourself with people with deformities. Even your limo driver is blind in one eye.''

''Hire the handicapped,'' he said, giggling.

''A pervert followed you into a rest room and pushed open your stall. That's how it happened, isn't it? What did he see that made you kill him?''

Alexei shook his head. ''You shouldn't talk this way.''

''The derelict, did he do the same thing? Maybe it was an accident. Did he push into the wrong stall and die because of what he saw? And the doctor? What did he see? Is that when you started playing nurse? To get to him?''

''The doctor made me what I am.'' His voice was very low, a barely audible whisper.

''What are you, Alexei? What are you hiding? What is so damn wrong that you have to leave a trail of murder behind you?''

He suddenly became calm and the panic left his eyes. Cocking his head, he stared at her as if looking at her for the first time.

''I was wrong about you,'' he said. ''I thought we were alike. Suppressed childhood, loners who never ran with a pack. But, Lara, I'm beginning to wonder if the psychiatrist wasn't right about your mental state.''

He leaned over and patted her knee. ''Don't worry, my dear, we'll have plenty of money wherever we end up and I'll get you the best treatment—''

His patronizing voice snapped her own icy calm and broke the wall that held back emotions buried since she had been abused and nearly murdered as a child. She was just a goddamned doll, another toy in his fantasy world.

When she got too close to his secret he would smash her, too.

Rage swept through her as a violent fever, wiping away all common sense, and before she knew what she was doing she hit him—her fists flying at him, beating at him. "Bastard! You killed my mother and you hurt me. You hurt me."

Alexei hit her, the blow catching her on the side of the head, throwing her back against the car door. Her hand clutched at the door handle and she fell out backward. He made a grab at her clothes as she dropped and hit the moving pavement at twenty miles an hour. The limo was in the second lane from the curb and she tumbled all the way to the gutter. A car moving down the curb lane swerved to avoid her, crashing into the car beside it.

Her stunned body reacted with a charge of adrenaline and she got herself out of the gutter and on the sidewalk as traffic went crazy with a chain reaction of crashes.

Her feet propelled her into a snow-covered park that ran alongside the road as her mind relived horrors.

> *Yuri crashing out of the window of the hotel.*
> *Her mother strapped to a bed in a psychiatric ward while Alexei dressed as a nurse gave her a lethal overdose.*
> *The freak show at the carnival. What did Belkin tell her? That he knew a freak?*
> *Black riders in the night, storming into villages, pulling the deformed out of houses and putting the sign of the cross on their hand.*

He was the director's woman, Yuri said.

A woman.

"The doctor made me what I am," Alexei told her.

Ugly thoughts raced around her mind. Bottled up tears broke loose and she cried, for Nina, for Yuri, for her mother, victims of the devil.

She staggered across the park, her eyes half-blinded by tears and the snow that beat at her. The night was freezing but her feverish rage kept her moving.

Through the haze of snow blurring the night she saw a riot of colors set aflame by powerful lights.

St. Basil's Cathedral.

The limo had been going along the Moscow River embankment with Red Square off to the side.

A burst of laughter—an hysterical giggle—escaped past her almost frozen lips. She was right back where it all started.

Life is a circle, she thought. I ran halfway around the world and came back again.

She turned and faced the path she had come.

Someone was out there, part of the white-out created by the fury of snow. The person was coming toward her, unhurried.

A moment passed before the person became visible enough for her to distinguish the shape and form of a nurse in a white uniform and hospital cap.

XXX

What can you do about killing?
Nothing.
You kill a dog, the master buys another—
that's all there is to it.

—Maxim Gorky

ONE

She ran, panic beating in her throat, terror winging her feet. The picture of Vera Swen's mutilated body flashed in her mind, cut and slashed and—

Anger fought with panic but she knew she had no chance against the strength of a madman with a knife.

What little she could see of Red Square was deserted, the great parade area dark and lost under the falling snow. She ran to the closest source of light, the cathedral built with the blood of a madman's enemies, and burst in.

An old man sitting on a wooden chair next to a table with his dinner laid out jumped up as she rushed into St. Basil's.

Breathing hard, she said, "There's a killer outside, he's coming."

The guard's eyes went wide. "A killer?"

"We have to call the police. Hurry. Where's the telephone?"

"On the wall." He pointed at the curtained alcove that led to the stairs to the main tower. "In there on the wall."

"Lock the doors," she told him. "I'll call the police."

The old man headed for the front door and she hurried into the alcove.

It was a pay phone.

She stared at it as if it had come from outer space. It took a damn coin and her purse was back at the hotel. Moscow police had an emergency number that didn't require a deposit but she didn't know the number.

She rushed back through the curtains. The old man was down the hallway leaning with his shoulder against the wall near the door.

"It's a pay phone," she said. "What's the—"

He turned with visible effort to face her. His face was twisted with pain and he held his abdomen as if he was keeping his guts from spilling out. Blood soaked through the cracks between his fingers. Pressed against the wall, he slowly slid to the floor.

Horrified, she turned and ran up the stairs, taking the steps two at a time, her heart racing, mindless panic driving her up.

And then it snapped, that terrible surge of panic, and she forced herself to stop running and catch her breath and get back her mind and senses.

She was doing exactly what he wanted.

He was driving her back up the stairs to where her nightmares were born. She was playing right into his hand but there were no other cards on the table.

She kept going up, getting angrier with each step. She didn't want to die and she would fight the bastard until her last breath. There were no more buried fears or even smothered passions. Fire within had swept it all away and now there was only cold, deadly anger.

The most dangerous of God's creatures was a trapped animal and she had her back to the wall and nothing to lose.

Somehow she would kill the bastard before he took her life.

Nearing the room at the top she heard the sound of footsteps below, feet shuffling, and she froze for a moment, wondering if she had heard more than one person. The sounds died and she continued up.

At the top landing she went into the dark room. Unlatching the window, she pushed open the shutters. A few feet below was a ledge no more than a couple feet wide. The bastard had been lucky, more luck than God should have given him . . . missing the ledge would have sent him a hundred feet to his death and her nightmares would have ended.

The wind suddenly blew the shutters closed as she stepped away from them.

She took one of the wooden crosses from the stack in the corner. If she could stun him with the cross and push him out of the window . . .

Panic rose choking her throat and she beat it back as she crouched in a corner and raised the wooden cross over her head.

Images flashed in her mind: her mother tucking an extra cookie in her side pocket and kissing her on the cheek as she bundled her off for school, the roses that Yuri brought her that had cost him a week's wages, Nina sneaking a Big Mac into the jail.

Footsteps reached the top of the steps and her heart beat wildly. Her hands tightened on the cross.

The steps came down the corridor and her throat began to throb. People she loved had been killed because of his madness. Now he was coming to kill her.

She saw the shadow first, a dark shape in the dim light outside the door. The shadow was vague but it wore a hat. Her hands on the cross trembled and she nearly dropped it.

Her lungs were on fire from holding her breath and her mind screamed *kill him kill him.*

The shadow paused in front of the doorway. As the shadow moved into the room she was so intently focused on the hat that her eyes froze and started to cross. The fire within blew the roof off her head and she screamed as she swung the cross at the person who had entered.

The cross slid against the person, scraping instead of striking, and she felt herself lose her balance. She fell forward, following her swing. Colliding into the person in the doorway she cried out and drew back, awkwardly raising the cross, her head coming up to face the person.

Her heart stopped and a scream broke in her throat.

"Yuri!"

She recoiled from him in shock, dropping the cross. The shutters at her back flew open as she hit them and her momentum carried her into the opening—

A pair of strong hands grabbed her by her coat and jerked her back inside. As Yuri pulled her back in, the cap he wore fell off. A chauffeur's cap.

"You bailed out of the car too fast. I was driving." His face and shirt were streaked with blood. "Alexei is back there somewhere. And just behind him will be Felix and his men."

"Yuri." She reached out and touched him. "I—I thought I lost you."

He hugged her. "It's a good thing you hate heights. A room on the tenth floor and I'd be dead."

"A temporary respite," a voice said.

Felix was in the doorway. A man beside him had a gun in hand. Sounds of other people on their way up came from the stairwell.

He stepped into the room and shone a flashlight around. "So this is the famous chamber where Alexei terrifies little girls and," he said to Lara, "young women."

The man with the gun stepped into the room and to one side as another man entered with Alexei in tow.

Alexei's hair was disheveled, blood ran from the top of his head down the side of his face. He looked ridiculous in a white nurse's uniform with a nurse's cap askew on his head.

Felix shook his head. "What would Russia think of their boy wonder if they saw him now? What would they think if they knew he liked to cut off other people's sex organs.''

Felix shot Lara a look. ''You realize of course that he was on his way here to finish off what he started over twenty years ago. And you were right about him. Your virginity was quite safe with him.''

He smiled with pleasure at the surprise on her face. ''We had the limo bugged and the driver on our payroll, the driver we found unconscious on the front floor of the limo.'' He gestured at Alexei with contempt. ''He's a freak, a man stuck in a woman's body. We called them sex freaks when I was a kid,'' Felix said, ''people born with the sex organs of both a man and a woman.

''During the age of Russian medical miracles, when they were sewing two heads on a dog and reprogramming brilliant minds with dulling drugs, they experimented with Alexei, cutting off his underdeveloped penis and testicles, and leaving him with a vagina. It was very clever of them and the process works quite nicely for a feminine personality trapped in a male body and needing a sex change, but—''

Felix turned back to his audience, Yuri and Lara; his tone was that reserved for speeches at medical conventions. ''You see the anomaly, don't you. You can turn a man with a feminine personality into a woman by cutting off his sex organs and feeding him female hormones. Alexei was a young teen when they did the operation. The surgeon thought he was doing Alexei a favor—cutting off the underdeveloped penis that was too small to be functional, increasing the size of the vagina to make it functional for sex, and giving the boy some female hormones.''

Sobs erupted from Alexei.

''It was the sort of quack medicine that went along with the quack psychiatry that you complained about during the trial,'' Felix told Lara. ''The problem of course is that not only is the operation irreversible, but nobody asked Alexei if he wanted to be a woman. Or even if he could be a woman. The female hormones merely messed up his mind more than it already was.''

"The first victim, the doctor?'' Lara asked.

"Yes, it was the doctor who did the surgery. You more or less guessed the rest. The two found in the public rest rooms had barged into the wrong stall. There have been others.''

"Why was Vera Swen killed?'' Lara asked.

"A very sexually liberated woman. She made the mistake of grabbing between Alexei's legs and laughing about not having felt anything.''

"You killed Nadia and Nina,'' Lara said.

"No, I don't kill people. I have them killed. Nadia was a security risk. She was getting too close to Alexei's secret. We thought she was just after the money. Had we known our friend the police officer, er, escaped murderer, was controlling her we would have taken him out instead. Your friend Nina we actually rescued from Alexei. He had gotten in one good slash before we grabbed her from him to use as a live witness against him if need be. Of course now we won't need any live witnesses . . .

"You should be grateful, Lara. I let you live and showed you the picture with Alexei and your mother to keep Alexei in line. Framing you for Nadia's death killed two birds with one stone.''

Felix grinned at his own wit. "The rest is history and I am afraid you two will soon be history, too. According to the official version being prepared right now, Detective Kirov kidnapped Lara from the limo, brought her here, and threw her out of the window before shooting himself.''

"What about Alexei?'' Lara asked the question.

Alexei lifted his head to meet Lara's eyes, his face painted with pain and shame.

"This piece of dog shit will be taken to a dacha belonging to one of our investors and will be coached into revealing where he has hidden the remaining assets of our cartel, those the bastard didn't squander playing prince.''

He gave Alexei a look of contempt. "I've always hated him. But he caught the eye of the head of the Finance Directorate of the KGB many years ago, when Alexei was in his late teens. The director had what you might call strange tastes in sexual partners. I suppose a sexual freak like Alexei doubled his pleasure by—"

"Stop it!" Alexei screamed.

The words caught everyone in the room by surprise. Alexei's actions were a blur to Lara as he launched himself at his tormentor, sweeping up the slender-framed Felix in his arms and rocketing him across the little room to the window.

Felix went backward out of the window, a death grip on Alexei, a cry of terror escaping from his mouth as he and Alexei both went out through the window in a free fall down to the pavement a hundred feet below.

The man holding the gun followed Alexei's movements across the room, trying unsuccessfully to grab him.

Yuri threw a shoulder block and hit the man on the side, sending him crashing against the opposite wall. As he bounced off the wall Yuri hit him with an elbow to the nose, shattering the nose, sending blood flying.

The man went down, still holding the gun. While Yuri dived for the gun, Lara threw herself at the man by the door.

Gunfire exploded in the room. The man by the door was knocked sideways before Lara reached him. She froze, staring as he started to recover and level his pistol at her. Another shot sounded and the man collapsed, the weapon spilling from his hand.

Stenka appeared in the doorway, gun in hand.

TWO

Lara and Yuri walked out of the front of St. Basil's. He took her hand and she leaned her head on his shoulder as they walked.

Twenty years of trouble had been shed in the cathedral. It wasn't a rebirth, there were wounds to heal, but for the first time since she had walked out of a classroom with someone masquerading as her mother over twenty years ago, she was free of fear.

And she was free of guilt, too. She now knew why seeing Alexei in the nurse's uniform coming out of Vera's apartment had been locked deeper in her mind than even the abuse Alexei had subjected her to as a child.

In her young mind she had concluded that her witnessing the nurse on the landing above had somehow led to losing her mother. It made no sense except to a traumatized seven-year-old, but the chains of that guilt were gone now. In her heart she knew her mother was at peace. She would carry the warm memories of her mother now without having them polluted by fear and horror.

Snow had stopped falling and a gloomy frozen mist shadowed Red Square. Stenka and other officers had left to retrieve Nina after a quick and ungentle persuasion to reveal her location was administered to Felix's surviving henchman.

As she walked side by side with Yuri, she heard the powerful voices of a mass rally coming from the other end of Red Square.

"I'm free," she said, squeezing Yuri's hand. Yuri, Alexander, Pasha, she didn't know what to call him but still thought of him as Yuri. "We're free. Do you hear that, Yuri? We're free to do anything we want, go anywhere."

"Are you going back to America?" he asked.

"Are you coming with me?"

The question popped out of her mouth. A few months ago she would have thrown herself on a bed of hot coals before she spoke to a man in that manner. She had not ended up as the world's oldest virgin by being forward with the opposite sex.

His answer was drowned out by the noise of the rally as thousands of feet and an army of voices invaded the square.

The rally poured by them, thousands of people marching shoulder to shoulder in a long column that extended back somewhere deep in the foggy mist. Hundreds of torches lit up the night sky. Flags illuminated by the torches showed a golden hammer and sickle on a red background.

"Hard-line Communists," Yuri told her. "They want to overthrow the new government, restore the Communist Party as the ruler of Russia, throw out the free economy movement, and bring back the Cold War."

"I know," she said. "I've seen them before."

They walked for a moment in silence, listening to the slogans of the political dead who wanted to rise from their graves and take their place once again among the living.

"Maybe I won't go back to America," she said. "Not right away, at least."

"I'm glad you said that. I don't want you to go back."

"Russia is the New Frontier. They can use a good lawyer in this town. Besides Nina. In fact, they need a whole damn legal system. My mother died needlessly because the system didn't work. I could help make one work, a jury system that safeguards the rights of defendants."

She thought for a moment. "And I'm going to kick the ass of Stalin's Breath again in the next trial I have with her."

He stopped and took her face in his hands. They were warm and heavenly on her cold cheeks. She wanted his whole body next to her.

"Is that how American women talk?" he asked. "Kick ass? Is that any way for a woman to talk?"

"Yuri . . . Yuri . . ." She spoke slowly, choosing her words very carefully. "I am not going to tell you that you are an old-fashioned Russian chauvinistic pig and get into a silly argument with you. I'm not going to argue with you about who won the Cold War. I'm not going to lecture you about smoking. I'm just going to be me and—"

"And I'll just be me."

She looked at his soulful eyes. She would never get used to the smoking and his insistence upon picking up the check in restaurants. "Well, we'll talk about that."

He kissed her tenderly and her whole body melted against his naturally, lovers meant for each other.

"Can they do it?" she asked.

"Do what?"

"Those people. The diehards. Can they take back Russia? Turn back the clock?"

"Ask the geese," he said.

Available by mail from

TOR/ FORGE

PEOPLE OF THE LIGHTNING • Kathleen O'Neal Gear and W. Michael Gear

The next novel in the First North American series by the bestselling authors Kathleen O'Neal Gear and W. Michael Gear.

SUMMER AT THE LAKE • Andrew M. Greeley

"[This] story of three friends who spend a memorable and life-altering summer at a lake near Chicago...is a riveting story of love, crime, and scandal laced with the Roman Catholic orientation that is Greeley's forté." —*The Chattanooga Times*

MAGNIFICENT SAVAGES • Fred Mustard Stewart

From China's opium trade to Garibaldi's Italy to the New York of Astor and Vanderbilt, comes this blockbuster, 19th century historical novel of the clipper ships and the men who made them.

DEEP AS THE MARROW • F. Paul Wilson

When the president decides to back the legalization of marijuana, organized crime decides that he must die and his best friend, his personal physician, must kill him.

A MAN'S GAME • Newton Thornburg

Another startling thriller from the author of *Cutter and Bone*, which *The New York Times* called "the best novel of its kind in ten years!"

SPOOKER • Dean Ing

It took the government a long time to figure out that someone was killing agents for their spookers—until that someone made one fatal mistake.

RELIQUARY • Lincoln Child and Douglas Preston

"The sequel to the popular *The Relic* hits all the right buttons for those looking for thrills and chills....Another page-turner that cries out for translation to the silver screen." —*The Orlando Sentinel*

Call toll-free 1-800-288-2131 to use your major credit card or clip and mail this form below to order by mail

- ✂

Send to: Publishers Book and Audio Mailing Service
PO Box 120159, Staten Island, NY 10312-0004

☐ 51556-0 **People of the Lightning** . . $6.99/$8.99 CAN   ☐ 55374-8 **A Man's Game** . . . . $6.99/$8.99 CAN
☐ 54442-0 **Summer at the Lake** . . . . $6.99/$8.99 CAN   ☐ 54842-6 **Spooker** . . . . $6.99/$8.99 CAN
☐ 56194-3 **Magnificent Savages** . . $6.99/$8.99 CAN   ☐ 54283-5 **Reliquary** . . . . $7.99/$9.99 CAN
☐ 57198-3 **Deep as the Marrow** . . . . $6.99/$8.99 CAN

Please send me the following books checked above. I am enclosing $_____. (Please add $1.50 for the first book, and 50¢ for each additional book to cover postage and handling. Send check or money order only—no CODs).

Name _____

Address _____ City _____ State _____ Zip_____